"The School for Brides
to add another strong, re:
It's wonderful to get reacquainted with past characters, and
the connection between them, as the plot—complete with
suspense, murder, and passion—unfolds."

—*Romantic Times*

"A very good love story as well as a well-written mystery.
It certainly held my interest from beginning to end."

—*The Book Binge*

"The story kept me on the edge the whole way through."

—*Night Owl Reviews*

The Accidental Courtesan

"With a dash of humor, plenty of sensuality, and a fast
pace, Smith's second School for Brides novel is a pure
delight. Readers will enjoy the charming cast of secondary
characters and the mystery." —*RT Book Reviews*

"A wonderful historical romance."

—*Genre Go Round Reviews*

"A fast-paced, amusing romantic historical filled with fun,
and a delight to read." —*Fresh Fiction*

continued . . .

"Will appeal to fans of historical romance . . . Passion, mystery, and intrigue, a fast-paced plot, and a dashing and worldly hero who knows how to work with his hands."

—*TwoLips Reviews*

"A charming story with characters that engaged you from the first sentence. Truly a joy!"   —*Night Owl Reviews*

The School for Brides

"Chockablock with plot twists . . . Plenty of passion and intrigue."   —*Publishers Weekly*

"Smith makes a dazzling entrance to the romance community with a charming, sexy, innovative tale that sparks the imagination. There's a bright future ahead of Smith."

—*RT Book Reviews*

"Delightful . . . And I loved the twists."

—*The Romance Dish*

"A great read."   —*Night Owl Reviews*

"Brings an interesting twist to this era of historical romance."   —*Fresh Fiction*

"I was completely captivated . . . Sharp and highly entertaining . . . Incredibly fun to read."   —*TwoLips Reviews*

"A warm gender-war historical romance . . . Fans will cheer."   —*Midwest Book Review*

Berkley Sensation titles by Cheryl Ann Smith

THE SCHOOL FOR BRIDES
THE ACCIDENTAL COURTESAN
THE SCARLET BRIDE
A CONVENIENT BRIDE

A Convenient Bride

CHERYL ANN SMITH

B

BERKLEY SENSATION, NEW YORK

THE BERKLEY PUBLISHING GROUP
Published by the Penguin Group
Penguin Group (USA) Inc.
375 Hudson Street, New York, New York 10014, USA

Penguin Group (Canada), 90 Eglinton Avenue East, Suite 700, Toronto, Ontario M4P 2Y3, Canada
(a division of Pearson Penguin Canada Inc.) • Penguin Books Ltd., 80 Strand, London WC2R 0RL,
England • Penguin Group Ireland, 25 St. Stephen's Green, Dublin 2, Ireland (a division of Penguin
Books Ltd.) • Penguin Group (Australia), 250 Camberwell Road, Camberwell, Victoria 3124, Australia
(a division of Pearson Australia Group Pty. Ltd.) • Penguin Books India Pvt. Ltd., 11 Community
Centre, Panchsheel Park, New Delhi—110 017, India • Penguin Group (NZ), 67 Apollo Drive,
Rosedale, Auckland 0632, New Zealand (a division of Pearson New Zealand Ltd.) • Penguin Books
(South Africa) (Pty.) Ltd., 24 Sturdee Avenue, Rosebank, Johannesburg 2196, South Africa •
Penguin China, B7 Jaiming Centre, 27 East Third Ring Road North,
Chaoyang District, Beijing 100020, China

Penguin Books Ltd., Registered Offices: 80 Strand, London WC2R 0RL, England

A CONVENIENT BRIDE

A Berkley Sensation Book / published by arrangement with the author

PUBLISHING HISTORY
Berkley Sensation mass-market paperback edition / January 2013

BERKLEY SENSATION®
Berkley Sensation Books are published by The Berkley Publishing Group,
a division of Penguin Group (USA) Inc.,
375 Hudson Street, New York, New York 10014.
BERKLEY SENSATION® is a registered trademark of Penguin Group (USA) Inc.
The "B" design is a trademark of Penguin Group (USA) Inc.

PRINTED IN THE UNITED STATES OF AMERICA

10 9 8 7 6 5 4 3 2 1

ALWAYS LEARNING   **PEARSON**

For my readers,
who continue to offer their encouragement and support,
this book is for you.

Chapter One

The first thing Lady Brenna Harrington noticed was the pistol. The second was the unusual shade of blue eyes of the man holding the pistol. The third was the way those eyes bore into her with such intensity that her heart beat at a rapid clip.

Then, without warning, the highwayman cursed, lowered the pistol, and slammed the coach door shut without demanding either bauble or coin.

It took a few deep breaths for her heart to stop pounding in her ears and to recover her senses.

"That was odd," she said, screwing up her face. "I may not know all the particulars of coach robberies, but I am certain highwaymen always steal valuables."

Her maid, Tippy, let out a whimper of relief.

Brenna had the opposite reaction. "What sort of thief steals nothing?" As puzzled as she was, it was her next thought that forced her from the seat with a burning sense of urgency. The solution to her woes had appeared in front of her, complete with a pair of bright blue eyes, and she was not about to let him get away!

He would make a perfect substitute suitor! If she pretended to be smitten with the unsuitable stranger, he'd provide the distraction needed to put off Father until she could find a way out of a marriage to the dreadful Chester Abbot.

The idea was perfect! Get the highwayman bathed, buy him some decent clothing, and teach him a few phrases of proper English. Once he was outfitted respectably, she might be able to successfully convince Father that she was deeply infatuated with the man.

Of course, Father would not be fooled for long. He would be outraged that a low-born stranger was courting his daughter, convinced the man was a rogue, out for her fortune, and would be fit to kill. Who knew better how to keep his neck safe from an irate father than an experienced highwayman?

The plan was flawless; now to convince the highwayman.

Taking a deep breath, Brenna carefully pushed the door open and peeked out. The thief was urging Brenna's coachman to continue his journey with clipped words and a wave.

Fletcher, an elderly coachman who'd served the Harrington family for as long as she could remember, was obviously in the throes of his first robbery, too. He sat frozen, with his hands still lifted over his head, in spite of the highwayman's insistence that all was well.

Her mouth twitched at the corners. Lud, the fact that he'd not shot Fletcher made him perfect. A killer of coachmen just would not do. She wasn't *that* desperate.

Gathering her skirt in one fist and clutching the doorframe with the other, she tamped down her reservations.

Taking advantage of her coachman's temporary paralysis, she made a hasty climb from the coach in a flurry of gray muslin and white petticoats. Mud squished beneath her boots from an earlier rain, but she ignored the possible ruination of the fine leather and focused instead on the back of the retreating thief.

"Pardon me. Sir?" Soiling her hem in her haste, she rushed over to him as he collected his waiting horse. She kept her eyes averted from the pistol in his waistband, so as not to lose her courage, and boldly faced him. "Sir, if I could have a moment."

The highwayman paused and scowled down at her. He was tall, though not overly so, and unshaven, with several days of beard growth marking his hard jaw. His clothes were those of a laboring man, though cleaner than most. Close enough to touch his dusty coat, Brenna realized that he smelled better than a groom or farmer, too, like strong soap, leather, and rain.

Most important, though, was his clear lack of wealth: worn gloves, scuffed boots, not a bit of lace on his cuffs. He was likely without the means to give up his life of thievery, even though he didn't steal her jewels. That information worked well in her favor.

"Please, I must speak to you privately." Emboldened by desperation, she pressed ahead and focused away from the fact he was a dangerous criminal and could kill her in an instant. "I'd like to propose a financially beneficial arrangement between us that will thicken your purse and keep my life from ruin."

His icy glare set her back on her heels. Why did he not seem intrigued with the offer?

He was an odd fellow. Perhaps he was new to thievery and inexperienced? She needed to do something to pique his interest.

Brenna tucked the stray hairs on either side of her face behind her ears so that the diamond ear bobs were clearly visible for his inspection. The pair, and her pearl necklace, were worth a tidy sum—certainly enough to intrigue a thief.

She braced herself and waited for him to pluck the necklace from her neck.

He ignored the expensive items and held his angry expression.

"Young lady, return to your coach." He claimed the loose reins and walked around his horse. Brenna stepped back as he passed her, her lips parted in disbelief. Her baubles were as uninteresting to him as stones on the muddy road.

Was the man daft?

Undeterred, she ducked under the horse's neck. "Wait, I beg of you. I am in a dire situation and am desperate for help. My father and brother intend to marry me off to a man I find intolerable. I cannot be his wife."

His expression didn't improve. "Perhaps your father and brother know what's best for you." He removed his gloves and jerked a stirrup into place. "Women often let emotion muddle their judgment."

Brenna grabbed the bridle and ignored the insulting comment. She wasn't about to chase this thief off by arguing with him.

Without the highwayman, she'd need weeks, maybe months, to find another disreputable character that wouldn't be intimidated by her father's title and wealth. By then, she could be Lord Chester's new marchioness.

"Release my horse," he demanded. She met his eyes and shook her head. She'd not be cowed.

"Not until you listen to my proposal." She tightened her grip on the bay gelding. Even if he shot her, it would be preferable to wedding Chester Abbot.

His exasperated sigh must have carried all the way to London. He briefly closed his eyes—she hoped for patience and not because he was about to shoot her—and crossed his arms across his chest.

"State your business and be quick about it," he said gruffly. His icy eyes peered out from beneath mussed sable hair. "I do not have time to waste while you whine about the unfairness of your life. If you need a sympathetic ear, look elsewhere."

Brenna's back stiffened. If she had any other choice, she'd tell this arrogant clod where to take his boorish manners and be done with him. But desperation held her tongue.

She pulled in a deep breath, knowing that what she did in these next few moments could either save or ruin her.

"As I previously explained, my family intends for me to marry this man, a dolt of high standing. He is dull and weak and about as exciting as the mud currently wetting my feet. I would rather throw myself under the hooves of your horse than to suffer that fate."

His jaw clenched. "What has this to do with me?"

Clearly his controlled temper was faltering. She rushed on, "The wedding cannot happen. I need you to compromise me."

The stranger started and his brows shot up.

Brenna's heart raced. Finally, she had his full attention. Her heart raced beneath the shocked surprise in his eyes. She prayed she'd not just made a grave, and possibly fatal, mistake.

"Have you lost your senses, young lady?" He shook his head slowly and stared as if she'd sprouted horns. "You think that my tossing up your skirts and violating you on this sodden ground will be a superior choice over wedding the man your family has chosen? Are you mad?"

The words and the way he looked at her left her feeling foolish and a bit childish. Still, Brenna held fast. Her brother, Simon, was already making overtures to Abbot. This man *was* her only option. It mattered not what he thought of her, only that he'd help her.

She fingered her expensive necklace. "You will not actually take my innocence," she clarified, her body recoiling at the thought of him touching her intimately. "You need only misbehave just enough to convince my father and brother that you are a cad, a bounder, out to ruin me. While they are focused on trying to rid me of you, I will be free to choose my own husband. And it will not be Lord Abbot."

"Lord Chester Abbot, the marquess?" His eyes lit with confusion. "You are intended for a marquess? Who are you?"

"That is not your concern. I will pay you well for any blackened eyes or loose teeth you may suffer at the hands of my father and brother. Then you will vanish before they recover their wits and see you flogged." She paused to allow him to catch up. "Surely a man in your profession would be happy to line his pockets with coin, even if it comes with a beating?"

He raked his hands over his head. "You *are* mad."

"I am as clear thinking as you are, sir," she countered tartly. The back of her neck prickled. "In fact, I think a man who robs coaches has no place to judge me."

A heartbeat or two passed before he spoke again. "You think I'm a highwayman, a desperate thief who would take your money and be grateful to have my face pummeled, so that you can avoid being leg-shackled to a marquess?" His stern face melted into a disbelieving smirk. He shook his head and laughed. "What an interesting turn. And I thought this day could get no worse."

His humor raised her hackles. She could no longer hold her temper. "How dare you find amusement in my situation! You, sir, are no gentleman."

The stranger chuckled again. "There you are wrong, Miss. I am indeed a gentleman."

The coach horses rattled their harnesses and brought Brenna's attention away from the highwayman. Fletcher, though far enough away not to have heard the exchange, was obviously distraught over her close proximity to the stranger.

"Miss Brenna, please come away from that man," Fletcher begged, when he noticed her attention turn away from the highwayman. His voice held barely concealed panic. "We must get you home before your mother worries."

Posh. Her parents were the reason she was in this fix.

After learning of the plot to wed her off to the marquess, she'd threatened to sail off with a pirate or some other such thing, and Father threatened to have any servant turned out if he or she took her out of London. Fletcher had finally given in to her pleas for fresh air and sunshine and had taken her on this secretive outing into the country.

The coach robbery had been an unintended and lucky turn of events.

"Miss Brenna?" The stranger's question returned her attention back to him. He'd lost his smirk. "Are you Brenna Harrington?"

Shocked that he knew her name, she refused to answer. He clearly took this as confirmation of her identity. Stepping toward her, he closed his hand over her wrist and wrenched it off the bridle. He held her in a tight grip and leaned to look directly into her face.

Brenna bit back a whimper. She'd underestimated him. He *was* dangerous. Could he be rethinking ravishment? Worse, would he kill her just for the enjoyment of doing so?

And for a moment, she thought that was her fate. Trapped in the grip of his dark gaze, her breath caught as his eyes trailed from her eyes to her breasts and back up again. Yet even as she braced herself to fight, she suddenly felt no fear.

His eyes spoke not of murder or rape but of something else she could not read. She would live another day.

"Forget this nonsense and go home before your father gives you a beating you well deserve." He released her, and she rubbed her chafed wrist. But it wasn't his callous treatment of her delicate bones that left her silent.

In those few seconds when his warm hand had touched her exposed skin above her glove, something upended inside her, and her body had snapped to attention. Beneath his drab and dusty clothing, Brenna became shockingly aware he was not just a highwayman but a man, a very virile and dangerous man.

Goodness.

Thankfully, he appeared unaware of his effect on her. Had he known how her body reacted from his simple touch, she might have been compromised in truth.

With a fluid motion, he swung up into the saddle and shot her one last glare as she stood stock-still, her skin still tingling from his grip.

"If I see you alone on these roads again, Miss Harrington, I'll paddle you myself."

Brenna gasped and watched him spin his horse around and race down the road, mud clumps flying up in their wake.

Time slowed. The smell of wet leaves, a distant bird call, the sound of Fletcher muttering, all blurred as she watched him race out of her life on a lathered horse.

Calling him back would serve no purpose. He'd made his decision not to help her. And she did have some pride left.

She rubbed her wrist and waited until he disappeared around a bend before slowly turning back toward the coach. It was then she realized there was more to his stunned reaction to her name. He'd looked at her with puzzled recognition.

Could the man have intimate knowledge of her family? Was he someone with whom Father or Mother were acquainted?

Surely not; he was a highwayman, after all. Yes, her family had many rogues and reprobates in their history. However, none recently—well, as far as she knew of anyway. Still, it was impossible to think that any of her extended family was closely connected with thieves.

Through gossip was likely how he'd gotten his recognition of the Harrington name. Her family was often the topic of whispers and speculation. Either way, this highwayman made his decision quite clear. He'd not rescue her.

Beneath crushing disappointment, she sloshed back to the coach and climbed inside, still feeling unsettled by the encounter and her stunning response to his touch.

Brenna Harrington. Richard found it difficult to believe the daughter of his good friend, Walter Harrington, had been wandering the countryside looking for a rogue to rescue her from a wedding to a marquess, even if he agreed with her description of Chester Abbot.

The man *was* a milksop.

But Brenna Harrington? He hadn't seen her since she was a gangly hellion who ran wild around the Harrington estate. And even then, their acquaintance had been brief and hardly worth noting.

The chit had certainly grown into a beauty with the sort of face that could get a man into all kinds of trouble.

He'd heard of the recent death of her uncle the earl and her father's ascent to the title. Therefore, the tart-tongued termagant with the seductive green eyes was Lady Brenna now. Even as he wanted to believe Walter's daughter would not be foolish enough to make a scandalous offer to a stranger, he knew without a doubt that Brenna was the image of her beautiful mother, Kathleen.

Though the Harringtons were a wild bunch and not prone to follow all the stiff rules of society, the chit's behavior went far beyond a bit of rule bending.

As soon as he returned home, he'd send off a note to Walter and let him know what his strong-willed daughter was up to before she put herself in real danger.

Returning his attention to more pressing matters, he urged his horse back toward Beckwith Hall and within minutes met his steward, Andrew, riding up in the opposite direction. The man clung to the reins with one hand while shoving his spectacles back into place with the other.

"Any luck?" Richard asked, eager for news of his runaway sister, Anne. He'd hoped that between the two of them, they'd get her home before anyone heard of her elopement and her reputation was ruined.

Now he feared it might already be too late. Before Richard had found her note, Anne had had a head start.

Andrew shook his head as the rain began anew. Beneath the brim of his hat, the young steward appeared defeated. "There's no sign of her or that bounder who made off with her. They have vanished."

A sickening dread chilled Richard's veins. Stewart Lockley was divorced, twice her age, and known for his taste for innocents. How his intelligent sister had ignored all warnings and fallen for his questionable charms was incomprehensible.

And now they were gone.

"We have to keep searching," Richard said, and ran a hand through his damp hair. He'd lost his hat in the wild chase after Brenna's coach. Catching a chill would be the perfect end to a disheartening day.

He'd run down and searched three coaches today, like the highwayman the exasperating Miss Harrington had accused him of being, and found no sign of Anne. Time was wasting, and he was losing hope.

A headache pressed against his temples.

"Where could they have gone?" Andrew said, his voice etched with concern. He and Anne were friends of long standing. His worry was second only to Richard's.

Richard looked north. "As far as I can discern, they haven't taken Great North Road toward Gretna Green, so that is some comfort. Whatever their destination, making the journey on less-traveled roads will be slower. I'll send out men in all directions, and we'll cover more ground. Until we get a hint of their route, we cannot take up their trail. I just hope we find her before she makes a run for Scotland."

Andrew scowled and twisted the reins in his gloved hands. "The bastard needs a thorough trouncing."

Richard nodded. "I will do that, and more, once I catch up with them. I can only hope I'll not be too late." He knew he needed luck and his swift horse if he was to save Anne from herself. "Until we have solid information of their direction, I intend to keep searching the surrounding area. I suspect Lockley has no real intention to wed her, so they may still be near. I'll take the road to—" He was cut off by the sight of his groom, Manny, racing up the road, panic on his face.

"What is it?" Richard asked, as the horse skidded to a stop.

"The Cooksons' cottage is burning. Mr. Cookson has been injured. He rushed in to save his youngest and was hurt. Milord, you must come quickly!"

Richard's stomach turned. Mr. Cookson was his tenant and a friend. He had five children and a wife heavy with child. "Did you send for the physician?"

"Aye, Milord."

Richard turned back to Andrew. "Take Great North Road and try to get in front of Anne, should she end up in Gretna Green. I will see to the Cooksons and continue my search here. If you discover she is indeed heading north, I'll meet you in Scotland as soon as I am able." He pulled the pistol from his waistband and handed it to his steward. "If you find them, shoot the bastard, Lockley, if you must."

Chapter Two

B renna!"
   Father's voice reverberated through the town house,
startling a pair of maids, who skittered off toward the kitchen
as if their skirts were ablaze.

Brenna winced. Walter Harrington seldom raised his voice
to his children, unless they'd done something outrageous. Her
father was generally a controlled man. For him to shout loud
enough to send servants fleeing did not bode well for her.

And there was a note of anger in his tone.

She rose up onto her slipper-covered toes, hoping to tiptoe
up the stairs and race to the safety of her room, when a second
bellow from his study, outmatching the first, boomed off the
walls and snapped her upright.

"Brenna!"

There was no escape. Two shouts indicated that she was
about to be flogged, figuratively speaking, for some misdeed.
A locked door wouldn't keep him from his course. When father summoned, you answered the call. There were no exceptions.

With weighted steps, she headed off in his direction. The
swish of satin and lace marked her passage down the suddenly
quiet hallway. A sense of doom rose with each step.

The only thing she could do was accept her punishment
and hope it wouldn't be dire. But what was causing his ire this

time? Since her list of infractions was lengthy, it was impossible to point in one direction.

"Yes, Father," she said sweetly, as she crossed the threshold into the study. "You wanted to see me?"

Slowly, he stood, and she froze. His face was angrier than she ever remembered seeing. A sheet of paper was gripped tightly in his hand as he rounded the desk and stalked toward her like a cat on a hapless mouse. It was all Brenna could do not to flinch backward when he reached her.

He thrust out his hand and handed over the note. "Explain this," he said, his checks flushed a deep puce.

With hands shaking, she took the crumpled missive and quickly read the first two paragraphs of the lengthy note. Her heart squeezed painfully in her chest as her eyes dropped past the bulk of the note to the name at the bottom. In spite of not recognizing the scrawled signature, she knew immediately who had sent her to the gallows.

Her highwayman. The details of her crime were too intimate for it to be anyone but him. Theirs had been a private conversation. The bastard had betrayed her.

"How—?" Her voice was a strangled squeak.

"The man you offered to pay to compromise you was not a thief but my dear friend Lord Richard Ellerby, the Viscount Ashwood, who stopped your hired coach while looking for his missing sister. He was worried you'd come to harm and sent around this note." His hands closed into fists in front of his mouth. "I cannot believe you've done such a thing, Daughter. Were you willing to risk your innocence, your life, just to avoid a marriage?"

Never had Brenna experienced such censure from her father. He was grievously disappointed in her. This realization twisted a hard knot in her stomach as tears threatened to spill. "I'm sorry, Father."

He snatched back the note and shook his head. "What am I to do with you? Lock you in a wardrobe? Place a guard on your door day and night?"

Brenna sniffed and whispered, "I cannot marry Chester Abbot. Please do not force me to, Father. He is horrid."

Father spun on his heel and returned to the desk. He dropped the paper on the surface and turned back. "It was never our intention to force you to marry that toad." His face softened, but only slightly. "We hoped that with Abbot looming as a potential mate, you'd finally accept a suitor, any suitor, and settle down with a family of your own."

Her eyes widened. "I do not have to marry the marquess?" She was free! "Thank you, Father," she exclaimed with relief. "You are the best father!"

When she opened her arms and took a step toward him, he raised his hand. She stopped.

"You may wish to reserve your glee until I have finished what I have to say." He crossed his arms. "Daughter, you are in clear need of more supervision than I can give. You managed to coerce poor Fletcher into defying my directive, and had the 'highwayman' not been a friend, I can only speculate about what might have happened to you. Thus, I have made a decision. A husband *is* what you need to rein in your impulsive nature."

She blanched. "Father, no!"

He leveled a hard stare on her. "For a moment, I considered a convent, but knew you'd never accept a pious life. So you will have one month to choose a man to wed. All I require is that he has some wealth to keep you in gowns, doesn't gamble, and is kind. Otherwise, the choice is yours."

Marriage. Though she was free of the marquess, she'd still be chained to some other man she didn't love. She couldn't fall in love in a month. It was impossible.

Several options raced through her head. She had to find a way out of this!

"Brenna . . . ," he warned, "I will not be dissuaded or tricked into changing my mind. You will be betrothed by month's end or off to the convent with you."

She swallowed. Hard. "Yes, Father."

Mentally scrolling through a quick list of men of her acquaintance, dread grew. Though most of the chaps were pleasant enough to dance or chat with, not one of those men made her heart race or her skin tingle—an affliction commonly known to happen when a person felt passionate about someone else.

It was the Viscount Ashwood who held that unwelcome distinction. The beast. He'd kept her from following through with one bout of poor judgment, only to throw her into another, slightly less unacceptable muddle.

Brenna's frustration with the highwayman over the last two days had turned to exasperation when she realized that several times since their encounter, his unshaven face and expressive blue eyes had drifted into her thoughts. She'd even caught herself caressing the spot on her wrist where he'd touched her.

And those caresses weren't to relieve an ache from his rough treatment of her wrist. His regretfully handsome features and male form had taken up a permanent place in her girlish dreams, like some dark knight of old, weighted with armor and ready to do battle for her affections. To learn he was not a thief but a peer, and Father's friend, served to make it worse. It was probable that during society functions in the future, she would have to socialize with the man. A dreary notion indeed!

Lud, she hated him!

As if noticing her woolgathering, Father cleared his throat. "I do not accept your promise as heartfelt, the way I would were you a more manageable daughter. Already, I suspect you are thinking of some way to thwart my plan."

Brenna looked down at her feet.

He waited a moment, then snorted. "You have been raised as a lady of quality and therefore have not been subjected to the harshness of life outside society. So I have taken it upon myself to arrange for you to learn what life is like for women without the benefit of your good fortune."

Brenna frowned.

"For the next week, you will be in the care of your cousin Eva's courtesan school. They are currently holding lessons, so there will be several courtesans in residence. Though I find the idea of putting my innocent daughter in the acquaintance of courtesans distasteful, I see no other option. Hopefully, by the end of the week, your eyes will be open to what can happen to unlucky young women who proposition strangers."

Brenna gaped. She'd only just become privy to Eva's secret school through her cousin Noelle and her brother Simon. She was still trying to get over that surprise news. Now her father wanted to send her off to Cheapside to live among the courtesans?

"Father, you cannot do this." Even now, her face burned. She'd never even been kissed, not really. A brush or two of male lips on hers did not count. What sorts of things would she learn in the company of women of loose moral character? What if the gossips discovered her whereabouts? She'd be ruined forever. What kind of man would marry her then? Even a highwayman would not have her!

"Father, please!"

His glare stopped further protest. "It has been arranged. As we speak, Tippy is packing what you'll need." He leaned to press a kiss on her forehead. "You need not plead to your mother. She is in agreement. And should you defy my wishes, I can still have you shackled to Abbot before the fortnight is over."

Blood drained from her face. He left her to contemplate her fate.

She walked to a chair and dropped into it, her mind jumbled. She was a lady. How dare Father foist her off into a household full of courtesans?

Eva. Cousin. Secret courtesan rescuer-matchmaker. Duchess. A woman of many faces.

Brenna liked her very much, and her husband, His Grace, was pleasing to look at. Still, just because Eva enjoyed rescuing courtesans it did not make it right for a woman of society to move among them.

The clock chimed and snapped her from her musing. Perhaps she could hide with a friend until Father gave up this idea? She looked at the window and wondered if she could squeeze through the sash without tearing her skirt.

"I would not attempt escape if I were you, Sister," Simon remarked dryly. "I would hate to ruin my boots racing after you across the damp grass."

Brenna turned in her seat to see her brother standing in the doorway, smoothing the wrinkles out of his coat. Simon had recently married and was living nearby with his wife, Laura. She was a delightful addition to the family and agreed with Brenna's mother, Kathleen, on the matter of Brenna marrying for love. It was the men who did not have the patience to wait for Brenna to make her own choice. They considered her a hoyden who needed a marital leash.

"I can still outrun you, Brother," she snapped, and sat back on the fine leather chair. "I suppose you have come to gloat. You will not convince me you did not know of Father's plan to imprison me at the courtesan school."

Simon cocked a brow and smirked. "Know about it? He has sent me to escort you. Only then can he be assured you'll not leap from the coach and vanish."

Brenna grumbled under her breath about traitorous brothers and obstinate fathers. Then, "When did I become the family menace?"

Simon shot her a wicked look. "At birth."

For a moment, she considered launching from the chair and chasing him around the study with Father's carved crystal paperweight. However, such a display of temper would serve to confirm to her father that she did indeed need supervision. Instead, she glared daggers at him and kept her seat.

"You have one hour to ready yourself." Simon looked at his pocket watch. "At two ten, I expect you to be waiting in the coach wearing your plainest gown."

This time Brenna couldn't contain herself. She pushed to her feet and stuck out her tongue in a most childish manner. His chuckle followed her out of the room.

T he distance to the courtesan school wasn't long, and Brenna spent the ride to Cheapside scowling at and plotting the untimely demise of her smug brother.

Eva had sent around an unadorned coach so as not to draw the attention of her neighbors on the quiet street. She liked to keep her work with the young women private, and having Brenna and Simon arrive in a fine coach would draw speculation.

The town house was a dull stone, without the guild of the houses in Mayfair and Berkeley Square. In fact, it was not so dissimilar to the other houses on the street, all perfectly ordinary. It was an ideal hiding place for courtesans fleeing their patrons.

Brenna sighed as the driver opened the door and helped

her down. She smoothed out her cloak over the simple gray traveling dress, and stared unhappily at the drab building looming before her. This was to be her prison for the week.

If one wanted to disappear into obscurity, this was the place to do it. For a moment, Brenna wondered if Simon truly intended to fetch her once her imprisonment was over. Knowing her brother as she did, she wasn't certain.

"Do not look so glum, Sister." Simon offered her his arm. "Your captivity will not be long. Once Father is convinced that your days of offering yourself up to criminals are over, you'll return home where you belong."

She peered up at him from beneath her bonnet. "It is difficult to understand how such a handsome man could hold such an evil heart."

He chuckled. "Your problems are of your own making."

"My exile will be worth a few days of suffering now that the threat of Chester Abbot is over," she said, through gritted teeth. "Thank goodness one of you has come to your senses. And it wasn't you."

"Father spoils you."

"Unlike you, he does not live to see me miserable."

They climbed the steps and stopped before the door. "You may not be marrying Abbot, Sister, but you will marry. It is high time you stopped your mischief and found a mate."

"I cannot believe Laura married you," she snapped. "How such a delightful woman could love you is beyond comprehension."

Simon laughed. "My charm won her."

Brenna refused to speak further with Simon as they were escorted inside by the butler and settled into a small parlor.

The house smelled of beeswax and perfume, and the simple furnishings had a feminine feel. It was neat and well kept, though Brenna thought the space could use a bit of color.

From somewhere in the house, women's laughing voices could be heard. Brenna's stomach tightened. How did one speak with courtesans? She knew nothing about courtesans except that they sold their bodies and that many wealthy men had one. And what had they been told about her? Certainly, her identity would be kept private?

A swish of skirts drew her attention as Eva, Miss Eva to the courtesans, came into the parlor with a smile of welcome.

For Brenna. Simon earned a grimace.

Disguised as a spinster, Brenna almost did not recognize her beautiful cousin. Even her rounding belly was hidden beneath the full cut of her drab brown gown.

"Simon," Eva said, frowning. "You cannot seem to resist invading my school. Will I ever be rid of you?"

He grinned and took her hand. Several months previous, Simon had rescued Laura from a dangerous situation and brought her here for her protection. The arrival of Laura had not irked Eva, as she would never turn away a young woman in need. No, it was Simon's continued desire to spend time with Laura that drew her ire. Men were not allowed at the school without an invitation. Simon thought nothing of breaking the rule.

And he called *Brenna* the family mischief maker.

Though Simon and Eva were now close, they liked to toss barbs at each other for their mutual amusement.

"Duchess, you are as lovely as ever." He kissed her hand. "And your mood as temperate as always."

"Hmm. Now leave." She withdrew her hand and turned to Brenna. Crossing the room, she joined her on the settee.

Amused, Simon quietly withdrew as a maid arrived with tea. Once they were alone, Eva said, "I know this is the last place you wish to be, Brenna. When your father proposed the idea, I hesitated. A household of courtesans is no place for a pedigreed young lady."

"On that we agree." Brenna wrinkled her nose.

"However," Eva said, ignoring Brenna's sharp tone. "After the mischief with the highwayman, your father has decided we can be of some benefit to you."

Brenna was now certain she'd find no sympathy here. "He wasn't actually a highwayman," she protested weakly. She silently cursed Lord Ashwood for interfering. If only she'd recognized him before she'd made her misguided proposal.

However, he'd been dressed in shabby garb, and it had been years since he'd last visited the Harrington town house. The man apparently preferred fresh air, and the company of sheep, to the entertainments of society. How would she have known him?

"Yes, a fact of which you were unaware." Eva poured the tea. "Now let us get started, shall we?" She talked about the school; Sophie, who helped run the school; the courtesans; and what was expected of Brenna. Brenna sipped the sweetened tea and felt some tension leave her. Eva was not at fault for her predicament. Brenna would not cause her any worry.

It was a viscount with unshaven cheeks and muddy boots who should be worried.

Deep inside the darkest part of her, she felt the desire for revenge grow for the man who'd stuck his nose in her affairs and locked her up here, almost as if he'd personally dragged her to this school himself.

Someday, somewhere, their paths would cross again, and she'd make him rue the moment he'd decided to chase down her coach.

Chapter Three

Helen, Iris, Alice, and Lucy. The four courtesans were gathered in the parlor, practicing stitchery, each with histories as varied as their appearances and backgrounds, all living in the courtesan school, trying to become wives. Ironic, Brenna thought, considering that her own desire was *not* to fall into that trap herself.

Though Brenna was new to the household, she'd managed to put together enough snippets of information about the women in a few hours to get a clearer picture of each.

Helen was the oldest, thirty, with dark hair shot through with threads of gray, and a trim figure. She was stoic, slow to smile, and preferred to keep her own company.

Iris was as lively as Helen was sober. She was twenty-three, blond, diminutive, and well read. So well read, in fact, she could chatter endlessly about any topic.

Alice was also blond, twenty-five, but was tall and plump. She enjoyed mothering the women like a hen with chicks.

And finally, there was Lucy. Lucy was the youngest, at twenty-one. Her hair was a medium brown, and her hazel eyes flashed mischief. Brenna suspected Lucy was the closest to her in temperament. If she ever wanted to make a nighttime raid to the pantry, Lucy would likely join in the fun.

"I cannot do this," Alice said, and plucked out her latest stitch. "I am hopeless with a needle."

"That is why you became a courtesan," Lucy teased, looking at her own project with a critical eye. "You'd make a horrible seamstress."

Alice shot Lucy a withering glare. "What, then, is your excuse, Lucy? You are excellent with a needle."

Lucy shrugged. "Misbehavior. I was a wicked child and never outgrew it," she said, with a wink. "Besides, if I had to spend my life making and mending clothing, I'd probably throw myself on my scissors and end it all."

"Oh, dear," Iris interjected. "I suppose being a courtesan is preferable to death by scissors."

Brenna bit her lip. These courtesans were a lively lot. Had she not known their history, and had the conversation not been about their scandalous former profession, this little group would resemble any other afternoon tea.

"Excellent point," Brenna said. She looked down at her own pitiful attempt to sew a straight line. "Some women are not suited for domestic pursuits."

Lucy smiled, and the women went back to work.

Unable to concentrate on her own stitches, Brenna watched them work on their needlepoint, while Sophie, a former courtesan herself, came in and out of the room, giving instructions and setting up the dining room for the next lesson.

Looking at the properly dressed and subdued young woman, it was almost impossible to believe she was seated amid courtesans. She wasn't certain what she'd expected, but it wasn't this. They all looked downright, dare she say it, ordinary.

After several more attempts to correct her mistakes, Alice finally asked Sophie for help.

"If you hold the needle thus, it makes a straighter stitch." Sophie adjusted the needle, and Alice nodded. After a minute, the young woman smiled.

"Yes, I see the difference." Alice showed her success to Lucy. Lucy changed the position of her hand. After a few stitches, the two shared a satisfied glance.

Brenna laid her needlepoint in her lap, and her eyes drifted to the window. If she were home, she might be playing chess with Father or practicing the pianoforte with Mother. She'd been imprisoned at the school for nearly three hours, and she was already feeling the loss of freedom.

It was entirely too quiet here.

"I wonder if His Lordship misses me? He always said I was his favorite mistress."

Brenna's attention snapped back with Iris's comment. She glanced around to see that Sophie had left the room again. Clearly the presence of Sophie kept the women proper. When she stepped out, there was no holding to propriety.

This was more interesting than stitches, Brenna thought. Her curiosity piqued, and she hoped Sophie would be delayed indefinitely.

"He misses tupping you," Helen said sharply. Brenna blushed. The rest of the women took the salacious comment without a blink. "I'm certain that you will be replaced, post-haste."

Iris pouted. "There is no need to be rude," she said. "He may actually miss me, you know."

"Fickle men are the nature of our profession," Helen added, ignoring the sudden silence of the other women. "Out of sight, we are soon forgotten when another woman falls into their beds. Sighing wistfully over the man will gain you nothing."

Lucy lowered her needlepoint. "I'm certain His Lordship cared for you, Iris. However, Helen is correct. We were all replaceable, despite any effusive declarations of affection. That is why we have come here. We all deserve something better for ourselves."

Curiosity overcame Brenna. Though she should hold her tongue, she knew very little about the shadowy world of courtesans. Now she had the opportunity to learn more from the women themselves and decided not to cling to propriety.

She turned to Helen. "I thought some men loved their courtesans?"

Eva had informed the women that Brenna was some poor relation from the country, come to stay for a time as she sought employment. Therefore, her ignorance of city life and all its scandals could be easily explained away.

Helen stared. "Men do not love their lovers. Most do not love their wives. Women serve to satisfy their needs or beget them children." She set aside her needlepoint and stood. Without another word, she left the room.

The courtesans exchanged a knowing glance.

"Did I say something wrong?" Brenna asked.

Lucy turned to Brenna and explained. "Helen was orphaned at a young age and was gently raised by her aunt and uncle. She fell in love with a steward and became pregnant. The cad left her, and she lost her baby. The uncle was so angry and disgraced by her mistake that he tossed her out. Becoming a courtesan was her only option."

"How dreadful," Brenna said. This explained much about Helen. She knew how strict society was about women and virtue. One small error in judgment, and a woman could be ruined.

"I, too, made that mistake," Lucy said, as if reading Brenna's thoughts. "Though, fortunately, my affair never produced a child. But I was caught in a situation with a young man by the lady of the household. He was her son." Lucy sighed. "He promised me marriage. Instead, I was left with nothing."

The room fell silent. Brenna had always assumed that courtesans went into the profession willingly. It surprised her to learn otherwise.

"You had no family to help you?" Brenna asked.

Lucy shook her head. "I was one of eleven children. My parents struggled on what my father made at the dairy. I could not return home and add to his burden."

For a long moment, Brenna pondered the story. She now understood why her father had sent her here. It was to teach her the consequences of bad choices. With these two grim stories, the reality of the hardship of life outside her sheltered world became painfully clear. These women had no one to support them when their situations became dire.

Yet her situation was not the same. She came from wealth, and one could not swing a stick nearly anywhere in England without hitting a Harrington, either by blood or by marriage. Surely her family would never put her out?

Still, scandal could ruin even a wealthy society miss. What if her plan had gone awry and she'd been forced to marry

Viscount Ashwood? Father would take any measure to keep her from ruin, even making her an unwilling viscountess.

Worse, what if Ashwood had been a highwayman in truth and had violated her in the ditch? She hated to think that perhaps the dreaded Viscount Ashwood *had* saved her from herself.

And yet that realization didn't make him any more palatable, nor did knowing he was a lord and not a criminal. He was despicable no matter what form he took. She still had to find a husband because of him.

"There are few choices for women seeking employment," Alice added. "Positions are filled as soon as they are posted. Poor women without employment often end up on the docks, servicing sailors. It is a lucky few who secure wealthy patrons."

Brenna thought about the women of the Harrington staff whose hard work made her life one of ease. One unfortunate turn, and any one of those women could have ended up here.

She'd no longer see the housemaids, Tippy, and even their cook the same way.

"Thankfully, we have Miss Eva," Iris said. She clasped her hands together and smiled. "She will give us husbands."

The grim conversation quickly turned lighter. Soon there was talk about a matching party and a Husbands Book. The women spoke about it in awed tones. Brenna assumed the latter was the way Eva found matches for her courtesans.

"I want a husband who is handsome and kind," Alice said, reaching to reclaim her needlepoint. She stabbed the cloth with the needle. "And a bit of wealth cannot hurt."

"I want a passionate man," Lucy said, smiling. At Alice's frown, she shrugged. "If I am to spend my life with one fellow, I want our beddings to be enthusiastic."

"Is sexual pleasure your only requirement?" Iris pressed. She frowned. "What if he has smelly breath or a large nose?"

"Then I shall have to hope another part of him is large as well. Then I can forgive his breath."

"Lucy!" Iris scolded. "You must not talk so!"

Lucy glanced sheepishly at Brenna. "I do apologize for my outspoken candor. I will try to behave."

Brenna tipped her face down and fiddled with her skirt to hide her blush. Where was Sophie?

The women continued to discuss men and the matching party, though they kept the topic suitable for all ears.

Brenna wished her own life was so easy to settle. She needed a husband, too, and thought society might fare well with its own Husbands Book. No matter how she put her mind to finding an acceptable partner, she had no success.

It was that unpleasant Lord Ashwood that continued to occupy her thoughts. He was crass and rude and unfortunately handsome, if one preferred a man who eschewed a razor. He likely enjoyed treating women poorly as a rule and took some fiendish pleasure in doing so.

If only he'd been less rude. If only he'd accepted her offer and helped her. If only he hadn't told on her to Father.

If only.

Growing weary of husband talk, Brenna excused herself and went to her room. The bedroom was barely large enough to spin around in, though a colorful coverlet on the narrow bed and soft blue curtains warmed the space. She wondered if this was the room Laura occupied after Simon had rescued her and left her in Eva's care.

For the first time all day, Brenna smiled. Her family certainly had its adventures. And secrets.

She went to the dressing table and sat on the chair. Her eyes looked back at her from the mirror; the same green eyes as her mother. It was the blue shadows under her eyes that were new. The stress of implementing her father's unwelcome plan was making her positively haggard.

What to do? Finding an unacceptable suitor was no longer an option. It was likely to end badly and would take up too much of her valuable month. Still, she needed a husband, a man who would not protest if she spent her time lost in the social whirl of London, who'd not ask much of her, who'd be content with small increments of her time in exchange for a large dowry.

Slowly the grim line of her mouth dissolved into a smile, and her eyes took on a wicked cast. A man who'd rather spend time buried in the country with his sheep.

* * *

Darkness disappeared into gold and orange hues as dawn drifted over the horizon. Brenna slipped over the sash of the first-floor parlor window and dropped to the ground, her boots making a soft thud on the damp grass.

She paused and listened for any sign that she'd been heard. Nothing indicated that her escape had been noted. Though the small staff of servants were beginning their day, Miss Sophie and the former courtesans were still abed.

This was the perfect time to escape. She'd not be noticed missing for several hours.

She adjusted her borrowed clothing. She'd found the blue skirt and soiled white shirt in a bin meant for charity, and she'd altered the skirt into a crude pair of trousers with scissors and two rows of crooked stitches.

A coach ambled down the street, and she pressed herself against the house. She breathed again only after the conveyance made a turn at the corner and faded off into the distance.

Thankfully, her father hadn't posted guards. She felt guilty breaking his trust but hoped that if her adventure went well, all would be forgiven when she returned.

Like a thief, she lowered the window behind her and crossed the small garden. The gate squawked when she pushed it open and stepped through. The groom from the house next door stood just outside the gate with her horse, Brontes, saddled and waiting.

Once she'd decided to run off, a quick trip into the mews after supper, and a brief search of the row of small stables, found her the perfect conspirator. The groom had no qualms about thievery for the right price.

"Yer late," he grumbled, and scratched his ear. He was a slovenly fellow of undetermined age, whose stained clothing smelled offensively of manure and ale.

"I overslept." She nuzzled the mare's white nose and smiled as the horse returned the nuzzling. "Were there any problems collecting her?"

He grinned, showing a missing tooth. In the dim light, he appeared a menacing character. Thankfully, Brenna was within screaming distance of several houses, should he decide to collect more than the agreed-upon payment.

"Not a one. The stable is not well watched. Only a fool does not guard 'is horses."

Brenna glared. "Lord Harrington does not expect anyone to steal from him." She scanned his unpleasant face. "You promised to speak about this to no one. I ask you now to renew that promise."

He shrugged and stuck out his calloused hand. "Yer reasons fer stealing the nag are no matter te me."

She showed him his payment. "You left the note?" At his nod, she pressed her ear bobs into his open palm. He grinned again, licked his lips, and ambled off.

Father would be livid when he received the note and realized she'd taken Brontes. Worse, that she'd fled the courtesan school and thwarted his orders. If this plan did not end as she hoped, it would be the convent, or Chester Abbot, for her. Either made her shudder.

Shaking off growing reservations, she quickly made certain the stirrups were at the right height, then wrapped the reins around Brontes's neck. With the skill of an experienced rider, Brenna mounted and settled into the saddle.

Riding astride was not difficult. As a child, she'd raced bareback around the fields with her brothers on whatever grazing horses they could catch. She knew this ride would take her some distance and hoped her disguise would keep her from recognition should she stumble upon someone she knew.

The saddle, her odd clothing, and the fact that she was traveling alone would be ruinous if she were caught.

Adjusting her hooded cloak to partially obscure her face from view, she made her way from London.

By the time she reached the outskirts, though still early, the road west was already filled with travelers. She waited until a pair of coaches passed her, heading in the right direction, and fell in behind them for safety.

If she kept up the brisk pace, she'd be at Beckwith Hall in about two hours. If her plotting came to fruition, she'd return in a day or two, none the worse for wear.

With a husband in tow.

Chapter Four

❧❧❧

T he inn was raucous, the sound of ribald laughter spilling from open windows and into the darkened yard.

Brenna slowed as she neared the squat and ramshackle building, her eyes and ears alert to possible danger. After discovering through his butler that her quarry, the now missing viscount, had left his home a half day earlier on a ride north to find his sister, she knew the simple trip to find her future husband had gotten much more complicated.

This was the third inn she'd stopped at today, and both she and Brontes were nearing the end of their stamina. If she did not find Ashwood here, she could be in serious trouble.

Clearly, by the looks of it, the inn was no place for a lady. Worse, the darkness that now shadowed the roads held all sorts of dangers to unwary travelers. A woman alone would be easy pickings for highwaymen and other scoundrels.

There was nowhere else to go. She'd have to take her chances with the inn and pray for luck to finally turn her way.

She'd not expected to have to chase down the viscount on muddy roads and through bouts of both blinding sun and brief showers. She longed for home and a bath to ease her aching muscles and clear travel grit from her hair and skin.

"Can I take yer 'orse from ye, Miss?" A small boy with

dirty cheeks and mussed hair peered up at her in the dim light spilling from the inn.

Brenna nodded. "See that she is fed and watered."

"Aye, Miss." The boy took Brontes and the proffered coin and ambled away. Brenna pulled her hood low to hide her face, traveled the short distance to the door, and pushed her way into the inn. Hers wasn't the best disguise, but it would have to do.

The smell of unwashed bodies and peat smoke assailed her senses, and she stumbled to a halt just inside the door. She resisted the urge to press a finger up under her nose. Showing weakness could encourage harassment from the coarse men seated around the common room.

A few travelers glanced in her direction, as she swept her gaze around the packed space. Thankfully, there were a few women scattered about, though not enough to ease her mind.

Quickly, so as not to draw more attention to herself than necessary, she sought out the innkeeper. She described Ashwood as she remembered him from their one brief encounter.

"There are several men who match that description, Miss." He shrugged and ran his gaze over her, his keen eyes taking her measure. "Maybe, if ye give me a moment to think on it, me mind will clear."

Brenna frowned. She understood quite well what would clear his mind. She reached into her pocket and pulled out a coin. She held it up. "The man has a small scar under his left eye."

The innkeeper reached for the coin. Brenna pulled it back. "The information first," she said. She wasn't a world traveler, but she had the intelligence to know the man would cheat her, had he the opportunity.

The innkeeper scratched his round belly under a soiled white shirt and snorted. "The bloke took a room upstairs, third door on the right."

Brenna tossed him the coin and retreated toward the staircase. She felt the heaviness of several pairs of eyes on her as she weaved through the common room and hurried up the staircase.

The corridor to the indicated room was dark. Brenna

shivered and pulled the hood of the cloak low over her forehead. She couldn't let panic overwhelm her. If this man wasn't Lord Ashwood, she didn't think she'd make it back out of the building unmolested.

Brenna paused outside the door and looked down at her travel-stained garments. She knew she smelled of horse and leather. Not the best condition in which to confront the man she intended to marry. Still, she had no choice but to forge onward.

A sharp rap on the scarred panel brought a shuffle of feet from inside. Her heart raced. The door jerked open, and Lord Ashwood stood before her, his face weary and his clothing rumpled from hard travel.

He grimaced. "I didn't order a woman. Find another bed to warm, wench."

Brenna stuck her boot in the door before it slammed closed. "Wait." He paused. She pushed back her hood. "I was not sent by the innkeeper, Milord."

It was impossible to guess whether it was the sound of her voice or the remembrance of her face that caused the look of utter surprise on his face. But she had only enough time for a short gasp as he grabbed her arm, jerked her inside the room, and slammed the door behind her.

"Brenna." His grip tightened, and she tried not to whimper. "What in the hell are you doing here?"

He left her no time to answer. He pushed her against the wall and pressed a hand over her mouth as muffled footsteps sounded from the corridor. Whoever the party was, he or she paused outside the room as if listening for . . . something. Low-voiced conversation followed. There were at least two men.

Brenna felt Ashwood's irregular breaths on her cheek as he pressed against her. Her heart raced, and her blood whooshed in her ears.

"Where'd the wench go off to?" a gruff voice asked.

"She has to be 'ere somewheres," said a second man. They went silent, as if listening for clues to her whereabouts.

Brenna pressed her face against the viscount's neck to help muffle her breathing. He smelled of male and fresh air and slightly of horse. His arm around her confirmed he was no milksop but a man of sinewy strength. If the two men wanted trouble, she'd be well protected.

After a moment, and several low curses, the men moved on.

Ashwood held her thus for another minute or two before slowly releasing her. Thankfully, she'd found the viscount, or the men might have spent the evening violating her.

Relief flooded through her.

Dragging her farther into the room, he pushed her down on the bed. Leaning forward, he met her eyes. "Have you lost your senses?" he whispered, his tone harsh. "Do you understand how dangerous this place is? There are men below who would kill me to have you."

She shuddered. The image of the men taking turns on her was too much to bear. "I did not know."

He straightened and raked his hands through his hair. His face tightened. "You have one minute to tell me why you're here."

It took nearly half of her allotted time to find her voice. Even then, with him glaring at her, it was low and thin.

"I came to ask you to marry me."

R ichard's expression instantly changed from angry to bemused. He'd been shocked to find her outside his door, dressed like a waif in a soiled shirt and oddly altered skirt. That was nothing compared to this statement.

"You have *what*?"

She stood and walked a few steps away. When she turned back to him, there was purpose in her eyes. "Thanks to your note to my father, and interference, I have less than a month to find a marriageable man to wed me. He has decided I need a husband to curb my mischievous ways." She met his eyes. "As it was you who set him on this unacceptable course, I have decided that it will be you who is the solution."

Weary from a long day of searching for Anne, it took him a moment to fully grasp her words. She wanted to marry him to satisfy her father's command?

Certain that she was crazier than he'd thought after their first encounter, he figured somewhere along her lineage was a

Harrington who was completely mad. And that relative had passed it on to Brenna.

"Any trouble you have gotten into was of your own doing, young lady. You'll not use me as a pawn against your father." He walked to the door and pressed his ear to the wood. Thankfully, the corridor was silent. The men had gone. "I will keep you here with me tonight, and in the morning I'll send you back to London on the first mail coach out."

Richard glanced to the one chair the room possessed. He collected it, tested it for worthiness, and jammed the high back under the door handle. "That should keep them out should they return."

When he turned, Brenna's arms were crossed over her curvy chest and her cloak was tossed on the edge of the bed. There was a stubborn set to her jaw. He braced himself for an argument.

"You will marry me," she said.

"I'll not." He reached for the tankard of cheap ale and took a deep swallow. If he'd known she'd show up, he would have asked the innkeeper for a barrel of the stuff. "You need to find yourself another victim."

In the firelight, her hair fell about her pretty face and shoulders in a tangle of dark waves, the mass having largely escaped the binding of her braid. Her expressive green eyes peered at him, heavy with defiance, and he knew he'd best settle in for a long night.

She sighed but held her tongue, which in no way gave comfort. He suspected that Brenna was working a new argument through her mind, another way to convince him to sacrifice himself on the sword for her.

If she expected him to give in to her demands, she was in for a very, very long wait.

Damn, but she was fetching, despite her dishevelment. The split skirt followed the lines of her body almost to the point of being indecent. And there was nothing decent about his thoughts at the moment.

He could still feel the fullness of her breasts where they'd pressed against him mere moments ago.

Ignoring the surprising attraction for the chit, he sat on the bed, pulled off his boots, and removed his cravat. Giving consideration to her virginal sensibilities, he left on his shirt and breeches.

Once comfortable, he walked over to stoke the fire and checked the chair. Satisfied he'd not have to fight other men for her tonight, he stretched out on the bed and closed his eyes.

The only sound in the room was her soft breathing as she, he suspected, plotted a way to make him miserable.

"You cannot expect us to share the bed?" she said finally. "A gentleman would take the floor."

He opened one lid and peered at her. She was clearly put out by his lack of manners. Good, let her stew. She should have stayed home. "A lady would not show up uninvited at the door of an unmarried man, with or without a chaperone." He closed his eye. He did not need to see her face to feel her frustration. "I have a long day ahead tomorrow and need my rest."

Richard almost smiled at her low growl. "You are impossible," she said. "You must marry me. If we are found together, I will be ruined."

Knowing he'd never be allowed to sleep until the matter was settled, he sighed and sat up. "You should have considered the consequences of your actions before you hunted me down and passed through a crowded common room to find me. You may have been recognized. You Harringtons are well known."

Defiance changed to worry. She bit her lip. "If I return to London without a husband, Father will kill me."

At that moment, he knew she'd finally realized the seriousness of her actions. He almost felt sorry for her.

Almost.

"Though you exaggerate, I agree, Walter will not be pleased that you've come to me or risked your neck, again, to defy him. Perhaps I can write him a note, explaining that you have not been compromised and your innocence is intact."

Like a feral cat caught in a cage, she hissed, "As if your note would soothe my outraged father. How would you convince him that you did not touch me? Once he discovers that we have spent the evening together, he will see us wed. You will be my husband."

Richard knew she was right. His stomach burned, and he

pushed from the bed. "You little minx. You planned this from the start. You knew you would force this wedding the minute you decided to follow me into this inn."

"I did no such thing." She lifted her hands as he approached her. Good, let her believe he'd strangle her. The girl deserved that, and more. "I swear I would not force you to marry me." She darted around the bed. "A compromise is all I ask."

This stopped him. "And what do you have to offer that would entice me to marry you?"

"I know you are searching for your missing sister. If I help you search for her, then you will agree to marry me."

A lock of hair slipped over her left eye. She pursed her deep pink lips and blew it aside. He went hard.

"How will you explain your absence from Walter?" He shifted to hide the evidence of his interest.

"I will tell him that I went off to Cornwall to visit my ancient aunt, Primrose, using the quiet of her country cottage to whittle down a list of potential suitors," she said. "He will never know I spent a few days chasing off to Gretna Green with you."

Though the plan was thin, it would keep him from damaging his friendship with Walter. He knew the hurt his old friend would feel knowing that he had a part in ruining his daughter, even if he was entirely innocent in the matter.

"Won't Aunt Primrose give you away?"

"She is a sweet soul but a touch forgetful," she said, shrugging. "It will not help him to ask her about my visit."

The exasperating Miss Harrington had an answer for every argument.

"I do not need your help," he said finally. "I have several men, loyal men, who are right now looking for Anne. You will only slow me down. Besides, what experience as an investigator do you have? What skills do you possess that will aid my hunt?"

She swallowed. "Er, none." A quick flash of panic crossed her face. The impulsive girl had clearly not thought this through. In her desire to thwart her father, she'd acted rashly—twice, if he counted the coach encounter. Perhaps her father was right. She needed a firm hand.

It would not be his.

He shook his head. "I think I shall take my chances with a note. You have nothing to offer that would make me willing to shackle us together for eternity."

For a long moment, she stood there, uncertain, and he was sure he could hear cogs turning in her brain.

"Nothing I can say or do will change your mind?" she asked softly.

"Nothing," he replied, confident of his win.

Then to his surprise, a slow smile crossed her perfect mouth, drawing him in and leaving him unable to turn away. He wasn't certain of her intentions until she crossed the space between them, hips swaying, eyes alight with mischief.

When she pressed her lush body against him and circled her arm around his neck, the soft scent of lilies and some other such flower teased his senses. He found that he did not even mind the hint of horse on her skin.

He was frozen in place. All he could think about was her hand tangled in his too long hair and the feel of her breasts teasing his chest—well, that and the slight parting of her perfect lips.

"Nothing?" she asked him again, in a breathless whisper, as she pulled his mouth down to hers.

Chapter Five

Scandalous, outrageous, delicious—Brenna slipped through every one of those emotions and more as she kissed the viscount's hard mouth, the length of her body draped against his. Though her previous chaste kisses had been with men who would be considered agreeable and charming, this man was anything but. He was hard and dangerous and completely unpleasant. Yet he made her body tingle all the way down to her toes.

She felt the moment when tension left him and he gave in to the kiss. And give in he did. One hand slid to her back, and the other weaved into her hair. Whatever control she thought she had changed the instant he deepened the chaste kiss by slanting his mouth over hers and showing her what it meant to kiss a man who was an expert in the matter.

His tongue dipped between her parted lips and sent a wave of both shock and heat through her senses.

Her throaty gasp was squelched by his mouth as his hand moved from back to buttock, pushing her against a hard ridge in his breeches, which she knew, from her brief time at the courtesan school, was an erection.

Her face burned with the knowledge.

Brenna felt the room tilt as he backed her up against the wall and trapped her in his embrace. The kiss was hot and his body overwhelming, as she finally gave up all thoughts of the scandalous placement of his hand and her body's innocent yet overwhelming reaction to his warmth. She succumbed to the kiss.

No boyish kiss was this. He tasted of ale and seduction. She whimpered low in her throat, wrapping her arms around his neck, seeking something . . . more.

Then just as quickly as the kiss began, she was freed. He stepped backward, his face hard, leaving her feverish flesh to the chill of the room.

"Tempting a man can have dire consequences, Milady. I could have easily taken the innocence you just offered so willingly." He turned and reclaimed the tankard, dismissing her.

Brenna stood there, held up by the wall, not knowing if she should claw out his eyes or throw a chair at him. The man was impossible—completely impossible!

Instead of launching an attack, she seethed.

"I was not offering you my innocence," she ground out.

She'd kissed him to show there was more to her than what he saw—an uncaring and spoiled noblewoman who would do anything to get her way. And she *was* spoiled, she knew. Her parents indulged her, the servants were there to fulfill her every whim, and she was used to getting her way. She wanted him to see her as a woman beneath her noble shell.

"Truly?" he said, clearly not believing a word she'd uttered. "I am certain I felt the invitation when you pressed your breasts against me."

"Oh, you are a horrible man!"

He smiled wryly. "So I've been told."

Brenna knew she was outmanned. She'd thought her chaste little kiss would entice him to beg to marry her. What a fool she'd been! She'd thoroughly misjudged him. This man was different, and her father was right. She knew nothing of the world outside her perfect existence. In that moment, with the feel of his hand still lingering on her bottom, Lady Brenna Harrington lost part of her innocence.

Accepting a momentary defeat, she pushed off the wall. He'd won a point, but she was not about to return to London without him. There was too much at stake.

If she'd learned anything from her brief time at the school, it was that women had more power than men suspected. They held the key to drive men to war, to take them to their knees. That key was seduction. She would use it now, driven by instinct, to make him want her, to marry her.

"You enjoyed the kiss," she said boldly. She shoved aside her anger and pretended experience she did not have. She had to make him mad for her or her plan would fail. "I felt your interest."

His body stiffened.

"You think of me as Walter's daughter and therefore untouchable." She walked to the bed and ran her fingertips over the coverlet. "At this moment, your body is warring with your sense of honor. You want me; I know you do."

"Do not press me, Brenna." He tossed back the remaining ale and kept his back to her. "I am a nudge away from paddling you."

Brenna hid her smile. "You treat me as if I am a child and you a man of advanced years. We are not so far apart. You are not yet thirty, not too old."

"A person's age is not always judged in years, but experiences. In that, you *are* a child." He finally turned to her, his face stoic. "I served my country, saw things a young man should never see. I married young and lost my wife and son in childbirth. My sister may be in danger, and I can do nothing for her." He walked to her. "So if you think I will easily succumb to your seduction, you need to rethink your game. I am world weary and hardened to the games of women."

Stunned by his confession, Brenna sat on the bed. She realized she knew very little about the man she intended to wed, and nothing about his lost wife and child.

"I didn't know," she said softly. She tried to imagine the pain of losing someone she loved. How he must have suffered.

Ashwood's jaw tightened. "I have much to accomplish tomorrow. While there is still a chance to save my sister from making a grave mistake, I'll continue onward." He returned to the bed and stretched out on the quilt. "For now, I need rest."

Brenna watched him for a moment before taking a second quilt from the foot of the bed and making a pallet on the floor. She'd not ask him for any consideration.

Blowing out the lamp, she lay on her hard bed and listened

to him breathe. "I want to help you find Anne. Though I have no experience in such matters, I can see things through a woman's eyes. If we are successful, perhaps you will do me my favor in return. As your wife, I would make no demands of you."

The silence stretched until Brenna was convinced he was asleep. Then, "Perhaps," he whispered in the darkness.

The first rays of sunlight stole through the darkness and peeked through a space in the worn curtains, the light teasing her lids. Brenna awoke to movement in the room, stretched, and startled upon realizing she was in the bed and tucked neatly beneath the quilt.

Sometime during the night, Lord Ashwood had placed her thus. There was no other explanation for her placement there or his kindness. She'd certainly given him no reason to treat her well.

"The maid brought bread with jam and tea," he said, from a shadowed corner of the room. "If you hope to break your fast before we leave, you'd better hurry. I'll wait below."

Before she could answer, he collected a small pack and left her alone. Brenna wasted no time dawdling and hurried from the bed. She took care of her needs, ate quickly, and fled the room. There was no guarantee he'd wait very long for her. He'd said he was in a hurry to find his sister. He'd not think twice about leaving her behind.

The common room was quiet, with only two men lingering over their breakfast. She worried that they might be the two men from last evening, but they paid her no mind.

Ashwood sat in the corner watching her with hooded eyes, a hat low on his head. He was dressed casually in workman's clothing and his dusty coat. He was obviously trying not to draw notice to himself, perhaps to protect his identity and therefore his sister's reputation. Or perhaps it was to keep from being robbed on the road. Either way, there was nothing about him that indicated his nobility or wealth.

He pushed up from his chair, and Brenna followed him outside.

Brontes was standing next to his horse, saddled and ready.

The mare bobbed her head as Ashwood gave the boy a coin and helped Brenna mount. Brenna patted Brontes's neck and stared down at her companion. "I thought I was to take the mail coach back to London."

He looked up from checking her stirrup. "I thought proper ladies rode sidesaddle."

She smiled. "Then we were both mistaken."

Ashwood snorted and stepped back. "The ride will be long and difficult. If you whine, whimper, or complain, I'll leave you off at the first coaching inn and be done with you."

Brenna shrugged. "Then do try to keep up."

Gathering the reins, she nudged Brontes. The mare took off as if she had wings, while Brenna laughed happily as a curse followed her flight. She was no simpering lass, and it was about time the viscount learned not to judge her only by her mistakes.

In the saddle, she was quite accomplished.

The path was easy to follow, and she slowed the horse to a walk when they came to the road, not wanting to tire her too quickly. Ashwood appeared around the bend, scowling. He drew up beside her.

They stopped.

"I already regret my decision to allow you to accompany me, but the mail coach is gone, and if I leave you behind, you'd only follow me anyway. Stubborn chit," he groused. "If I was ever fool enough to marry you, I'd never have peace."

"Oh, do not be grim," Brenna replied, her smile steady under his glower. "I was only setting your mind at ease. As you see, I am a skilled rider. I'll not whine, whimper, or complain even once, I assure you."

He moved his gaze down her, from her cloak, to her odd trousers, to her boots, and back. "I suppose I owe it to your father to return you to him in perfect order. I cannot watch you if you are straggling along behind me. So keep close. The road can be treacherous."

Not as treacherous as being with him, Brenna thought, if their kiss was the gauge on which to base her conclusion.

"So we are in agreement?" she asked, her tone hopeful. "We find your sister, and you marry me?"

"I agree to nothing. But I promise not to beat you. You

should consider that proof that I have forgiven you for your intrusion into my life."

Brenna scrunched up her face. "I do not like you."

He shrugged. "Then a marriage between us may work."

Not knowing how to read his moods, she took the comment, and the one about not beating her, as teasing, and left it at that. She was just pleased to be allowed to join his adventure. This would give her time to convince him to wed her.

If she returned to London without a spouse, it would not be for lack of trying.

Nudging his horse forward, he led on, and she fell in behind him. Taking advantage of the opportunity to observe him unnoticed, she let her attention roam.

His hair was a sort of mix of brown and light, a bit long and unkempt. She wondered what he would look like under the care of a valet and dressed in well-made clothing. He'd likely cut a fine figure. And she knew from spending time locked against his chest that the man hadn't an ounce of fat anywhere. He was a perfect male specimen.

A little tingle shivered through her as the kiss tugged at her mind. She wondered if, sometime during the next two or three days it would take to get to Gretna Green, they would share another kiss.

She certainly hoped so. If she were to marry the man, they'd share much more than that, even if their marriage was to be one of convenience, for his kiss was splendid, indeed.

The horses traveled onward for some time before Brenna's attention began to wander. The pace was steady, and Ashwood made no attempts to engage her in conversation.

They were on Great North Road, heading for Scotland, like an eloping couple eagerly seeking marriage, hurrying to keep ahead of outraged relatives.

Brenna glanced behind them, expecting to see her father racing after them, her brother Simon on his heels. There was nothing but road. She turned back, and her mind drifted.

Certainly Mother and Father were worried. She hated the idea of distressing them. Still, she could not return now, without an engagement in place, or Father would make good his threats.

Her neck prickled. She turned around again; this time

there were three riders, though she was confident none were Father or Simon.

She nudged Brontes to quicken her pace, remembering Ashwood's warning to stay close. A space had opened between them. The mare closed the gap, and Brenna took another glance behind her. The men had turned off. In their place, a large coach was visible in the distance and coming fast.

"Coach," she said, feeling foolish for worrying. They moved to the side of the road. There would be many travelers on the road today. She should not let her mind trick her into feeling danger. The inn was behind her, and there was no sign that the men from last evening had followed them and intended to abscond with her.

Brenna turned her face as the ornate coach sped past. She'd not risk recognition. Her family was well known in society.

Richard urged his horse into a lope. Brenna did the same. She'd thought this hunt for his sister would be a grand adventure. She'd see England in a way she'd never experienced. When her family traveled, it was always by coach. They stayed at the finest inns, or at the fine homes of friends.

Some adventure, this. He barely spoke to her.

After another hour, she'd reached the last thread of patience. When he drew his horse to a walk, she nudged Brontes up beside him.

"Are we heading for a particular destination, or are we just traveling north to Gretna Green with the hope of stumbling upon your sister?"

Ashwood looked around them and up at the sky before answering. "I was delayed from the search for a few days. My steward has gone ahead to Scotland. If he has news, he will leave word at the inns he visits. The first, if I am not mistaken, is not far ahead."

Brenna hid her relief. Though she'd promised not to complain, she did have to take care of certain needs.

The inn was small and tidy, and was far better than the one from last evening. Ashwood ordered a light repast and left Brenna at a table near a window. When he returned, he held a note that he tucked into his pocket.

"Andrew is certain that Anne passed this way by coach,

though there was no sign of Lockley. Perhaps they travel separately to keep from drawing attention." He took a chair across from her. "She will do anything to thwart me."

"She is headstrong like her brother," Brenna remarked, from behind the lip of her teacup.

He frowned. "I do not understand how a woman with good breeding and intelligence could desire to marry a man of such low character."

"She must love him. Perhaps she sees something you do not."

The frown deepened. "He has had two wives that were still in the schoolroom when he wed them, and the first he divorced to take the younger, second bride, who died last year of a fever. He has ruined two other young women in our village, one of whom was only fourteen." Ashwood shook his head. "Why he would want Anne is a mystery. At twenty-five, she is a full decade older than most of the girls he normally chooses."

The story left a sickening feeling inside Brenna. She did not know Anne but agreed with the viscount's concerns. A man who abused innocents would ruin his sister's life.

She reached to place a hand over his. "We will find her."

They locked eyes for a moment, and then he pulled away and stood. "Since you are both foolish enough to run away from your families, the least I can do is see to your care while you're under my protection and hope Anne is also safe." He tossed some coins on the table. "We must go."

Brenna took a last sip of tea, shoved a biscuit into her pocket, and scurried after her companion.

Chapter Six

It was almost noon, and two more inns behind them, when Richard eased his horse off the road and into a field, where a narrow creek wound its way through the weedy expanse.

They'd ridden hard, and the horses were tired. Truthfully, though he'd never admit it to Brenna, he needed rest, too. His back ached, and his eyes were losing focus. It was easier to use the horses as an excuse than to admit to his fatigue.

"We'll rest for a bit and eat." He slid off the horse.

He watched Brenna nod, her face weary. Her fortitude impressed him. Though he knew she had to be exhausted, she'd held to her promise and not complained.

"You find a spot to sit, and I'll retrieve the food," he said, and watched her dismount. She wobbled slightly but locked her knees and stayed upright. He kept his attention on her, expecting her to crumple, and when she did not, he snorted and turned away.

Brenna nodded a second time and ambled off. After slaking their thirst in the creek, he tied the pair of horses to a tree and untied the pack from behind his saddle. For a young woman who had been raised to a life of ease, she could certainly take a battering. Her bum alone had to ache.

As if to prove his point, she rubbed her backside as she

stepped into the shade of a large tree. He chuckled low. If nothing else, she had her father's strength.

The thought of Walter jerked his eyes from her backside. He could not forget who Brenna was. If anyone deserved his loyalty, it was Walter. He'd helped Richard when he was battling his demons and nearly everyone else had turned away from him. No matter how the kiss between them had left him out of sorts, he'd not betray his friend by taking liberties with his daughter.

This was easier to think than to actually carry out. Her appeal did not wane despite the layer of dust on her skin or the tangled locks of hair clinging to her damp skin.

He joined her where she leaned against the tree. Her eyes were half closed, the fan of black lashes shading her beautiful green eyes.

"The meal is sparse but should keep us until we stop for the night." He shook out his coat. "Come, eat."

She pushed from the tree and took a place on the coat. "I could eat a whole cow," she said, behind a yawn, and indicated a small group of bovines across the field.

"Unfortunately, we only have bread, cheese, and wine." He placed a cheese wedge between two bread slices and handed it to her. "The cows are thankful."

She paused in mid bite and stared. "Did you make a jest?"

He brought the wineskin to his mouth. "I have been known to do so now and then."

A smile weaved its way across her sun-kissed face. His breath caught with his focus on her mouth, the sort of full mouth that was made for wicked things.

Seeing the destruction of his friendship with her father looming, he cleared his throat and turned away.

Brenna shifted, and her knee came dangerously close to his thigh. "There is more to you than what you let me see."

He ate and said nothing. His silence did not discourage her attempt at conversation. She'd been quiet all morning. Whether it was the sunny meadow, the food, or her renewed energy from resting in the shade, something shook loose her tongue, and her target was him.

"I'd enjoy seeing you dressed in something other than

faded breeches and a dusty coat," she continued. Her gaze drifted over him. "You should find another tailor."

He frowned. Her look was pure innocence. "You clearly need a wife."

Manners kept him from looking skyward. "I promised to consider marrying you if you helped me find Anne. 'Consider' being the word of choice. Thus far, you have done nothing but follow along and test my patience."

The chance he'd marry her was minute. He'd vowed to never remarry, and he intended to keep to that promise.

Of course, a marriage of convenience would certainly chase off the several marriage-minded women of his acquaintance who had no qualms about openly seeking him out as a potential mate.

That alone should make him consider her proposal.

"And yet, you keep me with you. Why, I ask?" She took the wineskin and sipped. "Perhaps you are not finished kissing me?"

Richard scowled. Why couldn't Walter and Kathleen have whelped a less beguiling and aggravating child? By the time they reached Gretna Green, he'd likely be more inclined to strangle the chit than to wed her.

"Did you miss the lessons on proper behavior?" he said. His guilt weighed heavily on him. Her reminder did not ease his regret. "You must forget the kiss. It was a mistake, yours if I recall, and will not happen again. You are Walter's daughter. I will not ruin my friendship with him by kissing you again."

Brenna stared. "I talk of kissing, and you talk of my father. Interesting." Her eyes seemed to slip into his soul. "You have had too much darkness in your life. Once your sister has been returned home safely, and we are wed, I will make it my duty to see that you find happiness."

He crossed his arms. She was like a tiny dog attached to his boot by its sharp little teeth. No matter how much he tried to shake her off, she would not be dislodged. She planned to marry him, and that was that. "I have not agreed to wed you."

"You will." She smiled. "I always get what I want."

There were many ways to respond to her simple comment.

Even if she'd not carried the beauty of her mother, he'd still know her as a Harrington. Every one of them was born with a supreme confidence others lacked.

It was time to be honest with her before she turned her thoughts of marriage into a fanciful notion of happily ever after as his viscountess. There was no such thing as true happiness. Life was brutal, and marriage for love was a false illusion.

"I gave away my heart once, Brenna, and will not do so again," he said, with a harsh sigh. "If I do marry you, it would be a matter of convenience, nothing more. Do not ever expect me to love you."

T he bluntness of his comment took her aback like a slap. There was no questioning his feelings. When this adventure ended, she'd have a husband to satisfy her father, but Ashwood would not love her. Ever.

She'd not truly considered her life much further than the wedding. She assumed they would eventually grow fond of each other, and that would lead to love. Now even that had vanished under the brutality of his truth.

All her dreams of marrying for love would never come to fruition. Would a loveless marriage be the price worth paying to keep from having to marry Chester Abbot?

She tamped down her misgivings. She had no other options. She'd have to learn to live with her disappointment. "I do not ask for love," she said, hoping for an emotionless tone. "I have given up on that emotion. All I ask for now is a way out of my dilemma and for children someday. Certainly one does not need affection from one's husband to accomplish those goals."

Even as she said the words, defeat filled her. For years she'd avoided the trap of a loveless marriage. Now she'd agreed to one without argument.

"Then we have an understanding," he said, handing her the flask. "Let us eat. We have miles yet to travel today."

The bland meal stuck in her throat, to be followed by several more hours of searching, until her hands cramped on the reins and her back cried out for a soft bed. While Richard questioned the innkeepers, Brenna questioned the maids. At the Black Crow's Inn, she learned about a woman who fit Anne's description.

"I am not convinced it was Anne," he said, after talking to the maid himself. "Lockley has taken an interest in her that defies his unhealthy proclivities. I suspect it has to do with her sizable dowry. He will be with her to keep her from changing her mind and fleeing him."

Brenna led him out of the inn. "Could you be wrong about their elopement? Nothing we've learned thus far has led us to conclude they are heading for Gretna Green."

Richard helped her mount before answering. "I've searched hill and dale around our village. I've sent men in all directions. There are no clues to lead me to conclude they've gone anywhere else but north. Lockley must know I'll kill him if he ruins her. He will marry her to save his neck."

"Then we shall continue toward Scotland." Brenna wouldn't argue. She knew nothing about Anne. If Ashwood was certain Anne had run off with Lockley, then she would keep her doubts to herself.

The day aged as the sun began to set. They took a room just before dark. The innkeeper assured them he'd not seen Anne. Brenna felt her companion's frustration.

"We are two days from Scotland and still nothing. And my steward is still missing." He tossed his pack on the bed. The maids set out food, filled the bathtub with hot water, and withdrew. "We are on a fool's errand."

Brenna leaned to sniff the lamb stew. Her mouth watered. "You cannot give up. Even if we are too late to save her from the marriage, you will have tried."

Eager to eat, she laid out the meal on the scarred table. In addition to the stew, there was wine and bread.

He grumbled under his breath as Brenna ate with vigor. The meal infused her tired limbs with warmth. "I shall take the first bath," she said, not waiting for his reply. Her achy bones longed to soak in the hot water.

She stepped behind the screen and slipped out of her clothing. She wanted to kick her offensive garments into the fire, but thought that traveling the roads wearing nothing but her cloak might be pushing the boundaries of propriety. Even for her.

Bathing with Richard—as she'd begun to think of him—just outside the screen was scandalous enough. As she lowered herself into the tub, she did not care. A low groan escaped her as the water closed in around her.

Silence fell as she scrubbed with a chunk of crude soap. Though coarse enough to scrub pots clean, the soap left her skin tingling and her hair free of debris.

She knew by the clank of spoon against bowl that Richard was eating. She wondered if he was thinking of her naked in the tub as he spooned stew into his mouth.

If so, she hoped he was tortured by the image. It was the least he deserved for all the aggravation he'd caused her with his grumbles and scowls.

Once clean, she leaned back and closed her eyes, a wistful smile on her lips. The bath was heavenly.

A chair scraped on the wood floor. His gruff voice carried past the screen. "Do you plan to stay in the tub all evening? If not, you have two minutes to exit the tub or we will soon be sharing the space."

Brenna sat upright. Share the bath?

Scandalized by the thought of their bodies intertwined in the tub, her face warmed, and her body tingled. She stood quickly, letting the night air cool her tempestuous thoughts.

"I am getting out." She stood and scrubbed dry with a towel, untangled her hair with a brush left with the soap, and stepped into her chemise. Without a robe to cover the thin fabric, she kept the damp towel clutched against her as she walked from behind the screen. "I did not expect to be traveling or I would have packed a valise. I have nothing else to wear."

Richard nodded, his eyes on her. His mouth tightened. "Tomorrow we will get you a gown."

"Thank you." She walked over to stand by the bed. Contemplating the night ahead, and her troubling attraction for the man, she took a quilt from the chair, rolled it up as best she could with one free hand, and divided the bed with the makeshift barrier. Then without asking which side of the bed he preferred, she dropped the towel, scooted beneath the sheet and quilt, and pulled them up to her chin. "Good night."

"Good night, Brenna."

Richard watched her adjust the covers to her chin, her back to him, the shape of her curves not as well hidden beneath the faded quilt as he would have liked. She was like a siren leading him to his death, and he struggled to fight her silent call.

Even now, the image of her body barely hidden under her thin chemise caused him to harden beneath his breeches.

With a low curse, he tore his eyes away and walked behind the narrow screen. Doffing his clothes, he stepped into the rapidly cooling water. Knowing she'd been naked in that same bath moments previous hardened his cock a second time, and he silently cursed his lack of control.

He struggled to regain his wits, turning his thoughts to her father, to Anne, to parliament, anything that would keep him from thinking of Brenna lying warm and soft in the bed.

The effort gained him little, but he did manage to finish the bath without spilling his seed in the water.

After, he dried off and reclaimed his breeches. Brenna was breathing softly when he returned to her, her exhaustion from the day's ride having taken a toll. He watched her sleep, his arousal returning with a vengeance. Emitting a low frustrated growl, he snatched the rolled quilt from the bed, dragged the room's only chair to the window, put his bare feet on the sill, and jerked the blanket over him.

A night of suffering in the uncomfortable chair would be his penance for his heated thoughts. A mistake would be to share the bed with her. He knew better than to tempt fate.

With moonlight filtering over his face, he slowly drifted into a fitful sleep.

Chapter Seven

Richard waited downstairs while Brenna reluctantly climbed from the bed to dress. The crumpled shirt and makeshift trousers had smelled so much like horse and grime the previous night that they offended her senses. She blanched at the thought of putting them back on and wished she'd thought ahead to pack a gown. Unfortunately, without that option, she had no choice but to seek out the offending items.

With her resolve weakening, she forced herself toward the corner where she'd tossed the garments, but they were not to be found. Then she noticed a dress hung over the chair behind the screen. Upon further investigation, she found it to be nearly new, blue cotton, with the skirt divided for riding astride.

Beside it was her slightly frayed cloak, shaken free of road dust and pressed.

She smiled, delighted.

Richard. He'd obviously ordered the dress sometime after she'd fallen asleep so that they could continue north without the delay of searching for a shop, though she suspected a delay was not his only reason for the purchase. His senses were likely offended by her old clothing, too.

She didn't care where the dress came from, only that it was clean and the skirt altered for riding.

After hurrying through her toilet, she braided her hair into one plait down her back and stepped into the gown. Though slightly bigger than she, the item fit nicely.

When she joined him a few minutes later, she found him halfway through a breakfast of sausages, ham, and coddled eggs. A second plate awaited her arrival.

The great room was half full of travelers and surly characters, but she gave them little notice. Richard had chosen a table in a corner, his face still unshaven and looking far more handsome than he should. Her heart skipped a beat.

"Thank you for the dress," she said, taking a seat across from him and placing the cloak on an open chair. She picked up her fork and gave him a luminous smile. "I hoped you burned my old garments."

He grunted in reply. Brenna was certain she'd seen a brief flicker of appreciation over her fresh appearance, despite his surly mood.

"We should reach Gretna Green by tonight, then?" She took a bite of eggs, and he nodded. "I hope we find Anne. I would hate to think I'd spent these last few days enduring your foul moods for naught."

He paused and lifted his eyes to her. She stared innocently. He frowned and continued eating.

"And as I have been an excellent companion and investigator, I shall expect payment." She indicated the dress. "This dress will make an excellent wedding gown."

His fork clattered on his plate.

"Once we are wed," she continued unabated, "my father will have to accept you as my husband. Any anger he has over my running off to Scotland with you will dissipate under his happiness to see me successfully matched."

He grunted and spoke through a bite of ham. "Your father will despise me."

Brenna chewed down a nibble of sausage. "Once our first child is born, he will forgive you." She knew she shouldn't tease him but enjoyed it nonetheless. "By child five, you will have fully returned to his good graces."

Richard looked as though he wanted to paddle her. She reached for her teacup. "Oh, do not scowl so. I am teasing you. Truthfully, I need a husband, and you need a wife. If the worst happens and Anne married that bounder, you won't want his child inheriting Beckwith Hall, now would you?" She did not wait for an answer, as his deepening scowl was enough. "I promise not to make unreasonable demands on you. Your life will continue much as it was. You will live in the country, and I will reside in London. We will only need to suffer each other long enough to beget an heir and perhaps share an occasional Christmas goose to consider the union a rousing success."

Richard's hands twitched. Thankfully for her, they were in a common room with witnesses, making throttling her impossible. His orderly life had been tossed awry these last few days, and Brenna was at the top of the disorder.

The chit had planned out his life without considering his wishes. He did not want to marry her. Not now, not ever. The difficult part would be returning her to her father without Walter putting a bullet in him.

"The idea of spending the rest of my life with you strikes terror in my soul," he grumbled. "You are far too flighty to make a good wife, and the idea of you mothering my offspring makes me shudder."

Her mouth dropped open. She sputtered for a moment before collecting herself and leaning forward with a damning glare. "I am not flighty. Though I may be spirited, and sometimes act rashly, I am not without some intelligence," she snapped. "And I will make a kind and loving mother."

He pondered her for a moment. In spite of her impulsiveness, she was indeed well schooled. It was curbing the other that left him concerned.

"I do not wish for children," he said finally. "I have seen what happens when childbirth goes wrong. I will not have another wife die at my hands."

Brenna's face paled. He did not take any satisfaction from shocking her with his bluntness.

"Not all mothers die in childbirth," she said softly.

"Yet some do," he said. "I'll not take that risk again."

He stood abruptly, and the chair wobbled. This was a conversation he'd not have with her. His private pain was not her business. If he ever did marry her, she'd have to learn to keep her nose out of his history.

Paying the innkeeper for breakfast, he walked out of the inn, Brenna hurrying along behind him.

Expecting an argument, Brenna surprised him by saying nothing. Clearly, his sentiment about children had finally left her speechless. But he would not change his mind. The loss of his wife and son had sent him into a darkness that had fully consumed him. If it hadn't been for Walter Harrington, he would be dead.

Minutes ticked by as Brenna followed Richard, the horses plodding along the dusty path back to Great North Road. She hated the idea of another long day in the saddle but knew complaining would earn her a space in a mail coach heading south. That could not happen before a legal and binding marriage between them.

The abject sadness that edged his words when he spoke of his lost family had nearly knocked her flat. His determination to never risk another wife and child to death had almost brought her to tears.

It was the idea of marrying him and never having his love, or his children, that sent a full complement of emotions whirling through her mind and heart.

Could she make such a bargain to save herself from an unwanted marriage? Was she truly that desperate? These were certainly points to ponder.

The road seemed an endless line of pits and ruts as Brontes followed Richard's gelding with minimal guidance. Somewhere up ahead was Scotland. By the time they reached the border, her decision had to be made. How much could she sacrifice?

The weight of it filled her heart like a stone.

The morning aged, mist hanging over the low areas, refusing to give way to the sun. The road was eerily quiet but for an occasional coach rumbling past.

Richard rode in silence. She saw stiffness in his upright posture. She wanted to offer comfort but did not know how. Truthfully, she knew no matter what she said or how she said it, the topic of his lost family would make him angry. She was too weary to risk another argument. She wanted peace between them.

It was a full hour since they'd left the inn that she felt a prickle of unease on the back of her neck. Brontes spun her head around to peer back down the road. Brenna turned in the saddle to see what had interested the mare.

She saw a pair of riders coming up behind them, riding at a gentle lope, as if in no hurry. There was nothing outward about the men to cause alarm.

Perhaps they sought a runaway family member of their own. She'd heard that many fathers and brothers made this same desperate journey to rescue their daughters and sisters from their impulsive acts.

Still, she could not shake a feeling of unease. She felt it in her bones.

Turning forward, she urged Brontes to close the gap with Richard. It didn't take long before she looked back a second time, and her stomach dipped.

The men had narrowed the distance between them just enough for Brenna to realize they were a pair from the inn she'd seen that morning. She recognized the taller man's soiled green coat.

"That is odd," she said to herself. "They left before us." She watched them for another few seconds before a trill of alarm took root and spread through her. Their eyes were focused on her.

"Lord Ashwood. I think we may be in trouble."

He twisted in the saddle. His gaze darted to her, then past to the men. He cursed low, stopped his horse, and spun around. Brontes, surprised by the change, jumped sideways, almost unseating Brenna.

"Stay behind me," Richard commanded. He managed to put himself and his gelding between her and the men. As if understanding their stealthy attack had been thwarted, the pair urged their horses forward at a rapid clip.

One man pulled a pistol from his coat and aimed. Brenna gasped. A shot exploded, and Richard jerked sideways. The gelding startled and unseated his rider. Richard hit the ground with a thud and a pained grunt.

Brenna scrambled off Brontes and ran toward him. He had just enough time to get to his feet unaided when the men were upon them.

Whoops followed as the pair circled Brenna and Richard, their raucous calls breaking the quiet, their horses a blur of motion and slashing hooves. Brenna gripped Richard's uninjured right arm, fearing she'd be trampled.

"What do you want?" Richard ground out, holding his arm. A small patch of blood marked his coat. "We have little coin."

The men looked at each other, then back at Richard. The taller man grinned. "What luck. It appears we found us a nobleman to rob."

The other said, "Ye wouldna know it from 'is clothes."

Trying not to show fear, Brenna scowled. "Leave us be," she demanded forcefully. All she gained was lecherous grins. "We have nothing you want."

The tall man tugged his beard and rubbed himself through his trousers. His companion chortled. "I think we'll take both yer blunt . . . and yer woman."

The second man needed no further encouragement. He nudged his horse forward, right at Brenna. She darted sideways, releasing Richard. She cried out when a hand caught her hair and jerked her backward against the attacker's horse. Richard tried to get to her, but the excited horse spun about, making rescue impossible.

"Release me!" She clawed at his hand, pain tearing through her scalp. She bit back a cry.

"Release me," he mocked her in a high voice. Her capturer's laughter ended with a pistol shot. He arched backward, a bloody hole in the center of his chest, freeing her, his eyes startled and wide eyed.

With a strangled grunt, he flopped back off the horse.

Brenna jumped away, though not fast enough to avoid the panicked horse. The beast knocked her down. Her left wrist twisted, sending a sharp pain through her hand. She cried out as the riderless horse bunched up and bolted off down the road.

Through the pain, she saw Richard holding a smoking pistol. His face was hard-set and dangerous. She shivered.

The other man, wielding a knife, looked from his fallen companion, then to Richard, and decided he was outmanned. He jerked his horse about and dashed away in a trail of dust.

Brenna raced to Richard. He lowered the pistol and looked

down at his arm. Just above the elbow, a patch of blood grew through his coat sleeve.

"You're hurt." She gently touched the place with her good hand and swallowed to fight back a sob. He'd be dead had the bullet hit a handsbreath to the left. The idea was too horrible to imagine. "You need to see a surgeon."

He shook his head. "It is not deep." He looked at the dead man. "I should have taken better care to make certain we were not followed. We may have avoided this."

Brenna shook her head. "We had no reason to suspect we'd be robbed. The road is well traveled." As if to confirm her words, a coach appeared around the bend and rolled past them, the coachman not even casting a glance in their direction.

Apparently a dead man lying on the edge of the road was not enough reason to slow the speeding coach.

Sighing, Brenna turned back to him. He bent and straightened his arm, then winced. "We must get you patched up," she said. "Can you ride?"

He looked at her sidelong. "Truly, it is nothing."

She crossed her arms. "I don't care if it is nothing more than a burn. You will not help your sister or yourself if you die from an infection."

Frowning, he met her eyes. She refused to look away. The stubborn man had met his equal.

Finally, he nodded. "We will continue north to see if we can find an inn or a surgeon. Will that please you, Milady?"

Brenna nodded. "A short side trip will not put us too far behind. And your steward will be in Gretna Green to watch for Anne. I'm certain he'll not fail you, or face your wrath."

Grumbling under his breath, Richard went to collect Brontes and helped Brenna into the saddle. She whimpered softly and rubbed her hand. He reached for her arm.

"What have you done to yourself?" he asked.

"My wrist. I hurt it when the horse knocked me down."

He pushed back her sleeve. The wrist was slightly swollen. He probed it gently. She gritted her teeth.

"I do not suspect a break. More likely, it's sprained." He eased her sleeve down. "We will find shelter and tend to us both." He looked at the dead man. "First we need to tend to him."

A few minutes later, a farmer in a wagon appeared on the

road, and Richard waited until the man drew near. He waved the man down. "We were attacked by two men," he explained. "The other escaped. You would do me a great kindness if you could turn his body over to the nearest constable." He pulled a handful of coins from his pocket. The farmer nodded and took the payment. Between them, they loaded the dead man into the wagon.

"My thanks," Richard said.

With the transaction completed, Brenna held the reins in her good hand and watched Richard mount. He'd been correct. The bullet had not slowed him. He was as strong and confident as ever. It would take more than an ill-aimed bullet to break him. The man had strength aplenty.

It seemed like hours before they found an inn. The place was old and squat, and the term "inn" gave it an air of legitimacy it did not deserve. There were few travelers in the great room, and the place smelled little better than a stable.

"I apologize for the accommodations," Richard said.

"Do not concern yourself over me," Brenna said, glancing at his sleeve. "I could sleep in a barn."

Their eyes met and held. His mouth twitched, and he nodded. "Of that, I have no doubt."

Richard found the innkeeper, and he explained what they needed. The man walked back through an open door. A few minutes later he returned, followed by a maid worn by age and circumstance. She carried cloth strips for bandages and a tin of salve. "The salve will heal anything that ails ye," she said, and ambled back the way she'd come.

He took a key from the innkeeper and led Brenna up one flight of stairs to their room. The door hung on cracked leather hinges, and Richard both locked the door and pushed a chair up against it, not only for safety but for keeping the door from falling off its hinges.

"I stand a greater risk of catching an infection here than in the saddle," he said gruffly, shucking off his coat and taking a seat on the bed.

Brenna looked around the dusty space and found a basin of tepid water. It appeared to be fresh. "I agree. Still, it has a roof. Hopefully, our stay will be short."

Opening the tin, Brenna leaned forward to examine the

contents, and the pungent smell burned her eyes. She coughed and quickly replaced the lid. "It smells horrible."

She joined Richard on the bed. She lifted the lid just enough for him to sniff the salve. He grimaced and said, "I suspect the recipe includes cow dung and rotten food."

"I believe you may be correct." Brenna waited while Richard removed his shirt. The bare flesh took her aback. Though she'd assumed that in spite of his title and wealth, he'd lived a life mired in physical labor, the reality of his hard male form displayed for her viewing pleasure was breath stealing.

The expanse was touched by the sun and marked by angles and planes of rippled muscles.

"Oh, my," she said, before catching herself. He followed the path of her eyes down to where she stared at his flat stomach. Her cheeks burned.

"You blush like an innocent," he said softly.

"I am an innocent," she said, as the burn deepened. She knew her cheeks were bright red.

When he lifted his eyes, there was amusement there. "One would not know it from the way you asked me to compromise you, during our first meeting."

Brenna grimaced. "I was desperate. Certainly, you will not hold that against me forever."

Their eyes locked. Brenna's heartbeat thudded in her ears. She was close enough to touch him, feel his warmth. After the attack and the long ride, the longing to slip into his arms and ask to be held was great. But she knew it was also exceedingly inappropriate.

So she turned her attention to his arm. The wound was red, as the bullet had scraped along the skin to take off a layer of flesh. Richard was correct. It wasn't serious. The blood had caked in the shirt and stemmed its flow.

"Sadly, you'll live," she muttered, and took a piece of cloth to the basin to dampen it. When she returned, she washed the blood away and reached for the salve. He leaned to watch her work, and his breath caressed her face. His mouth was dangerously close—too close.

She silently scolded herself for the scandalous path of her thoughts. Her duty was to help him, not ogle his body and daydream of his kisses.

"Your concern is touching," he said.

"I have to keep you alive for the wedding." She handed him the tin to hold and stretched his arm out over her lap. His hand curled over her thigh. She almost leaped out of her skin with the intimate contact. Quickly, she used her good hand to spread the offensive goop on his arm. He didn't twitch, though his hand tightened on her leg. Tingles spread out from her thigh.

He was dreadfully attractive. She'd have to be dead not to notice. Lud help her!

She bit her lip to hold her concentration and to fight a sigh. He was too close and too deliciously warm. Her eyes lifted, saw his intense gaze on her face, and darted back to his wound. The weight of his stare, beneath a tangle of tousled hair, made her body flush.

"Hand me a cloth strip." Her voice wavered. She knew if she did not get the wound wrapped quickly and remove his arm from her leg, she'd melt all over him like warm honey. "And another." Working efficiently, the wound was soon covered.

"Perfect." She tucked the last end of the cloth under and nodded. "You were an excellent patient."

He thwarted her attempt to move away by linking her hand with his.

She froze, not knowing his intentions. She stared at his hard mouth. Would he kiss her? She desperately wanted another kiss!

Instead, he took her injured hand and turned it upright. She'd nearly forgotten about her wrist. She felt foolish for thinking he'd steal a kiss.

"It doesn't hurt." She tried to flex it and whimpered. "Perhaps it hurts a little bit."

She peered around his shoulder as he examined the wrist. It was swollen and a funny blue and purple color.

"We'll wrap it so that it will not bend, and hopefully in a few days, it will recover," Richard said. He reached for the remaining cloth strips. He laid her hand on his knee and gingerly wrapped the wrist. "Too tight?" he asked.

"Not too," she replied. The gentleness of his calloused

hands surprised her. For a bold man, his touch was feather light.

Taking the moment to examine him up close, she noticed small crinkles around his eyes, probably more from squinting in the sun than laughter. He was the sort who would find society frivolous and the usual amusements tiresome.

His hair looked impossibly soft and fell in disarray over his forehead. His nose was slightly crooked at the base, likely from an old break, and the small scar under his eye added to his rakish appeal. But it was his bright blue, expressive eyes that held her attention and tugged at her heart.

She wanted to kiss him so desperately. She wanted his perfect mouth on hers, his arms tightly around her, the breathless feeling that came from his touch.

"Finished," he said, low and deep. He rubbed the bandage with his thumb. He held her hand for a moment more before lifting his eyes. Her breath wavered, and her lips parted.

Whether it was the longing in her eyes he saw, or his own need, he drew her closer by her hand until they were almost nose to nose. He hesitated and looked into her eyes. With a groan of surrender, he captured her mouth in a searing kiss.

Chapter Eight

❧❧❧

Brenna clasped the smooth skin of his shoulder with her uninjured hand lest he recover his senses and break the kiss. She'd intended to make the most of the moment before guilt resurfaced. She was terribly tired of that unwelcome emotion ruining her kisses.

She moaned low in her throat. The sound came out closer to a purr. She slid against him, an awkward angle, surely, as they were seated side by side. Still, his arm was between her breasts, and his hand had reclaimed her thigh, inches away from her feminine core. It pulsed as if anticipating something Brenna, in her innocence, could not name.

Richard reached up to slide his hand along the side of her face, cupping her cheek as he teased her tongue with his.

Her senses frolicked over the scent of soap from last evening's bath and a hint of leather and horse. His muscled body arched forward, pushing her back onto the bed. She wasn't certain exactly how she ended up in the center, only that Richard was kissing her breathless and did not seem eager to end the kiss.

Aroused, he brushed against her with his hard body, and she responded in kind by arching upward, her covered breasts flattening against his bare chest.

Brenna smiled against his mouth. She kissed him with all

the need inside her, her body melding with his, her passion released. The kiss went on, his mouth tormenting her, teasing, tasting.

When he tore free, his eyes were troubled. "I cannot."

Frustrated, she pushed him off her and scrambled from the bed. "I'm taking my own room." She stomped to the door and reached for the chair. Richard caught her before she could jerk it free of the door handle.

"I cannot let you leave. It's too dangerous." He spun her around and pushed her against the wall. She felt the brush of his erection on her thigh. Her hand closed into a fist. Let him suffer from his unsatisfied passion. She was done with him.

"I am tired of guilt and games," she said, struggling for freedom. She hit him in the shoulder and twisted her body. He tightened his grip. "Unhand me."

He grabbed for her hand and clasped it tight to keep her from hitting him again. Brenna snarled and locked onto his eyes.

"I should never have come after you."

"It is too late for regrets," he countered, and leaned in until their breaths became one.

"I despise you," Brenna said, through gritted teeth.

His mouth softened into a wry smile. "Lud, you are a troublesome minx." His eyes drifted down to her lips, and he added roughly, "I am about to lead you to ruin."

Brenna, with a bold sensuality she did not know she possessed, pressed her breasts to his chest and pushed up to her toes to nip him on his neck. "Ruin me, Richard."

Richard let loose a curse and slammed his mouth over hers. He grasped her buttocks, jerked her hips forward, and ground his cock against her. "Is this what you want, Milady?"

"Yes," she breathed, against his mouth.

Bending, he swung her up into his arms and strode purposefully to the bed. He set her on her feet, unlaced her bodice, and jerked the dress down from neck to feet. The layers of undergarments followed, until she was bare to his view.

There would be no words of love, Brenna knew, no promises. But her skin was on fire. She knew somehow this night would be magical. A man who kissed as he did had the experience to extinguish the raw need inside her.

His hands caressed her, marking her, kneading her pliant skin. She felt him reach for his waistband, and he somehow removed his breeches without breaking the kiss. She knew that the moment he lost focus on her, the seduction would be over.

Though a war clearly raged inside him, she'd gotten her kiss, and his surrender.

Free of his clothing, he pressed her back on the bed. Brenna arched up, her modest yet perfect breasts drawing his attention. His mouth closed over one nipple, and she gasped. He teased the peak before moving to the other.

Seeking intimate knowledge of every part of him, she touched him all over, tempting him with her fingertips. He groaned as she ran her hand down his chest to the curls below his navel. She silently thanked the courtesans and their inappropriate conversations.

"Do not stop," he urged.

As commanded, Brenna began a slow exploration down his body. He reclaimed her mouth. Every part of her wanted his attention, every inch of her aching for this man.

Brenna kneaded his sculpted buttocks, the firm flesh smooth beneath her fingertips.

She had never touched bare male buttocks before and suspected his were perfect. However, it was the hard erection between them that drew her attention. She knew from the experienced courtesans that men enjoyed being touched down there.

Tentatively, she slid one hand around him to caress along the hard length. Richard groaned again, not from pain but pleasure. He allowed her touch for a moment. Then he eased back, out of reach, and began an exploration of her body. He trailed kisses and caresses over her, tasting her skin as if he were a man starved. Brenna's moans encouraged each new kiss, each touch.

When she was fully aroused, he poised between her legs and pressed his erection to her core.

Brenna sensed hesitation. "Please. I need—" The sentiment was left unfinished as he gently pressed inside her.

A brief moment of discomfort followed as her body adjusted to his presence. He pushed deep, and she whimpered softly. He trailed kisses up her neck, nipped her ear, and licked a nipple.

Slowly, he moved within her while teasing her with his mouth. Soon she forgot the initial discomfort as her body responded to his play. "Mmmmm," she said, "yes." She wasn't certain what she was searching for, but he knew. He slipped a hand between them and gently rubbed her core.

Brenna gasped and pressed against his hand. Richard teased her until she felt weightless, breathless. Crying out, she arched back on the bed as her body found her release.

His movements quickened. She returned her hands to his buttocks, encouraging his own release. Within moments, he let out a hoarse sound and shuddered, pumping twice more inside her.

The harsh sigh that followed, as he dropped onto the bed beside her, did not bode well for her. Brenna felt his emotions withdraw even before he'd moved from her body.

"Have we returned to guilt again, Milord?" she asked, staring up at the cracked ceiling. She'd just lost her innocence. She wanted to be held in his strong arms, have him whisper sweet sentiments in her ear. Instead, she said, "No one will know of this, save us."

He said nothing. Brenna sighed and pulled the worn sheet over her nakedness. She was too pleased with him to bicker. If he wanted to spend their time here thinking about her father, it was his issue. She rolled over and promptly fell asleep.

Richard listened to Brenna's breath even out and quietly called himself all sorts of names he'd not used since his days as a rebel at Cambridge. The shame of having taken her, the guilt over betraying her father, and his own lack of control left him angry and frustrated.

All his plans to never marry again were thwarted by one moment of bad judgment. In spite of Brenna's plan to help him find Anne and then marry him, he had no real intention of doing so. He'd let her think that in order to keep her from pressing the issue.

Now he had to marry her. There was no choice. He could not send her back to her father ruined.

His friend would be outraged. The moment Brenna had found him on that first day, he should have returned her to London on the morning coach and not looked back. He never should have allowed her to accompany him on this futile chase.

It had been the sweet scent of her skin and those damnable green eyes that made him lose all sense. One look into them and he'd agreed to throw himself blindly off a cliff.

Hell, her hands on him as she tended his wound, and the feel of his arm on her thigh, had almost caused him to spill himself in his breeches. His body had taken control, and his mind shut down. Her taste had driven him mad.

Lud. What had he done?

No excuse would satisfy Walter. Perhaps a wedding would save him from being murdered. Something he richly deserved.

He ran all sorts of excuses through his head, words needed to satisfy an outraged father. Nothing eased his conscience.

It was exhaustion that finally let him sleep.

Richard startled awake sometime later with a hand circling his erection. Befuddled, he sat upright to see Brenna, framed by the last threads of sunset trailing into the cracked window, smiling at him through a seductive mass of tangled hair.

He went steel hard. "Brenna, release my cock."

She tightened her hold. There was no pain, only pleasure. "I will not."

Richard closed his hand over hers. The stubborn set of her chin revealed her determination. "Can you not let me revel in my guilt without pushing the boundary further? I have already led you astray and have betrayed a man I greatly admire. Will you not leave me in peace?"

"I'm afraid not." Hunger filled her eyes.

She finally released him by fondling his shaft. She rose from where she lay, the sheet falling away to expose her beautiful, lush, and naked body to his gaze.

Dragging the sheet free of him, she straddled his hips and positioned his cock between her legs.

"Lud, Brenna," he groaned. She leaned forward until her breasts pressed against his chest. In an act of betrayal, his hands slid up her legs and clasped her delightful buttocks.

"You have already ruined me, Milord. You cannot ruin me

a second time. So why waste the hours between now and dawn arguing, when I give you permission to take me again and again?"

Richard wanted to protest, to ease her off and flee the room. Instead, he reached between them, adjusted her position, and impaled himself into her warmth.

Gasping, he was lost. Her slick heat wrapped around him, tormenting him with his desire.

Brenna moved up and down his length, her movements slow and unsure. Still, somewhere she'd learned something about the matters of sex, though he knew full well he'd stolen her virginity.

"You are destroying me," he gasped, as she brushed her fingertips over his nipples.

A seductive grin spread over her delightful mouth. Her lids lowered halfway. "I feel the same."

She kissed him then, her mouth taking his, her breasts flattening on his chest. Never had he felt such complete loss of control with a woman than he felt with this innocent temptress.

His own ruin was complete. He'd take her now, he'd take her later, and he'd take her as many times as he could between now and dawn, as she wished. And then when they crossed over into Scotland, he'd marry her, the impulsive and beautiful and exasperating chit with the bewitching green eyes.

Lord help him.

Chapter Nine

B renna awoke with a stiff neck and muscle aches all over her body. It felt as though she'd been dragged across a glen by her horse with her foot trapped in a stirrup. It was when she heard Richard breathing softly beside her that her body warmed and her heart tugged.

He'd made love to her three times. Three times! This proved he *did* care. How could he not? All his bluster had been a wall to guard his heart. But somehow she'd breached his defenses. The tender way he'd taken her certainly showed his affection.

Lud, Richard had even killed a man to protect her. He was her dangerous highwayman. They were fated to be together.

Relief welled in Brenna. Posh on the marriage of convenience! She'd wanted a love match, and a love match she would have. Just like her parents and Simon had.

She snuggled along his side and felt the tug of first love bloom inside her heart. He did not have to love her in return. Not yet. However, that would come in time. She just had to be patient. He'd suffered great loss. They'd have years together to overcome the last of the barriers around his heart.

She stretched and kissed his shoulder. Never again would she smell his particular scent without fondly remembering last evening.

She trailed kisses across his rib cage. When his hand came up to stop her progression, she noticed that his eyes were open, and it wasn't passion she saw there.

"Good morning," she said softly, and rose to steal a kiss. He avoided her mouth and rolled from the bed. He padded across the room to collect his breeches and gave her a delicious view of his backside. It was indeed perfect. "Come back to bed and warm me. The room is too cold—"

"Get dressed," he said sharply, interrupting her sentiment. "We leave immediately for Scotland."

"Richard?" This curt stranger had taken over the passionate and gentle man from last evening. She watched him jerk on his clothing and stuff his meager possessions into his pack. Throughout, he refused to look at her.

Brenna dressed, her stomach knotted, and she felt ill. Had she misread the situation? Perhaps the lack of sleep had left him cross. If she gave him time to soothe his temper, all would be well.

She desperately hoped for that outcome, her mind fighting against a growing sense of doom.

She braided her hair and stuffed it under her hood.

The breakfast was cold porridge and bread that formed a thick clot in her throat. She gave up eating after a few bites. Dread made the already tasteless meal unpalatable.

Once the horses had been collected and they were on the road, Brenna eased Brontes up beside him.

"Have I done something to anger you?" she asked. There was nothing from her memories to make such a conclusion. When last they'd slept, she'd been snuggled in his arms.

He finally looked at her. "You've done nothing. I am worried for Anne is all." He urged his horse to a faster clip.

Brenna felt the half truth in his words. He was back to guilt and regret. She wanted to remove her boot and launch it at his head. Unfortunately, that would not help her cause.

Instead of pressing the matter, she followed in silence until they reached the border. After crossing into Gretna Green, Richard left Brenna with the horses and inquired around the village after Anne and Lockley. He received no helpful information. Couples frequently came and left without leaving a mark. There was nothing that would stand out about his missing sister.

"Isn't it good that no one remembers her?" Brenna asked, when he returned with the news. "Perhaps she had a change of heart and is now awaiting your return to Beckwith Hall."

Richard rubbed his temples. "Then where is Andrew? He was to leave me word once he arrived here. Instead, he has vanished, too. I worry that he has come to harm."

"Is it possible he has found information about Anne to lead him in another direction?"

Staring off across the village, Richard sighed. "This trip has proven fruitless. Wherever Anne is, unless she has reclaimed her senses, I am too late to save her."

"Then we shall hope good sense has won out over the charms of a wicked man." Brenna forced a positive tone. "If she is as intelligent as you say, she will reach the correct conclusion about Lockley."

"I can only hope."

Richard collected the horses. He tugged their reins, and they followed him like well-trained dogs. "Come, we have an appointment."

Puzzled, Brenna hurried to keep up with his brisk strides. They came to a blacksmith's shop, and Richard tied the horses to a post. When they entered the building, a rough-looking man was wiping his dirty hands on a cloth, and a woman of middle years stood nearby, next to a young woman in braids. The older woman came over and took Brenna's hand. Her grip was strong, and her eyes were kind.

"Why, ye are lovely, lass," she said, with a smile. "I can see why yer man is so eager ta wed ye."

Wed? Brenna turned to Richard. He was speaking to the blacksmith, his back to her. There was nothing in his treatment of her, since rising this morning, to indicate he planned to wed her. Had the woman misread the situation?

Her confusion notched up. Was his sour mood related to the panic some men experienced on their wedding day?

A renewed flush of hope filled her, and the glum day brightened. He wanted to marry her! He *did* care!

"Bring the flowers, Cliona," the woman said to the girl, and Cliona hurried over with a small bouquet of fresh-cut flowers. "Now let us get ye married."

Brenna accepted the bouquet, lifted it to her nose, and

gazed over at Richard. He was a bit dusty and his hair was mussed, but in minutes he'd be her husband; every exasperating, irritating, frustrating, and devastatingly handsome part of him.

And she could not wait.

A blacksmith joining them together for eternity was certainly not the wedding she'd dreamed of. Still, she was marrying her viscount, and she was nearly giddy with anticipation.

When the ceremony commenced, Brenna said her vows in a wavering voice and stood silent as he said his. She accepted the brush of his mouth and signed the registry after. Richard declined the offer of tea and hurried Brenna out of the shop.

"Richard, wait." She had so many questions, so much to say to him. But he was off again, his brisk strides forcing her to trot to keep hold of his arm.

He did not stop. Instead, he said tersely, "We will eat and return to England. I have arranged for a coach to take us back to London."

All her girlish dreams of her happily ever after formed a hard lump in her heart. He hadn't softened toward her one whit.

The coldness in him followed them through a simple meal at an inn and as he secured their horses to the awaiting coach and helped her inside. Brenna shivered as she settled across from him on the bench seat, his eyes icy as they turned from her to stare out the window.

It was then that she shook off the fog of harsh reality and disappointment. With the clearing of her mind, heat prickled up her spine. She wasn't about to be cast aside, as if she were some doxy he'd found on a wharf and took up against the side of a warehouse. She was his wife, legal and binding, even if the ceremony had been performed by a man who shod horses.

"Why did you marry me, Richard?" she demanded.

"You told me I would, so I did," he said, his tone flat. His eyes bore into her. "Certainly that pleases you?"

Her spine stiffened. "Nothing about this pleases me. The romantic gesture of a surprise wedding fell away when I realized that I am now forever tied to a man who cannot give his wife a single word of kindness on their wedding day."

Richard leveled his frown on her. She inwardly blanched.

"If you wanted kindness, you should have picked another

groom. This marriage is one of convenience, nothing more. I have done my duty by you."

Brenna felt the slap of contempt as if he'd hit her. The night they'd shared meant nothing to him. Nothing. She blinked back tears. He'd not see her cry.

She felt foolish for thinking they would be happy. She'd known of his feelings about marriage. She did not expect grand declarations of love and devotion to come into their arrangement. However, she had expected him to accept the marriage with grace, as a gentleman would.

What a fool she was.

Turning away, the last vestiges of hopeful innocence faded. She'd mistaken his desire for her body as something more. She'd thought she was falling in love. Had she been worldly, she would have recognized the difference between the two.

It was a mistake she'd not make again.

For the next two days, they shared rooms and beds, but there was no intimacy. They were two strangers who spoke only when required. When they made their last overnight stop before reaching London, Brenna had come to a grim conclusion. The marriage was over.

She'd spent these last reflective hours looking into her heart and realized that she could not, would not, live within a marriage of convenience. She wanted love, and she'd find her way to it, even if she had to hunt down every eligible bachelor in all of London to find her perfect match.

"I have decided not to tell Father about our marriage," she said, her voice firm. He lifted his eyes from his supper. "Now that I am in no danger of being forced into a marriage to Chester Abbot, I will spend the next few weeks searching for an acceptable man to marry—a man who will love me desperately and with whom I can grow to love in return. Once I have made my choice, I'll grant you permission to have our marriage annulled. It should be easy to complete, as I will never share your marital bed."

"You cannot be serious." He stared, incredulous. "If your precious society found out that your husband had your marriage annulled, you'd be shunned."

"That is why you will arrange it quietly." Brenna's cheeks flushed. How could she have ever wanted to marry this man?

She never thought Chester Abbot could ever be a superior choice to what she had in Lord Ashwood. She was incorrect. "I will only tell Father if I am unable to find an acceptable replacement and he forces the issue. Otherwise, you will be rid of me, and your life will continue as it was."

Richard could not believe what he was hearing. Brenna did not want to be his wife? After all she'd done to get him to agree to the marriage, and the noble effort he'd made to correct his mistake for taking her innocence, she was setting him aside?

Blast. He'd been honest about his feelings on marriage from the start. Still, he *had* ruined her and done his duty by her, despite his misgivings. What more did she expect from him? She was the one who'd first proposed the arrangement.

"You are no longer a virgin," he said tightly. "How will you explain that to your husband?"

She lifted her pert nose. "That is my concern."

"And if there is a child?" he pressed. The idea of another man playing father to his child, or sharing a bed with her, left him cold. Despite his callous treatment of her these last few days, she'd gotten into his mind, taken control of his body. Even now, he ached to drag her upstairs and explore her lovely curves. Her icy tone told him that she did not feel the same.

Gone was the dewy expression she'd leveled on him the morning he'd awoken, satiated, in her arms. The look he'd quickly quelled before she'd had the chance to fancy herself in love with him.

"I do not think that is possible," Brenna said, dismissive. "We spent but one night together. By the time I have found a suitor, I should know if I will bear your offspring."

Richard's head pounded. He imagined a young nobleman climbing into Brenna's bed, kissing her breasts, pleasuring her, and reveling in her passionate nature.

He blinked to clear the image. If he was so eager to be free of his troublesome wife, why, then, did his stomach burn with the desire to strangle any man who touched her?

"What then?" he snapped. "Will you lead him to believe he's the father?"

Brenna took a sip of tea. "I will decide then what to do if your seed has planted in fertile ground. We will not worry about it now. All we can do is pray that fate has not settled upon us that grim hand."

Grim hand? She did not want his child?

The headache pounded in his temples. This emotionless woman was the same Brenna who'd made love to him so passionately? The same woman who'd begged him to take her while whispering encouragement as he'd explored every inch of her with his mouth?

Lud, what madness was this? He wanted to shake her, yet she was giving him his freedom. Why did he care what she did once she was out of his life?

Hell, she was correct. This marriage was a mistake. Richard knew if he did not distance himself from her, and soon, he would find himself fully besotted.

Resolve settled firmly in the pit of his stomach. Free her. Now. "Then we are in agreement," he said flatly. "Tomorrow we shall send you off to London, and I will return to Beckwith Hall to await news of your engagement. I will then contact a solicitor and see if I can arrange for an annulment. If the marriage does come to light, I will make myself the villain. It is the least I can do for you—and your father."

Richard thought he saw a flicker of sadness pass through her eyes but could not be certain. Her stoic expression had not changed.

Damn. He *was* a villain. The bad judgment he'd displayed since she'd arrived at his door on that first night had gotten them into this fix. He'd do anything he could to right his wrong, with no damage to her reputation.

Brenna nodded. "Thank you."

Brenna managed to keep her emotions in check through the rest of the evening and breakfast the next morning. When they reached the outskirts of London, she reclaimed Brontes. Richard sent the coach off and helped her mount.

She looked down at him from the saddle, memorizing the lines of his face, the crinkles around his eyes, his dusty coat. Years from now when she looked back on her adventure to

Scotland, she wanted to remember him, not as the rigid stranger standing before her now but as the man who'd taken her innocence in one glorious night of passion and who was, for one brief moment, her husband.

"How will you explain your absence when asked?" he pressed.

"The story about an unplanned visit to my ailing Aunt Primrose should suffice to satisfy the gossips." Brenna tightened her hands on the reins. "You need not concern yourself any further. I will be fine."

Richard nodded. "Be well, Brenna."

"You as well." With those last words, her marriage to her highwayman-stranger was over.

He released his hold on Brontes, and Brenna turned the horse toward home. She nudged the mare into a slow lope and did not look back, even once, as tears flowed freely down her face.

Chapter Ten

※♔♕♚※

I demand an accounting of every minute that you've been away, young lady. You cannot disappear and expect to reappear without a good explanation for your absence. You stole Brontes and ran away from the courtesan school," Father said, his eyes boring into her. "This is an outrage. Simon and I searched everywhere for you."

Brenna winced and glanced toward the closed parlor door. She wondered how many servants had heard the exchange and wasn't certain Father's upraised voice couldn't be heard all the way to Cheapside either. Her face flamed knowing the conversation was less than private.

Mother stood nearby, clearly torn between husband and child. Yet Brenna knew she'd not interfere.

"As I explained a few minutes ago, I went off to visit Aunt Primrose to collect my thoughts and whittle down my list of potential mates. And I did just that," Brenna said. She held out her hastily written list with the names of every unattached man she knew, having crossed off the most unsuitable. "I thought you wanted me to select a suitable suitor?"

"You were to stay in Cheapside, where Eva could guide you," he countered. "Your mother was frantic with worry."

Brenna turned to her mother. "I am sorry." She bit her

trembling lip. "It was not my intention to worry you, Mother. As usual, I was not thinking clearly."

Since returning late last evening and discovering that her parents were with Eva and the duke, Brenna had sequestered herself in her room to make her suitors list, eating very little and avoiding contact with anyone save Tippy. She suspected it would take time to repair an injured heart and was thankful this confrontation had been avoided until she had a few hours' rest and a chance to collect her jumbled emotions.

So she would tell no one the truth of her adventure and battle to drag herself out of her melancholia.

Lying to her parents would be harder to reconcile in her mind.

Father was not about to let the matter rest. "How can I be certain you did not get into some sort of mischief? You sneak out of the courtesan school in the middle of the night, steal Brontes, and then tell me it was all for a few days of quiet in the countryside? And you expect me to believe such hogwash?"

Mother placed her hand on Father's sleeve. "She has returned unharmed, Walter. Can we not leave it at that?"

"Is it not my place to know where my daughter has been and with whom?" he said to Mother. "How am I to know she was really with Primrose and not cavorting with pirates? She has made that threat, you know."

Brenna sighed. "I assure you, there were no pirates."

The weariness of the last week overwhelmed her. She dropped onto the settee. "I promise you, Father, that I will fulfill my duty, find an acceptable husband, and settle into my role as wife. I only ask that you give me time to comply with your wishes."

Father shook his head. "You have sent me into an early graying, Daughter." Brenna stood and walked to him.

"I will never again disappear. It was a mistake not to be repeated." Brenna meant every word. She'd had enough adventure for a lifetime.

Her eyes filled as she silently begged for forgiveness, and Father finally pulled her into his arms. Mother wrapped her arms around them both. "I truly am sorry," she said, and her voice caught.

After a moment, Father released her. "I spoke to Noelle this morning. She will be your chaperone while you husband hunt. Tomorrow you will attend the Wingate soiree, and whatever other parties and balls she has planned over the next month."

"Yes, Father."

He lifted her chin. "Do not look so glum, child. I am certain there is a man somewhere in London who will make you an excellent husband. You need only keep your mind open to the possibility."

I am concerned about her, my love," Kathleen said, as Walter helped her into the carriage. A ride in the country would give Walter time to settle his temper. "There was deep sadness in her eyes. Do you think something terrible has happened to her?"

Walter collected the reins from the groom. "I fear you are correct. Something has happened. I can feel it. She has matured in ways I did not expect when I sent her to this school. I just hope there will be no unwelcome repercussions from her missing week. I will despise having to hunt down and force a pirate to wed my daughter."

Kathleen shot him a quelling stare. "Should that happen, we shall accept him peg leg, parrot, and all." She closed her hand over his. "She is too much like you, my dearest husband. You are both thick skulled and stubborn. I would not get too comfortable with her new agreeable nature. I believe we have not seen the last of Brenna's hijinks."

Y ou do look lovely, Cousin," Noelle said, her left arm hooked through Brenna's and her right, through that of her handsome husband, Gavin, as he led them into Wingate House. "Men will be slavering all over themselves to dance with you."

The soiree was in full bloom as Gavin guided them through the doors and into the crush. He leaned in and took the women into his confidence. "Gossip has spread that Brenna is husband seeking. I may need some help to fight off the rogues and fortune hunters vying for her hand. I hope Simon and Laura are attending."

Brenna forced a smile. Gavin was a charming rake, born in England but raised in America. He and Noelle were deeply in love despite a rather bumpy start to their romance. Brenna was envious of their happiness and that of Simon and Laura and Eva and her duke. Love matches, all.

Sadly, she would not be so blessed.

As if hearing Gavin's comment, Simon and Laura appeared through the crowd. "There is my lovely sister." Simon took her hand and kissed her knuckles. "No worse for her misadventure."

Brenna pulled back her hand and frowned. "If not for you and Father, I would not have felt the need to flee."

He chuckled and took Laura's hand. She was beautiful in a deep emerald gown. Beside Noelle in blue silk, the two women made her feel perfectly dowdy. Father had insisted she wear white for her first evening of husband hunting.

If only she did not already have one.

A sharp pain twisted in her gut. Richard. The man she both hated and missed dreadfully. If he'd given her some kindness, offered her even a hint of hope that he could feel the slightest bit of affection for her, she'd have gone off to Beckwith Hall and spent the rest of her life learning to like sheep.

But he'd coldly cut her with his words and actions. He'd never feel more than disdain for having wed her.

Ire welled and with it a renewed determination to forget she'd ever met him. She'd find her perfect suitor, annul her marriage, and live happily ever after.

"Ah, but now you are back," Simon remarked. "Have you set your attention on a certain man, or is the list yet to be whittled down to one?"

"Alas, I have not picked a favorite, though Lord Chester has already been cut." A real smile tugged her mouth. "I have thwarted your dismal attempt to trap that man in the yoke. Who I choose can be no worse than him."

Simon shrugged. "I still think he is an excellent choice."

Laura grimaced. "If you were female, would you wish to be chained to that sop?" She didn't wait for an answer. His face showed his answer. "I thought not. Now leave your sister be. She will make her own decision."

With a warm smile for her sister-in-law, Brenna nodded. "Though you have the compassion of a vulture and the sense of an ox, you did manage to ensnare me a delightful new sister. How she fell in love with you will never be explained to my satisfaction."

Noelle and Gavin laughed, and Simon glared. Laura squeezed his arm. "It was his determination. He wore me down until I could do nothing but agree to marry him. He is most persuasive."

Though Laura teased, Brenna knew Laura and Simon loved each other dearly. They were a perfect match.

With her new resolve in place, and the distraction of her family to lift her spirits, the gray lens Brenna had been looking through since leaving Scotland cleared. She was done with Richard Ellerby, Viscount Ashwood. Forever.

"Lady Brenna. Aren't you a welcome sight?" Lord Manning came to stand before her. Tall and thin, he was a pleasant companion, and Brenna always enjoyed his company. Though he did not send her heart fluttering, he was the perfect man to start her evening on a good foot.

"My Lord. You look dashing this evening," Brenna said, taking his arm. "Is that a new coat?"

She led him away from her family, casting a frown over her shoulder at her brother. Simon grinned. For the rest of the evening, she'd keep her mind open and look at each man she met with new eyes. There had to be someone better than Lord Chester—or Lord Ashwood, for that matter—out there for her. And she'd do her level best to find him.

Lord Manning kept their conversation lively as he claimed the first dance, and after him, Brenna danced and laughed with a string of men. None were an immediate fit for her in either temperament or humor, but she did manage to find something pleasant about each.

The evening aged before the American, Jace Jones, claimed a dance. He was a friend of Simon's and a handsome, if slightly forward, gentleman. And an outrageous flirt.

"Simon told me you were husband hunting, beautiful Brenna," he said, taking her into his arms. "I would throw my hat in but fear I am not quite ready to be leg shackled. Though if I were, you'd be at the top of my list."

Brenna waited until they were away from prying ears before she said tartly, "As if I would settle on you, Mister Jones. You are positively barbaric."

He chuckled. "And in trade. Even if you were to fall desperately in love with me, Gavin already has the gossips atwitter with his shipping business. A second American businessman in the Harrington family would be too much for society to withstand. They will eject you all from the lords and ladies club."

"So true." Brenna smiled at his droll wit. "Thank goodness I'm in no danger of giving my heart to you. I would hate to give up my life of leisure for the hardships of toiling in your business ventures. Remind me again what you do?"

The music died. He eased her to a stop. "It would bore you. I think I shall depart now so that you may find more interesting and marriage-minded company." He bowed and left her.

Brenna watched him disappear into the crowd. She had met him a few times and found him charming. However, as with her brother, he enjoyed sparring with her in a brotherly manner. After the emotional upheaval of Richard, she was searching for a man less likely to prick her temper. So she mentally crossed Mister Jones off her list.

"Lady Harrington." The droll voice drifted over, and Brenna hid a wince. Mister Everhart. She turned and pasted on a smile.

"Mister Everhart." The man was nothing if not persistent. He was attractive enough to intrigue women but poor enough to send all but the dimmest running behind their mother's skirts. He was a fortune hunter of the highest order, and Brenna would not be ensnared.

She cocked up a brow and looked around him. "What? No wife? I thought you had Miss Tolson hooked?"

Everhart grinned. "She *is* lovely, and devilishly rich. Sadly, her father ran me off at the end of a pistol. Something about empty pockets and few prospects." He took her hand, tucked it under his arm, and led her in a stroll around the room. "Thankfully, Lady Brenna Harrington is still in need of a husband, and I am unattached."

Brenna felt the weight of his charm. "Alas, I am already promised to another life. My father thinks I would make an excellent nun."

"You?" He chuckled. "Tell me you are not taking vows? It will be a dark day indeed." He led her past a group of debutantes, who giggled when he nodded to them.

"According to Father, the convent will be far superior to spinsterhood. And I have yet to find a man to interest me enough to marry."

Before Brenna realized she'd just issued what he would see as a challenge, she was on the terrace. Unfortunately, the only other couple taking in the night air was some distance away.

Drat the long terrace. "I think we should return inside." Brenna removed her hand. It wasn't hers for long. Everhart reclaimed it quickly and drew her behind a column. "Mister Everhart. This is improper. Release me."

Everhart grinned as he pulled her into his arms. "I must show you what you will miss if you don the habit."

Brenna struggled, but it was too late. He kissed her.

The kiss was not unpleasant, though it was unwelcome. She managed to get her hands between them and push him back. Then, to prove her disinterest, she slapped him, too.

He jerked sideways.

His eyes flashed cold. Brenna shivered.

"If I wasn't clear during our previous encounters, then that should make things clearer for you, Mister Everhart." She flexed and closed her hand. "I am not interested in making you my husband. Now, if you will excuse me."

She stalked back to the ballroom.

For the rest of the evening, Brenna avoided the man. She needn't have worried he'd press his intentions. There were young women aplenty. In fact, he winked at her once as he squired a pretty thing past her. The man was a rogue. Had he been wealthy, and not so forward, she might have put him on her list . . . somewhere near the bottom, before tonight's kiss. She'd seen a brief glimpse of something in his eyes that she could not dismiss from her mind. Something darker than the charming side of him wanted her to see. It was best to avoid him from now on.

By evening's end, she'd collected the names of several nice

men and accepted three offers to call. Though none of the three suitors were interesting enough to eject Richard from her heart, she kept her mind open to the possibility of finding love this season. Certainly there was someone appealing she hadn't met yet?

"I am proud of you, Sister." Simon helped her on with her cloak as the clock struck two. "You managed not to repel a single potential suitor with your sharp tongue. I shall consider the evening a success."

Brenna sighed. She was too tired to squabble. "I made Father a promise. I intend to keep it."

Laura took her arm. "Do not let His Lordship or your brother bully you. Love will come. Keep your heart open."

As Simon led Brenna and Laura from the house, Brenna felt the return of gloom. How could she give her heart to anyone when it was already engaged?

Chapter Eleven

The school is so quiet," Brenna said, taking a seat in the parlor. She smoothed out her simple russet gown and looked over at Lucy. "I can hear the dust motes swirling."

Lucy poured tea. She was pretty in pale green. "The matching party was three days ago. The courtesans are all wed and gone. It's as silent as a mausoleum around here without them."

Brenna accepted a cup. She added sugar. "I'd forgotten about the matching party." During her week with Richard, she'd thought of nothing beyond her own troubles. She turned her focus on the former courtesan. "Did you not find a husband?"

"I did." Lucy added cream to her tea. "We married yesterday. I am now Mrs. Franklin Pruitt."

Puzzled, Brenna frowned. "And he has abandoned you already? Surely your wedding night was not as horrid as all that?"

Lucy laughed. "We spent a wonderful night at the Ritz before he had to run off to Paris to take care of a business concern. I did not want to stay in his town house alone, so Miss Eva said I could stay here for the month he will be away."

"A month?" Brenna said, aghast. "You are newly wed."

"The trip was planned before the party. Franklin almost

did not come to be matched. Yet I am pleased he did. He is handsome and charming and very sweet. I shall miss him dreadfully."

Brenna's story was not so dissimilar. She, too, had been abandoned shortly after her marriage.

At least Lucy's husband was returning for her.

Annoyed with herself for thinking of *him* at all, Brenna pulled in a deep breath for control. "Well, I am pleased you are here. It would be dreadfully dull without you."

Lucy smiled. "Miss Eva told me you'd be coming. We shall shop, help ready the household for the new courtesans, and tend the garden. Perhaps even stroll through the museums? Franklin left me funds enough to have a fine time."

"It sounds splendid," Brenna said, her spirits lifting. There was no better companion than Lucy to keep her distracted.

And for the next three weeks, Brenna spent her days at the school and her nights searching for a husband. Between the two, she was exhausted. Still, she dragged herself each day to Cheapside, determined to keep busy.

"I cannot go out today," she complained to Lucy, as the former courtesan tried to tug her from the settee after Brenna had drifted off during a conversation about fabrics.

With each day that passed, she found it harder and harder to get out of bed. In fact, she wouldn't have arrived at the school before noon at all if it weren't for Lucy's insistence that she needed Brenna to keep her from perishing from boredom in the quiet town house.

"It is almost noon," Lucy said, tightening her grip. "I have never seen you so weary. Perhaps you should feign a headache tonight and get some rest. Surely the parties will go on without you?"

"Perhaps you should go alone today, and I can nap now. My former room is empty. Sophie would not mind if I slept for a few hours here," Brenna suggested, and tried to put a pillow over her head, as if that would deter her friend. But she had to try. Her body craved sleep. "You are capable of choosing a frock without me. Just do not choose yellow. It is a horrid color on you."

Lucy finally relinquished Brenna's arm. "You have yawned

your way through the last few days and almost fell asleep in the coach yesterday. Your father can certainly give you one night off from your husband search."

Though Lucy knew Brenna was husband hunting, she did not know that Brenna was Lady Brenna, daughter of an earl.

"If only I could. My father is determined to see me wed. My days of finding a suitable suitor are dwindling. I cannot pass up a single party or poetry reading or ball, lest I miss the man I've been searching for my whole life." Brenna was having very little luck with her suitors. Not one of the dozen or so men she'd allowed to call had enticed her to anything but boredom. And she only had a week left to either find her perfect mate or summon up a suitable argument to convince Father to give her more time.

"It isn't as though you aren't trying," Lucy offered. She twirled a curl. "You should take me to the next party. I am an excellent judge of character. I'm sure I can find you a suitable match."

"If only I could." Brenna knew that taking a former courtesan to a society party was not an acceptable idea. Not only would Lucy discover her identity, but if anyone recognized Lucy from her former profession, Brenna would be ruined.

There were far too many rules to follow, too many ways to be ruined. Sometimes Brenna wished she was not of lofty birth.

She finally gave in to Lucy's pleading. "Help me up, and we will find something pretty for you to wear for your husband's homecoming." With a glad cry, Lucy pulled her from the settee. Brenna felt the room waver.

"Oh, dear." She dropped back on the cushion, her hand pressed to her forehead. "I fear I stood too quickly."

"You must be with child," Lucy teased. "My mother had six girls. She was always dizzy and tired when carrying a babe." She giggled and fanned Brenna with her hand.

"Oh, dear. Me with child?" Brenna repeated. Then her heart skipped. Could it be? She hadn't had her monthly course since three weeks before she'd bedded Richard, and it had been three weeks since that night. If she was with child, it was very early, not quite a month. "How early can a woman know she's been caught?"

Lucy shrugged. "My mother swore she knew the moment of conception with each of us, though most women know within two or three weeks after they miss their flow."

Closing her eyes, Brenna pressed her hands over her eyes and squelched a groan. Damn Richard and his bold, male seed. The crushing weight of the prospect of being pregnant with his child sent a tremor of fright through her veins.

She pressed her hands to her face, both stunned and terrified by the revelation. If she *was* pregnant, there would be no annulment. A baby changed everything.

"I should have known the virile bastard would not need more than one night to settle his offspring on me." When she realized she'd spoken aloud, her breath caught, and she darted a glance at Lucy. It was too late to take the comment back.

Lucy crossed the room, surprise on her face. "How can you be with child? I thought you had no prospects? Did you allow a footman to take liberties? A groom? A steward? Some of those men can charm their way under your skirts before you realize they have their hand untying your garters."

Brenna made a sound, half laugh, half groan. There was no reason to hide the truth anymore. "Oh, it is worse than all that. The father is a lord. And he's my husband."

Y ou are a scandalous flirt, Clive." Bethany giggled. She twirled her hair and glanced sidelong at Richard. "I'd guess you've left many broken hearts in your wake. I must take care to protect mine."

Richard ignored Bethany's obvious attempts to engage his interest. Three days ago she'd snuck into his room when he was abed, stolen a kiss, and been soundly rejected. Now she was trying another tactic that would also fail. He did not like games and was not interested in that certain piece of fluff.

He turned to Miriam. "I understand you have painted a picture of the north pond. Perhaps you can show it to me after supper?"

Miriam flushed. She was his late wife's cousin and had been foisted off on him two years ago by her social-climbing mother, who hoped he would fall in love with her daughter and make her his viscountess. Instead, she'd become a friend.

"I would like that very much."

The differences between Miriam and her friend Bethany could not be more pronounced; one was quiet and sweet natured, and the other a bold flirt. He much preferred the former.

Added to the mix was Bethany's brother, George, who did nothing of note and seemed content to live off Richard's good graces. He should toss the pair out on their collective ears, but he did not want to hurt his friendship with Miriam.

So he let them stay, hoping one day they'd tire of Beckwith Hall and leave on their own.

A trill of laughter drew his attention back to George and his friends: Clive Everhart, Silas Gimsby, and Lord Ponteby. Bethany had the attention of all the young bucks, and Richard silently hoped one would propose to the girl and run off with her. Her eyes on him told him he would not be so blessed.

If only he could tell them of his marriage. That would instantly take him off the list of eligible bachelors in the park and give him peace. But he could not.

His mind drifted to Brenna, as it often did, and he wondered if she'd found her next husband. He thought it unlikely, as he'd not received a note requesting an annulment.

For some reason, this pleased him, though he knew he should be eagerly checking the mail every day for her post. He did not want the marriage any more than she did. The sooner it was over, the sooner he could be rid of her haunting presence, a constant shadow over his life.

He could still taste her lush mouth, remember her scent, and feel the way her body fit his so perfectly. Though he tried to eject her from his mind, he could not. She'd taken hold and refused to release him. Perhaps he should take a lover, a widow with no hopes for marriage. Yet somehow he could not take that step while his wife was still his wife. The thought of betraying Brenna left him with a sour taste in his mouth.

"Would you care to share your thoughts, Richard?" Miriam interrupted his musings. "You've been quiet of late. Well, quieter than usual."

Smiling, he nodded. "I've not been a very attentive host," he agreed. "My mind has been occupied elsewhere."

Miriam scanned his face. "A woman perhaps?"

Richard met her gaze. Was it that obvious? "There is no woman. My mind is on business." The half truth came easily. Brenna was gone forever, and soon he would be free. "I have a small property in Kent that I'm selling, and I should know soon if the buyer has agreed to my price."

Whether she believed him or not, Miriam was too polite to question him. She was properly raised and would never consider proposing to a highwayman or chasing a runaway young woman all the way to Scotland. In truth, she was the perfect companion and would make an excellent wife.

Just not his.

G ood lord, Daughter. You are with child?" Father's face reddened, and Mother dropped onto the settee. The shock in their eyes and gaping mouths were to be expected. Brenna had known Lucy's surprise would be nothing compared to what she'd face from her parents. In fact, she'd waited another week, hoping desperately for her flow to appear, before sadly accepting her fate.

"When did this happen? How will we explain your condition?" Father continued. "If we cannot arrive at a plausible explanation, you'll be ruined."

"It is not as grim as it seems, Father." The sight of her father's disappointment pushed down on her already exhausted shoulders. "There is much that I have not yet explained. The father will accept the child."

"You are correct there, miss," he said, the bloom of outrage in his voice. "Whoever the rogue is, I'll see him horsewhipped and wed before sunset."

"Walter, please," Mother pleaded. She pulled Brenna down beside her and clasped her hand. "Let us speak of this rationally. We will save horsewhipping until Brenna has told us her story."

Father was not about to calm himself. Brenna slid closer to Mother until they were nearly one. The comforting hand was a lifeline she clung to. Mother would see her come to no harm, figuratively speaking, from facing her father's anger.

"I knew something was wrong when she went missing. Now we know why." Father ignored Brenna and spoke directly to Mother. "She was not with Primrose. She was traipsing all over who-knows-where with some scoundrel. And now he has stolen her innocence and left her carrying his bastard. I think horsewhipping should be the least of his worries."

Overwhelmed and overwrought, Brenna felt the sudden irrational urge to laugh. She'd married and given her parents the grandchild they'd wanted. Still, she'd made such a muddle of things that none of the three of them had cause to celebrate.

Perhaps she should finish the tale before her father's heart suffered a fatal seizure.

"There is no need to call the parson, Father." Brenna braced herself. There would no longer be a secret marriage. The hunt for her perfect mate was over. "I am already wed."

"What?" Mother gasped. Father stopped pacing.

Brenna nodded. "We wed in Scotland. It is a marriage of convenience, brought by his guilt over seducing me and the worry he may have gotten me with child." Brenna shook her head. Richard had cursed her by speaking aloud of his fear of impregnating her. "His concern has come to fruition."

Father stood frozen in place for several ticks of the clock. Mother stared at Brenna, worry on her face.

Finally, he said, "Tell me who he is, Daughter."

For a moment Brenna considered lying to him. She knew that her decision would ruin a friendship and risk Richard's life. Father was that angry. He would see Richard as having betrayed him. And Richard . . . he valued Father's friendship. The loss would affect him deeply.

"You have to promise not to kill him," she begged. "I do not want to raise this child alone."

"I cannot make that guarantee," Father said. His hands closed into fists.

Even now, Brenna knew her father was thinking of the worst possible way to make the man who ruined his child suffer.

"Then I will not tell you," she said, with a stubborn lift of her chin. "I will just vanish, and you will never see me again."

"Walter," Mother said. "The man did right by her. He married her. Can you not consider that his penance?"

"And where is this pillar of manhood, this man who

married my daughter and left her bearing the burden of his child? If he is such a fine man, why is he not here standing at her side, instead of letting her face my wrath alone?"

"I'm certain he has his reasons."

Both her parents stared at her. How could she explain without making the situation worse? "We realized rather quickly that we are not well suited. We both thought it best to keep our lives separate."

"Are you jesting?" Father said. "You thought you could keep this secret forever? What if you wanted to marry someone else? Would you have two husbands?"

"Father. I would never allow it to go that far. I would have had to confess then or secretly have the marriage annulled." She placed her hand on her stomach. "Clearly, there is no need for such measures now. The marriage will stand. The child *will* be claimed by his father. He has no choice."

"See, all will be well," Mother said softly. "Brenna is a wife, and soon she will be a mother." She kept her tone light. "Is that not what we have always wished for her?"

"At the moment, all I want is to know the name of the man who is responsible for this situation. I can only pray that he is not some penniless bounder of low character."

"Father, I am not so weak-minded as to fall for someone like that."

"Then who is he?"

She had no recourse but to be honest. So she sat straight on the cushioned surface of the settee, summoned up her courage, and looked directly into her father's eyes. "My husband is Richard Ellerby."

Chapter Twelve

✦

I'll kill him." Father's voice was so low that it took Brenna a moment to realize what he said. Mother was quicker.

"Walter, be reasonable," she said. "The deed has been done, and they are wed. We must look at this as a positive outcome. Our daughter is married to a fine man, and we will soon have a grandchild. This is excellent news."

"That reprobate ruined her," Father said. "He was my friend, and he did not hesitate to take advantage of my child."

"I am certain that Brenna had a hand in some of this," Mother replied, frowning at Brenna. "At least he is not a pirate."

Mother—always the reasonable one.

"When did this happen?" Father continued unabated. "Did he take you in the coach on the day you met? Was his letter a ruse to cover his misdeeds?"

"No, Father. He did not touch me then." How could Brenna explain this? She wrung her hands. "When you pressed me to find a husband, I thought he'd be perfect for a marriage of convenience. When I went to find him at Beckwith Hall, he was gone, on his way to Scotland to find his sister. I chased him down and insisted he take me with him."

"See, Walter, Brenna was equally responsible for what happened," Mother said.

"Tell me everything," Father pressed ahead.

"I made him a proposal. If I helped him find Anne, he would marry me. Unfortunately, we did not find Anne and were victims of a robbery. When we took shelter at this ghastly inn to tend our wounds, well, something happened—" Her voice caught. The rest of the story was too shameful to admit. "We married in Scotland."

"You were robbed?" Mother pressed a hand to her heart.

"We were." Brenna nodded. "Richard killed a man to save me from being kidnapped."

"Good lord." Father shook his head. "Could this get any worse?"

"The situation is more complicated than you think, Father," Brenna said. "Richard is an honorable man. I'm married and saved from disgrace." "Honorable" was carefully chosen to keep Father from going off to Beckwith Hall and strangling her husband. Brenna had different, less kind words for the man, her husband.

Husband and wife, that they would stay. There was no other way. Once society discovered her pregnancy, the news would be out, and she'd have to explain her actions. Her friends would be shocked, though not overly so. They considered her a rule breaker. The rest of the Ton, well, she did not give a fig what they thought.

Her hand slid down to her flat belly. She had greater concerns now than her reputation. She was to be a mother. This terrified her more than facing the wrath of her father.

"He married and abandoned her," Father was saying, when Brenna returned her attention to the conversation.

"We both know Richard," Mother interjected. "He does not race around England seducing young innocents. I am certain he has an explanation for what he's done, and we will hear of it soon enough. For now, we need to decide what is best for Brenna and the babe."

Brenna stood. She crossed her arms and faced her parents with firm resolve. "The decision is mine, and I have made it. Tomorrow I leave for Beckwith Hall. It is time to take my place as Richard's wife."

"I think that is best," Mother said, before Father could voice his opinion. She smiled. "I cannot believe I'm to be a grandmother." She glanced at Father. "And you a grandfather. What a blessing."

Father grumbled under his breath. "The only blessing here should be for Ashwood's continued good health. If he mistreats my child, he will know the full wrath of an outraged father."

"Yes, dear," Mother said, with a wink at Brenna. "I know just the right story to spread about this unexpected marriage." She rubbed her hands together. "We shall tell everyone that you and Richard met last January when we were in Brighton for the holidays. He was instantly smitten, but you were not yet ready to accept his suit. When he discovered you were with Primrose, he took the opportunity to see you again, away from the protective eyes of your overbearing father." She smiled at Father. "It was then that you realized you desperately loved Richard, could not wait to be married, and ran off to Gretna Green."

"This will keep her reputation unsullied?" Father said, clearly skeptical.

Mother nodded. "Even the most vicious gossip will not be able to overcome such a grand love story. By the time I am finished weaving this unbelievable tale, Brenna and Richard's story will have everyone, down to the most stalwart heart, swooning."

Brenna sniffed and slipped into her mother's arms. "You are simply the greatest mother."

"I will not allow my precious child to be shunned for one misstep in judgment. It will all work out. I promise."

Brenna left her parents and went off to direct the maids to begin packing. With nothing for her to do at the moment, she decided to return to the courtesan school and make her good-byes. She knew the likelihood of ever returning there was slim, and she'd grown fond of Sophie, Cook, and Lucy. Even the butler, Primm, and the ever-stoic man-of-all-positions, Thomas, had found their way into her affections.

I shall miss you, Brenna," Lucy said, hugging her tight. "It is dull here without you." She drew Brenna down on the set-tee. "And with my husband delayed for a few more weeks in Paris, I will have no one to share my adventures." She scanned

Brenna's face and dropped into an exaggerated curtsy. "I suppose I should call you Your Ladyship, Your Ladyship."

Brenna screwed up her face. "I shall be put out if you do. This is the only place where I can be myself without my title. Lady Brenna has no place here."

Having said her good-byes to everyone else, she'd saved Lucy for last. They'd become close over the last weeks, and the former courtesan would be the hardest to leave behind.

What a turn her life had taken.

"You have been a good friend," Brenna said. She blinked to keep back tears. "I will miss your wicked humor and the way you manage to make even a dark day brighter."

Lucy took her hand and snorted. "We are a pair. The lady and the courtesan."

"Former courtesan," Brenna reminded her. "You are a wife now, Mrs. Pruitt. Soon you'll have ten children and your past will be all but forgotten."

"Ten children." Lucy groaned. "I dearly hope not."

Touching her stomach, Brenna could not believe she was with child herself. "Perhaps we should both begin with one." Her thoughts turned foreboding. What would Richard think when his unwanted wife showed up bearing his heir?

Hoping to keep from pulling a pillow over her head and letting her trepidation overwhelm her, she tried to keep positive. Certainly her husband would not turn her away.

They chatted about Brenna's impending trip and what life would be like at the hall. "I shall soon be the Lady of the Sheep," Brenna groaned. "The whirl of London will soon be a distant memory."

Lucy giggled. "You make it sound positively grim."

"How can I look at this any other way?"

The former courtesan squeezed her hand. "I'm certain you will love the dusty old hall once you have spent time there. As for the sheep, well, I think there are worse things. Be grateful that your husband does not raise hogs."

"Hogs?" She shuddered. Then an idea popped into Brenna's head. "You should come with me! Your husband is away, and you do like adventure. Oh, do promise you'll come!"

Lucy leaned back against the cushions. "Do I dare?"

"We will keep each other company for the next few weeks,"

Brenna urged. "You can send your husband a letter. He should not mind your change of household. When he comes back to England, he can fetch you there."

A smile graced Lucy's face. "I will do it."

The strain of venturing into the unknown lifted from Brenna, knowing she'd have one friend at Beckwith Hall—at least for a few weeks, while she got her footing. There was no telling what Richard would do when she rolled up to his home, buried in luggage, with her "companion" in tow. But she was ready to put up a fight. Her baby deserved that and more.

R ichard put down the ledger and looked up at Miriam. For a moment, his heart stopped. In the shadows, outside the light from the lamp and fireplace, she looked much like his Millicent, before their marriage had ended so tragically. He shook off the memory and focused on Miriam.

"I hope I am not disturbing you, Richard," Miriam said, with a smile. "I was wondering if you would like to drive into the village tomorrow with Bethany and me. We both require a visit to the dressmakers."

Richard wanted to refuse. He knew that family and friends had hoped they would wed, but he could not abide the idea of replacing his late wife with her cousin. And Bethany left no question what she was after. Though Miriam seemed content to wait for him to decide, Bethany was as calculating as a snake. She wasn't concerned with propriety or the fact that she and Miriam were friends. She was eager to get Richard under a yoke and was not concerned who she stepped over to get her wish.

"I should be able to spare a few hours in the early afternoon," he said kindly. "Shall we say one o'clock?"

"One o'clock is perfect." Miriam curtsied and rushed from the room.

Richard stared into the fireplace and wondered what his trio of guests would think if they knew he was already married. They thought nothing of living indefinitely off his generosity in the hope that one of the young women would eventually be his bride. Would that change if they learned the truth?

Two years under this roof. Ever since Miriam's mother

realized he'd been dragged out of mourning and had given up his life of drunken debauchery, she'd made it her mission to snag Richard for her daughter. About six months ago, she'd finally given up and returned to London.

But she was not a complete fool. She'd left Miriam, and her friends, behind.

There were times when he'd thought of casting them out. However, they brought life into the house, as it were, and he had enough wealth to feed them.

Truthfully, he didn't care what they did, as long as they respected his privacy. Besides, he admitted to himself, having them under his roof kept him from becoming too used to his own company, or a crazy bearded hermit who scared small children.

"Your Lordship?" Joseph stepped into the library. The butler looked befuddled. "Several coaches are coming up the drive at a rapid clip."

"Coaches?" Richard rose and went to the window. It was just dark enough to hide whatever markings might have given a clue to the identity of the visitors. "Are we expecting guests?"

"Not that I am aware," Joseph replied. "I shall have the cook warm what is left of supper and the maids ready several rooms, in case your company decides to take shelter for the night." He rushed out, put out by the unexpected visitors.

Richard watched the first coach stop before the house, and a second soon followed suit. Curious, he left the library and almost collided with Bethany in the hallway.

"We have guests," she tittered happily, and took his arm. "I do hope it is someone lively. This park can be quite dull."

He bit back a snide remark about how she could leave at any time, but decided instead to say nothing. He led her out the door and onto the drive as a flurry of servants came out behind him. They went to the coaches as the coachmen swung open the doors and the process of unloading the coaches began.

Miriam joined them. "Who is it?"

Richard shook his head. The coaches bore no identifying crests. "All we have seen thus far are the trunks. Whoever our uninvited guest, or guests, are remains a mystery."

Crunching wheels marked the arrival of another coach,

this one grander than the other two. The coach looked new, and the coachman was bedecked in dark blue livery. "Whoever it is, he, or she, has an excessive amount of luggage."

Bethany tightened her possessive hold on his arm. Richard was about to shake free of her grip when the coach came to a halt before them and a footman climbed down to open the door.

The large feathered hat appeared in the opening. "It's a woman," Miriam said, as the visitor was helped from the coach. Another woman, less expensively dressed, climbed down behind her. There was something about the figure underneath the finely cut hat and gown that struck a cord of familiarity in him.

Richard tensed as she lifted her face to the lamplight. Dressed in a deep plum gown and looking as beautiful as ever, Brenna adjusted her hat and looked into his eyes. "Hello, Richard."

"Brenna." The world disappeared around them. She took his breath. How had he ever thought he could forget her? She captivated him before, and she captivated him now. It took will to find his voice. "You look well."

"As do you." Her voice was strained. She glanced at Miriam and then at Bethany. Brenna's eyes took her measure.

For a moment, Bethany seemed taken aback by Brenna's beauty. Then she lifted her chin in a lofty manner and tightened her hold on his arm. Brenna's fine brows came together.

His mouth twitched. Clearly Brenna recognized a rival when she saw one. Life in society had sharpened her instincts. Though he wondered at her purpose for coming, he was even more curious about how long it would take before she pushed Bethany down on her bum.

"Richard, who is she?" Bethany said sharply, clearly tired of being ignored. The whine in her voice grated.

By the amount of trunks and the determined set of her chin, he knew that his wife intended to stay for an indefinite length of time. Brenna wasn't about to do anything half measure. She had not come to Beckwith Hall by mistake. She had an agenda, and he was about to find out what it was. Until then, he had introductions to make.

Richard met Brenna's eyes and saw a mischievous glint in

the green depths. She knew exactly what she was doing when she'd arrived unannounced. She wanted to surprise him, and she had. Now she waited for him to put Bethany in her place.

He willingly obliged. "Miriam, Bethany, meet Lady Brenna Harrington Ellerby, the Viscountess Ashwood. My wife."

Chapter Thirteen

Gasps erupted from both women. Brenna was satisfied to see the thin blonde release Richard. The calculating look in the woman's eyes was replaced by shock. Whatever she thought her position was in this household, it had just been usurped by a stranger. Worse yet, the stranger was Richard's wife.

Excellent. Brenna did not try to hide her satisfaction. She'd not come all this way to see her husband claimed by another woman. Whatever their connection, it was over. Brenna would not accept Richard's mistress living in *her* house. And Beckwith Hall was *her* house now.

"Leave us," Richard said. The two women stumbled off toward the manor, half supporting each other. Lucy walked over to stand on the steps, far enough away to give them some privacy yet close enough to satisfy her protective nature.

Richard took Brenna's arm. Drawing her away from the curious servants unloading her luggage, he positioned them face-to-face. Brenna inhaled his spicy scent, and her mind went back to that night at the inn. She remembered how his hands and mouth felt on her and how he tasted beneath her lips. Her skin tingled with the memory.

"Brenna, why have you come?" he asked, and then understanding quickly filled his eyes. "Am I to assume that your parents know the truth about our marriage?" At her nod, he expelled a harsh breath. "I'd supposed that the truth would come out eventually. When am I to expect Walter to arrive and exact his revenge?" He glanced up the drive.

"He wanted to kill you. Mother reasoned him down to a whipping," Brenna said. Her emotions where tangled. She was so pleased to see him, more than she'd expected. She'd hoped her infatuation for him was over. She was wrong. If he took her hand and led her to his bed, she'd offer no protest. "I think it's a satisfactory compromise. Don't you?"

Several emotions flashed across his face: guilt, anger, acceptance. Her father knew the truth. Richard had to accept his punishment, no matter what her father decided to mete out. It was no less than any other outraged father would do.

He ran a hand over his head. "I thought you wanted an annulment? I assume your husband hunt was unsuccessful?"

She fell into his eyes. She wanted to throw herself against him and feel his arms around her. She wanted him to declare his desire for her here in the drive. She wanted him to kiss her passionately without reservation or guilt.

Lud! What was wrong with her?

Truthfully, she did not know what she wanted, but his indifference was not high on her list. He treated her as though she were a casual acquaintance, as if their night together and their marriage meant nothing to him.

Perhaps it didn't. Had he missed her at all? Had he lain awake nights missing her naked body against his?

From his hard expression, she suspected not. Well, she was not about to be brushed off like lint on his jacket. She was his wife! She'd shake him to his core and shock some emotion out of him before the evening ended. The life of the staid Viscount Ashwood, as he knew it to be, was over.

So she straightened her spine, lifted her chin, and locked her knees. "Richard, I am with child."

Surprise widened his bright blue eyes. "You cannot be."

Finally, she'd chipped through his reserve. She placed a hand on her abdomen. "I assure you that I am. I'm approximately a month along. You should know that since you were there for the deflowering."

He looked as if she'd hit him. "This is not happening," he whispered. "Not again."

Brenna knew his history, but she was not his late wife. "I know you have concerns. However, I come from sturdy Irish stock. I have no intention of dying in childbirth."

The words were sharper than she'd intended. Still, they performed the desired consequence. Anger tightened his jaw. "You know my feelings on the matter. I did not want a child."

A rush of annoyance stiffened her spine. "You speak as if I chose to bear your child." She pointed a finger at his chest. "As I recall, you were equally involved with making our baby. I'll not allow you to shift the blame onto my shoulders, nor did Lucy and I come all the way from London to be turned away." She put her hands on her hips. "You will learn to accept this. You have no other option."

Richard's jaw pulsed. He glanced over her shoulder at Lucy. She did not need to turn to know her friend was intently listening to the exchange.

"What are your plans?" he asked finally.

"I intend to make Beckwith Hall my home."

He sighed. "Nothing has changed between us, Brenna. We both know this marriage is a mistake, though if the child lives, I will do my duty as its father. However, our agreement stands. Our marriage will be in name only."

He turned on his heel and returned to the house.

"Bastard," Lucy said, behind her. She moved up and placed a comforting hand on Brenna's shoulder. "I see why you fled him. He is a tyrant."

Brenna's lids narrowed. "He can be grim," she agreed, and faced Lucy. If Richard thought a bit of marital discord would send her fleeing back to her parents, he was wrong. She meant to fight for this marriage, his feelings be damned.

"Will you stay?" Lucy asked.

"Of course I'm staying." Brenna looked up at the manor. "Richard married me of his free will." She sighed. "The night we conceived this child, he was tender, almost loving. I hope to find that again. There is much in Lord Ashwood yet to discover."

Lucy appeared skeptical. She crinkled up her nose. "You will face many challenges in your journey to uncover his good qualities."

Brenna grinned. "I do enjoy a challenge." She hooked her arm with Lucy's, and together they presented a formidable force. "Now, shall we inspect my new home together?"

If Brenna expected the hall to be a dusty old manor, she was mistaken. The maids were well trained, as there was no dust, or cobwebs, to be seen. The foyer gleamed.

"Beautiful," Lucy breathed, agog at the splendor of the entryway. The ceiling was three stories high in the five-story house and was painted with a mural of angels at play. There were tapestries on the walls and tall windows to let in the sunlight.

Brenna nodded. "It is lovely." During her brief stop in her search for Richard, she'd not gotten past the stoop. Now she'd be living here, and she wanted to see it all.

She and Lucy stepped aside as a pair of footmen entered with one of Brenna's trunks, another pair on their heels. The foursome easily carried the two trunks up the curved staircase as if they were not packed to bursting with her possessions.

"I do not know where to start." Brenna held tight to Lucy's hand. She glanced about for a maid, but she and Lucy appeared forgotten in the chaos of their arrival. "My husband needs to be taught manners."

"Richard can be a bore." The pair turned to find the blonde, recovered from her shock, standing in an open doorway. Her loveliness was even more apparent in the lamplight. Though her eyes were sharp, she smiled. "I shall show you to your rooms. Tomorrow, I'll give you a tour of the hall."

Fatigued and overwhelmed, Brenna did not argue. The trip had taken a toll, and her body craved sleep. "Thank you—?"

"Bethany." She took Brenna by the elbow, pointedly ignoring Lucy. "I shall explain all about our little group once you have rested. You look positively peaked."

Lucy made a disgusted sound behind them, and Brenna's hand went to her face. How bad did she look?

"This way," Bethany said, and led her down a shadowed

hallway. They passed several rooms and stopped at the second to the last at the end. Bethany pushed the door open. "Here we are."

The bedroom was large and decorated in yellow and white. A door off to one side led to a small sitting room and past that to what she assumed was the master's chamber. Brenna had not considered that she and her reluctant husband would be quartered so closely together. She'd have thought Richard would want her in another wing.

"A maid will be assigned to you. If you need anything, she will fetch it for you," Bethany said. "Your companion will be one floor up. I will show her to her room."

"Thank you," Brenna replied.

Lucy sent her one last glance for courage and followed Bethany out.

Brenna removed her hat and sat it on a narrow settee. The sitting room shared the same yellow as the bedroom. In a moment of pique, she walked into the sitting room, pulled over a chair, and shoved it up under the door handle to the master's chamber. If Richard intended to sneak in during the night and have his way with her, he had better reconsider. While she ached to share a bed again, she'd not do so until his attitude about her, and their baby, changed.

"I will show him I am not some delicate daisy," she grumbled, and glared at the door. "And I will make this marriage work . . . or expire trying."

She heard the maid arrive and sighed. "Stubborn man," she whispered, and left the sitting room.

It was nearly ten when Richard heard the maid leave his wife. Brenna moved around for a few minutes more before blowing out the lamp, extinguishing the thin patch of light under the door.

He leaned against the headboard and listened intently for sounds, any sounds, coming from her room. Aside from the rustle of bedding as she moved on the bed, there was nothing.

His cock twitched. The image of her, clad in only her bedclothes with her hair tumbling about her shoulders in coal-dark disarray, left him feverish. She was no longer hours away in

London. Only footsteps separated them now. If he wanted to, he could take her as was his right. Damn his vow to keep her out of his bed.

Dressed only in his boots, trousers, and shirt, his hands behind his head, he jerked his mind from thoughts of her naked and writhing beneath him and contemplated her news—news that in an instant had changed his life forever.

Brenna. He should have known the minx couldn't keep her part of the bargain. Only she would agree to end the marriage, then show up pregnant.

A baby. They were having a baby. His heart clenched. Born too early for survival, his son had lived for only a few minutes while Millicent, who had lost so much blood, followed their son shortly thereafter. The midwife had done all she could to save them both, but the effort proved futile. Over the course of an afternoon, he'd lost them both.

Now Brenna was carrying his child.

How had he allowed that to happen? He'd been so careful with previous lovers. There were ways to prevent conception. The first virgin who finds her way into his bed gets with child on their first and only night together. And what a night it was. She'd upended his world and changed everything. Not a day had passed over the last month when he'd not thought of her in his arms. Now she was under his roof to torment him in person.

He closed his eyes. Fate had dealt him a cruel hand.

With effort, he pushed aside thoughts of what he'd lost and focused instead on what to do about Brenna. Knowing the stubborn chit as he did, she had a reason for coming, and it was not just about the babe. She had another agenda—he was certain of it.

He stared at her closed door. He'd heard her drag the chair over and push it under the handle. The lady may have shown up unannounced with some unspoken plan for him, but she wasn't ready to forgive him for his perceived misbehavior. He suspected over the next months he'd see more of her fiery temper.

Unbidden images returned. Brenna naked in bed, her eyes smoky from lovemaking, her kisses on his chest, and a sultry smile etched on her mouth.

He'd never seen anything so beautiful—and so dangerous. If he did not protect himself, in a short time she'd have him chasing after her like a besotted fool.

Love had no place in marriage; he'd learned a harsh lesson there. Once a heart was engaged, pain followed.

Chapter Fourteen

❧

Morning came with sunshine on her face and the distant bleating of sheep. Brenna grumbled when the bleating came again. She rolled over and stretched, the scent of tea filling her senses.

One lid lifted to find the curtains open and a tea tray sitting on a table by the bed. Though she couldn't immediately find a clock, by the lack of full daylight, she assumed it was still early—far too early to get up. With a groan, she pulled the coverlet over her head. The sound of male voices drifted from the bedroom next door. Obviously, Richard awoke with the roosters—or the sheep—and expected the same from her. Otherwise, the curtains would be closed and the tea still downstairs in the pot.

She'd have to convince him that the morning was for sleeping. She was on a London schedule; if he wanted to roam the dales with his sheep at sunrise, that was his concern. She'd sleep in until eleven.

Pushing from the bed, she shivered when her feet hit the cold floor, and she grumbled, realizing that her slippers were not yet unpacked.

Fall was arriving. Soon winter would be upon them. She wondered what it would be like confined here in the country all winter with her unhappy husband. The idea was dismal, indeed.

Hurrying into the sitting room lest he leave without speaking to her, she removed the chair and pulled the door open, startling the valet. The man stood stock-still, a pair of uplifted shirts clutched in his hands.

Richard was bare chested, his perfect chest golden in the sunlight. Unable to find her voice, she stared a bit too long. Her cheeks warmed.

"Excuse us, Miles," Richard said. The valet left, carrying the shirts.

Crossing his arms, Richard leaned back on his heels. "Is there a reason you have invaded my room?"

"I . . . I wanted to talk to you about an urgent matter." He was too distracting as he was, half dressed. She swallowed deeply as her gaze dropped to his hands, his very skilled hands.

"It could not wait until breakfast?"

She tore her attention away from his hands and back to his face. She blinked. "It could not. I wish to be allowed to sleep in late. I am used to a certain schedule and find early rising unsatisfactory to my good health."

His mouth curled downward. "Is that true? Or could it be that living a pampered existence has made you lazy?"

Her chin lifted. "I am not lazy!" She stepped into the room. "I have a full schedule: visits, charities, I even volunteer at a school." He did not need to know she helped at a courtesan school. "Because I like to sleep to a reasonable hour does not make me lazy."

Richard grunted, and Brenna seethed. "Would you rather see me up to my knees in cow waste, milking from dawn to dusk until my hands are gnarled and my back stooped? Or plowing fields behind an ox until I drop dead from exhaustion? Would that prove I'm worth my keep?"

His gaze drifted slowly down her and back up again. Was there a touch of humor in his eyes?

"Were you not carrying my child, I'm certain we could find a cow or two needing milking." He walked to her, his face blank. He ran a fingertip across the cream lace at the neckline of her nightdress. "If I see you so much as lift anything heavier than a teapot, I'll paddle your perfect little rump."

Brenna's breath caught. She watched his face as he looked down at her thinly covered breasts. There was heat in his eyes.

Knowing he still wanted her brought some comfort. Passion was a powerful thing. He was unhappy with the pregnancy, and with her, but she had months to convince him this was not the disaster he anticipated. Passion might be the key to building closeness between them.

First she desired to change the tone of this conversation. Arguing would get them nowhere and lead to more discord. She'd be pleasant even if it killed her.

She squelched the image of her lying dead on the polished floor, having succumbed to death by good humor, and forced a smile.

"Yes, My Lord." She pushed onto her toes and pressed a kiss on his cheek. Spice tickled her senses as she spoke softly in his ear, "I promise to remain hale and hearty."

For a heartbeat, his hands came to rest on her hips. Brenna stepped out of reach. He needed to get used to her, and she'd not rush him. By the time the babe came, she vowed he'd be hers in both mind and heart.

"I shall leave you to dress." With that, she walked from the room and closed the door behind her.

She pressed her back to the panel and listened for a moment as he called for his valet. Her heart fluttered as his rich voice drifted through the door. She placed her hand over her flat abdomen and wondered if the babe would share her dark hair and green eyes or Richard's fairer features and blue eyes.

Either way, she already loved the little mite. "He will love you, too," she whispered. "I promise."

Richard felt Brenna's presence in his bedroom long after she returned through the sitting room. The softness of her mouth on his face and the feel of her hips beneath his hands left his emotions muddled.

Why did Brenna, and Brenna alone, possess the ability to encompass his mind and give him no peace? He'd once lived a rogue's life and bedded many women, moving on after the passion waned, without a single qualm.

Even now, if pressed, he couldn't think of one woman, outside of Millicent, who'd shared his bed who stood out as particularly memorable. And he'd been with some celebrated beauties. Why, then, did it have to be Walter's virgin daughter who knocked him free of his determination to live the life of a quiet country bachelor?

Oh, right. He'd seduced her and got her with child. If anything was made to ruin carefully laid plans, it was that.

"Now that I have you, what am I to do with you?" he grumbled, under his breath.

"My Lord?" Miles paused from brushing off his coat.

"It's nothing, Miles." He sighed and glanced at the closed sitting-room door. "I was talking to myself."

The valet followed his gaze. "You do seem distracted this morning. Her ladyship's unexpected arrival has the household in a dither. The fact that there is a Lady Ashwood at all has come as quite a shock to everyone."

Richard turned back to Miles. "It was unexpected to me, too." What to tell the man? If the staff knew the truth about the marriage, it might undermine Brenna's position here. He could not have that. It was better to let them believe the marriage a love match. "I fear I was taken with the lady at first sight. What could I do but marry her?"

Miles nodded slowly, clearly not convinced. Richard had long vowed to never wed again. His valet knew his feelings more than anyone else who lived under this roof.

"I do find it odd that we are just now learning of her, when by my calculations, the wedding had to have happened sometime during your search for the still missing Lady Anne," Miles remarked. "One would think the joyous news would be brought to us, before her ladyship showed up at our door last evening with her luggage, and companion, in tow. It's almost as if the marriage were meant to be kept secret."

Richard frowned. Miles was teetering on the edge of crossing some servant-employer barrier. Still, he could not fault the man for his observation. It was correct.

"My wife needed time to explain this unexpected marriage to her family and to come to terms with it herself. The whirlwind nature of the matter left her a bit off-kilter. And as her devoted husband, I was willing to wait."

He expected Miles wanted to call the explanation utter rubbish. His face said the words he couldn't mutter aloud, out of respect for his position. However, Richard knew his valet. Though the man might think the story a lie, he'd do whatever he could to smooth Brenna's transition into the household.

Miles nodded soberly. "You are truly a most understanding husband, Milord."

Richard took note of Miles's struggle to keep his sober expression, and then smiled at the valet. The matter was settled between them. Miles would keep his curiosity to himself.

"I shall introduce my lady to the staff at breakfast," Richard said, as Miles helped him into his coat. "If you'll assemble in the breakfast room, I shall fetch my wife."

"Yes, My Lord."

Though expecting the sitting-room door to be barricaded, he was pleased to find he'd not have to knock. A man should never find the door to his wife's bedroom locked.

To his surprise, she was not abed but dressing for the day.

Brenna stood in her chemise and corset, her breasts pushed up to an enticing degree, while the maid was making ready to pull a pale blue gown over her head. Brenna raised her silky white arms over her head. The motion further threatened to send her breasts toppling over her corset.

His breath caught, his eyes eagerly waiting. But it was not to be. Her damned undergarments worked far too well.

Tearing his eyes from those perfect mounds, he continued exploring her body with his hungry gaze. In spite of her condition, she was still a slip of a girl. There was no sign of the babe in the curves he remembered, most vividly, exploring.

She lifted her hem to adjust her stocking, and he roused beneath his trousers. All too quickly, she dropped the hem. His disappointment tugged at his cock.

The presence of the maid proved to be a blessing. Seducing Brenna was the very last thing he should be doing. A marriage of convenience could not be accomplished if he was making love to his wife.

It took a moment to realize Brenna was watching him in the mirror while the maid buttoned her into the dress. The amusement in her pretty eyes told him she knew exactly where his thoughts were. The slight bulge in his breeches was further confirmation.

He cleared his throat. "I have come to take you to breakfast. Will you be finished soon?"

"I will have the lady ready in a moment, My Lord." The woman worked with quiet efficiency, and as promised, Brenna was ready before he had the chance to grow impatient. "You look lovely, My Lady."

"Thank you, Agnes." She smoothed the bodice, bringing Richard's eyes back to the place. "Can you bring Lucy down to the breakfast room? I fear she will get lost without assistance."

The maid curtsied. "Yes, Milady."

Richard waited for the maid to leave before speaking. "Do companions not usually eat with the staff?"

Brenna turned away from the mirror. "Lucy is more than a companion; she is my dear friend. If she is not welcome at your table, I shall eat with her in the kitchen."

Neither marriage nor impending motherhood had clipped her claws. If anything, she was more stubborn than he remembered.

This was one small battle he'd not fight. He'd save his ammunition for the bigger skirmishes he suspected were ahead. "I will not have my wife dining in the kitchen. Your Lucy will eat with us."

She smiled, and he felt the warmth from across the room. "Thank you, Richard."

She walked to him, her hips swaying. The sunlight from the window framed her in light, and his cock tightened again. She was a delectable piece who strained his willpower.

Damn his vow of celibacy. For a moment, he reconsidered taking her. It wasn't as if he could get her with child. He'd already done that deed. Still, if they were to live separate lives after the baby arrived, he needed to practice controlling his baser needs now.

"You must learn to dress more quickly. I hate to wait for my breakfast." He took her arm and felt her stiffen.

"Agnes is an excellent lady's maid," Brenna snapped. "I'll not have you cause her to fret with your impatience. If you'd like to breakfast by yourself, I will be more than willing to sleep until after the sun rises."

Richard cocked a brow and peered down at her. "I think you need to learn to follow my directives, as a compliant wife should."

She held his stare. "Truly? And at what point during our short time together did you ever find me compliant? I think you have confused me with another woman."

He snorted. "Your father should not have spared the switch when he could have beaten the insufferable tartness out of you, before it became forever part of your troublesome nature."

Smiling wickedly, she leaned against his arm. "Interesting that you find me so difficult, Husband. Why, just two weeks ago, a man kissed me in the corner of a darkened terrace. He did not find me the least bit troublesome."

B renna watched his face cloud. She knew she was treading into muddy waters, but he'd piqued her temper. She *was* troublesome and stubborn and outspoken. She did not need him to point it out, as if the three were negatives.

She could not be shy and sweet and simpering. And she suspected that, in spite of his protests to the contrary, Richard would not be happy with her as a scared little mouse.

"When you were playing the coquette for the rogue, did you consider the vows we took?" He stopped her at the top of the staircase. "Or were you too taken with his insipid poetry and the moonlight to think about our marriage?"

"Of all the—! Oh! You are insufferable!" She forced her voice down. "You did not want to marry me. You never wanted to marry at all. And you were happy to send me off to find another husband so you could be free. Now that I have done my best to replace you, you have the audacity to judge me for trying to take myself out of your life?"

Brenna stepped back, wanting to get away from him, when she caught her heel on the edge of the staircase. She wobbled and cried out as the floor beneath her foot fell away.

She saw the horror in Richard's face as she tumbled backward. The world became a blur. But her near fall down the stairs ended with his hands grabbing her arms. He jerked her against his chest.

Beneath her ribs, her heart pounded as the terror of the moment caught her in its grip. She let out a small sob as she clutched his shirt and held tight.

"I'm sorry, Brenna. So sorry," he said into her hair, his strong arms holding her tight, his heart racing beneath his rib cage.

"I could have lost the baby," she sobbed into his shirt. "I cannot lose the baby."

"No, love," he shushed her. "The baby is safe; you are unhurt. When I saw you falling backward—" The rest of his thought was left unsaid. He kissed her forehead, his breathing unsteady.

Brenna saw the hurt, the fear, in his eyes. For the first time she understood the heartbreaking moment when he'd lost his family, felt the grief that had taken him to that very dark place, where her father had found and rescued him.

And her moment of clumsy inattention had brought those awful memories back.

"I will not be foolish again." She pulled him down and kissed him once, twice, and again, while her salty tears mixed with her kisses. "It is I who am sorry, Richard. I promise you we will be safe. This baby will be born strong and healthy," she said against his mouth.

Slowly, she felt the tension leave him as he eased her farther away from the staircase, matching her kiss for kiss. "If you scare me like that again, I will lock you in a pillory until the babe is born."

She shook her head. "There will be no need. I have learned a terrifying lesson."

He looked deep into her eyes. "We both have." He lowered his head and kissed her long and deep.

Brenna's heart lightened just enough to feel hope. The feeling lasted only for a moment. He lifted his head and looked away. "We should go down."

Taking her arm, the cool Richard returned, and Brenna bit back a wave of disappointment. He escorted her down the staircase with great care.

Dozens of servants stood in the hall, and Richard introduced them all. Her mind whirled. There were so many.

The middle-aged housekeeper, Mrs. Beal, stepped forward. She leaned to take Brenna into her confidence. Her eyes twinkled. "I will help you remember each name, Milady. It will be my pleasure."

Relieved, Brenna took her hand. "Thank you, Mrs. Beal. I will need all the assistance you can offer."

When introductions were finished, Richard led her to the breakfast room. The space was grand as befitting a house of this size, and the table long enough to seat a large family.

Bethany was seated at one end, next to where the master would sit, and the other woman she'd seen last evening was opposite her. Bethany quickly masked her displeasure over seeing them together. The other woman focused on her plate.

Brenna knew that Bethany saw her as a rival for Richard's affections. He was rich and handsome. There were likely many other women in their village who would despise her on sight for the same reason Bethany resented her. She was his wife.

Thankfully, Agnes told her enough, while dressing her, for Brenna to conclude that Bethany was not Richard's mistress.

Lucy was seated near the middle of the table. Brenna released Richard's arm and moved to the sideboard. She did not have the will to fight the two other women for a place at his side. If Bethany and her companion expected her to fly into a rage over the seating arrangements, they'd be disappointed. She would not push her position until she was fully aware of what she faced here at Beckwith Hall.

When her plate was full, she joined Lucy. Her friend smiled knowingly. "Less than a day as mistress of the hall, and you've already made enemies. That is quite admirable."

They both looked down the long table to see two pairs of eyes staring at them as if they were some sort of carnival curiosity.

"A new and unexpected bride cannot be welcome," Brenna said, cutting into a slice of ham. Her stomach rumbled beneath her gown. "They will quickly learn that Harrington women do not share their men with anyone."

Brenna looked over at Richard. He was turning away from the sideboard, his plate piled high. In spite of her confident words, she wasn't sure what Richard planned to do with her. He went from hot to frosty cold in a blink.

Looking at the seating arrangement, he frowned. She held her breath, waiting for him to choose. Then, without hesitation, he walked to her and took a place at her side.

Happiness flooded her veins. She may be an unwanted bride, but he had just solidified her position as mistress of the hall.

Lucy grinned wide, and she and Brenna shared a smile.

"Lord Ashwood, I would like to introduce you to my friend Lucy, Mrs. Franklin Pruitt. She will be staying with us for a few weeks, until her husband returns from Paris."

Richard nodded to Lucy, and she simpered slightly under his regard. "It is my pleasure, My Lord."

"I hope you enjoy your stay, Mrs. Pruitt," he said companionably, and reached for a pastry. "I'm sure my wife will enjoy having a friend close while she navigates her new position here."

Brenna bit her lip to hide her smile as she and Lucy exchanged satisfied glances. Richard understood her worries more than she'd expected. It would be nice to have someone, besides just Lucy, watching her back, lest she find a knife sticking out of it.

The meal progressed with Richard giving them a history of the hall and information about the park, the neighbors, and the village beyond. Sometime during the hour, Bethany and Miriam—which Brenna learned was the quiet woman's name—left them without joining the conversation.

This pleased Brenna immensely. She sat back in her chair and pondered her husband. Though often sober, he was an entertaining host. After the meal concluded, Lucy excused herself, leaving Brenna and Richard alone.

"I will never remember all this," she said, taking a last sip of tea. "I pray for your patience as I learn the names of your neighbors and navigate myself about the grounds."

Richard stared, his expression unreadable. "I shall have someone find you a map. Andrew would know where they're kept, but he is still missing."

His comment brought her hand to her lips. "I apologize, My Lord. I have not asked about Anne. I'd assumed she'd been found."

His face darkened. "There has been no sign of her or that bastard she ran off with. The whispers surrounding her disappearance have kicked up to a humiliating degree. She is now ruined."

Though she did not know Anne, she felt for the missing woman. Even if she were found to be wed, the circumstances of her elopement would be the fodder for gossip for years to come.

"We must hope she is safe," Brenna said softly. She knew how worried Richard was for his sister. "You mentioned Andrew is still missing, too? May he have continued the search?"

She knew that Andrew was her husband's steward and was terribly concerned for Anne's safety, too.

"The last note I received from him was that he was following a lead into Scotland. He wasn't even sure the woman he was searching for was Anne. Though there was no sign of her marrying in Gretna Green, there are many other places to wed." He paused and sighed. "There is nothing I can do if she's wed Lockley. I just want to know she is in good health."

Brenna reached out to touch his hand. They locked eyes. "Have faith. I am certain Andrew will find something. You may soon have your sister returned."

Richard looked down at her hand. He rubbed a thumb over her fingertip. "If anything has happened to Anne, I will kill Lockley myself."

Chapter Fifteen

A shiver slipped down her spine. The emotion in his words left her troubled. She had to pray Anne was hale and happy. The idea of raising her child alone, after Richard was hanged for the murder of Mister Lockley, knotted her stomach.

"You must put aside the notion of killing the man," she scolded. "And keep your mind looking for the positive. For now you must accept that your steward is still searching for her and all will be well."

He looked at her sidelong. "I do not remember you seeing the world with such optimism," he said, his tone flat. "I thought you a bit of a termagant from our first meeting."

Her thoughts turned dark. "How dare you call me shrewish? I am a woman of good humor. It was your grim expressions and grumbles that were the source of my sour moods. Anyone who had to spend that many days traveling with you would feel the same."

"I had very little cause to be happy," he admitted, to her surprise. He pulled his hand free. "Even you could not expect levity when my sister was missing at the hands of a letch. I think a sour mood was acceptable, considering the situation."

Brenna sat for a long pause, processing his comment. She

knew he was not talking only about his missing sister. Much of his history was bleak. There *was* very little in his life for him to smile about.

Finally, she said, "I vow to change that, Husband. I intend to bring laughter into this household. Our child will not be raised in a grim mausoleum."

She rose and left him to take her words as he would.

They both needed happiness. It was some months since she'd laughed wholeheartedly just for the sheer joy of doing so. It was Lucy and her teasing that kept her from becoming quite sour.

Though she'd been out of sorts and angry after learning of Simon's plans to wed her to Lord Abbot, she vowed to reclaim her joy. She was married to a man she, oddly enough, felt great affection for and was about to be a mother. What was there not to be happy about?

R ichard stared out the open door. His wife had not lost her headstrong nature. Though she'd accepted Miriam's and Bethany's places at the head of the table without comment, he'd seen the agitation in her eyes. The two women had no idea what a formidable foe they had in his wife. If they expected weakness in the city-born Brenna, they would soon learn their mistake.

For a moment, he considered warning the pair, then changed his mind.

Bethany had gotten too used to playing mistress of the house, and Miriam, well, he was not entirely sure what went on in her head. Whatever their plans had been regarding him had been shattered with Brenna's arrival. It would be interesting to see how this all played out.

He smiled. Lud help the person who underestimated his bride.

"Can I get you anything else, My Lord?" the maid asked, turning his attention back to the moment.

"No thank you, Fanny. I feel the need for a ride this morning. Can you ask one of the footmen to call for my horse?"

"Yes, Milord." She curtsied and trotted off.

A ride on this cool fall morning would go far to clear his head. Brenna's arrival and the surprising news of the babe left him unsettled. Wanting her with stunning intensity was not the same as loving her or wanting the marriage.

And he knew that not all women died in childbirth. It was the almost violent nature of Millicent's death that gave him nightmares for a long time afterward.

He'd loved her as one loves a childhood friend. Now, years later, he still couldn't shake the irrational fear that he might fall in love with, and lose, Brenna.

He wasn't certain he could survive it.

W ith Lucy keeping her company and acting as a watchdog of sorts, Brenna—with the help of Mrs. Beal and the butler, Joseph, who had found a map of the hall buried in Andrew's desk—was off.

Brenna and Lucy took almost three hours exploring the upper two floors, including the attic, even chasing a mouse, leading Brenna to make a note to request more household cats.

"I do so hate those little creatures. I would be content to leave them be if they just stayed outside," she said, climbing off the chair after Lucy chased it under a wardrobe.

"Let us pray there are no rats," Lucy remarked dryly.

Brenna grimaced. "Do not tease."

Lucy giggled. "I am surprised there is even one mouse. This house is so clean that even the dust motes are fearful of making an appearance, lest they end up in the ash bin."

Looking around the upstairs parlor, Brenna nodded. "I wonder what the maids would do if I left my stockings scattered on the floor?"

A male voice interrupted. "You would be locked in the closet until you vowed to pick up after yourself."

Brenna startled, and Lucy squeaked. They spun around in unison to see Richard standing in the open doorway.

Wearing dusty riding clothes, Brenna's heart fluttered as she scanned his handsome face.

"Mrs. Beal worried you might have become lost, and I offered to launch a search." He stepped into the room and walked over to Brenna. He looked down at the map in her hand. "Are you enjoying your exploration?"

"Very much so," Brenna replied, holding his gaze. "There is much to discover."

Richard looked around the room, allowing her to examine his profile. He had the small scar under his left eye and a few crinkles at the corners of his eyes. Both gave him a rakish air.

When his attention returned to her, he locked onto her gaze. Brenna wetted her bottom lip with her tongue. Richard watched the movement with great interest. Brenna stopped breathing.

Lucy cleared her throat. "I'd forgotten that I was to help Mrs. Beal with . . . something. Perhaps we can continue our tour after lunch?" Without waiting for a reply, Lucy sent her a knowing look and hurried out the door.

"You have an interesting companion," Richard said, frowning. "Wherever did you find her?"

"She has decided to match us," Brenna admitted, ignoring his question. Lucy's past was their secret. "She has a romantic heart."

"Hmm." He moved closer. "I thought we were already matched." He reached out to finger the ribbon at her waist. "I think the child is proof of that."

Brenna wanted to slip her hands around his waist and bury her face in his dusty coat. "Strangers marry. Romantics hope for the emotional attachment. Love."

"Romeo and Juliet had romantic love," he offered. "See what that got them."

Smiling, Brenna shook her head. "You truly are a man who keeps his heart carefully guarded."

"It is better than the man who thinks he loves every woman who crosses his path. That man is a fool."

She thought for a moment. She knew such men. "Perhaps." A movement caught her eye. The mouse had darted out from under the wardrobe and was running along the wall to the door. She squawked and scrambled back onto the recently vacated chair.

Richard spun around. Clearly not knowing what to expect, he backed up to shield her from harm. She grabbed the shoulder of his coat with one hand and pointed a shaky finger with the other.

"Mouse!" Brenna cried, as the furry body scurried from beneath the wardrobe to the open doorway and vanished out the door.

The tension in his body eased. It took another moment to realize he was shaking. At first she thought perhaps the mouse had frightened him, also, until she realized he was laughing.

She smacked him on the shoulder. "This is not funny. Have you ever had a mouse run up your skirt?" He turned, his chuckle filling the room. Cad. "Well, I have. It is positively terrifying."

He shook his head and scooped her into his arms. "It isn't the mouse that amuses me, my dear, it is knowing that my fearless wife can be terrorized by a creature small enough to fit into a teacup."

She wanted to struggle, but the fear of the mouse returning kept her from demanding release. "When an eight-year-old girl suffers the feel of tiny claws climbing up her stocking, she should not be ridiculed for her girlish screams."

"I assume you are speaking of your brothers?"

She scowled. "They are an unsympathetic pair; Simon more than Gabriel. He did enjoy tormenting me for my fear. I still think he was working together with that mouse."

Richard chuckled again, and Brenna realized that although it was at her expense, she liked the sound. He seldom found amusement around her, and she silently thanked the mouse for its intervention on her behalf.

Perhaps she should skip adding more cats to the household.

Taking advantage of the turn of events, she snuggled against him and pressed her face against his neck. He smelled of spice and outdoors.

"Do you think the mouse is gone?" she asked. He murmured something to the affirmative but did not release her. She played with his hair. "I certainly hope so. Maybe you should hold me for another minute in case it returns."

If he sensed her game, he said nothing. The clock clicked for a moment. Then, "I believe you are safe now." Slowly, he lowered her to the floor.

Disappointment welled. Still, she'd stolen a moment and would be satisfied with that. For now.

Stepping back, she met his eyes. "I should find Lucy and continue the tour."

Richard tucked her hand under his arm. "Not until you've eaten. I'll not have you starve my child."

The concern in his voice sent a rush of warmth through her bones. She smiled. "I promise not to miss a single meal, My Lord. Our babe will be born plump and hearty."

Those words came back to haunt her a week later when the chamber pot became her most treasured companion.

B renna brushed her hair back from her face and slowly pushed, wobbling, to her feet. "I wish I had not eaten those eggs for breakfast." She walked to the basin to clean her teeth while Lucy watched.

"Poor dear," Lucy said. "You are so pale."

Peering in the mirror, Brenna grimaced. There was no color in her cheeks. "The last two mornings have been trying. But it does not stop with the arrival of the noon hour."

"I thought pregnancy nausea only came in the morning?"

"Morning, afternoon, evening," Brenna grumbled. "I spent most of last evening racing for the chamber pot. We must ask Cook not to make pickled fish."

Lucy bit her lip. "I will make a note to tell her."

Beneath her gown, Brenna's stomach recoiled. It took all her will not to return to the pot. "You will understand my misery when you are caught with a child of your own. I certainly do not look forward to the months ahead."

Lucy walked over and put her hands on her friend's shoulders. "I shall ask that your breakfast be limited to toast and tea. Eggs shall be banned from your plate."

Brenna smiled and turned to hug her friend. "What would I do without you?"

"It will be another week or two before you have to find out," Lucy replied. "I should hear from Franklin soon."

The idea of losing Lucy was disheartening. But she would not be selfish and voice her regrets aloud. Lucy had her own family to build. She could not live here at the hall forever.

"Have you heard from your husband?"

"I have only that one letter. I assume he is still in France and will return by the end of the month."

Part of Brenna hoped his return would be delayed, but she squashed the wish. Though Bethany and Miriam had been on good behavior, she'd seen them whispering together and sending unhappy glances her way when they thought she wasn't looking. She worried that they were plotting some misdeeds and liked that Lucy was watching over her.

She took Lucy's hands and smiled brightly for her friend. "We shall pray he finds a swift ship home."

The rest of the morning was spent going over the menu for the week and banning fish and eggs. Brenna also made an effort to talk to the maids and footmen, trying to set names to faces. It wasn't easy, as there were so many, but she felt she had most of it conquered by lunch.

"I don't know why you concern yourself with knowing their names," Bethany said, as she daintily nibbled a pastry. " 'You there' has always worked well for me."

Bethany was quite a snob.

"Funny," Brenna said. "I have always found using someone's proper name more productive when making a request than a grunt and finger point."

A snort sounded from the direction of the waiting footmen, but when she and Bethany glanced over, there was no hint of guilt on the trio of set faces.

Bethany glared at each in turn. Brenna smiled at the men and quickly regained her sober expression before the woman turned back.

"I have learned from my mother's teachings," Brenna continued, "that the staff is more amiable when treated with respect."

The woman stared at Brenna as though she were a blithering idiot, then said, "Perhaps the threat of dismissal would work just as well."

Brenna had no time to answer the ridiculous comment. She reached for her teacup, and the staff set upon her as if she were the queen.

"Would you care for more tea, My Lady? Is the pudding to your liking? Perhaps I can find you a tart. Cook makes excellent tarts." This went on and on for several minutes, as each servant who'd overheard her exchange with Bethany offered to assist in her comfort, while Bethany couldn't get even another sugar for her tea.

Richard joined them. He stared at the effusive staff with puzzlement while Bethany stewed.

And Brenna watched it all with serenity on her face. The other woman finally stood, threw down her napkin, and quit the room.

"Should I dare ask what has brought this overwhelming display of devotion?" Richard asked.

Her sweeping smile encompassed the staff, and they smiled in return. "I have set in place a new rule. All servants must be called by their names. Anyone who fails to adhere to this rule will be sent on their way."

Brenna braced herself for his objection. Instead, he nodded. "That is an excellent rule. I do prefer my staff be treated with respect."

She beamed. She had won her first battle with the support of her husband, though it was won without one shot fired.

"Thank you."

Richard shrugged and reached for his newspaper. "This is your home, Brenna. If you'd like to pass a rule that we all come to meals in our nightclothes, I shall make sure mine are pressed."

The idea deepened her happiness. "While you are so agreeable, I hoped that perhaps I could put new drapes in the third-floor guest rooms. It is entirely too dark up there."

"Do as you wish." He lifted the paper, and she considered herself dismissed.

There were several other changes she hoped to implement but decided to wait until another time to ask.

Instead, she finished her tea, bid him a good day, and left him to his reading.

The newspaper was not nearly as appealing as his wife as he lowered *The Times* and watched her exit the room, his eyes trained on her trim backside.

It was impossible to ignore the hardening in his breeches.

It was impossible to ignore her. He'd kissed her several times already. Without getting a firm hold on his desires, he'd have her bedded by the close of the week.

His appalling lack of control worried him. If this was to be a marriage of convenience, he needed to tighten his control on his lust. Once the babe was born, Brenna would certainly tire of life in the country and beg to return to London. If he allowed himself to share her bed, the separation would be all the more difficult for them both.

"Good morning, Richard," Miriam said, as she swept through the open door and glanced toward the open windows. She giggled. "Though I suppose it is afternoon now. I do not know how I slept so late."

Richard watched her walk over to the sideboard to examine the fare. Frowning, it took him a minute or two to realize there was something different about her.

Her favored costume of choice, a simple high-necked gown in an uninteresting color, was gone. In place was a bright green dress, cut low to showcase her small bosom and to skim over her thin frame.

"I have never seen you in green," Richard said.

"Do you like the dress?" she asked, and turned around for his inspection. Though she possessed none of Brenna's delightful curves, the dress was certainly better suited to her coloring than the drab colors she usually preferred.

"It is quite fetching," he replied, and was rewarded with a smile. "You should wear color more often. You might entice the unattached young bucks in the park to call." As her guardian of sorts, he realized he'd been neglectful of his duties toward her. Her future needed consideration. "I think it high time you think about courtship. You have spent too much time fussing over me. You should have a husband and family of your own."

Her smile slipped. Richard continued, "Once Brenna familiarizes herself with the household, your duties will be eased. It will free you up to pursue your own interests."

Any hope she may have had toward him was over. Though he never saw her in a romantic way, he'd enjoyed her company and felt some fondness for her.

He watched her over the top of the newspaper as her face

began to crumble. She placed a hand over her mouth and hurried from the room, thus confirming the change of appearance had been for him.

Sighing, he lowered the paper. Miriam needed to forget any fanciful notions she had and find a suitor of her own. Brenna was his wife, and his wife she would stay.

Even if it meant the death of his sanity.

Chapter Sixteen

❧

"I have never seen a house so clean," Brenna said to Mrs. Beal. She dropped the edge of the coverlet and straightened. Just for her own amusement, she'd looked under several beds while she and Mrs. Beal chatted about the staff. Expecting to find at least one dust ball, she was happily disappointed. "Your master must carry a large whip."

Mrs. Beal startled. "His Lordship is a kind master, My Lady!" she protested. Then, as if realizing Brenna was jesting, she clucked her tongue, shook her head, and muttered, "That cannot be said for others who reside under this roof."

Brenna's brows arched up. "Is there something you'd like to tell me, Mrs. Beal? Certainly you cannot be speaking about me?" she asked innocently.

"Oh no, My Lady. You are very kind." The housekeeper flushed. "Some people do like to elevate themselves far above their station."

Curiosity welled in Brenna. "I will not pretend that I do not know who you mean. Miss Bethany is not pleased with my arrival. I think she had other plans for my husband."

"That woman could try the patience of Job," Mrs. Beal snapped, and her flush deepened. "Oh, dear. I should not speak so."

Brenna reached to touch her arm. "Your secret is safe." She realized Mrs. Beal was very protective of her employer and had clearly feared Bethany would get her talons into Richard. "I'm certain my husband appreciates having such a staunch ally in you."

Mrs. Beal nodded. "After his wife died, he was lost, trapped with his demons. A friend saved him. Then two years ago, those women, and Miss Bethany's brother, George Bentley, came to stay. I worried His Lordship would be taken by Miss Bethany's face and not see the wickedness inside her." She peered askance at Brenna. "I am pleased to see his heart has turned in another direction."

The comment brought forward an ache in Brenna's stomach. Mrs. Beal was so happy that Richard had taken a wife that Brenna could not destroy the housekeeper's romantic notions.

"What of Miss Miriam?" Brenna asked. "I see the way she looks at my husband."

Mrs. Beal waved the comment away. "She is better off finding a more settled sort. A vicar perhaps. His Lordship was right not to encourage her."

Brenna knew she should not gossip about people she'd only just met. However, as unsettled as she was in her new position as Lady of Beckwith Hall, she wanted to know the players in the game to better prepare herself for what may come.

"Tell me about Mister George," she said.

Appearing to struggle with what she should say against what she wanted to say, Mrs. Beal finally sighed. "Mister George has charmed the entire park. The ladies love him, and their mamas all want him to marry their daughters."

The housekeeper's face tightened. This gave Brenna the impression that she was holding something back. "You do not like him?" she said. "Why?"

"He is a wily fox, that one," Mrs. Beal said. "He and his sister are cut from the same soiled cloth."

"Interesting," Brenna said. "Thank you."

She thought about all she had learned as the housekeeper excused herself. Alone, Brenna sat on the bed, fatigue bearing down on her. She lay back on the coverlet, her hand open on her abdomen, and stared at the ceiling. "You do take much from me, little one. Soon I will sleep all day and eat everything in sight. I'll be both tired and fat. For that, I'll thank you."

Smiling softly, she yawned and gently caressed her still-flat belly. "I cannot wait to meet you."

R ichard stood in the hallway outside the guest bedroom and watched quietly as Brenna's eyelids drooped closed. It did not take long before her breathing evened out and she slept.

He turned to shush Lucy as she walked up behind him. "Tell the maids to no longer awaken my wife in the mornings. It appears she and the baby need more sleep."

Lucy peered around him and smiled. "My Lady wants to please you, My Lord. She thinks a country wife should rise early."

He remembered the conversation with Brenna her first morning here. He woke her early to pique her temper. He did not expect her to follow his directives.

"She can sleep all day if she wishes." She looked so peaceful in sleep. An ache grew in his chest. He'd overheard her words to their child and knew she'd do anything to keep the babe safe. And as hard as he tried to steel himself against the worry that he'd lose them, fear still lingered. "I want her pampered. Give her anything she desires."

"Yes, Milord." Lucy nodded. She glanced back at Brenna. "When will you tell the household about the baby?"

"Soon. I thought it best to wait for a bit, and Brenna agrees. We will allow her to settle here before the fussing begins. There has not been a new babe at the hall in many years. The staff will be in a dither once they discover I am to be a father. So for her sake, and mine, we will give Brenna a few more weeks of peace."

Lucy rubbed her palms together. "She has been a dear friend to me," she said softly. "I long for her happiness." She looked up at Richard. "I hope she can find it with you."

Richard stared into her pretty face. There was fierce loyalty in her eyes. More, she had just handed him the duty to ensure Brenna's happiness.

He slowly turned back to watch Brenna sleep. She was stunningly lovely against the backdrop of the bright yellow coverlet and the sunshine from the open window.

Could she be happy here? Could she be happy as his wife? What did *he* want from her?

Taking a step backward, Richard turned. "Send a maid up to wake her in two hours. That should give her enough time to rest before supper." In spite of the overwhelming desire to join his wife on the bed, he knew it would only complicate matters.

He left Lucy to do his bidding.

When he returned downstairs, he found Joseph waiting with a letter. "This just arrived, Milord." He handed over the missive.

Richard tore it open and read the brief note. "It is from the Runner I hired to find Anne. He confirms that she went missing in Scotland. Nothing more." He crumpled the paper and stuffed it into his pocket.

"Will you rejoin the search?" Joseph asked.

"I will not." Richard had done all he could. Although he hated knowing she was out there somewhere, unprotected, he had hit a wall in the search. "She clearly does not want to be found. I can do nothing more but pray for her eventual safe return."

He spent the rest of the day going over estate books. Thankfully, Andrew kept perfect records.

The evening meal was quiet, and he was satisfied that the seating arrangement had been settled. He took his rightful place at the head of the table, with Brenna at his side and Lucy next to her. Bethany and Miriam took places nearby. After, he excused himself and went to the library for some much-needed libation.

Brenna found him there. She walked over as he poured himself a brandy and touched his arm. "I understand you received word about Anne."

He tossed back the contents and poured another. "Yes. If you consider no news as news."

Brenna winced at the bitterness in his voice and stepped away. Moving to the nearest bookshelf, she ran her fingertips over several volumes about proper crop planting and harvesting.

"These last weeks have been trying for you," she said

softly. "Your sister ran off with a bounder, you betrayed my father by bedding me, and now you are stuck with a wife and child you do not want. Could your life get any worse?"

Her words took him aback as they pounded into his brain. Was she mocking him for feeling sorry for himself?

With only one side of her face to see, he was certain there was wickedness in her expression. The little witch!

Suddenly, and without warning, a chuckle welled up in him. "You are a wicked wench, Brenna Ashwood."

"And you feel entirely too sorry for yourself, Husband." She returned to him. "Your sister is an adult, free to make her own mistakes. I do not know her, but I think she will find her way through her own life." She drew in a deep breath. "I promise you that I will come through this pregnancy unscathed and give you a perfect little Ellerby heir for you to brag about to everyone. As for Bethany and Miriam, I will leave them to you and do my best to understand their bitter disappointment over losing you."

The chuckle deepened. "How can I enjoy my misery properly when you continue to poke fun at my expense? I knew that I should have found a more agreeable wife."

Brenna scoffed. "You did not want a wife, agreeable or otherwise. And I found you."

She was too close and too lovely in her spring green frock. The fabric flowed over her delightful curves, enticing him with the fullness of her breasts. Unable to compel himself to walk away, he reached out and pulled her to his chest. Her soft floral scent tweaked his senses. "I shouldn't kiss you."

"You should not," she agreed, and splayed her hands over his chest. Her touch pushed him over the last barrier of resistance.

"But I will kiss you anyway."

"If you must," she replied.

With a low growl, he kissed her soundly.

A whisper of a sigh escaped her. His arms slipped around her, holding her tight, and every inch of her body welcomed his embrace.

She felt him harden against her. Her feminine core responded with tingles of need. She kissed him passionately, knowing that the moment would end far too soon and wanting to enjoy his kiss for as long as he allowed.

When he did break the kiss, his voice was low and harsh. "What you do to me, Wife, can only be called torture."

"Take me, Richard," she begged, pulling at his shirt. She desperately wanted to see him naked, feel his body against hers.

"I cannot." He released her. "It was not our agreement."

"Damn our agreement," she said. Feeling his disconnect, she couldn't bear his rejection. "We are husband and wife."

Without waiting for further comment, she went to close the door, locked it, and reached for the laces at the front of her gown. She tugged open the bow.

"Brenna," he warned.

She did not stop until the bodice gaped open and her full breasts were teetering at the edge of spilling over her corset and chemise. His heated eyes were locked on her, his breathing shallow. She trailed her fingertips over the soft tops of her breasts.

"You want me," she said, and pushed her gown down over her hips to puddle at her feet. She reached for the corset. Thankfully, this one laced at the front. Soon, the item joined the gown on the floor.

"You must stop this." His protest was without bite.

"I will not." She tugged at the chemise, and the straps fell down her arms. Her breasts were covered with only the thin fabric. She lifted the hem and removed her stockings. She thought she heard a low groan. Soon, she was wearing nothing but her chemise.

Slowly, and what she hoped was seductively, she strolled toward him, her eyes locked on his. "We will not leave this room until you have loved me passionately and thoroughly."

He grumbled under his breath, but his eyes were already removing the chemise. She stopped and let one side of the chemise slip down, exposing one breast. Without hesitation, his hand closed over the rounded flesh in a firm caress.

"How thorough is thorough?" His mouth followed his hand as he bent and tugged her nipple gently between his teeth. She moaned and tangled her fingertips in his hair.

"At least once," she breathed. "Possibly twice, if you are willing."

Expelling an exasperated sound, he bent and carried her to the desk. "You are a temptress, a witch."

Richard sat her on the surface and reached for the neckline of the chemise. Renting it easily with a jerk, the cloth fell away. A laugh-gasp escaped her. He leaned to kiss her other breast, kneading the first with his hand.

"You are a seductive rogue," she countered, breathlessly.

The rain of kisses and caresses sent shivers through her as he moved eagerly down her body, like a man feasting after a long period of deprivation. He was no fop, her husband. His calloused hands, rough and certain, teased and tempted her, moving to places they ought not. When his fingertips found and breached her feminine folds, she nearly came off the desk.

"Richard," she breathed. "Yes, please."

She was certain she heard him chuckle as he teased her to little delighted moans. When she climaxed, she slumped back on the smooth surface, watching him through half-open eyelids as he jerked off his cravat and his remaining clothes.

Before she could offer encouragement, he was inside her, holding her legs as he plundered her heat. She reached for him as he leaned over her, rocking against her, her eyes watching the passion build on his face.

For a second time, her pleasure peaked. She offered little nonsensical words of encouragement, giving a final gasp as they found release together.

Expecting him to close himself off from her as was his want, instead he reached to lift her into his arms and carried her to the rug before the fireplace. Lowering her onto the plush surface, he joined her, rolling onto his back and staring up at the ceiling.

Brenna curled up against him and laid her head on his chest. His hand caressed her back.

"We are quite a pair," she said softly. "When I chased after you, I never expected this."

"Our marriage of convenience is proving anything but convenient," he agreed. "It would be better for us both if you went back to London. It would ease the temptation."

Rising up slightly, she looked into his eyes. "I know you have doubts about me, our baby, everything. You steel yourself against us, unwilling to risk your heart. But I am not going back to London, not when I have everything I want here." She paused and took a deep breath. "I do not ask for your love. I only ask that you give this marriage your full consideration."

He held her gaze for a long moment, then nodded. "I suppose I owe you that much."

It wasn't a declaration of affection or a strong affirmation that she was not foolish for thinking they had a chance at happiness. However, he wasn't pushing her away and reaching for his clothes. That in itself was a victory.

Smiling, she rose onto her knees and straddled him. She leaned to press a light kiss on his mouth. Her breasts teased him, and she felt his cock twitch.

"I know we agreed to a marriage of convenience, yet I think denying our pleasure is foolish. It isn't as though we risk a child. That deed is done." Brenna wriggled against his erection. He reached for her breasts. "I will not lock my door. You are welcome to have me whenever you wish."

Mischief welled in his eyes. "You may not want to make that offer, mistress. I can be most demanding."

She slid her hand between them and eased him inside her. "I shall take my chances," she said softly, and impaled herself on his manly sword.

G ood evening, my dears, Richard." The man paused and stared at Brenna, his handsome face showing his surprise. "And the lovely new addition to our supper table." The stranger crossed the room and stopped beside Brenna's chair.

Bending, he took her hand and brought it to his mouth. "Had I known what was awaiting me at home, I'd have returned sooner."

Knowing a rake when she heard one, Brenna accepted his attention with patience, as she suspected this was the missing George. Dressed impeccably in a dark blue coat and matching waistcoat, she wondered if her husband paid the bills for the expensive clothing.

"Please do tell me you have come to marry me and make me the happiest man in all England?"

Brenna resisted rolling her eyes. She suspected that there were dozens of women all over these fair shores who had received the same proposal. Still, he was charming.

This explained why Mrs. Beal did not like him. Effusive charm would not appeal to the sensible housekeeper.

"I fear you are too late," she said, amused, as his face fell. "I am already wed."

"She is my wife." Richard's voice was tight. Clearly, he did not appreciate George fawning over his wife. "Lady Ashwood, this is Mister George Bentley."

With a most exaggerated sigh, George bowed low over her hand and returned it to her. "Such is the bane of my existence. I am always a step behind."

A feminine cough from down the table saved Brenna from a response. She knew nothing about the man and wasn't certain what to think of him or how to proceed without giving encouragement. She suspected he was the sort who'd not let marriage vows deter a courtship.

"Brother, do sit down," Bethany said sharply. "You have already disrupted our meal."

George glowered at his sister, who returned the gesture in kind. Then he claimed the seat across from Brenna and sat.

The rest of the meal was taken up with news of George's adventure to Dover. While Richard scowled at his houseguest, the three women enjoyed tales of horse races and gambling and an ill-fated courtship; most of his animated buffoonery was directed at Brenna and the reason for Richard's scowl.

Once his tale was told, his face grew grim. "Alas, there was one sad note, in an otherwise enjoyable adventure." He paused dramatically until all eyes were upon him. "A maid was found dead at the base of the cliffs. The constable believed she either fell . . . or was pushed."

Miriam gasped. "How horrible."

"Indeed it was," George agreed. "My friend Stewart, who lives in Dover, has promised to keep me abreast of the investigation."

A sober mood fell over the room. Brenna leaned forward

and frowned. "Another maid was found at the bottom of the stairs in Bath last spring. It was determined to be an accident."

"I remember that case," Bethany added. She twirled a ring on her finger. "Do you think neither was an accident, and that a killer is murdering maids all over England?"

"Nonsense," Richard interjected. "The two incidents were in two different cities, far apart. It wouldn't be the first time a woman has taken a tumble down a flight of stairs or gotten too close to the edge of a cliff. To take a leap to a crazed killer of maids is ridiculous."

"Still . . . ," George said low and for dramatic affect. "We must make sure our doors and windows are locked and our maids safely tucked in behind these walls at night, lest the grim reaper comes to call."

Miriam's eyes were wide. "I shan't sleep a wink tonight."

"See what you have done with your tale of murder?" Richard said, with his eyes hard on George. "Every time a shutter rattles, the hall will be filled with terrified female shrieks."

Brenna reached for her teacup. "I promise I'll not shriek over rattling shutters, if that sets your mind at ease."

Richard motioned for dessert to be served. "Unless there is proof a killer is connected to the two cases, we should accept that these are two unfortunate accidents and be done with this silly speculation."

Taken to task, the foursome let the matter drop. Still, even Brenna wondered how well she would sleep.

As a child, she had loved ghost stories and tales of the grim fates of unwary travelers who vanished on fog-shrouded roads. Still, no matter how much she enjoyed having her wits scared out of her, she could never sleep well for several nights after. And though what Richard said made sense, she suspected her night would be spent listening for those rattling shutters.

When the last dish was cleared away, the group gathered in the parlor. Bethany played the pianoforte with skill, and the rest of the conversations progressed on a lighter note.

Later, when Brenna was abed and Richard joined her there, she rolled onto her side and watched him stoke the fire.

"Isn't there a small part of you who thinks a grim reaper

could be wandering around England killing unsuspecting maids?" she asked, drawing an exasperated stare. She smiled. "It certainly made for entertaining supper fare."

"George is a dolt. He takes pleasure from commanding the attention of the room." Richard stood and walked barefoot, and naked, to the bed. Brenna watched him, admiring his perfect male form. He climbed in beside her. "When I was a child, my uncle used to tell us tales of young boys gone missing on moonless nights, to keep us from sneaking out of our beds and making mischief. Not once do I recall a single missing boy, here or elsewhere."

He lowered himself over her and kissed her nose. Brenna circled his neck with her hands and pulled his mouth to hers. Richard grinned under her seeking mouth.

"If you promise not to talk about murder, I promise to give you something else to occupy your mind."

When she nodded happily, he did as he vowed, and later, she slept quite soundly.

Chapter Seventeen

***

Brenna spent the rest of the week certain she was dying, while Lucy assured her that the nausea would pass and all would be well. Richard removed anything pickled or curdled from her sight, but nothing eased her symptoms.

"You are not dying," Richard assured her.

Lifting the damp cloth from her face, she narrowed her lids. "You do not know that."

He tried desperately to keep a sober expression. "Unless you are crushed beneath a tipping chamber pot, we can assume you are in no immediate threat of expiration."

Groaning, she dropped the cloth back over her eyes. "I can see I'm to expect no sympathy from you." She felt the bed move under his weight. He lifted a corner of the cloth.

"I would take your misery upon myself if I could."

His sincerity touched her. "I believe you mean what you say, Husband."

"That I do." He patted her thigh and took his leave. Brenna replaced the cloth over her closed eyes.

A few minutes later, Lucy climbed onto the bed with her. "I see there will be no more pickled eel." She sighed deeply. "I do adore eel."

Brenna grumbled. "How much longer can I keep the babe a secret? George, Bethany, and Miriam didn't seem to notice the change in fare, but the maids will begin to wonder why my stomach ailment has no end."

"Thankfully, as a new member of the household, you can eat as many pastries as you wish without drawing notice."

Brenna tossed the cloth away. "Though I am still slender, the laces of my corset do not cinch as tightly as before. By my calculation, it won't be long before I can no longer hide beneath high waistlines and a flowing skirt."

Lucy pulled her from the bed, and they left the room. "You will strain His Lordship's purse strings with the excess cloth needed to make your gowns."

"I do not find you amusing. I cannot imagine waddling about the house like a pregnant bovine," Brenna groused, as she and Lucy walked down the staircase, arm in arm. Richard was talking to a maid in the foyer. "My cousin Eva is barely able to rise from a chair without a pair of footmen and her husband helping her up."

Lucy gave her a sidelong look. "I am certain that is an exaggeration."

"Not by far." Brenna looked at her husband, casually dressed in dun-colored trousers and a deep blue coat. Her breath caught. Then, "My mother said she could clear a wide path when she was pregnant with me. I expect to be the same."

"You will be lovely."

Brenna smiled for Richard as they neared. "I hope my husband thinks so," she whispered.

Richard stepped forward. "I know what will lift your mood, Brenna. A picnic. It is a fine day, and I have advised Cook to only pack the blandest food available."

An outing did sound fun. Perhaps fresh air would settle her stomach. "I shall get my bonnet and pelisse."

Minutes later, Richard helped Brenna into the curricle, and they were on their way. "The clouds are gathering," she said. "I hope it doesn't rain."

"Hmm." Richard looked up. "I think we will return before we get wet. I promised you a picnic, and I expect the weather to help me keep my word."

"Where are we going?"

"There is an old ruin just down the road," he said, taking a right at the end of the drive. "It used to be a small abbey but was abandoned long ago, when a larger one was built closer to London. It is interesting architecturally, and I thought you might enjoy exploring the place."

Brenna nodded eagerly. "I would, very much. Perhaps we might even see a ghost."

He flicked his gaze to her. "There is an old cemetery on the grounds, kept up by a caretaker. I am convinced that there are ghosts aplenty inside those iron gates."

The idea of a haunted abbey sent a trill of excitement through her. She rubbed her hands together and eagerly looked about for a first sight of the ruin.

"Do you think we could ask one to rattle a chain or moan dramatically?" Brenna asked, with mock seriousness. "I do adore chain-rattling ghosts."

"We shall have to wait and see." Richard made another turn, and soon the abbey came into view. It was three stories tall, with a large bell tower in the center that added another tall story. The rest was made up of lower wings, jutting out this way and that. The roof was gone, but the rest of the building seemed to have withstood the elements quite well. Though there were small cracks in several places in the stonework, the place appeared sound.

"This is the perfect place for a picnic," Brenna said, in awe. "It is charming."

Richard drew the horse to a stop and helped her down. "Would you like to explore first, or eat?"

"Explore." She did not hesitate. She hurried toward the building, Richard on her heels. "I can't wait to find the first ghost."

The wood door to what she supposed was a foyer of sorts was nothing more than a few broken bits of ancient wood from the missing roof scattered in the grass. Brenna stepped over them and through the open doorway. The room went clear up the full three stories and opened up to the sky beyond.

Several crows took flight, soaring skyward without a roof to block their passage, their black bodies disappearing against the backdrop of gray clouds.

Instead of seeing the birds as a grim omen, Brenna clapped her hands. "Perfect. I am convinced a ghost is nearby."

Richard shook his head. "Next you will be talking about

dead maids and murderers. Who knew you had such a dark imagination, my dear Brenna."

She glanced up toward the second floor. "Is that a chain I hear rattling?" she said, and grinned. "We'd better hurry before the ghost gets away." She lifted her skirts and hurried for the stone staircase, her laughter echoing off the walls.

Keeping close to the wall, as the crumbling stone railing appeared to be unsafe, she climbed the stairs and entered the first room to her right.

The space was sparse, as expected, and full of cobwebs. A brick and stone alter stood at one end, and Brenna wondered how many pairs of knees ached while kneeling for hours on the stone floor before it. Hundreds, she suspected.

Richard came in beside her, brushing a web away from his head. "You really must let me lead this exploration." He held up his cane. "There could be rats or raccoons living in these rooms. I'd hate to see you bitten."

Rats? Brenna shuddered and peered around for any sign of the furry critters. "If there is one thing I hate more than mice, it is rats. Perhaps I will let you lead."

They explored the rooms for an hour or so, Richard scaring off two mice and startling a wren from its nest. As with the foyer, the third story was missing much of its roof. With rain threatening, they moved back down to the second floor.

There were no ghosts, though Brenna was certain that once darkness fell, there would be spirits aplenty.

"This is the last room," Richard said. It was the largest, with a huge stone fireplace and the biggest collection of spiderwebs. They fluttered in the breeze coming in through the chimney and missing window glass.

Brenna paused in the doorway, her ears picking up a noise. It sounded like shuffling feet. "Did you hear that?"

Richard went silent and listened. "Is it your ghost?"

She wasn't certain what she heard, but she did hear something. It was coming from the staircase. "Perhaps it is." She motioned with her hand, and Richard joined her in the hallway as her imagination took flight.

Clutching his arm, she waited for a ghost to appear. When he did, she bit back a gasp. The spirit was old and stooped and wheezing from the effort of climbing the stairs.

Wheezing? "Do ghosts wheeze?" she whispered, as the apparition paused, bending over to place his hands on his knees while struggling to reclaim his breath.

Richard chuckled. "I fear you have mistaken something earthbound for a ghost. Hello, Mister Crane!"

The elderly man righted himself and peered through the dim light. "Is that you, Lord Ashwood? I thought that was your curricle."

"Mister Crane is the caretaker here," Richard muttered, under his breath. Brenna hid her disappointment. She had really hoped for a ghost. "You have caught us trespassing," he said, as the man approached. "I thought my wife would enjoy exploring the grounds. Lady Ashwood, this is Mister Crane."

A pair of kind eyes scanned Brenna's face. "I'd heard you'd married. A lovely one is this new Lady Ashwood."

Brenna smiled. "Thank you, sir, though I am certain the dim light flatters me."

"Nonsense," he replied. "My eyes may be old and tired, but I can see His Lordship made a fine choice. And high time it was. I'd worried that boy would never bring home a new missus."

Glancing at Richard, she saw him sober. Though they'd seldom missed a night of lovemaking, he held part of himself from her, and she always woke up alone in her bed. Now he was reminded that he hadn't chosen her, not really. Her stomach knotted.

"I was waiting for my perfect viscountess," Richard smiled tightly. "When I met Lady Harrington, I knew I had to make her my wife."

The truth had been twisted to appear as if theirs was a love match. Brenna's heart ached. Good breeding kept her smile in place. She'd not crumble in front of a stranger.

When Mister Crane grinned, she saw that his upper two front teeth were missing. "A fine choice, indeed." He winked at Brenna. "I shall leave you two lovers to your exploring. I have some weeds that need my attention."

Brenna listened to his old bones pop and crackle as he walked away. She worried about him on the stairs but soon heard him whistling below.

"Mister Crane is a nice man," Brenna said. "Though we are still missing a ghost."

Richard nodded absently and took her arm. "My stomach is rumbling. Shall we eat?"

He led her down to the ground floor, taking care on the stairs. He left her waiting inside the building while he retrieved the basket. After spreading the blanket out on the grass and laying out the contents of the basket, they were soon eating the delicious fare.

"I do love dining outside," Brenna said, and looked around her at the stone walls. "Of course, this isn't exactly outside."

Richard nodded. "The missing roof does lend to the feeling of being out in nature."

The polite conversation left her wanting to both shake and kiss him, anything to rid them of the wall that had gone up between them as a result of a few innocent words spoken by an elderly caretaker. She knew he was trying to be a good husband, but she did not want him feeling resignation over what he could not change. She wanted him to be happy in their marriage.

Taking him to bed seemed to be the only time she saw true emotion in his eyes.

Still, she could not force his affection. It had to grow naturally. For now, she'd do whatever it took to shake some emotion from him, even if it meant taking the risk of him closing off to her.

So she drew in a deep breath and braced herself. "Tell me about Millicent."

His eyes snapped up. He frowned. "No."

Brenna crossed her arms and matched his frown. "I am competing with a woman I know nothing about. I think I am entitled to know her."

Richard stood. "You are entitled to nothing. She is dead."

Scrambling to her feet, Brenna wasn't about to give in so easily. "I live in her house, I sleep in her bed, and I am married to her husband. She haunts everything you do. I see her in your eyes every time you look at me."

Richard bent to shove the remnants of their picnic into the basket and snapped the lid closed. "Leave this alone, Brenna."

She stepped back off the blanket. He jerked it up, gave it a hard shake, and shoved it under his arm.

"I will not." She set her jaw. "I cannot."

He was angry. It was something. "The subject is closed." He turned on his heel and stalked away.

It took an effort to catch up with his long, angry strides. "You need to bury her, Richard. You cannot live with her haunting you." He dropped the basket and blanket into the curricle. "I know you were hurt—"

"You know nothing," he snapped. His glare was cold on her.

"Then tell me," she pleaded.

"You want to know why I cannot forget her or forgive myself for her death?" At her weak nod, he leaned down and met her eyes. "Because I killed her."

Chapter Eighteen

Stunned into silence, Brenna allowed him to help her into the curricle. She winced as the small conveyance swayed under the weight of his body as he climbed aboard and took up the reins.

He killed Millicent? That couldn't be!

Shivering, she clutched her hands against her body. Though the rational part of her mind knew that if he'd committed murder, he'd have been hanged. Still, she could not bring herself to ask why he believed his wife's death was his fault. Hadn't she died in childbirth? She wasn't certain she wanted to know the details. Would it make her think differently about him?

She needed time to collect her thoughts.

The short ride back to Beckwith Hall took an eternity. She could feel the tension in him and knew she'd pushed too hard.

Worse, the confession shook her to her soul.

When they reached the hall, she murmured her thanks when he helped her down, then hurried inside. She went to her room, passing Bethany on the stairs. She barely gave her notice. Her emotions were scrambled, and she needed time alone.

Two hours later, Lucy joined her. The former courtesan sat beside her on the bed. "Am I to assume the picnic did not go well? You have been locked up here since your return."

Brenna sighed. "Oh, Lucy. What have I gotten myself into?" She pushed up and leaned against the headboard. "I thought if I wished it hard enough, and used a bit of seduction, then all would be well between Richard and me. I was very wrong."

Lucy waited patiently for her to continue.

"I knew Richard felt guilty over the deaths of his wife and son." She worried her thumbnail between her teeth. "Lucy, he thinks he killed them!"

Eyes widening, Lucy rubbed her temple. "That certainly explains why his behavior became so destructive afterward. Did he tell you why he thinks so?"

"He did not," Brenna replied. "And I was afraid to ask."

There were so many questions. "The deeper I delve into my husband's past, the more complicated it becomes. With each passing day, I feel I am taking a few steps forward and many steps back. By the time the babe is born, we could be bitter strangers living under the same roof."

"I do hope not."

"What can I do?" Brenna continued. She was desperate to help him, but her inexperience with men and marriage left her without a solution.

"Your husband needs healing." Lucy nodded. "I do not know if there is anything you can do, save being patient."

"And here I thought you would impart some wisdom that would instantly make everything better." Brenna's thoughts drifted to Richard's tortured expression during the confession. "Instead, you suggest patience. I have never been good at waiting."

Lucy touched her foot and met her eyes. "I see the way he looks at you, the way he seems to listen for your footsteps when you aren't in the room. I think you *are* the solution that will cast out his demons. However, it will take time."

"Time is what I do not have."

For the next week, Richard avoided her except at meals and did not come to her bed. According to Lucy, the entire household felt the tension, none more so than Bethany. Brenna hated her knowing smirk, which she made little attempt to hide.

"I do hate to see you and Richard so unhappy," Bethany said

one afternoon, when she found Brenna alone in the library. "Perhaps I can assist. I know Richard's moods quite well."

"Thank you, but no." Brenna took a book off the shelf. "My marriage is my concern."

"Come, Brenna. Richard is a complicated man." Bethany walked across the room. Clad in sunny yellow, she was lovely. It was unfortunate that her disposition did not match her deceptively sweet face. "Certainly I can answer any questions you may have."

Brenna did not trust her in the least. Though the other woman seemed to accept her place as mistress of the hall, Brenna did not believe for a moment that she wasn't plotting ways to ruin the marriage.

"There is something I am curious about." Brenna tucked the book under her arm. "I suspect that both you and Miriam hoped to marry Richard. Now that I am his wife, why are you still here?"

If she expected to pique Bethany's temper, she failed. The woman laughed. "You are a delight, my dear."

The woman closed the distance between them. She gave Brenna a thorough look over, perhaps calculating her qualities as a rival.

"I suspect Richard married you out of duty or guilt, or under the threat of death," Bethany said. "It matters not why, only that he did not willingly agree to your marriage."

Brenna winced, the truth cutting deeply. She quickly tried to mask her hurt, but it was too late.

Smiling knowingly, Bethany pounced. "Ah, it *is* true!" She placed her hands on her hips. "Your pretty face will only keep him interested for so long. His heart belongs to Millicent. Soon you will tire of always living under her gloomy shadow and run back to London, where you belong."

Beneath her corset, Brenna's stomach recoiled, yet she managed to keep her eyes locked on Bethany's. "Once I am gone, what do you expect to get from him that you could not achieve over the last two years?"

Her brown eyes darkened, but her smile held. "Did Richard tell you that he kissed me? I know that once you've gone, and the marriage is annulled, I will seduce him into making me his next, and last, wife."

Hatred burned hot in Brenna's bones. "You have this all planned out, do you?" A slow smug smile curled her mouth up. "There is only one problem with your plot."

"And that is?"

Brenna placed a hand over her stomach. "Richard will never leave the woman who is carrying his child."

Bethany looked down, and her face went white. "You are pregnant?"

She did not need to answer. The satisfied smile was all it took to convince Bethany that her words rang true. "I suggest you look elsewhere for a husband. You cannot have mine."

And with as much confidence as she could manage, Brenna glided from the room.

Only after she was safely away from that witch did the tears come. Richard had kissed Bethany. He clearly found the woman attractive. That shattered her confidence.

No matter what he felt for her, what she'd said to Bethany about him not leaving her was correct. He had too much honor to cast out the mother of his child. But he could take a mistress. Nothing would stop him if he wanted Bethany.

Their marriage vows were just words. Men of his ilk took mistresses without qualms or concerns for their wives.

And Richard did not love her.

In a few months, she'd be well rounded, not the seductive wife he married. Could she trust him not to look elsewhere?

Brushing away the tears with her sleeve, she headed for the back of the house and out into the garden.

The sun was hidden beneath blanketing clouds as she found the path to the pond. Once there, she sat on the stone bench and looked out over the water. A pair of ducks dove for fish, their antics drawing a smile.

"When did my life become such a muddle?" she said softly, and placed her hands over her stomach. "How do I fix this?"

"Can I join you, or is this a private conversation?" Brenna startled, and turned to find George walking up behind her. "I would hate to intrude."

Brenna slid her skirt aside to make room on the bench. "I was just pondering the meaning of my existence," she said, in half jest. He took a seat beside her. "I am troubled with what I see."

George looked into her face and rubbed his chin. "I think most of your troubles begin with that grim man you wed."

"Partially," she admitted. "And there are other forces at work to darken my mood."

"My sister," George said, without hesitation. "She is desperately jealous of you. She wanted to be Lady Ashwood. She would have tromped over anyone to make that happen. Unfortunately for her, Richard was not of a similar mind."

"She seems to think she was very close to seeing that come to fruition," Brenna said. She looked back at the ducks. "Her confidence concerns me."

"Hmm." George rubbed at his cuff. A spot of dirt marked the lace. "Bethany holds herself in high regard. There is nothing she wants that she cannot have. Except Ashwood. I do not know what you did to hook him, but you have succeeded where my sister, and many other women, have failed."

This was turning into a very interesting conversation. "Are you including Miriam in that group? I suspect she was also hoping for a proposal."

George snorted. "Miriam is a mouse. Bethany would have pushed her under a coach before she'd allow a wedding between them to happen. It was Miriam's mother who hoped for that match."

Brenna stared. "I thought Bethany and Miriam were friends?"

"Bethany has no friends," George said, snickering. "Miriam's mother and our mother are friends. Bethany found out about Richard, and Mrs. Prindle's hope that Miriam would one day be Lady Ashwood, and manipulated an invitation to the hall. She only tolerates Miriam to keep her place here."

Interesting. She wanted to delve further into the relationships but felt she'd snooped enough already.

"And what of you?" she asked. "What do you gain from living here at the hall?"

A bright grin split his face. "Balls, soirees, and all the women I can charm." He chuckled. "Richard may prefer his own company to the social whirl, but living here affords me invitations to events for which I would otherwise be overlooked. And I do enjoy a good party."

"And yet you remain unmarried?" she pressed. He probably had mothers all over the park hoping to gain his favor for their daughters. "There must be women who've captured your interest?"

"Alas, I have difficulty settling for one," he admitted. "Though if you decide to leave that cranky husband of yours, I would gladly give up my bachelorhood for a cottage in the country and a passel of sniveling children with you as my bride."

Brenna laughed. "You make it sound so charming."

He made a face and shuddered dramatically. "It does sound horrid, does it not? Perhaps I shall remain a bachelor after all. Your marriage is safe from me."

"For that, I am thankful," Brenna teased.

They chatted for a time, until the hour grew late. Brenna excused herself to change for supper. The afternoon had taken an upward turn. George certainly amused.

The maid had just finished fastening her gown when she heard Richard moving around next door. She decided to take the opportunity to speak to him privately. She walked through the sitting room and knocked.

Her stomach fluttered when he opened the door. It took a moment to regain her composure. She lifted her chin.

"I came to speak to you about a matter of great importance," she said, hoping he'd not refuse her. "It cannot wait until later."

He sighed and stepped back. "Then do come in." Brenna passed him, keeping her hands to herself. She wanted desperately to drag him down on his bed and forget their quarrel, everything but finding pleasure in each other.

Instead, she knitted her fingers together and turned. "I owe you an apology. I should not have insisted you tell me about your wife. It was not my place."

He tugged at his cravat. "Some memories should be left buried."

"Oh, I do not think so," she said. "I am only sorry I pushed you, not that I felt I should not know. I just want you to tell me on your own."

He released the cravat and scowled. "This is an apology?"

Brenna shrugged. "I grow weary of your silence. I am with child. As I understand from Mrs. Beal, I should keep my emotions even. Otherwise, I will have a temperamental child."

"Your mother must have suffered much trauma when she was carrying you," he said gruffly.

Laughter bubbled up. "I suspect you are correct." She did not wait for a reply. She walked over and took his arm. "Come, let us eat before the baby starves."

The evening meal passed along the same light vein as the afternoon in the garden, when George told story after story, his supply of humorous adventures seemingly endless. Even Richard smiled now and again when something amusing was said.

Brenna watched Richard, uncertain of his thoughts but hoping their talk helped to ease the strain between them.

Occasionally she caught him looking at her with a heated gaze that he quickly masked. This gave her hope that he might join her in bed that evening. She eagerly anticipated the moment. However, and without explanation, he left her with a kiss on the forehead before moving on to his solitary bed.

Disappointed and frustrated, she followed him through the sitting room and placed herself in the doorway before he could close the panel.

"I thought we had settled our differences," she said, puzzled at his abrupt dismissal.

"We have. For the moment." He tugged at his cravat. "This last week has given me time to conclude that you and I are very different. And it goes beyond the obvious. You enjoy parties and shopping and attention. I enjoy quiet and country and . . . sheep."

He gave her a funny look. She flushed. Somehow he must have overheard her jest about him preferring the company of the woolly creatures over people.

"You make me sound frivolous, like I possess only fluff in my head," she said, annoyed. "I do maintain some intelligence, meager though it may be."

"You are very intelligent, Brenna," he said. "My point was that we both know you will never be happy living this life here. You will miss the gaiety of London and the social whirl, your friends, your family, everything I cannot give you at Beckwith Hall."

Wanting to deny this, she opened her mouth to speak, then snapped it closed just as quickly. Was she entirely certain he was incorrect? She was currently focused on giving him a healthy child and trying to find some common ground between them on which to build a marriage.

What about after the babe was born? Would she be satisfied to spend the rest of her days in this lovely but somewhat isolated manor house?

He continued. "I loved once, Brenna, and you know how that ended. I cannot give you the love you deserve. Will you be happy to share my bed and carry my children without love?" He paused. "I know not wanting a loveless marriage was one of the reasons you offered the bargain to the highwayman. Now you are in one."

Deep inside her, she knew he was right. He'd never lied to her or promised anything. And in spite of his moods and ill humors, she was already half in love with him. Loving a man who did not return that love was a hopeless prospect indeed.

"I assume from your silence that I have struck a cord in you." He came to her and touched the side of her face. "I think it best if we return to our marriage of convenience and accept what we cannot change."

She wanted to deny everything, to convince him she was fully devoted to her marriage. But she was not entirely convinced herself. Success in bed did not a perfect marriage make.

Thankfully, she was no longer the moony-eyed innocent she was after the first night they'd spent together, thinking she was in love with a stranger, hoping her prince had finally come to rescue her. As a grown woman, she had to accept her fate. Everything she'd fought her father against had come to fruition. How she went forward with her life depended on her.

Still, falling in love was not a dream easily forgotten. Not when Richard was standing in front of her now, as handsome as any fairy-tale prince.

She could not let him see how deeply hurt she was that he could so easily dismiss her. She had her pride. She'd lean on that pride during the months ahead.

"I agree," she forced out, her heart breaking. "I accept your terms. From this night forward, my door will be locked to keep temptation in check."

With her spine straight and her head high, Brenna walked

into the sitting room, locked the door behind her, and allowed silent tears to fall.

H e might well have slapped her. The sadness in her eyes made him long to go to her, to say something to ease her pain.

She was carrying his child and deserved better than he could offer. She should be in London, falling in love. Instead she was married to a man who held himself from her.

He was a coldhearted bastard.

If only he *could* love her. She had everything a man could want in a wife: beauty, good humor, strength. Even the temperamental side of her intrigued him. He knew she'd be an excellent mother, too. She had much love to give.

Sadly, she'd come too late into his life. Millicent's betrayal and the death of the baby had hardened his heart.

And not even Brenna could heal his damaged soul.

Chapter Nineteen

✦

"Sara, have you seen my silver brush?" Brenna was on her hands and knees, looking under the bed for the item, when a maid arrived with freshly washed linens for the bed. "I used it this morning, and now it is missing."

Sara sat the linens on the bed and dropped down beside her. She glanced around the space. "I don't see it, Milady. Have you asked Agnes?"

"I have not. She has gone into the village. Perhaps you will have better luck than I am having." They stood and began a thorough search of the room. The brush was nowhere to be found. "This is odd," Brenna screwed up her face. "It could not have walked away."

After checking the sitting room, Brenna was certain something was amiss. She always lined up her brushes in a neat row on her dressing table. It was a habit she'd picked up from her mother. And neither of them ever lost a brush.

"This *is* odd," Sara agreed.

Brenna puzzled over the missing brush. "It is possible someone borrowed it." Though she thought it unlikely, she could not accuse anyone of thievery without first excluding every other option. "Could you please ask the maids if they've seen it, and please assure them that I only suspect it was accidentally misplaced."

"Yes, Milady." Sara hurried off to do her bidding.

While she was gone, Brenna made another cursory look around both rooms again. She was coming out of the sitting room when Lucy arrived.

"Is that dust on your chin?" Lucy asked, and Brenna scrubbed the spot. "I see you have found the only few dust particles in the entire manor. And put your face in them."

Frowning at her friend, Brenna brushed the dust off her hand. "I was looking under the furniture for my silver brush. It has vanished."

"How strange." Lucy walked to the dressing table. She looked down at the array of combs and brushes. "Are you talking about the silver brush with the swans carved into the handle?"

Brenna nodded. "It was a birthday gift. I'd hate to lose—"

Her mouth dropped open as Lucy turned, the brush gripped in her hand.

"The brush has been found," Lucy said.

"How . . . where . . . ?" She took the brush, her eyes wide. "I swear it was not here a moment ago." Completely befuddled, she tried to make sense of the sudden reappearance.

Lucy smiled indulgently. "I've heard that women can be scatterbrained when with child. Perhaps your eyes were tricking you? After all, you do have several brushes. You may have overlooked this one."

"Could that be true?" Brenna wasn't so sure. Though her thoughts were taken up with the babe, and Richard, her mind remained sharp. Still, what other explanation was there?

Sara returned. "The maids have not seen the brush, Milady."

She, too, looked astonished when Brenna held the item up for her to see. "Where did you find it?"

"On the dressing table," Lucy said, with a chuckle. "I think your mistress has suffered some malady of the eyes."

The maid smiled wide. "She does have many brushes." Her words echoed Lucy's sentiment.

"I think you are both correct." As there was no other explanation, Brenna took it as a moment of her eyes playing tricks on her. "Either that, or a mischievous spirit has followed me home from the abbey."

The three women shared a smile. Sara took the brush and returned it to the table. "All is well, then."

A flurry of rushing feet drew Brenna's eyes to the open door. A footman and a maid passed, moving at a rapid clip.

"Something is amiss," Brenna said. A second maid, Brigit, stopped as Brenna appeared in the hall. "What is this excitement about, Brigit?"

"Coaches are arriving, My Lady. Lots of coaches. Everyone is having fits." She hurried off in a bustle of gray cotton without offering any further information.

"Are we expecting guests?" Lucy asked, as the three women followed on Brigit's heels.

"We are not." In the two weeks since she and Richard agreed to a sexless and emotionless marriage, he'd taken on a polite and distant demeanor with her, and she'd done the same with him. There had been no discussion about entertaining guests. "I suppose we will find out the identity of our mystery visitors soon enough."

"Oh, how exciting," Lucy said. "Perhaps the Prince Regent has come to call."

Sara gasped. Brenna turned to the maid after sending Lucy a shaming glare. "It is not the Prince Regent. Please do not start gossip and frighten Mrs. Beal with that nonsense."

"Yes, Milady."

Though she and Richard were no longer more than two distant parties conversing over a meal, or passing in the hall, Brenna doubted that he'd invite anyone, much less the Prince Regent, without advising her of his plans.

When they reached the foyer, she found him standing in the open doorway, staring out at the drive. Several members of the staff lingered behind him, in position, ready to hustle off to help the guests.

"Who has come?" she asked, trying to look around him for clues. Brigit was correct; there were several coaches coming up the drive.

He stepped aside so she could see the caravan kick up dust in their wake. "Your father, I suspect."

"Oh, dear," she replied. Her stomach flipped. She hoped her father was unarmed. A dead husband would make her a widow and leave their child fatherless. She did not care for that option.

"Do you Harringtons ever send notice when planning a visit?" Richard said drolly.

Brenna shrugged. She, too, had shown up at the hall uninvited. "We do like our surprises."

Brenna watched a coach, with the Harrington crest, roll to a stop in front of the manor. Two more followed. Father did not wait for the coachman to climb down but pushed the door open and stepped down, turning to help Mother alight.

"Shall I sneak out through the kitchen?" Richard jested, his voice tight. "I can certainly get into the forest before your father has the house searched for me."

Brenna knew he'd not cower from her father, and smiled. "You are a dangerous highwayman," she quipped. "I think you can stand your ground with one angry father."

He looked down at her, a smile tugging at his mouth. She wondered if he even realized that in the light of Father's arrival, he'd lost the mask of indifference he often adopted in her presence. She thought not. Not even under the threat of her father's wrath.

Father did not come all this way for renewed friendship and brandy. He wanted to confront Richard, the man who'd ruined his daughter.

She slipped her hand in Richard's and turned back to her parents. He allowed the gesture, as if they both instinctively knew that a show of unity would fare better with her parents.

"There you are, darling," Mother said, as she released Father's arm and hurried up the steps. They came together and fell into a tight embrace.

Mother's favorite lavender scent swirled around Brenna and brought tears. "I've missed you terribly, Mother."

"I've missed you." Mother pulled back and looked her over with a critical eye. "The level of mischief in our home has receded greatly since you've been gone." She took Brenna's hands and spread her arms wide. Her eyes dipped to Brenna's stomach. "I cannot wait for this grandchild to come. It will bring fun back into that quiet old town house."

Several gasps sounded from the lurking servants. The pregnancy was no longer a secret.

Brenna ignored them and stepped between her father and Richard. The few steps distancing them from each other did not give her comfort. Father's glare was dark enough to murder.

"I've missed you, Father," she said softly, and moved close. He tore his glare from her husband and looked into her face.

"All is well, girl?"

"Yes, Father." She slid into his embrace. "All is well." He held her for a moment, then coughed and released her. She took him by the forearms when she realized the glare was back. "Please do not kill my husband," she whispered.

"I cannot make that promise."

Fearing trouble, Brenna sent a silent appeal to Lucy. Lucy nodded, shooed the servants into the house, and closed the door behind them.

Father eased Brenna aside and walked the last few steps up to Richard. Mother and daughter clutched each other, unsure of what to expect.

Walter ignored Richard's outstretched hand and instead let a fist fly. The blow caught Richard in the right eye, and he grunted but kept on his feet.

"That is for compromising my daughter." The second blow hit him in the chin. Richard's head snapped to the side. Still he did nothing to defend himself. "And that one is for betraying our friendship."

"I suppose I deserved that." Richard worked his jaw with his hand. "You may be old, my friend, but you can still hit like a younger man." His hand moved to his reddened eye. He winced. "I accept my punishment as my due."

Brenna felt the tension leave her mother. Father had taken his pound of flesh. There would be no further violence.

Richard reached out a hand to Brenna, and she took it, thankful she'd not have to purchase widow's weeds.

"Come, we shall retire to the library for a drink," Richard said. "I think we could both use one."

The foursome walked into the house, the puzzled servants making a path. Miriam cowered back when Walter passed, and Bethany smiled, her eyes both amused and calculating as she noted Richard's injuries.

Brenna ignored them all as Richard led them into the library and closed the door tightly behind them.

"Brandy?" he asked, and filled two glasses.

Brenna and her mother shared a glance and took seats on the settee. They held hands and watched their husbands.

Once the men drank the first brandy and then a second, Richard finally broke the silence. "Nothing I can say will repair the damage I've done to Brenna, or our friendship. I can only hope that one day you will forgive me."

Walter grunted and walked to the fireplace. He stared into the flames for several minutes. Then, "Why my daughter?"

Richard turned his gaze to Brenna. She saw the struggle in his eyes. How do you explain to a father how you got mixed up in such a muddle without looking like a virgin-seducing cad?

"I was smitten," he said finally. "One look in her green eyes, and I was hooked."

Surprised by the warmth of his comment, Brenna's heart lurched until she realized the words were chosen to assuage her father. She forced herself to smile under his regard.

Mother sighed. "We Harrington women do entice men."

Father and Mother shared an affectionate glance. The love between them was evident and open.

Richard, with his attention still on her, missed the exchange. His eye was swollen halfway shut, and his chin sported a red welt. Whether by accident or by design, he'd be wearing the mark of the Harrington crest from Father's ring for days to come.

Glancing back at her parents, he spoke again. "I was so taken with your daughter that I lost my senses. As soon as I realized the gravity of my actions, I knew I had to marry her."

Father said nothing. Richard shook his head.

"It was unfortunate that we quarreled after the wedding, and through anger, we parted, vowing to keep the marriage secret." Richard walked over to Brenna and took her hand. "Fortunately, the babe did what his stubborn parents would not do. He brought us back together."

If Brenna were not well aware of his ruse, she would have found the story charming. Clearly her mother did, as her eyes softened as she glanced from husband to wife.

He did spin a compelling story of lust, loss, and love. She could almost believe their tale a grand love story, if she was not living the opposite.

"So you see, Father, our romance began under unusual circumstances, true. However, now that we have spent these last weeks together, we have learned we are indeed well suited," Brenna said, and rubbed her cheek against the back of Richard's hand. She hoped her parents would see them as a devoted couple. "So your fears have proved unfounded. I did not need help finding a husband. He found me."

"Or, rather, robbed your coach," Richard interjected, and smiled down at Brenna. "It was fate."

The maid arrived with tea, saving Brenna from continuing the farce. She hated lying to her parents, even if the tale *was* largely true.

"How long will you be staying?" Brenna asked, after sipping the tea to quell a wave of nausea.

"No more than a week," Mother replied. "Eva is due to give birth soon, and we would like to be there for the occasion."

Though the matter of their relationship was not entirely settled to her father's satisfaction, Brenna thought her father seemed willing to accept that he had a new son-in-law, and a baby to be born in the spring, and let the matter rest. The two men turned their conversation to new farming techniques, and only the damage to Richard's face was left as a reminder of a fractured friendship.

The two women slipped into easy chatter about the new Harrington heir and how Brenna's own pregnancy was progressing. Just when Brenna thought the matter settled, her mother set her teacup down, crossed her arms, and frowned.

"I want you to tell me the truth about this marriage, Daughter," Mother said quietly, so as not to be overheard. "That tale of love may have fooled your father, but not me. Something is amiss, and I want to know what it is."

Chapter Twenty

🕸

"Mother, I do not know what you mean." Brenna tried to keep her eyes level but found her gaze drifting downward to the floor. She really needed to practice the art of dodging Mother's truth-detecting stare.

Kathleen made a small triumphant sound. "I knew that story was rubbish. The only thing missing from this Shakespearean farce was a funny neck collar for Richard and a lute strumming in the background."

Warmth crept up Brenna's neck. She nodded. "There are some issues we have yet to resolve." Insurmountable issues. But her marriage was a private matter. And she had Richard's continued good health in her hands. Father needed to think she was happy.

"Would you like to embellish on that comment?"

"Mother, nothing is so serious that it cannot be resolved. Neither myself nor Richard were prepared for this marriage. We were strangers. I suspect over the next few months, we will settle in to a contented life."

"A contented life? That sounds perfectly dismal. You could have married that milksop, Abbot, and had 'contented.' What about passion?" Mother darted a glance at Father. "Your father and I are still passionate about each other. And it has been thirty years."

Brenna drew in a deep breath. "There is more to a marriage than passion, Mother." She held back regret. Looking at Richard dressed in gray, his hair slightly mussed and his damaged eye almost completely closed, she couldn't think of anything more appealing than dragging him upstairs to bed. "What about companionship, or a shared love of books?"

Even to her ears, the argument fell flat.

Mother stared, aghast. "You cannot look forward to discussing books for the next forty years over bedding the handsome man you married?" Her eyes widened. "Has Richard suffered a malady that makes him no longer capable of performing his husbandly duties?"

"What? Mother, no!" The two men glanced over. Brenna lowered her voice. "Richard is perfectly capable of . . . Lud, must we discuss this? I am content with my position here. Can we not leave it at that?"

Even as she pleaded for understanding, she knew her mother would not leave the issue alone. Mother was happy with Father and wanted the same for her children.

Despite Father and Simon threatening her with an unwanted marriage, Mother would never have allowed them to marry Brenna off to Chester Abbot.

After adding another sugar to her tea, Mother finally broke the silence. "You have several months before the baby is born to make Richard fall in love with you. After you have recovered from the birth, I expect you to drag him into your bed and solidify your place as his cherished wife."

Brenna's flush deepened. It was impossible to speak so frankly with her mother without blushing. She knew her parents had a loving marriage; it was the idea of two people their age still sharing intimacies in bed that was, well, unseemly.

"Can we not talk about the weather?" Brenna begged. "I think the sky is threatening rain."

Mother frowned. "Just remember what I said. If a man loves his wife, he is less likely to stray. If a man fears the wrath of his wife, he will either behave or sleep with his eyes open." Mother smiled over her cup. "Ask your father the last time he had a peaceful night's sleep."

A groan was Brenna's answer.

* * *

From across the room, Richard watched Brenna flush at something her mother said. He suspected they were talking about him by the frequency of glances cast in his direction.

If Brenna did not hold up his story, he'd need to prepare for Walter's displeasure. Walter was not the sort of man who'd let his daughter be ignored or mistreated by her husband, and he was no exception. He suspected Walter would spend the next week looking for any infraction on his part so that he could express his disapproval.

The pain in his face was his penance for his sins. He'd not defended himself, as he deserved no less.

Walter's voice faded as Richard watched the charming flush grow on Brenna's cheeks. She was as lovely as she was the day he stopped her coach. Carrying his child had not taken away her appeal, nor did it lessen his interest in her. In fact, if not for the deep seat of the chair, everyone would be privy to his obvious desire for his wife.

"Am I boring you?" Walter's voice broke his musing. "Or is there something more interesting here than a discussion of horse breeding?"

Tearing his attention away from his wife, he let Walter think him besotted with Brenna. In some regards he was. She was a seductive woman, beautiful and passionate. If only she could accept a loveless marriage, they could share a bed, and a life, without complications.

Sadly, that was not Brenna. She'd said as much. She would be miserable with a husband who did not cherish and love her.

"I wonder what sort of mischief they are plotting," he said to Walter, taking on a lighter tone.

"Knowing Kathleen, it could be anything." Walter frowned. "Hang on to your purse and watch your wife. Once Kathleen gets a notion in her head, she plows forward, and there is no changing her course. And if she involves Brenna in her scheme, disaster could loom on the horizon."

Richard hoped the two women were *only* plotting to spend loads of his money. He suspected otherwise.

There were dark forces at work, in the form of a pair of lovely Harrington women. He sensed it to his bones.

How much longer can we play this game?" Brenna grumbled two days later, when Richard came through the sitting room to collect her for breakfast. "I grow weary of acting as if nothing is amiss."

The strain of keeping Father from knowing their secret mixed up her emotions. Pretending to be a loving wife was easy enough. Keeping her father content while fending off snide little comments from Bethany made her long to shriek from the rafters. The woman was horrid. If not for Richard's friendship with Miriam, Brenna would have already chased her off the property.

She peered in the mirror from her seat at the dressing table. Dark smudges rimmed her lower lids.

"I admire your fortitude." He kissed the top of her head. "I know you can hold up for a few more days."

"If only I had your confidence," she muttered. Restless sleep left her fatigued and cranky. She stood and smoothed her yellow dress. "Agnes, where is that shawl?"

"The white shawl is not here, Milady," Agnes said, turning from the wardrobe. "Perhaps one of the maids took it down to clean?"

Brenna walked over and peered inside. After inspecting the contents and looking on the floor, in case it had fallen there, she came to the same conclusion. No shawl.

"It was there last evening," she said softly, confused. I returned it myself." Glancing back at Richard, she said, "I shall wear the cream shawl. I'm sure the other will turn up."

Agnes collected the item and settled it around her shoulders. Richard took her arm and led her into the hallway. "Is there something amiss? You look unsettled, Brenna."

How do you tell the father of your child that you suspect you are losing your mind, that for three days this week your possessions have vanished, only to reappear later, as if nothing had happened? And there was no sign anyone had been in her room, other than the maids, her mother, and Lucy. And Mother had not arrived until after the first incident.

"It is nothing to worry over," she assured him. She could not admit the truth. "I'm certain the shawl will be found."

At first she'd thought it was simple forgetfulness. Then she'd suspected someone was up to mischief. Now she wasn't certain that it wasn't the pregnancy at work.

During the last few weeks she'd been ill, quick to tears, and was now misplacing things. None of these symptoms were an issue before the pregnancy. Could there be any other explanation?

She slid a hand over her belly. There was a slight curve now. Soon even strangers would know her condition. "The babe must enjoy the fuss he puts me through."

Richard stared at her hand. He reached out to touch her stomach, paused, and pulled back. He cleared his throat. "He has already inherited your spirit and love of mischief."

Brenna smiled. "It is the Irish in me. We do enjoy a good bit of trickery."

His brows went up. "Truly?"

The teasing in his voice deepened her smile. "You may find that surprising, I know. I am usually quite subdued and retiring. In fact, I find devilry most distressing."

Her quip softened his bruised face. Oddly, as much as she found Father's presence stressful, Richard seemed to enjoy having her father near. He smiled more often, and she'd heard his laughter several times over the last two days—a rare treat indeed. The two men had rediscovered some of the closeness they'd once shared.

The pair were slowly rebuilding their friendship. This pleased both wives immensely. Still, it would take Walter some time to regain his full trust of Richard.

"I have decided to visit the Cooksons today," Richard said, changing the topic. "Mister Cookson is one of my tenants and was burned in a fire. He is yet struggling to recover. I would like to see if his sons require any assistance with the farm."

"How horrible," Brenna said. "I have a cousin who burned her arm badly as a child, when a pot of heated water tipped over onto her. It was awful to see her suffer through the lengthy recovery. She still bares scars that never faded."

"It is tragic." Richard agreed. "I check on them at least twice a week to see how they are managing."

"I would like to join you. I shall ask Cook to prepare a basket for the family."

Richard stared at her for a moment and nodded. "I know they will appreciate your kindness."

Warming under his soft expression, she held his gaze. "It is my place to know the tenants and their families. They are now under my care, too."

A slow smile spread across his face. "Most women do not want to know the names of anyone below their notice. You are a puzzle, Lady Ashwood."

"I was born to a mother who as a child wore patched gowns and worked for her meals. If not for fate, she would never have met and married my wealthy father." Brenna shrugged. "She raised us to appreciate what we have and to be respectful of those not as fortunate."

"Your mother is a treasure," Richard said. "Walter is a very lucky man."

"My brothers and I believe so. I am lucky to have come from a close and loving family."

Richard had no comment, and instead took her hand and led her down to breakfast. She wondered if he missed his parents. They had died, several years apart, when he was still quite young. She hoped their child would be the beginning of building a new family, together.

Her parents were seated for breakfast when they arrived. The servants hurried over to offer Brenna their assistance. Since learning about the baby, they were overly eager to help her with even the smallest tasks, much to the amusement of her parents.

"If you asked, I think one or more of them would spoon-feed you, dearest," Mother jested, and Brenna took her seat. "Perhaps you would enjoy a foot rub later?"

Brenna laughed softly. "Mother, be kind. There hasn't been an heir born here for ages. They cannot help their excitement."

Mother leaned close and whispered, "Then perhaps you can ask one of your handsome footmen to give *me* a foot rub. My toes ache something terrible."

"You are scandalous, Mother." Brenna, laughing, shook her head. "You saw what Father did to Richard. I would hate to see him pummel a footman for touching your bare feet."

Brenna watched as her mother's bright laughter drew eyes from family and staff alike. Though well into her forties, Kathleen was as stunningly beautiful as she ever was, and entirely devoted to her husband. The footmen were safe from a pummeling.

Settling in to eat, Brenna devoured two plates of food before deciding she'd better stop. She'd already given up her corsets. Soon she'd have to ask a seamstress to take out her gowns.

"I've decided to have Walter drive me into your village today," Mother said. "We passed a quaint little dress shop on the way here. I'd like to see what the proprietress offers by way of fashion."

Father rolled up his eyes. "Watching your mother fuss over gowns and fripperies is how I like to spend my mornings."

"Posh," Mother scolded. "You know I would have asked Brenna to accompany me, but she and Richard have plans." She winked at him. "If you behave, I will give you a private showing of my purchases."

Dear lord. "Mother, really." Brenna glanced at Richard, who was clearly amused.

"Are your parents always so openly affectionate?" he asked.

"Always." Brenna dropped her napkin on the table. "Not even the presence of my friends kept them from their flirtations. It was highly humiliating, to say the least."

Mother laughed. "It is the curse of being married to such a virile man."

Brenna placed her hands over her ears. "Husband, if you wish to keep me from throwing myself from the roof, I ask you to take me away. Now."

Richard chuckled and pulled out her chair. Brenna mumbled a cross good-bye to her parents, collected the basket, and left the manor with Richard.

The fall day was crisp, and Brenna tucked the shawl around her. The sun shone through white clouds, against a backdrop of blue sky. It was a perfect morning for driving and calling on the Cooksons.

"There may not be many more days like this," she said, lifting her face to the sun. "Soon we will have snow."

Richard clucked his tongue to the horse, and they were off.

"Summer seems to want to linger this year, though I hope it will get cooler soon. I do appreciate a bit of snow."

Brenna tucked her hands under the shawl. "My beastly brothers used to throw snowballs at me whenever our nanny wasn't looking. No matter how much she scolded them, I always returned to the house with snow down the back of my dress."

Richard turned to her, his expression guilty. "I used to do the same to Anne. All boys do like to torment their sisters."

She shot him a mock-scathing glare. "I think boys are born mischief makers." She thought about the babe and suspected that if it were a boy, he'd keep her, and his nanny, exhausted while trying to keep up with his antics. "Tell me about her. Anne. You speak so seldom of her. What is she like?"

He turned the horse onto a side lane. "Anne is much like you. She's headstrong and stubborn, pretty, and taller than you. I thought her intelligence admirable until she ran off with Lockley. Now I am not certain I ever knew her."

"Does she also like sheep?" Brenna asked, one brow up.

Her teasing was rewarded with a frown. "There is nothing wrong with sheep. They keep us in food and comfort."

As if on cue, they passed a field with what seemed like a hundred of the woolly creatures scattered about the grass. Brenna smiled. "They do paint a pretty picture, with all that white against the green field. I have decided I like sheep, too. We are lord and lady of the sheep."

There was a brief silence, until his laughter startled the horse. The beast quickly settled with his firm grip on the reins. He stopped the carriage and peered down at her. "What am I to do with you, Wife? You do try my patience."

Brenna joined his laughter. "But I do amuse you. You will keep me around if for nothing more than my jests."

His mouth twisted, yet there was humor in his eyes. "You do have your uses." His attention flicked to her mouth, and Brenna held her breath. She desperately wanted him to kiss her.

Sobering, he cleared his throat. Brenna was not about to lose the opportunity to steal a kiss. She pushed up, leaned toward him, and quickly brushed her mouth over his, startling him. Then she dropped back down on the seat, tucked her shawl back around her, and stared straight forward.

"Onward, Richard. The Cooksons are waiting."

A moment passed, then he clicked his tongue, and the horse continued on. If a simple kiss unsettled him, what would he do if she asked him to pull into the nearest field and have his way with her in the grass?

Mischief welled as she remembered Mother's advice. If she wanted a happy marriage, she'd have to reintroduce him to seduction.

By this time next year, she hoped to have Richard so besotted that he'd not refuse her no matter where she asked him to take her, be it bed, floor, or open field.

Chapter Twenty-one

What to do about his wife? Richard sighed. Brenna had agreed to keep their relationship friendly and out of bed. However, she'd just kissed him without invitation. It was clear that she had no intention of keeping her word.

Staring down at her, with an unobstructed view of her lovely breasts where the shawl gaped away, he knew the next few months would be torture. If she did not adhere to the bargain, he wasn't certain he could keep from pushing her down on the bed and burying himself into her sweet body.

"You cannot kiss me, Brenna," he scolded. "Kissing leads to other things, and we have a bargain."

"I like the other things, and I hate bargains."

As he suspected, she wasn't a bit contrite. He grumbled under his breath. "I should send you back to London with your parents when they leave."

"You won't," she replied. "In spite of everything, you want me here. I have brought light into your musty and cobweb-filled old manor, and you would be lonely if I was gone."

"The manor does not have cobwebs."

He felt her silent laughter as she shook beside him. She was a minx. All he could think about when she was near was the way her body responded to his when he made love to her.

Hell, she only had to come into his thoughts and he suffered the same malady.

He shifted on the seat, hardening beneath his breeches. His wife was torture in its purest form.

Perhaps the solution to his torment was cold baths. When they returned to the hall, he'd instruct Miles to begin new bathing procedures. If icy water could not cool his ardor, nothing could.

"I should pull over and paddle you for teasing me," he ground out, his hands tightening on the reins.

"I would not protest."

This was becoming an argument he could not win, and his erection was becoming an uncomfortable distraction. Thankfully, relief came in the form of a tidy stone cottage. "Ah, there is the Cookson home." Grateful for the interruption, he eased the horse up the narrow lane to the cottage.

Smoke rose in a thin gray plume from the chimney and dissipated on the light breeze. Richard slowed the carriage, and a pair of little girls with matching gold hair hurried from the house to welcome the visitors.

Molly and Mary were bright girls who took lessons with the children of his staff in a small schoolhouse on the property. Richard believed all children should know how to read and write and had hired the best instructor available to take over the school, after the last man retired.

"They are adorable," Brenna said. The girls ran over, a pair of matching smiles on their faces. They jumped around like excited puppies as Richard helped Brenna down from the carriage.

"Did you bring us a treat, Lord Ashwood?" Mary asked. One year older than her sister, at eight, she was also the more outspoken of the two.

"Let me see what I can find." He patted one pocket, then another. His brows came together. "Hmm. I was certain the candy fairy visited last evening."

The girls giggled. "There is no candy fairy," Mary said.

"Oh, there is a candy fairy," Richard assured her. "You have to believe, or she won't visit."

"I believe, Your Lordship," Molly replied, around the thumb in her mouth.

"Then I should keep looking, for surely she would not

deprive little girls of candy." He reached into his pocket and pulled out a bag of maple candy that the kitchen staff had made the day before. He handed it to Mary.

"See!" Molly cried. "There is a candy fairy!"

The girls squealed with delight and darted off toward the house. He shouted after them, "Make certain you share with your brothers!"

"Yes, Milord!"

He chuckled. When he turned back to Brenna, she was staring at him with a soft expression.

"Those girls worship you," she said, blinking as if she had dust in her eye. She appeared on the verge of tears. "You are a kind man, Lord Ashwood."

"It was just candy," he replied. Brenna's emotions swung wildly back and forth like the wind. "Please don't cry."

"I cannot help myself. It is part of my condition." She sniffed and dabbed at her eyes with her gloved knuckles. "You will make a fine father," she said, and held his gaze.

He removed his glove and brushed a tear off her cheek. "You are not planning to kiss me again, are you?"

"I may. You have certainly earned a kiss."

Richard knew he should step away but discovered his feet would not move. Her sweet expression held him enraptured. Truthfully, he wanted to taste her mouth.

Her sneeze broke the moment. A second sneeze caused him to reach for his handkerchief. A third brought her laughter.

"Sometimes when I am outside, my nose tickles," she explained, and waved away the handkerchief. She scrunched up her face and paused. No more sneezes. "There, I believe I am finished."

Shaking his head, Richard collected the large basket the cook had prepared. "Perhaps we should get you inside before the sneezes begin anew."

"Excellent idea." She made a funny sound and sneezed again. This time when he held out his handkerchief, she did not refuse.

The cottage was clean and tidy. A small fire burned in the fireplace, and the scent of baking bread permeated the room. The interior wasn't spacious, and Brenna marveled at how such a large family could fit within the walls without constantly tromping over one another.

Mrs. Cookson, a small woman in the last stages of pregnancy, with a warm smile and tired eyes, waddled over with a baby in her arms, the little mite shyly turning his head to his mother's shoulder.

"So pleased I am to meet you, Lady Ashwood." She curtsied awkwardly. Her protruding stomach, and the baby in her arms, made the effort a chore.

"Please do sit, Mrs. Cookson." Brenna hurried over to help her into a chair, fearful the woman would topple over onto her face if she dipped too far forward. "We can dispense with formalities today."

The woman smiled gratefully. "Mary, can you take baby and put him down for his nap?" The older girl who'd met them outside popped a piece of candy into her mouth and collected her brother. She made faces at the boy, who offered a toothless grin for his sister.

"You have lovely children, Mrs. Cookson."

"I have two more outside. My older boys are working in the fields to bring in the hay before the snow comes. His Lordship has sent over workers to help." Mrs. Cookson indicated a chair, and Brenna sat. "Your husband is a fine man, Milady."

Brenna nodded as Richard sat the basket near the fireplace. She was discovering much about him this day. There was another side of her husband she was just learning about.

"He is," she agreed.

A shuffle brought her attention around. A man of middle years came from a back room, leaning heavily on a cane. The left side of his face was scarred, as well as his left hand. Brenna assumed the rest of that side of his body, covered by his shirt, was similarly afflicted.

He waved off Richard, who walked over to assist him.

"I can manage," he said, and limped to the table. Easing into the chair, he looked at Brenna. "I see you 'ave finally brought your missus, Milord," he said. "I thought she was made up by gossips."

Brenna smiled. "I assure you, I am very real, Mr. Cookson."

The man nodded. "It pleases us to 'ave a new Lady at the manor to keep 'is Lordship 'opping."

"Thank you," she said. "I will do my best."

Covertly, Brenna examined his scars when he turned away to speak with Richard, feeling for what he'd suffered. For him to have survived such a tragic event spoke of his fortitude and a strong will to live.

For the next hour, the women talked of babies and the Cookson children, Brenna envying the large brood. Though Mrs. Cookson was weary from the burdens she carried, it was clear she loved her family.

The men spoke of crops and the coming winter, and it quickly became clear that the two men were more than land-lord and tenant but friends.

When Richard finally stood and made their good-byes, Mrs. Cookson took Brenna's hand. "Please visit again, Milady."

"I will; I promise."

Once seated in the carriage, Brenna stared off at the cottage. For the first time, she noticed the soot stains on the roof where it had recently been patched. Thankfully, the cottage had not been fully destroyed.

"Their burdens are great," she said softly, her eyes troubled. "It is tragic what happened."

"It is," Richard agreed. "I have known Alfred since I was a child. He worked for my father. He is a prideful man. I've offered to do more, but he does not want too much charity. Thankfully, his sons are strong and capable lads."

She touched her stomach. "If we have a son, I hope he is like his father. You, too, are strong and capable."

The horse rattled his harness. Richard eased them back onto the road. He shot her a quick glance.

"If she is a daughter, I pray she has a gentle temperament and does not cause her father grief." He snapped the reins. "One termagant in the family is more than one man can take."

The comment ruffled her feathers, but she knew it was in good fun. "Truly? You managed to get past my prickly nature to get me with this child. There must be something you found appealing about me. Please do tell me what it was."

"Hmm." He made a play of deep thought. Then, "If I were to choose one thing appealing about you to me, it has to be your breasts. They are immensely pleasing."

Brenna's mouth snapped open. What on earth could she say in reply to such a bawdy comment?

Laughter bubbled up. "You are scandalous, Richard Ellerby."

"You asked, and I replied." He shrugged. "If I cannot bed you, I can certainly enjoy the view of the perfect pair at my leisure."

She placed both open hands over her mouth but could not staunch the ripple of laughter. "What has happened to my staid country gentleman husband? Did my father rattle something loose in your head when he hit you?"

"I just thought you of all people appreciated honesty," he said. His mouth curled up.

"Oh, I do," she said. "Feel free to ogle at will."

He chuckled. They fell into a companionable silence as the clip-clop of horse hooves and the squeaks and rattles of the carriage filled the silence. The wind began to pick up, and leaves fell slowly off the trees. Though still warm enough for a light shawl, the trees shedding their leaves indicated that the weather was changing.

The manor came into view just as a loud snap sounded, followed instantly by a sideways jerk of the carriage. Brenna cried out, just managing to catch the side of the seat as the carriage dropped sideways, the harness trapping the horse to the disabled carriage and keeping it from flipping over.

The panicked horse tried to free itself, spinning the carriage. Richard fought for control and to keep his seat.

Brenna struggled to keep from being thrown. The effort wrenched her back, and she slid sideways against Richard. The carriage rattled and the horse kicked, trying to free itself from the harness. It seemed as if the battle went on forever, as Richard tried to soothe the terrified animal. Finally he gained control, though the horse shook, sweat foaming on his skin.

"Easy now." Richard quickly climbed down from the carriage. He gripped the reins in one hand lest the horse bolt. He reached for Brenna. She wasted no time launching herself awkwardly off the conveyance. He released the reins and caught her against him.

A distant call sounded, and several men came running down the drive. "What happened?" one asked. The men took hold of the skittish horse.

"I think we broke a bolt." Richard scooped a trembling Brenna into his arms.

She whimpered. "My back, it hurts."

Without further conversation, he left the men to take care of the horse and carriage, and walked briskly but carefully toward the manor. The butler heard the commotion and swung the door wide open.

"Get the physician," Richard bellowed, as he hurried through the foyer and up the staircase. With great care, he went to her room and laid her gingerly down on the bed.

It wasn't a moment later when her mother rushed in. "What happened?" She crossed to Brenna and reached for her. "She is sheet-white."

"We broke a wheel." Richard sat on the bed and touched Brenna's belly. "How is the baby?"

Brenna gripped his hand. "I'm not certain. I think he is fine." She looked into his eyes. Through tears, she pleaded, "Richard, he has to be fine."

He pressed her hand to his mouth. Brenna knew he was fighting to be strong for her. "The babe will survive. Have faith," he said. She clung to the conviction in his voice. She had to.

Mother sat beside her and tucked Brenna into her arms. The familiar scent of lavender swirled around her. Brenna let silent tears fall. She was terrified.

While they waited for the physician, family and servants gathered in the bedroom and hallway. Several maids sniffed softly, and the household prayed for their new mistress and the unborn heir.

There was a collective sense of relief when the man finally showed, examined Brenna, and was reasonably certain the babe was uninjured. Still, he took Richard and Kathleen aside.

"Her Ladyship needs to stay abed until her strained back heals. If she cramps, there will be nothing we can do for the baby." He collected his bag. "Someone should watch her day and night for the next few days."

"We will." Kathleen returned to the bed. Richard walked the physician out, and Kathleen pressed a kiss on Brenna's forehead.

Brenna's lip trembled. "I cannot lose this baby."

"Do not think such a thing, darling," Mother scolded gently. "You are both strong. You will have a healthy baby. I promise."

Caressing her belly while mouthing a silent prayer, Brenna took from her mother's strength. Then, exhausted, Brenna held her mother tightly and drifted off into a troubled sleep.

Kathleen looked up to see Walter standing in the doorway. He shooed everyone away and closed the door behind him.

"How is she?" he whispered.

"She is trying to be strong." Kathleen's lip trembled. "If she loses this baby, I don't know how she will survive. She loves it so."

Walter reached for her hand. "Our daughter does nothing at half measure. She knows this baby is what holds this marriage together. She will not lose him."

Eyes widening, Kathleen stared. "You know?"

"That the marriage is no love match?" He shook his head. "I am not nearly as dense as you two think. But I also see the way Brenna and Richard look at each other. This gives me hope."

Kathleen rubbed her cheek against his knuckles. "I thank you for giving Richard a chance. He does not yet realize how much he needs her."

"He will." Walter brushed Brenna's hair back from her face. "I do love this girl."

"I know you do." Kathleen looked from daughter to husband, her eyes soft. "Now go and pour Richard a tall drink. I think the man could use one."

Chapter Twenty-two

Rage burned hot inside Richard as he stared down at the broken bolt. A break from normal wear was not what happened to the wheel. From the condition of the item, the metal had been damaged intentionally and nearly cut through. It was enough to become an accident when the last of the undamaged part finally gave way during travel.

And he and Brenna could have been killed.

"I don't know what happened, Milord," Freddy said. He was shocked, upset, and frightened. "I checked the equipment myself a few days ago. There was nothing amiss."

Richard held up a hand. "I do not blame you." Freddy had been with him for many years. He excelled at his job of keeping the coaches and carriages in top form. He trusted the man with his life every time he took out a conveyance. No, this was the act of a deranged mind. "Have there been any other incidents, any other failures?"

"None, Milord."

"Hell." Richard walked around the carriage, his stomach knotted. If not for good luck, a slow pace, and a great deal of driving skill, well, he could not think about how close they had come to tragic consequences. "The carriage could have been used by anyone. Was it targeted at me or my wife, or at another member of the household?"

Freddy wrung his cap. "Everyone uses this carriage. If the culprit targeted a certain person, there would be more accurate ways to create a fatal accident."

The man was correct. "They could damage a saddle or use a weapon when the target was out walking. There are three ponds on the property. Any one of the ponds would be perfect for an 'accidental' drowning."

Richard pondered what might have happened had Brenna taken the carriage out alone; she wouldn't have had the strength to control the frightened horse.

He rubbed his eyes. "We must keep this news to ourselves for now. Check each coach, carriage, and dog cart immediately for sabotage." He ran his hand over the carriage wheel. "From now forward, when someone requests to go out, I need you to personally check the equipage for tampering right before they leave. I want it to be impossible for this to happen again."

"Yes, Milord."

Knowing his instructions would be followed exactly, he left the stable and walked to the house. He checked on Brenna and found her sleeping. Lucy was sitting in the chair, and Lady Kathleen was looking out the window. He needn't worry about his wife for the moment. She was in good care.

Richard went down to the library. The desire to drink to excess was overwhelming. He knew getting soused was not in his best interest, nor would it ease his anger.

However, one brandy would not send him into a downward spiral. He poured a liberal amount in a glass.

"My wife instructed me to pour you a drink." Walter came into the room. "I see you have started without me."

"Five years ago, I would have had half the carafe finished already." Pouring another glass, he walked to the fireplace and stared into the flames. "You taught me control."

Walter snorted. "You taught yourself." He leaned back against the sideboard and crossed his arms. "I am proud of you, son. Your father would be, too."

Richard's head jerked up. "You knew my father well?" This was the first time they'd ever discussed the late viscount.

"He was some years older than me, but we traveled in the

same circles. The first time I saw you, you were in short pants and I was not yet thirty. You were tormenting Anne with a toad, and she was screaming to rattle the dead." His eyes took a faraway cast with the memory. "The night you challenged me at the inn, I hardly recognized you. Many years had passed since your father died and I'd seen you last. Sadly, I'd not gone to you after Edmond's death or the subsequent loss of your family and felt guilty for my neglect. This, added to my desire not to see you drink yourself to death, spurred me to take you in hand and help drag you from your melancholia."

There was so much Richard did not know about his friend. "Most men would have left me to rot. You will forever have my thanks for what you did for me."

Walter shrugged, picked up his drink, and tossed it back. "All I ask is that you take care of my daughter." Walter left him without waiting for an answer.

This was a simple request from a friend who'd asked for nothing since rescuing Richard from despair's black grip.

Take care of Brenna. The weighted words carried more than a command to keep her safe. Walter did not know the depths of what he was asking. There was danger lurking in his home, and he vowed the culprit would not get away with what happened today. Worse yet, he hadn't a clue as to who would want to hurt someone in this household.

They lived quietly here at Beckwith Hall. Neighbors were scattered far and wide across the park, entertaining with parties or dinners when the urge to socialize struck. Richard would reciprocate a few times a year but mostly kept to himself. George, Miriam, and Bethany would occasionally invite in friends, but he seldom joined their youthful revelry, as he preferred keeping his own company.

There was no gambling or fights or general misbehavior under his roof. If he encountered trouble with a member of his staff, the offending party would be dismissed immediately. He'd not let anyone go in well over a year.

His mind drifted up the stairs, and rage welled again. He'd lost one wife and child, and he'd not lose another. He'd kill to keep them safe.

With a growl he hauled back and threw the glass into the flames.

Night came before Brenna awakened to the sound of some-one setting a tray on the night table. She opened her eyes to find the room dimly lit by only the fireplace, and the shad-owy form of her husband leaning over the tray.

"Have you taken over the duties of the maids, Husband?" she said, and carefully stretched out her sore back. The mus-cles contracted, and she winced.

He took a seat on the bed. "How are you feeling?"

Brenna reached beneath the sheet and found everything in order. "There is no cramping or bleeding. I suspect your son or daughter has decided not to let a carriage accident keep him, or her, from continuing to grow." She smiled softly. "I told you that we Harringtons are a hearty lot."

Richard took her hand. "I have noticed as much. You held on to the carriage seat with the grip of ten men. The courage you displayed was admirable."

"I had to hold on. You were otherwise occupied and could not do the deed yourself."

His face clouded. "You frightened years off my life, My Lady. Please take better care of yourself in the future."

Shifting on the bed to ease her back, Brenna frowned play-fully. "Am I to blame for a broken wheel? Did you find the reason for the trouble?"

"It was a rusty bolt. The matter has been taken care of and will not be repeated." He leaned to fluff her pillows. His arm brushed against her. She smiled.

Satisfied with his explanation, she pulled the sheet and quilt up. "Where are Mother and Lucy?"

"I sent them off to bed. I am taking the evening shift." He stood and collected the tray. "Since you missed supper, I thought we could eat together."

With his assistance, she slid up against the pillows and waited for him to serve them. She watched him smooth out the quilt and placed the tray near her hip. As he removed the napkin covering the tray, the scents of meat pie and creamed vegetables drifted up.

Her stomach grumbled, and she chuckled. "The babe has a hearty appetite. Soon, I will be unable to walk."

"Then I shall carry you wherever you need to go." Richard smoothed the napkin over her lap and handed her the pie.

"I see myself held in your arms, your legs bowed under my great weight, stumbling up and down the stairs." Brenna bit into the delicious food. "Perhaps a craftsman could make me a cart and add a pony to pull it. It will save your back."

Richard nodded, clearly seeing the idea as having merit. "Perhaps. It will be some months before we need to worry about your expanding girth."

Brenna kicked him with her sheet-covered foot. "Even when I am as big as a donkey, as my husband, you must compliment me on my lithe beauty and pretend not to notice my waddling walk and extra chins."

"I shall do my best," he teased.

The rest of the meal went on with light conversation as Brenna enjoyed the companionship of her husband. With her parents eager to spend as much time with her as possible during this short visit, they seldom had time alone.

Once the food was consumed, he cleaned up and helped her stretch out on the bed. "I shall return this to the kitchen while you try to sleep."

"I am weary of sleep," she said, then smiled at her choice of words. She did not want him to leave her, even long enough to walk to the kitchen and back.

"Regardless," he said, "you must do whatever you can to get well, and sleep is medicinal."

Brenna squelched a yawn. Her full belly did make her sleepy. "Did you make that up?"

"It does not matter whether it is true or not; I am lord of the manor, and you must do what I say." He gathered up the tray. "I expect you to be sleeping when I return."

"Yes, My Lord."

Dressed only in his white shirt, buff trousers, and boots, he cut a fine figure. His broad shoulders flexed as he adjusted the tray and disappeared out the door.

She placed a hand on her belly. "Your father is a cut above other men," she whispered. "He will love us. Wait and see."

She closed her eyes and went to sleep.

* * *

"How is your wife?" Bethany asked. She met Richard coming down the stairs. Dressed in a thin robe and obviously very little beneath it, her hair tumbled around her shoulders.

He wondered if she was tupping one of his footmen.

Outside of her brother and himself, there were no other men in the household to choose from but the footmen and his elderly butler. And with Richard not interested, and in spite of her hints at her innocence, he was certain she was not as virginal as she wanted him to believe.

The night she snuck into his bed and kissed him confirmed that notion. No innocent would be so bold. Thankfully, he'd run her off before he'd ended up married to the chit.

"It appears as if all is well. Thank you for your concern."

She shrugged, and the robe slid down to expose the top of one breast. "Thankfully, you managed to control the horse and save you both."

Richard kept his eyes averted. Her obvious ploy to entice him left him flat. There was only one woman who roused him to passion, and she was resting upstairs. "It was odd how the bolt broke clean through. We must have hit a rut."

He watched her closely, but her face gave nothing away. If she was involved in the accident, she was a very good actress.

"If you will excuse me." He left her and continued on to the kitchen. He sent the cook off to bed and returned to Brenna's room.

Staring down at her for several minutes, he found that he enjoyed watching her sleep. She was lovely with her dark lashes fanned out on her cheeks and her dark hair spread around her face. However, it was her full mouth that held his interest.

Though he'd earlier claimed it was her breasts that he liked most, there were so many things about her to intrigue him that, truthfully, he could not name only one.

He smiled with the memory of their discussion about her breasts. The shock she'd displayed over his brash comment still had the ability to amuse. He'd enjoyed setting his bold wife back on her heels.

Lud, she was a troubling piece of strength and fluff. It took determination, and her injury, to keep him from climbing into bed beside her.

The next few days saw Brenna's health improve as her family and Richard kept her entertained. Even Bethany visited—Brenna thought more from curiosity than concern—and Miriam brought her a plate of flaky chocolate pastries that she'd made herself.

"Thank you very much," Brenna said, and bit into one. Chocolate teased her tongue, and she groaned happily. "Delicious."

Miriam flushed. "Mother's cook taught me. He was once employed by a German prince, or so he says. He fled when the prince discovered he was doing more than cooking for the princess, his wife."

"What an interesting story," Brenna said. "If he baked like this for the princess, I can see why she would be smitten."

Nodding, Miriam stood up from the chair. "I should go now. Richard wants to go over the household accounts. With Andrew missing, the books need updating. I have a way with numbers."

Brenna waited until she was alone again and ate three more pastries. Though she'd jested with Richard about her growing girth, she knew that once she was allowed out of bed, she'd plan daily walks around the grounds to keep from becoming a sloth.

"I cannot become so big that I will not be able to walk through doors." Brenna caressed her stomach bump. "Such a humiliating thought that is."

I will miss you so much. I wish we did not have to leave," Kathleen said, squeezing Brenna tight. Her parents had already stayed almost an extra week, waiting for Brenna to be up and about, before Father insisted they needed to return to London soon or miss the birth of Eva's baby. "We will be back before Christmas, I promise."

"I'll miss you both," Brenna said, her eyes filling. "You must give Eva and the duke my love. Noelle, Gavin, and Laura, too." She scrunched up her face. "Even Simon, I suppose."

Kathleen smiled. "Will your brother and you ever make peace? Or will this war between you rage on until you are both too old to remember all the reasons you squabbled in the first place?"

"Simon and I take pleasure in our arguments," Brenna said lightly. She loved her brother dearly, though she seldom admitted to it aloud. "I suspect they will go on until one of us drops over dead."

Mother shook her head. "Then I am pleased you two are miles away from each other to keep your bickering to a minimum." She hugged Brenna again. "Be well, my darling girl."

"You too, Mother."

Brenna kissed her father and watched her parents and servants load into the coaches. She brushed away a tear and waved, clinging heavily to Richard's arm with her other hand.

She'd been out of bed for short trips over the past two days but still felt somewhat weak. So when the coaches disappeared down the lane, Richard scooped her into his arms and carried her back to bed.

"I feel so helpless," she grumbled. He bussed the top of her head. "If I do not recover soon, Bethany will reclaim my place at the table."

Richard frowned. "She'd not dare. I think deep inside her confident exterior, she fears you. In a fight, my wager would be on you, Wife."

Picturing them wrestling on the floor, shirts tangled, hairpins flying, lifted her spirits. She chuckled softly. "Let us hope our feud does not come to a brawl. A well-bred viscountess must always behave."

"Dearest, you have never behaved," Richard jested.

L ucy found her reading a very dull book about gardening a few hours later, when she came into Brenna's room. Lucy's face was white and her eyes red rimmed. She clutched a letter against her bosom.

Brenna tossed the book aside and slid up on her bottom. "Lucy, what is it? You look like a ghost."

Lucy's lip trembled, and she stumbled over to the bed. Brenna collected her into an embrace as sobs overtook her friend. "Lucy, you are scaring me. Tell me what has happened."

It took a minute for Lucy's sobs to subside. She eased back and faced Brenna. "Franklin is dead."

Shocked, Brenna gaped. "What?"

"My husband is dead." Lucy held out the note. "He took a fever in Paris and died." Her voice rose. "I was barely a wife, and now I am a widow." Her voice caught. Brenna hugged her close. "We never got a chance to know each other. We were married one night when he left. Now he's buried in Paris. The government will not allow his body to be returned because of the contagious nature of his illness."

"Oh, my darling Lucy." Brenna rubbed her back while she cried for the loss of the husband she hardly knew.

After a time, the tears subsided, and they opened and read a second letter together. "As his widow, you will receive a portion of what he owns and stipends from his business ventures," Brenna said. "According to the bankers, it should be enough for you to live on comfortably, if you spend wisely."

Lucy dropped back on the bed and stared at the ceiling. "I never met his family. I only know he had elderly parents and no siblings. It appears that they are content to let the bankers handle their correspondence and have no interest in meeting me."

Brenna touched her knee. "It is their loss."

Nodding, Lucy puffed out her cheeks and expelled the breath. "What am I to do now? Do I wait for a year, then ask Miss Eva to match me again? Do I find a small town house and live out the rest of my days in quiet seclusion with dozens of cats?"

"You are welcome to stay here until you decide," Brenna said. "I enjoy your company, and I know you want to see the baby."

Lucy met her eyes. "I suppose I can tolerate you for a few more months." Her lips trembled. "I cannot believe I am a widow. I was a courtesan longer than I was Mrs. Pruitt."

Brenna took her hand and lay down beside her. The two of

them stared at the ceiling together and talked about the complexity of life. Lucy lost her husband before they had a chance to fall in love, and she had a husband who promised to never love her.

What a pair they were.

Chapter Twenty-three

❦

The days aged onward as fall turned into winter, with the arrival of the cold weather and occasional whirls of falling snow. The duchess, Eva, had her baby, and she and the duke named their daughter Catherine Victoria. The sometimes hard-edged duke was said to be a doting father.

Richard kept vigilant for any further signs of trouble, but the culprit seemed to have satisfied his desire to make mischief. Either that or he preferred to limit his crimes to times when the weather was temperate.

Watching the arrival of the last party guests, he glanced over at his wife, resplendent in red velvet, her dark hair swept up into a fetching twist on top of her head.

Brenna grew lovelier as her belly rounded out, making her condition obvious to everyone around her. Against the backdrop of Christmas decorations, Richard could not keep his eyes from her soft beauty.

And with each day, he grew fonder of his wife.

"I cannot believe how well you look, my dear," Mrs. Turner was saying from her place across the table from Brenna. "How far along are you now?"

"Almost five months," Brenna said. "It feels like twenty."

"Posh," the elderly woman replied. "When I was carrying

my Doris, I could hardly leave the bed. A trial, that one was." She looked down the table at the eldest of her six daughters. "You, my dear, are the picture of health."

Brenna glanced at Richard, and he smiled. Though Brenna had met most of the guests at previous parties, this was her first time hosting. The nausea had passed, her back had recovered, and she was back to the lively Brenna he knew well.

Mrs. Turner also peered down the table at him. "Tell your wife how the babe gives her a certain happy glow."

He nodded and rested his warm gaze on Brenna. "I have never seen an expectant mother quite so content, or lovely, as my wife."

Brenna flushed, her cheeks pink in the candlelight. "Thank you, Mrs. Turner, Lord Ashwood." Her eyes sparkled in the candlelight.

Duties as host required he charm the ladies seated at either side of him. If not for that, he'd be quite content to spend the evening staring at Brenna.

The Christmas party had been her idea, and she'd spent weeks fretting over the decorations. Bows and ribbons and pine branches gave the house a festive air, and she'd had the footmen cut a small tree that was set up on a table in the library as a surprise for the children who would join them on Christmas Eve.

"I wonder if the snow will ever stop," Lady Allen said, as Richard returned his attention to the lady seated beside him.

"I suspect so, though it looks like we are in for a snowy Christmas." He tried to focus on talk of the weather, but his mind, and eyes, continued to drift back to his wife.

She laughed at some witticism from Mister Gray, and their handsome neighbor appeared besotted. Richard scowled and wondered why he ever agreed to invite him.

Not sharing a bed with Brenna was torture. Watching other men flirt with his wife made it worse.

The cold baths had done nothing to ease his suffering. Who knew one could get aroused while racked with shivers?

Whoever came up with that cure for male sexual frustration had obviously never met his wife.

*   *   *

Mister Gray was an entertaining sort. Brenna found his stories amusing. However, what amused her more was the way Richard glared at her companion as though he wanted to yank him from his chair and toss him out into the snow.

She did not have to look at him to know he was watching her. It seemed to be his favorite pastime. Though it was impossible to know what he was thinking, she'd sometimes catch him watching her with the heated intensity he'd previously reserved for the times they'd shared a bed. She suspected he was regretting his choice to keep his distance.

This encouraged her and gave her hope.

"Milady Brenna." Mister Gray leaned to take her into his confidence. "You have not yet agreed to run away with me. I have a coach waiting outside for your word."

Brenna shook her head. "I fear, Mister Gray, that I cannot run away with you. Waddling is the best I can do. And I think my husband might protest to find me gone. I carry his heir."

He grinned. "Pity. Then I shall have to wait until summer, when you are otherwise, er, unencumbered."

Knowing the man was an outrageous flirt, she did not take his offer seriously. Instead, she rolled her eyes dramatically and drew laughter from her companion.

"You are a delight, Lady Ashwood," he said. "Your husband is very lucky."

Brenna shook her head. "It is I who is lucky. Richard is a devoted husband."

When the meal was finished, the guests moved to the ballroom, where a small orchestra played. There was no dancing, but conversation and laughter kept the evening light.

By the time the clock chimed twelve, the last of the guests were collecting their outerwear and bracing for the cold.

George and Miriam had already gone to bed, and Bethany was sharing a farewell with Mister Gray. By the flush on her cheeks, he was saying something outlandish. Brenna wondered if it was another proposal to run away. One could hope.

"You look exhausted," Richard said, as the last guest hurried out into the night. He took her arm and led her toward the stairs. She leaned to put her head on his shoulder.

"I am tired," she admitted.

He patted her hand. "The party was a success. That is quite an accomplishment, Lady Ashwood."

"I think everyone enjoyed themselves," she agreed. Brenna rubbed her lower back. It ached from standing most of the night. "All my worries have come to naught. No soup was spilled and no arguments over political differences. I am certain I have you to thank for the latter."

"I threatened any gentleman who dared ruin your party with lashings. They all promised to behave."

Brenna smiled. She knew he was teasing. Still, he had been watching over her. She took comfort in that.

They got to the top of the staircase when she felt a small fluttering in her belly. She pulled Richard to a stop and released his arm. She placed both her hands over her belly.

"I felt something." Her eyes widened. The fluttering came again. "I think the baby is moving."

Without thinking, she reached and placed his hand over the spot. The movement abated. "Drat."

Richard stood frozen, as if waiting for the babe to move again. Then he blinked and pulled his hand away.

In her excitement, she'd forgotten about the son he'd lost. Surely, he'd also felt that baby move. The memory had to ache deep within his heart.

He often appeared uncomfortable when she spoke at length about the baby, his worry over losing another child tempering his anticipation of the impending birth. She tried to reassure him, but until their child was born healthy, he'd still suffer from the malady of fear.

"Soon we will feel him kick," she said, and reclaimed his arm. "Mother said I was prone to hiccups. It often kept her up at night."

A longing filtered through his eyes. It was then that Brenna realized how desperately he wanted to be a father.

Hoping to keep him from turning sober, Brenna continued on in a mock-serious tone. "Soon, we will need to choose names. I was thinking Daisy, Petunia, or Nettle if it's a girl, and Horace, Newlin, or Percy for a boy."

He frowned. "You cannot be serious?"

A brow went up. "You do not like Nettle or Newlin? I am quite fond of Newlin Ellerby."

"We are not naming our daughter after weeds, or giving our son a name better suited for an ancient uncle than a robust young man. I think you need to rethink your choices, madam."

She feigned insult, though she agreed wholeheartedly with his assessment of the names. She chose them to tease him.

"If you think my choices dismal, then perhaps you should try to come up with a few of your own." Choosing names would further establish his role as a father.

"I shall put thought into it." He grimaced. "Newlin? How dreadful."

They stopped before her bedroom door. "We do have a few months to decide." She lifted to her toes and kissed him, a brief brush of her mouth, a press of her breasts against his arm, just enough to remind him that she was still his wife.

One day soon, after the baby was born, she'd find her way into his bed, permanently, if she had to use all her femininity and seductive wiles to do so.

She did not like sleeping alone. "Good night, Richard."

"Good night, Brenna."

Christmas Eve came with the excited squeals of children, as all the little ones who resided on the property came to collect the presents and treats prepared for each. The servants and tenants were not left out of the celebrating. Each received a gift and a side of pork or a turkey; and the household staff, a Christmas bonus.

Brenna made Richard a robe of deep blue velvet, and he gave her a pendant of emeralds and diamonds. But her most cherished gift of the holiday was watching Richard watch the children open their gifts and to see the happiness in his eyes.

"Your husband is more at ease than I've ever seen him," Lucy said. She and Brenna stood back from the melee. They would exchange their gifts the next morning, when Brenna's parents arrived late from London.

"He does take well to the children."

Lucy shook her head. "It is more than that. He is not nearly as sober as when we first came, and he smiles more often. I believe the man has accepted you and the marriage, though I do not think he realizes it yet."

"Perhaps." Brenna wanted so much for Lucy's words to be true. "However, he still keeps me at arm's length."

"That will change."

Brenna looked at her friend. "I hope so."

The evening grew late. The tenants left for home, and the servants retired to their rooms, leaving the household quiet again. Lucy yawned and went off to bed. Richard took Brenna up and saw her settled for the evening.

"It was a very nice day," she said, squelching a yawn of her own. "I enjoyed the children's laughter."

"As did I." Richard kissed her cheek. "I shall see you in the morning." He prepared to leave through the sitting room.

"Wait." He turned, and Brenna walked to him. "I have one last gift." She stood up on her toes and kissed him full on the mouth. He seemed hesitant for a moment. However, it did not last. He swept her against him and deepened the kiss with a hungry sweep of his tongue.

Brenna melted. She wrapped one arm around his neck and splayed the other flat on his chest. She felt his rapid heartbeat beneath her hand.

A shout broke them apart.

There was commotion from somewhere below. Richard left Brenna and went to the staircase. Taking the stairs down two at a time, he was shocked to see smoke coming from the library. A footman ran by, clad in only his trousers and shirt, carrying a pair of buckets filled with water.

Richard darted after him. The children's tree was ablaze. Luckily the tree was small, and the water buckets doused most of the flames rather quickly. A second footman and his buckets took care of the final smoldering branches.

"What happened here?" he asked. Luckily the fire was limited to the tree, though there was some minor soot damage to the ceiling.

"I do not know, Milord," Mrs. Beal said, her voice high. I came down for a glass of milk and found the tree burning."

She pointed to a melted candle beneath the black branches. "When I retired upstairs, I know the candle was not there."

She seemed so certain that Richard believed her.

Could this be the work of the culprit who damaged the wheel? The idea could not be dismissed easily.

"Oh, dear. The tree," Brenna said from the doorway, her hand over her mouth. "Thank goodness the fire was contained before it spread."

"Someone accidentally left a candle burning near the tree." He walked over and took her by the arm. "Go back to bed. I will see to the cleanup."

"Such a shame," she said, as he led her out. He watched her go back upstairs.

The footmen filed out with empty buckets in hand. When he and Mrs. Beal were alone, he joined her by the tree.

"I am certain about the candle," she said.

Richard pulled the blackened candleholder from under the tree with the edge of his sleeve. The metal was hot. "I believe you."

"Do you think someone set this on purpose?" she asked. "Who would do such a terrible thing?"

"We do not know what happened," he said. "Unless we have proof of mischief, we must take this as an accident. Please do not say anything about your suspicions to my wife."

"Yes, Milord." Mrs. Beal frowned and left him.

The dull ache of dread settled into his stomach. From a place in the back of his mind, he knew this fire was no accident.

The holidays passed, and the new year came with several inches of snow. Richard had taken to getting up during the night and walking the halls, just to reassure himself that all was well. After weeks and then months passed without further trouble, he began to convince himself that the fire *had* been accidental.

Spring planting began in earnest with the arrival of warmer weather, and Richard was often out overseeing the work on the property as soon as the sun came up.

This left Brenna and Lucy time alone to prepare for the

baby. There was so much to do. With Mrs. Beal's assistance, the nursery was aired out and a nanny hired. Clothes were made and Richard's old cradle brought down from the attic and repaired.

"I think my feet have swollen to twice their previous size," Brenna groused during a quiet moment, as she put her feet up on the stool in her sitting room. "I do not know how I am expected to attend the spring ball tonight when I cannot see my feet."

"You could beg off and spend the evening in front of the fire with a book," Lucy said, dropping into a chair beside her. Her friend looked trim and youthful in a dress of pale pink cotton. Brenna felt a slight twist of jealousy. Beside Lucy, she was positively bovine.

"I cannot. If I do not keep an eye on *that* woman, she will snatch Richard away from me. Did you see her last evening? That gown barely concealed her nipples."

Lucy rolled her eyes heavenward. "Nonsense. Your husband has no interest in Bethany and never will, in spite of her nipple display. You worry too much about her."

"You saw the gown she wore three evenings ago," Brenna said, annoyed. "I am quite certain I caught a glimpse of her nipples at least twice. It will not be long before Richard finds comfort in her bed."

"He only notices you," Lucy insisted. "The man would not take so many cold baths if he was enjoying the favors of other women."

Brenna's interest perked up. "What is this news?"

Shrugging, Lucy examined her fingernails. "I may have overheard a whisper or two about how His Lordship has taken to cold baths these last few months. That does not sound like a man who plans to cuckold his wife. It sounds like a sexually frustrated man who is waiting for his child to be born before taking his rightful place in her bed."

The idea was both preposterous and endearing all at once.

"I think your imagination has taken flight," Brenna said, and stood. She walked into her bedroom and stared down at the silver dress laid out on the bed. "Richard knows he can come to me at any time and has not done so. If he found me so desirable, why then does he not press his intentions?" She felt the baby move and looked down. Her shoulders slumped. "Only a bull elephant would find me appealing."

Lucy giggled. "Patience, dearest. Your time draws near. Soon you will have your husband on his knees begging for your favors."

T he ball was festive and fun, as everyone from the park, and beyond, came to celebrate. Within the next few weeks, most of the citizenry—particularly those with marriageable daughters—would be leaving for London to partake in the new season.

"Oh, to be young," Mrs. Turner said, from her seat beside Brenna. "I have not danced in years. My ancient bones will not allow such activity."

Brenna murmured something unintelligible as she watched Richard and Miriam join a line of dancers. Envy filled her. The shy spinster was dressed in a gown of cream and rose and was smiling brightly at Richard. Why had Brenna never noticed how pretty she was?

Mrs. Turner must have noted that her attention had wandered as well as who was the focus of her perusal. "What have you done with that girl? She has certainly blossomed since I last saw her at Christmas."

There had been a change in Miriam over the last few weeks. Brenna had been so busy she had not done more than take casual notice. Miriam was positively glowing with happiness and good cheer.

"I have done nothing to her," Brenna said glumly. Miriam smiled brightly at Richard. He responded in kind.

"Does she have a beau?" Mrs. Turner pressed. Not waiting for an answer, she went on. "She must have a beau. She has the look of a girl who is smitten."

Brenna had a ready denial, but it failed to materialize. Truthfully, Miriam could have had ten beaus, and Brenna wouldn't have noticed. She was focused on the baby.

Frowning, Brenna watched Miriam look at Richard like a love-struck schoolgirl. Her stomach dropped. Richard did not find Miriam attractive. Or did he?

Before her mind could put the pair into a steamy affair,

George approached, a young man in tow. He bowed before Mrs. Turner. "Mrs. Turner, you look lovely tonight. Perhaps I can persuade you to give up that chair and dance with me?"

Mrs. Turner harrumphed. "You know I do not dance, and not with the likes of you, George Bentley. You have too much charm for your own good."

George grinned. He turned to Brenna. "Lady Ashwood, this is Mister Clive Ever—" A drunken guest jostled against him, and his smile wavered. He watched the guest stumble off and darted a tense glance at his companion. She suspected the two men had been arguing. George continued, "He is visiting the park and staying with Lord Ponteby."

Brenna allowed the young man to bow over her hand. There was something familiar about him. An unpleasant feeling came over her.

"A pleasure, Lady Ashwood."

The man was tall and blond and impeccably, if not expensively, dressed as a young man of some means.

He released her hand and straightened. "I see you find me familiar." He winked, and she frowned. "You probably notice my resemblance to my uncle, who you do know. Mister Everhart?"

Brenna winced.

Chapter Twenty-four

※

How much did Clive know about his uncle's kiss at the ball and her subsequent slap? She was sure she'd seen something calculating in his eyes when he mentioned his uncle, as if he knew the entire tale in detail.

"Yes, Mister Everhart and I have met," she said. If he expected some emotional reaction, he'd not get one. She kept her features bland. "You do look much like him."

Their appearance was not the only thing the two men shared. Clive, whether intentionally or not, shared his uncle's ability to pique her temper.

"Why don't you two run along," Mrs. Turner said. She pointed across the ballroom. "I believe I see some frilly young things better suited for your attentions."

Bowing, the two men left. "You do not like the older Mister Everhart," Mrs. Turner said. "Nor do you like the nephew."

Brenna nodded. "No, I do not like the elder Everhart. He is charming, yet I'm not entirely comfortable in his presence." She watched the two men approach a gaggle of girls, and soon they were all laughing together. "He is very forward with his attentions."

The baby kicked. Brenna instantly forgot anything but the child. She placed a hand over her abdomen.

"The baby comes soon."

"He does," Brenna said. She scanned the room for Richard. He was speaking to a gentleman in dusty travel clothes. Curious, she watched, realizing there was something familiar about the man, though she could not see his face.

The music died, and Richard's companion turned.

Jace Jones? She blinked. It *was* him. Why was he here? Had something happened to Simon?

Richard noticed Brenna's interest in Jones. "We need to find a private place to talk. You have drawn the attention of my wife."

He turned and led Jones from the ballroom and out of the house. He'd never met the man before Jones approached him in the ballroom, but the stranger knew him and insisted they speak privately.

The brisk air was welcome after the heat of the ballroom. The bright stars and lamplight from the windows lit the garden as Richard led Jones away from prying eyes. Jones followed him to a small courtyard.

Once he was certain they'd not be overheard, he faced his companion. "Now tell me what this is about."

"Simon Harrington sent me to check up on Brenna."

"What? Why?" His temper flared. Did Harrington think Richard incapable of tending to his own wife? "Brenna is my concern," he said bluntly. "Tell Simon he need not worry about her."

He stalked a few steps away before Jones's voice brought him upright. "Wait. There is more."

Richard released a harsh sigh and turned back.

Jones rubbed his eyes with his palms. There was weariness in the man that came from a hard ride from London. "A few weeks past, there was a murder at the Mayfair home of a client. A maid was found strangled in the mews behind the house," Jones began. "Bow Street is investigating, but they are unable to come up with a suspect at this time."

Another death? His interest peaked as his mind drifted to the dead maid from Dover. "We've heard nothing of this murder."

Jones settled back on his heels. "It was kept quiet. The Runners think it might be part of a rash of murders. They are hoping not to cause panic."

This was interesting. "We have heard of the deaths of a maid from Bath and the other in Dover. Are they connected? We were under the assumption that those were accidents."

"The Runners believe the incident in Bath was accidental. The girl had fallen before."

"And Dover?" Richard pressed. Though he had no idea what this had to do with Simon's concern for Brenna, it was a bleak and fascinating story.

"They are convinced that one was murder."

Richard glanced back at the house. "Two murders so far apart does not mean the same man has killed both women. The man would have to have the means to travel to commit those crimes. It would be no common killer."

Jones stared at him in the darkness. "True. But when you add another maid in Hastings and a tavern wench in Oxford, it makes a compelling case."

This was a surprising turn. "Four murders?" Richard shook his head to clear it. Jace Jones had not come all the way out here on a lark. There was more to this story; he knew it in his knotted gut. "Why don't you tell me the real reason Simon sent you here. I suspect it was not to see if I am mistreating my wife."

The stranger took a step closer, the light filtering over his hard features. "I have reason to believe the killer is somewhere in or near this park."

B renna froze. A killer in the park? She stepped from the shadows into the small opening in a circle of hedges leading to the fountain outside the meeting hall. The two men turned to her, clearly startled by her appearance.

"There is a murderer. Here?"

Richard came to her and took her by the arm. He walked her to a bench and eased her onto the surface. "You should have stayed inside, Brenna. There is no need to alarm yourself. This is all speculation, with no proof."

She shook off his arm and faced Jones. "I am not a child. Tell me what is happening, Jace."

"You know each other?" Richard asked, but Brenna was focused on Jones. He should have known that they'd be acquainted. The man knew Simon Harrington. It wasn't a stretch for Brenna to know him, too.

Jace nodded. "There is a series of killings of women."

"Jones," Richard interjected. The warning in his voice carried no weight. It earned an exasperated sigh from his wife.

"Continue," she said, unabated by Richard's desire to protect her from this dark news. "I am no wilting flower in need of protecting."

Jones nodded. "Four women have been murdered." He moved to take a seat beside her and glanced at her stomach. His face grew troubled. "Perhaps you *should* return inside, Brenna."

"You do not need to coddle me, Jace." She encompassed both men in her glare. "I want to know everything you know. If there is a chance the women of this park are in danger, I should make sure they are warned."

Jace glanced at Richard, who shrugged. Brenna knew neither man wanted to tangle with her. She might be close to birthing, but she was still a formidable opponent.

"Two years ago, a maid was murdered in Hastings. She was found strangled in a meadow. The case was never solved. Last year, another woman suffered a similar fate, though her body was discovered in a churchyard. The Dover maid fell from the cliffs, but she had marks on her neck. The constable thinks she may have fought off her attacker and fallen while trying to flee him."

"And the maid in London?" Brenna pressed.

"That is where the story takes a turn. She was stabbed to death." Jace paused. "There seemed to be no connection. It was after the girl had been dead for two days that marks became visible on her neck. The culprit had tried to strangle her but could not finish the deed. So he stabbed her."

Brenna clasped her hands, saddened by the tale. She knew every maid in her family's employ and here at Beckwith Hall, too. It frightened her to think that any one of the girls could suffer a similar fate.

"What leads the Runners to believe the killer has come here?" Richard asked.

"Underneath the last victim was part of a torn note. There was only enough to deduce that it was directions to an inn about a half hour from here. We have no proof that the note was lost by the killer; it could have blown into the alley at any time before the murder. But it is too big a clue to leave uninvestigated. The Runners have gone to the inn to see what they can find."

A moment of quiet followed. Then Richard spoke. "The killer could be out of the country by now. There is no reason to believe he has come here."

"True," Jace conceded.

"Why, then, do you think we need to be dragged into this sordid business?" Richard said.

Jace leaned his elbows on his knees and stared at the ground for a minute. When he lifted his eyes, he met Brenna's gaze. "Though the note was torn, I recognized the letterhead from letters Simon received from you and shared with me. The paper was yours, Brenna."

The shock could not have been greater had he told Brenna that someone had witnessed her murdering the maid. She had to take a moment to collect her thoughts before she could speak. When she did, her voice was no more than a whisper.

"How can that be?" She often wrote her family and friends; thus, the paper could have come from anywhere and anyone. Still, it worried her that a killer may have dropped her writing paper during the murder. "Are you certain?"

"Simon confirmed it. I have a Runner friend who let me see the note. I described it to your brother. It contains the same swan pattern as the notes you send."

Brenna turned to Richard. Her stomach burned. "Mother had the paper printed for my twentieth birthday. She designed it herself, as she knows I adore swans. No one else shares that design. Simon would know it well."

"The Runners know it, too," Jace said. "I have come ahead to warn you. After they have checked out the inn, they will come here. I thought you should be ready."

Richard reached for her hand. "They cannot suspect Brenna."

Jace shook his head. "They do not, for many reasons. They

want to speak to you about your friends, family, and acquaintances. They think the killer is someone you know."

The many people she'd met through her lifetime blurred through her mind. She tried to think of anyone who could be capable of these horrible deaths and could not name a single man who stood out.

"I don't believe this," Brenna said. "Surely this man could not walk among us as if nothing were amiss. He has to be a monster."

"He is," Jace said. "But on the outside he could appear quite normal." He stood and walked to the fountain. "Some years ago a bookkeeper in New York was arrested for killing two prostitutes. He buried the first in his garden and was caught with the body of the second one in his home. He was small and meek, not what you would picture in a killer. Yet he did kill."

Crickets chirped in the night while Brenna pondered all she'd heard. Suddenly, she wished she had stayed inside after all.

Chapter Twenty-five

❧❧❧

Richard paced the clearing, fear gripping him to his bones. He'd thought the incident with the carriage had been a onetime dangerous prank, by someone with a grudge against him or someone at the hall, and the tree fire, an accident.

Now a killer was loose and may be stalking his wife?

He turned to stare into the darkness, unsure of what he expected to see. All he knew was that he needed to tell Jones about the incidents. The time for keeping secrets from Brenna was over.

He raked his hands through his hair. "There is something you should know." He pulled in a deep breath. "Last fall someone tampered with one of our carriages by cutting a bolt. The wheel broke when Brenna and I were out. It was through God's good grace that we were largely uninjured."

Brenna shifted on the seat. "You told me the broken bolt was accidental." Anger flashed in her eyes. "You kept the truth from me?"

Jace stepped between them before Brenna could start an argument. "That is odd. If the cut bolt was meant to harm someone and failed, why didn't the culprit try again?"

Glancing past Jace to Brenna, Richard gritted his teeth and knew his wife would take off his head for keeping the truth from her. Still, he had to tell Jace. There was no way around it.

"Last Christmas we had a fire. Someone put a candle under the children's tree, and it burned. Mrs. Beal was certain the candle was not there when she went to bed."

"Lud," Brenna bit out.

"Could it have been accidental?" Jace interjected.

"We do not know," Richard said. "No one came forward to confess. It remains a mystery."

Silence fell. Richard wondered if Brenna was plotting his demise. She hated being coddled, and he'd kept two very big secrets from her.

When he looked past Jones, there was no anger on her face. In fact, she looked rather controlled.

"Richard?" Brenna shifted again and rubbed her back. "There is something I have not told you, either."

"What is it?"

"Last fall, and a few times over the winter, things of mine disappeared and were later put back, like my favorite brush or shawl. I'd notice the item missing, and then when the search turned up nothing, it would mysteriously return."

"And you did not tell me this until now?" Richard said. He tamped down his temper. They'd both kept secrets.

"I thought it was either my own forgetfulness or someone playing pranks." She stretched her back. "My arrival was not exactly welcomed by everyone in the household."

The two men shared a glance. "I find it difficult to believe a killer would stoop to such a spiteful game," Jace said. "Still, if the prankster is our killer, then the person lives in or has access to your household."

"I suspected it was Bethany and still hold that belief," Brenna admitted. "She would like nothing more than to see me flee to London and never return."

"It is possible," Richard agreed. "I'd rather consider a jealous woman behind the matter than a killer roaming my household unnoticed." Richard paused and tried to put all the incidents together. The pieces did not match. "The hidden brush sounds like a petty prank that Bethany would do. The fire and the carriage accident caused real danger. I'm convinced they are separate matters."

Jace nodded. "As do I, though it is best to keep vigilant in case we are mistaken."

Brenna stood. "The baby is restless." She bent forward and kneaded her back. Richard went to her and took her arm. With her large belly hindering her balance, he worried she might topple forward.

"We can continue this conversation tomorrow," Richard said. "Jones, will you stay at Beckwith Hall tonight?"

"I'd be grateful. The inn is currently overrun with Bow Street Runners. My friend, Freemont, will not be pleased to know I have come to you first. It ruins their surprise arrival."

The trio returned to the common room and found Lucy. They left George, Bethany, and Miriam to enjoy the rest of the evening and took Brenna home.

Once Jace was sent off to a guest room with a maid, Richard swung Brenna into his arms and carried her up the stairs.

"I am able to walk," she protested, but snuggled against him anyway. Lucy trailed along behind.

Her belly made the effort of carrying her challenging, though she was still quite light. "Indulge me. The evening was long, and you are tired. I'd rather carry you than have you fall asleep halfway up the stairs."

Brenna pressed her face to his neck, and her warm breath stirred interest below. Well, that and the fullness of her breast pushing up from the neckline of her gown. Their growth had been one aspect of her pregnancy that he had enjoyed, even if they were only lusted over from a distance.

Damn. He hated cold baths.

"I can stay with her tonight, My Lord," Lucy offered, when they entered Brenna's room. She helped Brenna out of her gown. "I think her time is close."

"No, thank you, Lucy. I'll stay."

Lucy nodded. "Yes, Milord."

He walked through to his room and found Miles waiting. The valet stripped him down to his trousers and shirt. "Miles, have you seen anything unusual in the hall over the last few months? A stranger lurking or unusual incidents that brought questions?"

Miles hung the coat in the wardrobe. "I have not. Has something happened, Milord?"

Richard briefly filled him in on Jones's news.

"That *is* troubling," Miles said. "There has been no hint of anything untoward that I can recall. Should I alert the staff to keep watch for strangers on the property?"

"I think you should," Richard agreed. "Try not to start a panic, especially among the maids. Tell them to keep vigilant and not to wander the grounds alone."

"Yes, Milord."

Richard left Miles and returned to Brenna. She was abed, dressed in a nightdress of white. She was so beautiful. "You look virginal in white, Wife."

Brenna smiled and cupped her belly. "You jest, Husband. I'd not be mistaken for virginal in this condition."

He walked to the bed. "I should sleep in the chair."

"Please sleep with me." She reached out her hand. "My back hurts. It would pleasure me greatly if you'd rub out the aches."

He allowed her to tug him down beside her. "It is comforting to know I can be of use. Roll over."

Propping herself at as much of an angle as manageable, Brenna groaned happily as he kneaded her back for several minutes with gentle strokes. "I am in heaven," she purred.

The husky sound raced from his ears to his cock, stirring an erection. He struggled not to let his hands roam at will over her softer parts. "Your feet are swollen, your back pains you, and you complain of burning in your chest. What part of this is heaven?"

She chuckled. "If you rubbed my back whenever I asked, I would have no more complaints."

Snorting, he pressed harder into her lower back with his fingertips. She groaned again. He wanted desperately to ease her onto her back and push up her nightdress. Living under this roof with Brenna was driving him mad. He couldn't sleep, nor could he concentrate on anything but her.

The sooner she returned to London, the better it would be for them both.

When his hands grew tired, he lay down beside her. She turned around and snuggled against him. Soon her breathing evened out, and she fell asleep.

He knew he should go to the chair, but the night was chilly, and Brenna was warm. He pulled the quilt up and relaxed back, hoping sleep would find him as easily.

The baby had other plans. He felt movement where her belly pressed his rib cage. He froze and was rewarded with a sharp kick. Surprised, he held his breath. The little mite never seemed willing to show himself around his father, though Brenna occasionally, and futilely, put his hand over the places where the baby kicked.

Now he was kicking quite vigorously. Richard slid a hand between them and marveled at the wonder of the new life.

Had his worries been unjustified? Would Brenna and the baby survive the birth? Would she give him a healthy son or daughter as she promised?

"Our child cannot wait to meet you," Brenna whispered.

"I thought you were sleeping."

"I was, until the babe decided to kick up a ruckus." She closed her hand over his. She knitted their fingertips together. "You are thinking about Millicent and your lost son."

He said nothing.

Brenna lifted her head and rested it on her hand. "Tell me about them."

For a moment he thought to refuse. Then just as suddenly, he wanted to unburden himself to Brenna. Tonight was a time to share secrets. He might as well tell her the story she desperately wanted to hear.

He rolled over to face her and began his tale. "Millicent was the first girl I ever loved. Her father was a baron and friends with one of my neighbors. We met at a picnic, and I was taken with her. The friendship grew with the years until we were old enough to wed."

"You were happy?"

"I was. I think she married me not for love but for security. Her father was a wastrel who gambled them into debt." He sighed. "The marriage was troubled from the first. She was fragile, moody, and sometimes withdrawn. Eventually, I suspected an affair with a soldier she'd met at a party, but there was no proof, only my own jealous mind." He closed his eyes. "When she announced her pregnancy, I was pleased. I refused to consider that the baby was not mine."

"She told you it wasn't?"

"No. She assured me I was the father and she'd not been unfaithful." His face hardened. "Then one night, I caught her

sneaking out the kitchen door wearing only a nightdress. I
confronted her. She denied that she was going out to meet a
lover. We argued, and she ran from the hall. It was raining. By
the time I found her some two hours later, she'd collapsed in
the garden, racked with chills from the cold."

"Oh, Richard." She squeezed his hand.

"She caught a fever and went into labor the next afternoon.
The physician tried to save them, but the babe came too early
and Millicent was too weak. They did not survive the night."

A tear rolled down her face. "How tragic. And you blame
yourself."

"I killed them, Brenna," he said softly. "The same as if I'd
taken a gun to her."

B renna touched the side of his face. He closed his lids.
"This was not your fault. You could not have known she
would run away into the night."

"We should not have quarreled," he countered. "If not for
the nightdress and her lack of a reasonable explanation for her
actions, I had no solid proof that she had a lover. Nor was
there proof the baby was not mine. Whispered gossip was all
it was. I just did not trust her."

"Yet you loved her."

Richard met her eyes. "I believe I did. I was a child when
we met and became infatuated with her beauty. I think part of
our unhappiness came from being married young and my
father's death soon after. I was weighted with responsibilities
and frequently left her alone while I tried to untangle the
financial mess my father had left behind."

It was a sad bit of history. "When did you meet my father?"

"After the burial, I took to drinking, gaming, and whoring
in an attempt to assuage my guilt and blur the pain. I was well
on my way to killing myself when I ran, literally, into your
father coming out of a tavern. I was drunk and took offense
when he refused to apologize for what was my fault. When I
swung at him, he hit me in the jaw, hard, and I went out."

Brenna smiled. "My father is tough."

He nodded. "I woke up at his town house. Your parents

nursed me through days, maybe weeks, while my body cleared away the whiskey and ale, and my mind regained focus. Once I was sober, your father gave me a choice. Either I stop my destructive behavior or he'd dump me back where he found me and be done with the entire affair."

"Father can be forceful."

"I chose the first, and though there were dark times, your parents had faith. They watched over me and became two of my dearest friends."

Brenna could not remember him. Mother and Father must have kept him away from her and her brothers. Then, she was on the cusp of her first season and her mind was on young men. She would not have noticed if there had been a giraffe living in the study.

This story explained much about his closeness to her parents and why he'd been so guilt-ridden after he'd taken her innocence. "That is why you married me. You felt you betrayed them."

"I still do." He pulled his hand from hers. "I knew what I was doing that night in the inn. I could have stopped it. But you were so enticing, so lovely."

Brenna's expression softened. "Thank you for telling me this." She slid closer to him and leaned her head on his arm. "Soon we will revisit what we want for our own marriage. But first, we have a baby to welcome into the world."

The next three days tried Brenna's patience, as everything seemed to go awry. Her back hurt, food tasted bland, and Bethany seemed to take joy in wearing her most scandalous dresses and flirting outrageously with Richard. The wench knew Brenna was feeling large and unattractive, and it was her want to stand near Brenna, as if to show Richard the marked difference between them.

"Do not worry, dearest," Lucy said, during a moment after supper on the third day when Brenna was near tears. "You will soon be giving your husband a gift she cannot. His heir. He cares for you and barely gives her notice. She is a desperate and grasping woman, and it shows."

The comment was made to give comfort, but it fell flat when Bethany touched Richard's arm and leaned in, giving him a full view of her pushed-up cleavage.

From Brenna's point of view, she could not see whether he was taking advantage of the moment for a peek or keeping his attention on Bethany's face. All she knew was that she'd had enough of the woman flaunting herself before her husband. Heat burned up her neck to flame across her face.

She took one step forward, then two, ready to kill.

Without warning, a sharp pain doubled her over. She whimpered, the urge to wring Bethany's neck instantly forgotten. A second pain came, and she cried out.

"Brenna!" Lucy hurried over and took her by the elbow.

"It's the baby," Brenna said, struggling to keep on her feet. "I think the baby is coming!"

In a flash, Richard was at her side. "It's the baby," Lucy told him, and he swept Brenna into his arms.

"Send for the midwife and a messenger to the Harringtons in London," he ordered. "Get Mrs. Beal. She will know what to do."

Lucy hurried off to do his bidding. He raced from the room, weighted down by her swollen belly. "No arguments, love, I intend to carry you, and that is final."

Brenna winced as another pain came, and she gripped his coat. "It hurts too much to do anything but whimper." Her attempt at levity failed when another pain gripped her.

"Richard, it hurts."

"I know, love." Once he got to her room, he paused, then continued down the hallway to his bedroom. "The baby will be born here."

"A footman has been sent for the midwife," Lucy said, arriving on their heels. "We need to get her out of her gown."

By the time Richard and Lucy got her undressed and into a nightdress, Mrs. Beal had come in, several maids in tow, each carrying the supplies needed for the birth. She directed two of the girls to smooth out a thick pad on the bed to protect the mattress, and Richard helped Brenna into bed.

"With a first baby, it will be some time before he or she makes an appearance," Mrs. Beal said, and tucked Brenna under a warm blanket. "The pains will be irregular, then come more frequently as the birth progresses."

While the women flittered around, Brenna pulled Richard down on the bed beside her. He clasped her hands in his.

"We are having a baby," she said softly, her eyes welling up. She was soon to be a mother. "The idea both thrills and terrifies me."

"From what I understand, pregnancy does usually end with the arrival of a baby," he teased. His eyes did not match his jest. There was deep worry in the blue depths.

Brenna reached up to circle his neck. She pulled him down until they were eye to eye. "I vow to give you a healthy baby, my husband. You'll see."

He nodded and cupped her face. "I'll keep you to that promise." He leaned to kiss her forehead.

Brenna touched her forehead to his and smiled weakly. "If you do not come up with names soon, we shall have to settle for Nettle or Newlin."

Shaking his head, Richard grimaced. "I am not needed here, so I shall go downstairs and start a list before my son or daughter is forever cursed with either of those monikers."

Through the whirl of activity, Brenna watched him go. Lucy took his place on the bed. "I have to give him this child," Brenna said softly. "If I lose the baby, our marriage will not survive."

"Do not be so sour," Lucy said, frowning. "This is a joyous day. You will look on it as such."

Brenna nodded. "You are right. I am about to be a mother. What a change a few months has made in my life."

Even as hope rose in her breast, her stomach tightened, and she slid her hand over the place just as another pain ripped through her. Her future rested on these next few hours.

Chapter Twenty-six

❧

Richard paced. When he wasn't pacing, he was walking to the doorway and looking up the stairs. A flurry of activity sounded from above. Birthing was women's work. Men were banned to their brandy. . . and pacing.

After several visits with Brenna, and his many questions concerning the birth and Brenna's condition, the housekeeper finally shooed him from the room.

"Go now before you fray my lady's nerves," Mrs. Beal scolded. "She cannot worry about you worrying."

He wanted to fall into the brandy and allow it to soothe him, but thought it best if he got through the evening with a clear head. He wanted to be helpful to Brenna should a need arise.

Now that he pondered the decision, he was not convinced it was the wisest choice.

"If anything happens to Brenna and the baby—" he mumbled to himself. He cupped his hands behind his neck and looked down. He must think positive thoughts.

"Lady Brenna will be fine," Miriam replied.

Richard looked around, not realizing she was standing at his elbow. She placed a hand on his arm.

"The child will come in due time," she assured him. "Soon you will have your heir."

He looked for something—jealousy, envy, anger—in her

face but found only compassion. Since discovering a killer may be in the park, he was suspicious of everyone. It pleased him to see nothing calculating in her expression. Unless she was an accomplished actress, Miriam was truly happy for him.

"Yes. I guess you are right."

Hours passed with the loud clicks of the clock. Lucy came down at intervals to assure him that all was well.

"You might need to replace your rug," she teased, pointing down at the scuffed fabric beneath his feet. Without waiting for a reply, she added, "Brenna would like to see you."

When Richard stepped over the bedroom threshold, he noticed that the room had been cleared of all unnecessary maids, and the midwife was standing off to the side, conversing quietly with Mrs. Beal. Brenna lay on the bed, her hair damp and matted, her face flushed.

His heart skipped. She gave him a small smile as he sat beside her. "The babe has your stubborn nature. He's making us wait until he is ready. He cares not what I wish."

"Then you are well?"

Brenna nodded. "I've told you that we Irish are made of stern stock. We'll give birth in a field and go right back to plowing soon after." In spite of her obvious pain, her eyes danced. "And have supper ready that evening."

He forced a light tone. "Perhaps, then, I should have a plow brought around if you think it will hurry things along."

Despite her confidence, she looked frail, exhausted.

"Ask me again in a few hours," she said. "I might take you up on—oh!" She let out a mewling cry. Richard had no time to react to her suffering when Mrs. Beal ushered him back out into the hallway.

"It shouldn't be long now, My Lord," she assured him, and slipped back inside the room.

Richard managed, somehow, to make it halfway down the stairs when the front door banged open and a woman, resplendent in a rose hat and gown, blew in with the wind.

"Where is my daughter?" Kathleen demanded, giving Joseph only enough time to catch her hat and cloak up against his chest, when she was off again.

The butler pointed up. She shot Richard a quick smile as she passed him on the staircase and was gone.

He turned to find Walter removing his silk top hat. "We were at a party when we got word. She did not even stop at home to change. I assume our luggage will arrive sometime tomorrow."

Richard joined him.

Walter shucked off his overcoat, looked him over, and clamped a hand down on his shoulder. "Point me to the brandy, my friend. I think we can both use one."

B renna tried to be brave but lost the battle sometime near dawn, when the pushing began in earnest. She cried out with each pain and gripped her mother's hand, certain she was about to be torn asunder.

"That's it, darling," Mother said. "The babe is coming."

Lucy dabbed her damp forehead with a cloth and brushed back her hair. "You are so brave."

"Push!" the midwife commanded. She pushed. "Push again!"

Brenna gritted her teeth and pushed. A scream tore from her, and the room whirled. She slumped back against the pillows, the world going gray.

"It's a boy," Lucy exclaimed. Then, "Oh, dear. I think she's fainted."

Mother leaned over her. "Brenna? Brenna?"

Slowly, the fog dissipated as Brenna roused with a lusty baby cry filling the room. Clarity slowly worked its way into her exhausted mind. Relief filled her with warmth to her toes. "I have a son?" she asked, awed.

"A beautiful son." Mother smiled. She smoothed Brenna's damp hair out of her face. "Your husband will be pleased."

Brenna sighed and closed her eyes. "I told him we would be fine." Then the room went black.

R ichard rushed to the doorway as the robust cry of a babe sounded overhead. His knees went weak. The doorframe, and sheer determination, kept him upright.

"Go to her," Walter urged, and Richard needed no further encouragement. He took the stairs two at a time.

The hallway was filled with maids, who stepped aside as he approached. Words of congratulations barely registered in his mind. Unsure of the protocol for husbands, he paused just inside the doorway to take stock of the scene. He could not see Brenna on the bed, but Kathleen caught sight of him and walked over, a wrapped bundle in her arms.

"You have a son, Richard." She tipped the baby so he could get a glimpse of the tiny red face beneath a thin patch of black hair. She cooed and rocked him. "You sure did take your time, young man."

"And Brenna?" Richard asked.

"She fainted, but she is fine." Kathleen stepped out of the way, and Richard walked past her.

Brenna was pale but breathing softly as he approached. Mrs. Beal smiled. "She worked very hard, our Lady Brenna did," she said. "She is resting."

Richard nodded. He watched her breathe for several minutes, relief filling him to his bones. Months of worry had come to naught. Brenna and their son had survived.

From behind him, he heard Mrs. Beal chase the maids off and Kathleen thank the midwife for her efforts.

The room went quiet. So intent was he to watch her sleep, it took a moment to realize she was awake and peering at him through laden eyelids.

"Did you see him?" she asked softly.

"I did."

"I understand he is quite handsome."

"He resembles me," he said, and was rewarded with a weak smile. It took his breath. "Well done, Wife."

Their eyes met and held. She lifted her face, and Richard did not hesitate. He lowered his mouth and brushed his lips over hers. Her sweet taste infused him.

"Thank you for my son."

"You're welcome," she replied.

Kathleen walked over, and between he and Lucy, they helped Brenna get into position to hold the baby. Once he was snuggled against her, she stared at him, overwhelmed with emotion.

"His head is oddly shaped," Brenna noted, as it seemed a bit elongated. She looked up in alarm.

"Yours was the same," Kathleen remarked. "That often happens. It will be round and perfect in a few days."

Brenna relaxed back. She brushed her fingertip over his cheek and across his bottom lip. He opened his mouth.

"He's hungry," Lucy said. She leaned over for a better look. The baby scrunched up his face and let out a cry.

"I shall leave you now." Richard ran his hand over his son's soft head. "Later we will have to decide what to name him. I was thinking Horace."

Brenna grinned. "You, Husband, will think again."

James Richard Ellerby became the focus of the household from the moment his father presented him to the staff. Brenna stayed abed for a week after his birth, and then a second week to make certain all was well. She was pampered by everyone as she recovered her strength.

"He will be spoiled if this does not come to an end," Brenna said, her eyes on the stack of gifts from both family and neighbors alike. "He is barely two weeks old, and already he is being treated like a prince. Noble arrogance will soon follow."

Richard placed James into his crib and turned to Brenna. For a moment, she thought of pulling up her gown, as it was askew from nursing their son, but decided to leave her bodice hanging low. In a few weeks, she would be able to resume her life normally, and the first thing on her list was to work diligently on getting her marriage in order. Though Richard had not mentioned her return to London in weeks, she knew he expected her to do so in good time.

He would have to rethink this. She was going nowhere.

The social whirl of London no longer intrigued her. She was a mother now. Though she knew they would spend time visiting her family in town, she had not expected to find contentment in the country . . . with the sheep.

"Is there something remiss about noble arrogance?" Richard asked. "It has suited me well."

He was casually dressed in his breeches and open-necked shirt, his boots polished and gleaming. She liked him best like this, when his hair was askew from sleep and his face softened from spending the hours before breakfast alone with her and James.

"Certainly not," she reassured him. She pushed up from the bed and walked to the crib. James was sleeping. She turned to Richard and laid her palm flat on his chest. "If he grows up like you, I will be content. Now go. I have to change."

As if on cue, Agnes arrived to assist.

Richard seemed reluctant to leave them but gave a slight bow and left. It heartened Brenna to know that Richard adored his son. She hoped the fatherly devotion would make it harder for him to see them go.

"Will you choose the blue or the pink today, Milady?" Agnes asked, as she dug through the wardrobe.

Brenna mumbled something, as her mind was elsewhere.

Always polite, Richard allowed her a light kiss now and again, but nothing more. He spent time with her, talking about the weather, farming, the goings-on in London, but nothing personal. Her frustration welled with each passing day, despite Lucy's assurances that he was not as indifferent as he appeared.

"There you are." Lucy glided in, her pleasant personality lighting the room like morning sunshine. She'd gone through bouts of gloom after losing her husband so tragically. However, she was back to her old self again, and Brenna was happy she'd chosen to stay on, for now, rather than return to London for another matching. "What is on the schedule for today? Lying about eating chocolates? Fittings with the dressmaker? Needlepoint?"

"None of those things." Brenna looked to the window, where the cloudy sky had just a hint of sunshine breaking through, and another activity came to mind. She called for Agnes to get out a walking dress. "The physician has declared me fit, and I have decided to begin a regimen of walking; brisk walking, each morning that the weather allows. And when I am allowed to ride again, I will do that, too." She moved over to the crib and leaned to kiss James's downy head. "I ate far too many sweets over the last months, and my backside is as wide as a coach."

"Nonsense, though you did keep the kitchen busy," Lucy teased, and watched Agnes pull a yellow walking dress over

Brenna's head. "Still, you are almost as trim as you were before the babe. It should not be long before you are in top form."

Brenna waited to reply until she was laced into her dress and Agnes sent off to fetch the nanny. She whispered so Agnes could not hear her next comment. "Then I will be ready to seduce my husband."

Lucy nodded, and they shared a conspiratorial glance. "That Bethany is certainly forward. With any other man, she'd have already been taken up on her blatant offer for a romp. Thankfully, His Lordship has his eyes elsewhere."

Reaching for her bonnet, Brenna said, "Then let us get our breakfast and start the morning with a stroll around the park. The fresh air is calling."

O ver the next few weeks, Brenna walked with her mother and Lucy, and after her parents returned to London, she and Lucy kept up their walks, occasionally adding in a ride. Lucy was only a fair rider, and Brenna was ordered by Richard not to overdo, so they kept their rides sedate. Still, Brenna longed to race around the park and decided one early morning to sneak out before breakfast to do just that.

She fed James, and Agnes put her in a dark blue riding habit. She tiptoed down the stairs and slipped out of the house. The morning was damp from an overnight rain, and a slight haze clung to the lowlands. She inhaled the damp air, smiling to herself and eager for her ride.

The groom startled as she arrived at the stable, rubbing his hand over his unshaven face. "Milady?"

"Good morning, Carl." She strolled past the sleepy man, down to the stall where Brontes was finishing her breakfast. "I would like to take Brontes out. Could you saddle her for me, please?"

"Aye, Milady." He hurried to do her bidding. A quick brush and a few minutes to get Brontes saddled, and the mare was ready. "I will rouse Elliott to ride with you."

"That will not be necessary. I know the way."

Carl stood, clearly uncertain, before nodding. "Aye, Milady."

He moved to help her mount, and they rode toward the rose and orange sunrise.

Brenna waited until they were out of sight of the stable, so as not to alarm the groom, before nudging Brontes into a run. The mare was as eager as she to stretch her muscles and raced down the path toward the woodland at the back of the property.

Laughing with the sheer joy of the ride, Brenna let Brontes have her head, and the mare did not disappoint. Soon they were both breathless from the effort.

Finally slowing the mare, Brenna leaned over and scratched her gloved hand over Brontes's sleek neck. "You are such a beautiful girl. Yes, you are."

She continued to fuss over the horse, their shared affection showing. Brontes had been a gift from her parents some years ago, and Brenna was fond of the steed.

Once they both had a chance to rest, Brenna leaned up and nudged the mare forward. She wanted to return before breakfast.

A flash of something bright near the woods caught her attention. By the time she was able to focus, it was gone. But she was fairly positive what she'd seen was a flash of fabric from a gown. A woman was in the woods.

"That is odd." It was far too early for a stroll, and they were quite a distance from the manor to make it reasonable for someone from the household to be out this far.

She glanced around for signs of a horse. There was nothing to indicate another rider had come this way.

After a brief hesitation, she nudged Brontes forward. Her heart beat loudly in her ears. From Jace's warning of a killer, and the visit the day after the party from the Bow Street Runners, she knew that she needed to be cautious when settling her curiosity.

As they neared the trees, Brontes paused, her ears alert. Brenna tapped her heels, but the horse was unwilling to go forward. Brenna peered into the trees, watching for danger.

"Is anyone there?" she called out.

Silence met her call. She waited for a moment for any signs of a woman in distress, then turned Brontes around and headed back to the manor.

An hour later, changed into a clean blue day dress, Brenna walked into the breakfast room, the troubling morning still vividly fresh in her mind. She kept the encounter to herself until she could get Richard alone. They ate. After, she followed him out into the hall and took him aside. She quickly explained what she'd seen.

"I am not entirely certain it was a woman," she said. "I did not see more than a flash of color. My eyes may have tricked me."

"You said your horse reacted when you went near the trees?"

"She did. She has been in the woods before, when Lucy and I ride, and has never hesitated. I did find that disturbing."

Richard crossed his arms. "I've found that horses have a keen sense of self-preservation. If Brontes was fearful, then something was amiss." He scanned her face. "I will see that the woods are thoroughly checked and think you should stay clear of them for now when you ride. If you intend to wander the park, do so with Lucy and a groom."

The idea of not riding pell-mell over the grounds was a crushing disappointment. Richard must have read regret in her eyes.

"If you want a heartier ride, I'll go with you."

Brenna took a happy step forward. She pressed a kiss on his cheek. "Thank you, Richard."

For an instant, she felt his hands on her hips, his fingers tightening, and then they were gone. She managed to hide a look of pure feminine satisfaction after garnering an instinctive reaction from him, no matter how brief.

Perhaps Lucy was right. He was not as indifferent as he appeared. Though she'd taken up residence in his bed since the birth, and he'd moved into her vacated room, they were still separated by the sitting room. Soon, she'd launch a war on his senses, and the battle to return to his bed would be won.

Chapter Twenty-seven

Richard watched Brenna walk away, the sway of her hips drawing his eyes and stirring a part of him that he tried to ignore.

Motherhood did not detract from her beauty. In fact, her new curves enticed him almost to the point of madness. If not for the cold baths, he would have already succumbed to his baser needs and taken her wherever and whenever he pleased.

It was getting impossible to resist her pull.

He knew it was his right to take her to bed. It had been he who wanted a marriage of convenience. But he knew that in spite of her current contentment with motherhood and Beckwith Hall, eventually her youth would crave more excitement than he could give her.

And once they shared a bed, it would be impossible to let her go. Eventually, she'd grow to hate him, feeling trapped here, and any chance of a comfortable existence between them would be gone.

Once again settled into the notion of not seducing his wife, he set off for the stable. Gathering up some men on horseback, they headed off for the woodland.

When they reached the area Brenna had indicated, the only hoof prints he saw were one set, Brontes's. There was no sign of anyone else. He wanted to believe that Brenna was correct and the flash of color was a trick of her eyes, but in the back of his mind, he could not dismiss the reaction of the horse.

Animals had a keen sense of danger.

"Spread out," he said, and the half dozen men dismounted. "Look for anything untoward. If you find clues that someone has been here, collect what you find and bring it to me."

It took over an hour to cover the acreage and for Richard to be reassured that if someone had been there, they were gone. It was when he stepped out of the trees on the far side of the forest that the investigation changed.

In the still-dewy grass was a clear set of hoof prints. As he followed them back toward the trees, he discovered something more disturbing: two sets of boot prints, one several sizes smaller than the other.

The clues had all the trappings of a lovers' tryst.

Looking around, he followed the path of the footprints, heading off in the direction of the distant road. He should be relieved not to find evidence of trespassers living on his property. However, they were so isolated here that he found it odd that someone would come all this way for a tryst. The next closest neighbor was several miles away.

The groom, Carl, joined him. "I see you've found your evidence," he said, noting the boot prints. "Your Ladyship did see something."

"She did indeed," Richard said. "Unfortunately, I have no idea what to make of it. It appears that someone was meeting here, though I have no idea why."

"It's a puzzle." Carl shook his head.

Richard had to agree. "Ask two of the men to follow the tracks to make sure they end up at the road. I want to make certain whoever was here is gone."

"Aye, Milord."

With one last look around him, Richard headed back up the wooded path toward his horse, his mind troubled. He did not want to make a fuss over something that may just be two lovers seeking privacy. Perhaps one or both were married, and his property was far enough away from wherever they were from to make discovery impossible.

Or it was someone from his household, up to mischief

perhaps, as he was well aware that at least two of the house-maids were involved with other members of his staff: a footman and one of the grooms.

It was unlikely that any clandestine relationships would require such secrecy. He was not against his servants courting and marrying, as long as it did not interfere with their employment.

A level of concern kept him from finding peace that the matter was concluded. It was time to take precautions.

T here were two sets of footprints on the far side of the forest, those of a woman and a man," Richard said, when he met Brenna in the foyer holding the baby. "Unfortunately, there is no indication of the identity of the trespassers."

"So my eyes were not playing tricks." The news pleased her. "Let us hope the pair decides to tryst elsewhere. We have enough worries keeping our maids safe."

Jace had gone off to meet with his Bow Street Runner friend, and Richard had learned that the Runners had spoken to his neighbors. This alerted the citizenry to watch for strangers and to keep their women close.

James yawned. "I think your son needs a nap," Brenna said. "I shall take him up." She smiled and walked away, certain she felt Richard's eyes follow her. In case she was right, she added just a little extra sway to her hips. Why waste a moment to entice her husband?

Brenna felt a sniffle coming on during supper, and by the time she awoke the next day, her muscles ached and her head felt stuffed with fluff. Weakened, all she could do was tend to the baby and sleep. By the second night, Nanny had taken over much of James's care, even taking him into the nursery at night so Brenna could sleep. Nanny only returned him for nighttime feedings, for which Brenna was grateful.

For three days, Brenna stayed abed, sipping broth and wallowing in her misery. It was late into the evening on the third night when Richard came in to check on her one last time before bed.

"I am fine," she assured him. "My head has cleared, and my strength has returned. I should be quite fit in the morning."

She glanced at the crib. "I look forward to getting our son back. I miss him when he isn't here—"

A shriek broke the night. Then a second. Brenna untangled herself from the coverlet and came to her feet.

Screams came from overhead.

"Richard, the baby!" Brenna cried, as she darted after him and up the stairs. They met several servants in nightclothes as they breached the upper floor and raced to the nursery. They found Nanny in her cotton nightdress, hysterical, cuddling the baby against her ample bosom.

"I saw someone, Milady," she said, sobbing, only outdone by the cries of her charge. Brenna rushed over to take him and spoke in low soothing tones. Richard took Nanny by the arms and gave her a gentle shake to stop her sobs.

"What happened?" he demanded. "Who did you see?"

"A man," she said, pointing toward the crib. "He was leaning over the little master."

Brenna gasped. She began a thorough search of her son, relieved to find he'd not been harmed. After a moment, he settled from crying to hiccups.

"Are you certain you saw someone?" Richard pressed. He released her and walked over to put an arm around Brenna. He stared down at James. "Could it have been a dream?"

"No, Milord," she said. "When I screamed, he ran out. I heard his footsteps. It was no dream."

"Did you recognize him?" Brenna asked.

"It was dark," Nanny said. "But I am certain I did not know him. I think he was a housebreaker."

Richard turned to the footmen standing in the open doorway. "Search the house."

The men hurried off. Richard touched Brenna's face and followed the footmen out.

Mrs. Beal arrived wrapped in a dressing gown. Brenna quickly explained the situation. After she assured herself that the baby was fine, she took the shaking nanny into her arms.

"There, there. You saved little master," Mrs. Beal said softly. "You have done well, Mary."

Nanny brushed tears from her face. "I could not let him harm the baby. He is such a sweet little love."

Brenna walked to them and held out her hand. Nanny took

it. "You showed your loyalty to my son tonight, possibly at your own peril. For that I will always be grateful."

There was a commotion in the hallway. George, Miriam, and Bethany appeared. George stepped forward, his shirttails hanging untucked, as he'd hastily dressed.

"What has happened?" he asked.

"A stranger was in the nursery with the baby," Brenna said. She snuggled James against her shoulder. "Nanny scared him off."

George went white. "A stranger?"

At her nod, he looked down at the bundled baby. "Why would anyone want to do such a thing?"

Brenna did not realize how much their guest had grown fond of her son. She touched his arm. "He is fine. I think I will take him to my room now. He needs quiet."

Once in her room, Lucy joined her, having awakened late to the excitement. Brenna told the tale, and the two women stood on either side of the crib and cooed over the brave little boy.

"If His Lordship finds the culprit, he needs to be thrown into Newgate and the key tossed out," Lucy said. She made a silly face at James, who kicked his feet, obviously recovered from his distress. "He deserves nothing less."

Tucking a blanket around him, Brenna sighed. "First there were people in the forest, and now a stranger has broken into the house. I'm terribly worried. Could one of them be a killer?"

Lucy met her gaze. "Please do not distress yourself." She paused, and her expression softened. "His Lordship will not let anything happen to you or the baby."

Do you think we are in danger?" Bethany asked, her voice trembling. She clutched her robe around her and watched the footmen head for the upper floor.

Richard had no clear answer. "I don't know what to think," he said honestly. "There is no reason for this madness." He skimmed his eyes over her face and then glanced at Miriam, who was standing a few feet away, next to George. Both women were worried, as they all were. "From the pranks against Brenna last year to the carriage accident and tree fire, and now the happenings this week, it's difficult to know the mind of this culprit."

Bethany glanced away. This convinced Richard of her guilt for the pranks.

"Certainly you cannot think the same person is responsible for all this?" Miriam asked. She clutched her robe closed at the neck. "That would mean someone has been sneaking into the house for months."

"I do not think so," Richard said. "The man in the nursery, and the other incidents, are at a higher level of mischief than moving things around to harass my wife."

The two women shared a glance. Miriam, too?

He wanted to shake them both. However, without proof, they would deny their guilt. And since the pranks ended months ago, he had more pressing matters to worry him. He believed the person who snuck into the house could very well be dangerous.

George placed a hand on his sister's shoulder. "I should join the footmen," he said, and walked away.

"Is there anything we can do?" Miriam stepped closer to Bethany. They clasped hands.

"Go to your rooms and lock your doors," Richard replied. "Do not open up unless you know who is knocking."

Nodding, they hurried off. Richard watched as they made their way down the hall. Miriam was almost to her door when something odd caught his eye. The hem of her nightdress was damp and slightly soiled.

The only explanation for that condition was if she had been out wandering the dew-covered grounds.

A feeling of dread crept through him. Could she be the woman in the forest? Did she have a lover?

He wanted to dismiss the idea. Meek and shy Miriam was not the bold sort of woman who would tryst in the darkness with a lover. Or was she?

Could he answer that definitively? She'd lived in his house for almost three years, but how much had he really paid attention to her comings and goings? Next to the opulent Bethany, she faded into the background. If there was something to be learned about his houseguest, it was time he found out what.

Tomorrow, he'd get answers. Tonight, they had a house-breaker to find. Richard went to join the hunt.

The entire house was searched, from the lowest level to the attic above. Not a nook or corner, a bed or a wardrobe was missed. Whoever had invaded his household had made his escape.

Richard ordered every window and door to be locked, then sent the staff off to bed. Frustrated, he finally walked with heavy footfalls back to his room, to Brenna and his son.

The room was lit with firelight and one candle. He locked both the hallway and the sitting-room doors. In the dim light, he could see James sleeping peacefully in his crib and Brenna curled up on the bed.

Her eyes were closed, and her cheeks were tear streaked. Evidently, she'd cried herself to sleep.

His heart tugged. Brenna was a woman who could face down nearly any adversary and come out the victor. She would kill to keep their son from harm. But when it came down to the frightening events of this evening, she was still a mother first and terrified for the welfare of her child.

Richard glanced to the chair and back down at his wife. Without hesitation, he climbed in next to her on the bed and wrapped her snuggly in his arms.

And spent the rest of the evening alert for danger.

Chapter Twenty-eight

❦

Brenna awoke to her son fussing and her husband asleep beside her. She went to James and fed him. It was still dark outside, and she heard a light patter of rain on the window glass. Another damp day was ahead.

Thankfully, once his belly was full, the baby fell back to sleep. She returned him to his crib and stoked the fire.

Unable to resist the pull of her husband's warmth, she quickly climbed back under the coverlet and snuggled close. If not for her daily responsibilities, she'd be content to stay hidden away with Richard and James all day.

"Your feet are cold," Richard grumbled, when she worked her feet under his breeches-clad legs.

"I was feeding your son," she said. "Surely you cannot begrudge me a bit of warmth on this stormy morning."

He opened his eyelids just enough to frown before twisting her legs with his. Brenna let out a happy sound. Her toes started to warm up.

"Thank you, Richard." The feeling of rightness lying beside him was not lost on her, and she hoped he felt the same. But she'd not press the issue for fear of running him off. Wanting to bed her and loving her were two difference issues. And she'd not be satisfied until she had both.

"Did you find any sign of the housebreaker?" she asked softly, so as not to wake James.

"We did not. Nanny's screams sent him fleeing the house."

"That is disappointing." She stared into the fire. "What can you do next?"

"I will post guards and send for Jones. From our conversations, I learned that he has an investigative background of his own. We need to take the story of the dead maids seriously. We can no longer dismiss his concerns. The killer may be here."

Brenna pushed up onto her elbows. Her stomach knotted. "You cannot think those crimes are connected to our housebreaker?"

"It cannot be ruled out," Richard said. "A torn piece of your writing paper was found under the body in London. I am not one to believe in coincidences. Whoever killed that girl is connected to you through the killing, either by accident or by design. The question remains, why?"

"Yes, why?" Brenna echoed. She glanced at the crib.

"James will be carefully guarded," Richard assured her. "When he is not with us, Nanny and a footman will be watching him. There will not be a repeat of last night."

She took some comfort in his words and tried to hold back her fear of the unknown culprit. "It terrifies me to think the housebreaker might also be a killer. Had Nanny not awoken and screamed—" She could not finish the thought.

Richard pressed his mouth to her temple. "Fretting over what did not happen will make you ill, love. James is safe."

"I know you are right." She reached deep for strength. They faced a faceless foe. Richard needed her to be strong. "Nanny made a formidable guard. The housebreaker is lucky to have escaped uninjured."

"He is, indeed." Richard kissed her head, then rolled from the bed. He padded barefoot to the window. "I want to ride the property this morning to look for clues the housebreaker may have left behind." He leaned to peer up at the sky. "Excellent. The rain has abated."

"I am coming with you." Brenna kicked off the coverlet and gained her feet. The cold floor made her hesitate, but only for a moment. Chilled feet were not worth crawling back into bed. She wanted to help catch the culprit.

"You will stay here with James."

She ignored his command, went to the wardrobe, and pulled out a habit in dark green. "Our son might have been kidnapped. I'll not sit by and let some evildoer threaten my family. I will ride with you. Two pairs of eyes are better for searching."

"Will it help me to argue?"

She glanced sidelong. "It will not. However, if you want to assist, you can call for Agnes to help me dress and for Nanny and the footman to watch the baby. Then I shall be ready posthaste."

Muttering under his breath, Richard pulled the bell cord. Soon both husband and wife were dressed and ready.

Brontes and Richard's gelding were brought around. James was in safe care, so Brenna focused on the mission ahead. She and Richard rode the perimeter of the manor, finding nothing in the wet grass. Any boot prints had been washed away.

They expanded the search in a wider circle. Brenna went one way and Richard the other. They met near the garden.

"Nothing," Brenna said.

"You check the south pond, and I'll follow the creek north," he said, turning his horse about.

Brenna followed the south path and rode around the pond. Disappointment welled over the lack of clues. She did a second cursory ride around the pond before giving up. She headed in Richard's direction. He was some distance from where he'd left her. She urged Brontes into a run to catch up. As she approached, he swung down from the gelding.

"There is a partial hoof print here in the mud." He touched the print and rolled wet soil between his fingers. "It's impossible to know how fresh it is. The rain damaged much of it. It could be days old."

"Or made last night," Brenna countered. She nudged Brontes closer. "If it was our housebreaker, it appears he went that way."

"I agree. We should check the forest." Richard urged his horse into a lope. Brenna followed. She kept her attention focused on the ground for hoof marks.

The forest gave up no obvious clues. Though a man could easily hide in the brambles, a horse would be exposed. And there was no sign of a horse as they peered through the trees.

Richard took off his hat and rubbed his forehead. "Next is the dower house. It has been locked for years. Still, if someone was determined to break the lock, it would not be difficult."

"I didn't know you had a dower house."

Richard led onward. "My mother would go there when Father slipped into one of his rages. She considered it her sanctuary. I closed it up after she died. I had no use for it."

Ten minutes later, the two-story cottage came into view. Set back in a small grove, Brenna could see that it had once been pretty, an ideal place for solitude. Though it still stood, it had fallen into disrepair. The weeds had taken over the small yard, and the roof looked ramshackle.

"Damn," Richard muttered, as he swung down from his horse. "I should have taken better care of the house."

He walked over to help Brenna down. "I suspect it was lovely when your mother came here. The stone is still in good condition. It wouldn't take much to fix it up."

"Hmm." Richard steered Brenna around a fallen tree. "I'll send workmen to make the repairs. We might want to use it someday."

Brenna thought it a perfect place for her and Richard to be alone. Someday when they had half a dozen children, they'd want somewhere to steal some privacy.

"The lock is broken." Richard cursed low and pushed the door open. The door squeaked on its hinges. They stepped gingerly over the threshold. There was no sign of wild animals.

"This house is surprisingly clean," Brenna remarked, and swiped her glove over the top of a narrow table. A minimal layer of dust clung to her fingertips.

"Hmm. Something is amiss." Richard walked through the house, Brenna behind him. He pushed open the door to a large bedroom and cursed. "It is as I suspected. Someone has recently used the cottage."

The bed was unmade, and a pair of candles stood on the bedside table. At the foot of the bed, half-eaten food lay on two plates, sitting on a tray next to a wineskin.

"I think we've found where our lovers meet." Brenna walked over to the tray. "The food is not old."

"We will post guards should they return and send maids to clean up this mess." He examined the room, taking care to look under the bed and anywhere clues might have been left. "Our trespassers were careful. Nothing personal was left behind."

Brenna touched his arm. "We will catch them, and our housebreaker. I am sure of it."

Richard stared down at the bed. Suspicion led in one direction. "I think I can name one of the lovers."

"Who?"

He looked down at her. "Miriam's nightdress was damp last night. I suspected she'd met someone outside the hall but have not had a chance to interview her today."

"Miriam?" Brenna shook her head. "Not Bethany?"

"I was just as puzzled as you. But there is no other reason for her to be wandering the grounds at night. Everyone was warned by the Runners to stay inside after dark. She'd not risk her safety unless she knew the party she was meeting."

This was a strange turn. Brenna tried and failed to imagine Miriam and her secret lover tangled together on these sheets.

"She'd not have the courage to venture out alone. You are correct; she must have met someone." Brenna glanced at the bed. "However, this cottage is quite a distance from the manor. It would take almost an hour to cover this much ground on foot."

"Unless he met her on horseback by the creek."

"That is possible," she agreed. "We only found that one print and assumed they'd gone back to the forest. Yet they could have veered west and come here."

Richard stared at her and smiled. "You have a very deductive mind, Wife. I wonder if I need to send for Jones at all. By the end of the week, you should have this case solved."

Brenna matched his smile. "We make a very good pair of investigators." She reached out and put her hand on his chest. He peered down at her hand, his eyes warming. When he did not step back, she became emboldened. What better place to steal a kiss, a real kiss, than an empty cottage?

"Kiss me, Richard." She gave him no time to protest. She

rose up onto her toes, gripped his coat lapels tightly in both fists, and pressed her mouth to his.

Any hesitation lasted no more than one breath. His arms came around her, locking her body against his. He groaned and plunged his tongue into her mouth. Brenna moaned in agreement.

The kiss was hot and deep. Brenna felt herself walked backward until her legs hit the dressing table. Richard picked her up and sat her on the surface, pressing himself between her legs. She pushed his coat off his shoulders as he tried to get his fingers around the lace at her bodice.

"Brenna," he breathed, tugging the laces open.

"Love me, please, Richard," she begged, breathless as he reclaimed her mouth.

A shout from outside tore them apart. "Milord! Milord!" Footsteps breached the cottage door.

Panicked, Brenna pulled her bodice together, and Richard quickly shucked back into his coat, where it hung at his elbows.

He turned and walked to the bedroom door, blocking her from view. She quickly put herself to rights.

"What is it, Carl?" He called out. The servant joined him.

"There is a body, Milord," Carl said, his breath coming in harsh gasps. "Down in the meadow near the sheep barn. It's a woman. She's been murdered."

Brenna's breath caught.

"Damn," Richard growled. Brenna tied her bow and hurried after the two men, who were halfway down the hallway. The three of them rushed from the house. Richard helped her onto the saddle, and they were off at a run.

"The shepherd's dog found her," Carl shouted, to be heard over the horses. "I knew you'd want to be contacted first. I followed your tracks to the dower house."

"Do you know who she is?" Richard asked.

"I do not," Carl replied. "She was dressed in nightclothes. She could be either a noblewoman or a servant."

A small crowd gathered in the meadow. Brenna did not wait to be assisted down but slid off Brontes. She could see the nearly nude woman lying on the grass.

Bile burned at the back of her throat, but she forced herself not to turn away.

"Stand back," Richard said, and she stopped. He walked to the woman. "Get something to cover her."

The shepherd went into the sheep barn and returned with a tattered blanket. When she was covered, all but her head, Richard waved Brenna over. She braced herself.

"Is she familiar to you?"

Brenna carefully examined her pale face. Her heart tugged for the loss of life.

There was a bruise under the young woman's eye and red marks on her neck. No question, it was not an accidental death.

"I am not certain. I may have seen her in the village." She walked around to look at the undamaged side of her face. "I'm certain now that I've seen her, but I cannot think where."

Richard nodded. "Get her back to the hall, and send men into the village—and to our neighbors—to see if anyone is missing."

"Yes, Milord."

Taking Brenna by the hand, Richard drew her away from the terrible scene. "We must find out who she is and return her to her family."

Nodding, Brenna put a hand over her mouth to quell her trembling lips. "How can someone be so evil? She did not deserve this."

He put his arm around her. "The killer will be punished. I will see to it, if I have to hang the bastard myself."

"Mister Jones has arrived, Milord." Joseph stepped back and allowed Jace to pass him and move into the parlor, where Richard, Brenna, and Lucy sat. Richard rose from his chair. Behind Jace came another man, similarly dressed in serviceable clothes and half a head taller. His pleasing features were framed with black hair.

Both men were grim faced.

Jace introduced his companion. "Mister Freemont is my friend and former Bow Street Runner. You may have met him when the Runners came after finding the note. As of three days ago, he now works for me."

"Of course," Brenna said. He did look familiar, but the day had been chaotic.

Brenna introduced Lucy to the men. After the brief introductions, Jace got to business. "I understand you've found a body," he said, with a harsh sigh. "Was she a maid?"

Richard went to pour port for the men. "We aren't certain. She was in a simple nightdress. I have sent my men to ask around for missing women. If she is from here, we should know her identity soon."

He handed out the drinks and briefly explained the morning's events, including the findings at the dower house.

"She may have met her killer there, or the two are not connected. It seems as though every time we go in one direction, the path veers in another."

Jace paced. "It is odd that you found her that far away from any house. The killer either lured her to the sheep barn or brought her body with him and dumped her there."

"The next house is nearly three miles to the east," Richard said. "That is too far to travel afoot at night. Also, she would have to know my property to find the sheep barn without assistance. It is not within sight of the hall."

"Then we can rule out her being lured," Mister Freemont said. "The killer placed her there."

"Is it possible that she is the woman I saw?" Brenna asked.

"That would explain why she may be familiar with the property," Richard replied. "If she's been meeting someone in the forest, and my dower house, then she would feel comfortable with her killer."

"Or the killer stumbled upon her as she was meeting her lover and took advantage of the situation," Lucy said, her eyes on the handsome Mister Freemont. "Though that would be an unfortunate and unlikely coincidence."

"True," Richard said. "The killer would have to have followed her or been lurking in just the right place."

"It's possible he saw her meeting her lover in the dower house, became intrigued with her, and waited for his chance to confront her," Jace offered.

"She did appear fair of face," Brenna offered.

"Or we can go back to the idea that he was her lover, became tired of her, and killed her," Richard said. "She would innocently follow him to her death."

"We can go on like this all night," Jace said, "and still come up with no answers."

"Excuse me, My Lord, but Lady Phillips is here," Joseph said, his expression tight. "She is missing a maid."

Richard nodded. "Send her in."

The Lady was somewhere near sixty, what most people would consider a handsome woman for her age, and very tall. She leaned on a cane as she entered the room.

"Lady Phillips. I wish we were meeting again under happier circumstances," Richard said. He took her elbow and led her over to Brenna, who stood. "This is my wife, Brenna, Lady Ashwood."

"A pleasure, Lady Phillips," Brenna said.

"I've heard much about the new Lady Ashwood." Lady Phillips accepted Brenna's hand. "A tragic business, our first meeting."

"It is," Brenna agreed. "So tragic."

They shared a moment of silence.

"Perhaps we should show Lady Phillips the girl," Richard said. "She is laid out in the upstairs parlor."

The party, save Lucy, filed out. Richard led the way to the parlor, and Lady Phillips walked over to the dead woman. She stared long into the young woman's face, then crossed herself. Brenna stepped up behind her and put a comforting hand on her shoulder.

"It's Clara," Lady Phillips said, and her voice caught.

Chapter Twenty-nine

"I met Clara when I was in Germany last month," Lady Phillips said, once they had returned downstairs and were seated. Her hands shook, rattling her teacup. "She spoke English and needed employment, so I brought her back with me. She was a good maid and a sweet-natured girl. I am sad to see her come to such a tragic end."

"Do you know if she had a beau, Milady?" Jace asked. "We believe she met with someone last evening."

Lady Phillips shook her head. "I am unaware of a beau, though she never talked of anything personal to me. I had a feeling her past was an unhappy one."

"Did she have anyone on your staff whom she was close to?" Richard pressed. He hoped someone knew Clara's secrets. "A close friend, perhaps?"

The elderly woman touched two fingertips to her lips. "She was very new to my household. I do not think she was close to anyone yet. She did go often to the village and may have met someone there. I could ask and send around a note if I discover anything of interest."

"That would be helpful," Jace said. He asked her a few more questions, but Lady Phillips had nothing new to add. Richard led her out and arranged for Clara to be returned to her.

Brenna excused herself and went in search of James. Lucy followed on her heels.

Once the men were alone, Richard slumped onto a chair. He faced Jace, who had claimed a second chair, and frowned. "I want to know everything you have on this investigation. Leave nothing out. A killer is loose, putting my family in danger."

Jace rubbed his chin. He glanced at Mister Freemont and back to Richard. "The Runners have offered little by way of additional information. Freemont is no longer privy to the investigation now that he is no longer working for them."

"Still, you do know something."

Nodding, Jace leaned forward. "I told you most of what I learned when I was here last. Dead maids, a tavern wench— similar deaths, and all were suspected of meeting lovers. It is the piece of writing paper that I just cannot figure out. At first I thought Lady Brenna might be targeted, but that makes no sense. All the other victims were servants."

"And Clara did not work for me," Richard added. "There is no connection between her and Beckwith Hall."

"Other than the fact she worked for your neighbor," Freemont said. "It is possible that the killer is a nobleman who moves among your social circle. It would give him access to homes and the servants. Perhaps he chooses one he likes, seduces her, and kills her."

Richard glanced at Jones. "Is that a plausible theory?" he asked. Jones nodded. "Someone who travels makes sense. The killings have been all over the country."

"Correct," Jace said. "Another theory is that the killer is a servant. Perhaps a footman or a coachman? He would also travel and be in closer contact with a household staff."

Wanting to believe that Brenna was safe, Richard couldn't be confident until the man was caught. "How would that tie into my housebreaker?"

"The incident might be just that; a common housebreaker broke in to steal jewels and accidentally stumbled into the nursery. It may not be tied to the killer at all."

"I want to believe that," Richard said. "However, my mind tells me otherwise."

By the glance the two men shared, Richard knew they

thought the same. Beckwith Hall was a peaceful place. Nothing untoward ever happened here.

Soon after Brenna arrived was when these strange happenings started. Though he did not think she was the cause, it was impossible to dismiss her involvement, even if indirectly.

He stared at Jones. What did he know about the man? He knew Brenna and her brother, but how? His involvement in this investigation had never been explained, other than that he'd worked for someone in London whose maid had been killed.

Suspicions pricked his mind. Could Jones be involved in the crimes himself? He was nearby when Clara was murdered.

Richard put his elbows on the chair arms and locked his fingers together. "You have certainly interjected yourself into this investigation, Mister Jones. What exactly is your profession, sir?"

Jones met and held his stare. For a minute, Richard wondered if he would answer. Clearly the man had secrets.

Then, Jones grinned, as if he could read the suspicion in Richard's thoughts. "I provide a service. Protection for certain, shall we say, individuals who have done things in their pasts that could bring danger to themselves or their families."

Protection? "You did not save the maid in London." Richard could not keep the irony out of his voice.

"She was not under my protection," Jones said, defensive. "The girl had a suitor in Cheapside, the butler of an elderly baron. She did not take care and often met him at night. It was late when she was returning home, after a visit, when she was killed in the mews, several houses down from my employer's town house." He twirled his glass and admitted, "It is my regret that I knew nothing of the danger she faced."

"And you do not think the murder was connected to your employer?" Richard pressed.

Jones shook his head. "The danger he faced had nothing to do with a killer of maids but political enemies."

Though Richard wanted to press for more information, by the set of Jones's jaw, he suspected the man would not be forthright with any further questions about his business. Discretion would be required from his employers.

If what Jones said about his profession were true, it was

unlikely he'd be wandering England killing women. Still, at this moment, Richard trusted no one. It was his connection to the Harrington family, and his knowledge of the case, that kept Richard from sending him away.

Jones was not finished. He leaned forward in his chair. "Truthfully, I'm irate about a murder taking place under my watch, and that the killer may be somehow connected to Brenna. Simon is my friend. I have to solve the case before anyone else dies, and for Brenna."

Finally, honesty. Richard stared at the man through narrowed lids. A similar goal connected them: to keep Brenna safe. He had to trust Jones.

"You and Mister Freemont are welcome to stay," Richard said. "The inn is too distant, and I prefer to have you here. Hopefully, your presence will deter the housebreaker from another trespass."

Nodding, Jones sat down his glass and stood. "We will start by asking questions of your staff. Someone may have seen something they did not think was important." He inclined his head toward the door, and Mister Freemont followed him out.

With the two men on the case and Brenna with the baby, Richard went to seek out Miriam. It was time to find out what she was doing wandering the grounds at night.

"Miss Miriam left right after the footman told us of the murder," Miriam's maid, Doris, said. "She dressed in a habit. I believe she was taking a horse into the village."

Richard gritted his teeth. He'd already put off this interrogation long enough. Now another delay loomed. He was tired of the games, the secrets, everything. As soon as the case was over, Bethany and Miriam would be sent home, something he should have done months ago.

"Did she indicate when she'd return?"

"No, Milord." Doris fluffed a pillow and placed it on the bed. "She said she may be late and would sup in the village."

When she returned, he'd be waiting. Lives were at risk. He'd shake answers out of her if he had to. The timid woman had secrets, and he'd ferret out each and every one.

He went to seek out Bethany. He found her in the library. She was standing at the window, looking out in the direction of the sheep barn. Dressed in blue, she made a pretty picture. He'd just never found her forwardness enticing.

"It is terrible what has happened," she said, and he realized she'd seen his reflection in the glass. "I cannot believe a killer is stalking Beckwith Hall."

"I am doing what I can to keep everyone safe," he assured her. "I think it best if you stay close to the house and do not travel into the village without a groom."

She turned. "I'm frightened, Richard." She hurried across the room and launched herself into his arms. Unprepared, Richard stumbled back and caught her against him to keep them both upright. "I'm pleased to know you will keep me protected."

"You, and everyone under my care." The strong scent of flowers whirled around her. There was nothing subtle about Bethany. Not even her perfume.

He suspected that she wasn't as frightened as she claimed. Her hands had somehow found their way under his coat, and one was settled just above his left buttock.

He tried to dislodge her, but she held tight.

"Hold me, Richard."

"Bethany." He managed to clutch her upper arms and push her back slightly. As he'd predicted, there was no terror in her eyes. In fact, she was smiling.

"I've imagined your embrace since the night of our kiss." She released him enough to run her hands up his chest and around his neck. "You want me as I want you." She lifted onto her toes and moved in for a kiss. He barely avoided contact by turning his head.

"Enough!" he said, and jerked free.

Her smile dissolved into a pout. "Why do you fight me, Richard? I know you are not sleeping with Brenna. If you came to my bed, I would not refuse you. You have to know of my love."

"Love? You jest." He held out a hand lest she launch another attack. "You love my fortune. That is not the same as loving me."

The smile faded. "How dare you accuse me of being a

fortune hunter? I have devoted nearly three years to loving you, and this is my repayment? You push me aside for that bitch you married? What does she possess that I do not?"

"Cease your prattle, woman," he commanded. "You tried to seduce me once and failed. It is time you found another wealthy man more receptive to your charms."

Her eyes flashed anger. "You are a bastard."

"I am Brenna's bastard."

She slapped him. Hard. "I despise you." She gathered her skirts and stalked from the room.

Richard sighed. Hopefully she'd be gone by nightfall. Hell, it was high time for Miriam and George to return home, too. He was no longer in danger of becoming a recluse, and their youthful antics had lost their ability to amuse him. This was Brenna's home now, for as long as she wanted to stay, and he'd put running the trio off long enough.

As soon as everyone was questioned in the case, he'd give them a week or two to gather their things and make other arrangements. He realized, then, that he was looking forward to having Beckwith Hall, and Brenna, all to himself.

Brenna's heart broke. To discover Richard in the library, locked in a lover's embrace with Bethany, was too much to bear. It was clear why he did not come to her bed. He was already finding his ease with another woman.

She brushed her tears away with the back of her hand.

Why had she thought he cared for her? How could she have been so foolish? How many times did he have to tell her theirs was a marriage in name only and that he'd never love her? Why had she not listened?

James was the reason he had not sent her away. He adored his son. She'd seen the way he looked at the boy. Someday, they would be inseparable.

She'd been nothing but James's mother to him. How fortunate for him that his seed had found fertile ground so easily. Otherwise, she'd still be in London, likely with their marriage annulled and married to someone else. And he'd be happily keeping company with Bethany here at the hall, having pushed aside all memories of her. Forever.

"Why so glum, Brenna?" Lucy asked, when she found her brooding in her sitting room.

"I found Richard and Bethany together, in the library." Tears welled again. "Embracing."

Lucy sat next to her on the settee. "You must be mistaken."

"I am not," Brenna said, her tears turning to anger. She swiped her face. "She was in his arms, and they acted like lovers. Her hand was on his bum."

"I cannot believe that," Lucy said. "He is mad for you. I've told you that a dozen times. He never so much as gives Bethany a second glance, even when she prances around him like an overheated bitch."

Brenna caught up a pillow to her chest and twisted it in her hands. "I know what I saw."

"I believe you. Yet there must be some explanation."

"Yes, and I know what it is," Brenna sniped. "He sees me as nothing more than the mother of his child. Any passion he once felt for me is gone. I am nothing but a frumpy broodmare, with none of Bethany's trim appeal."

Lucy shook her head. "You are as lovely as you ever were. Why would he choose that scrawny pigeon over you? He would not. I think he just needs to be reminded that you are seductive and passionate . . . and his wife. It is time he moves past his reservations and realizes you two are meant to be together, now and always."

"What about Bethany?" Brenna asked. "I hate him for betraying me."

Lucy stood and pulled Brenna to her feet. "Whatever you saw was Bethany's doing. She is a calculating bitch. She probably saw you in the hall and decided to torment you."

"I cannot be certain of that." Brenna wanted to believe Richard had not betrayed her. "Men have needs, and he is not slaking them with me."

"We will discover the truth easily enough." Lucy led her into Brenna's bedroom. She walked to the wardrobe and pulled out the rose ball gown with the tiny crystals on the bodice. She'd ordered the gown last month and had yet to wear it. The dress shimmered in the light. "You will wear this to the Pomerantz ball tomorrow night. You will flirt and dance with every handsome man assembled there. If His

Lordship is not insane with jealousy by evening's end, then you know his feelings are for Bethany alone."

Brenna fingered the cloth. It *was* a stunning gown. If this did not entice him, she'd turn to wearing sackcloth. "You truly think this will work?"

"If I am wrong about this, I will spend the next month emptying the hall's chamber pots myself." The two women locked gazes and screwed up their faces.

"Ick," Brenna said.

"Your husband had better prove me right," Lucy said, with a clipped laugh. "Or the next month will be miserable for me."

That evening, Brenna was cool to Richard and refused to explain why. Though she'd allowed Lucy to give her hope, she still could not be certain he was not sneaking into Bethany's room at night.

Bethany came down to supper in a sour mood. This was curious. She craved male attention. George's friends Clive and Lord Ponteby, who lived nearby, arrived to join them for supper. This would have normally put her in good spirits. Instead, she cast gloom over the evening. Since she'd met with Richard in the library, something had changed in her.

Brenna took some satisfaction in knowing the other woman was unhappy as she.

Friday came, and in spite of the murder, the ball went on. Brenna played with and fed James before returning him to Nanny.

Lucy helped Agnes dress Brenna, putting her own touches into place. She slid diamond clips in Brenna's upswept hair. Against her dark tresses, the clips sparkled.

"His Lordship will not take his eyes from you, Milady," Agnes said, smiling. "He will have to keep his guard up lest some young buck steals you away."

Nodding her agreement over the sentiment, Lucy handed Brenna her gloves. "You are stunning."

Once she was ready, Agnes left them to collect Brenna's cloak, to hide the dress from Richard. He would not see her in her full finery until the ball.

"I wish you were coming with me," Brenna said.

"I am still in mourning," Lucy replied. "Besides, you need to be alone with Lord Ashwood. You cannot entice him with me underfoot."

Brenna looked into the mirror, and her shoulders slumped. "I hope this helps me seduce my husband."

"It will." Lucy put her hands on Brenna's shoulders and turned her around. "As soon as the cloak comes off, he will spill himself in his trousers."

Chapter Thirty

❧

Brenna shot her a look meant to shame her, but Lucy only laughed and hugged her tight. "You are disgraceful."

"Disgraceful? Half the young bucks will have the same reaction when they see you," Lucy teased, and released her. "The other half will need stronger glasses."

"Clearly Miss Eva has more work to do with you before she can match you again," Brenna scolded, fighting her own urge to giggle. "You need to learn to curb your tongue, lest you get yourself into trouble."

Lucy waved a hand. "Posh. Life would be dull without women like me to make things lively."

Agnes returned, and Lucy took the cloak from her. She settled it around Brenna's shoulders. "Besides, I'm not certain I want to be matched again. I think I might want to match myself."

"Oh?" Brenna's brows went up. "Could a certain Mister Freemont be the reason for this change?"

Lucy's eyes lit up. She tried to shrug off Brenna's question, but her face gave her away. "He is handsome," she finally admitted. "But he is far too quiet. Unless he is speaking of thugs and murders, he has very little to say."

"He may be shy," Brenna offered.

"Perhaps. If not for his face and fine form, I would not give him a second glance. I do prefer a bolder fellow."

"Hmm." Brenna was certain there was more to Mister Freemont than Lucy saw. Any man who chased criminals and murderers as his profession was not timid. "I noticed you ignoring him at supper. Your indifference has worked in your favor. He has noticed you in return."

With a quick glance at Agnes, Lucy leaned in to whisper in Brenna's ear. "I did learn some tricks as a courtesan."

Brenna smiled. "If this gown and playing coquette tonight does not work for me, I think tomorrow you can begin my lessons on how to seduce my husband as a courtesan would."

They laughed, drawing Agnes's attention. She frowned as Lucy took Brenna's hand and pulled her from the room.

Richard waited at the bottom of the stairs, and Brenna's heart fluttered. He was dressed in gray trousers, a matching coat, a gray and white striped waistcoat, and a white shirt and cravat. He was so very handsome.

"You look lovely, Brenna," he said politely.

Irked, she held back her temper. She did not want polite. She was entirely sick of polite. She wanted him to toss her onto a dressing table, as he had in the dower house, and take her with sensual abandon—without the interruption this time.

"Thank you," she managed, with a placid smile. By the end of the evening, he'd be anything but polite. She planned to unleash the dangerous highwayman inside her staid husband.

"Shall we go?" Richard took her by the elbow and led her toward the door. She glanced over her shoulder and matched the wicked glance in Lucy's eyes.

"I cannot wait," she said, and watched Lucy cover her mouth with one hand. Brenna winked at her friend as Richard ushered her into the night.

The ball was in full bloom when they arrived, though the gaiety was somewhat tempered in deference to the murder. The house was lit with candles and decorated in silver and gold.

Mister and Mrs. Pomerantz welcomed them warmly. The

middle-aged couple had moved from Austria to England some years earlier, and Brenna had to listen closely in order to understand their heavily accented words. "Welcome to our home," Mrs. Pomerantz said, and took Brenna's hands. "We are happy you could come."

"Thank you for inviting us," Brenna said. "I seldom get out, with our son so young."

"Yes, you are a new mother," the hostess said. She squeezed Brenna's hands. "Congratulations to you and Lord Ashwood."

"Thank you," Brenna replied. Due to the crush of arriving guests, the footman was a bit late collecting her cloak. When he swept it off her shoulders, Brenna heard Richard suck in his breath. The dress shimmered in the candlelight.

She scored her first point.

"Your gown is beautiful, Lady Ashwood," Mrs. Pomerantz said, and glanced at Richard. "Your husband had better stay close. We have a wealth of young gentlemen in attendance tonight."

Several people lingered behind them, waiting for introductions, so Richard only had time to mutter, "I certainly will," as he led her away.

They weaved through the guests to a less crowded corner, and Richard faced her. "Isn't that gown a bit low in the bodice?"

Brenna glanced down at the full press of her breasts straining the limits of her corset. It was low, indeed. Still, the gown was entirely proper. "I think not. Several women we passed wore necklines much lower."

"I do not care about other women. You are my wife."

Glancing around, Brenna took note of the attention of several men. "I do not see anyone scandalized by my gown."

Richard followed her eyes and scowled. "Perhaps a maid can find you a shawl."

"You are being ridiculous," Brenna snapped. "I assure you that I will not fall out of my dress and shame us both. Now let us greet our neighbors."

Without waiting for his reply, Brenna headed off in the direction of Mrs. Turner, forcing Richard to follow. She stepped lively, knowing he was put out by the fact that there wasn't a single thing he could do about her dress.

"Good evening, Lady Ashwood," Ellard Smith said, as she passed. The gangly lad was barely out of the schoolroom.

"Good evening, Mister Smith."

"Good evening, Lady Ashwood," Lord Brighton said, his gaze falling well below her eyes.

"Good evening, Lord Brighton," she replied, fighting the urge to take him to task for his rudeness. She'd wanted Richard jealous. This sort of man fit perfectly into her plan.

On and on the greetings went, along the same vein, as Brenna walked across the room. When Richard finally caught her elbow, his grip was tight . . . and possessive. "You are causing a stir," he hissed.

She smiled brightly. "Truly? Then I have chosen my gown well." She stepped toward Mrs. Turner. She was dressed from head to hem in orange, with matching feathers in her hair.

"Good evening, Mrs. Turner. You look fetching tonight." She did not wait for Richard but took an open seat beside her friend. She indicated the packed ballroom. "Murder has not kept the guests home."

"Sad business, that," Mrs. Turner agreed. She looked up at Richard. "Would you mind getting us some punch, Richard?"

Clearly, he did not want to let Brenna out of his sight. But he could not be rude to Mrs. Turner. He bowed, frowned one last time at Brenna, and left.

"Your husband is in a sour state," Mrs. Turner said. She gave Brenna a look over. "He does not like your gown. He is the only man who doesn't."

Eyes widening, Brenna stared. Mrs. Turner shrugged. "I was not always an old woman. There was once a time when I wore things to shock my husband. Sometimes a man needs a reminder that his wife is still able to turn heads."

Brenna bit her lip. "He is angry."

"Let him be. His eyes will be on you all night."

Richard returned with the punch, managed several minutes of polite conversation with Mrs. Turner, then led Brenna away. They greeted friends and acquaintances, and he introduced her to several guests she had not yet met.

"Lady Brenna?" Brenna turned, and her heart skipped.

"Mister Everhart?" Her shock was genuine. After he'd

stolen that kiss and she'd slapped him, she'd hoped to never see him again. Clearly, she hadn't wished hard enough. "I am surprised to see you here. We are quite a distance from London."

"I am visiting my nephew, Clive." He bowed over her hand. His eyes bore into her, as if they shared a salacious secret. "He is staying with his friend Percy, Lord Ponteby. Of course, you know that. I understand that they are frequent guests in your home."

"Yes, they are." She broke contact with his eyes and turned to Richard. She introduced the men. They nodded.

"How do you know my wife?" Richard said. Brenna felt his tension. He was jealous of the handsome Mister Everhart.

"We met several times in London."

Everhart kept his tone even, but Brenna knew he was thinking of the kiss. His eyes were too heated for comfort. The cad.

"We danced," she said, by way of explanation. She wanted to drag Richard away from the man. However, to do so would raise her husband's curiosity. Though she did not have any reason to feel shamed or guilty, she did not think Richard would let the matter rest. He'd want to know every detail, and she did not want to discuss the unpleasant encounter.

"I hope you will save me a place on your dance card, Milady," Everhart said. "I do look forward to dancing with the loveliest woman at the ball."

He nodded and walked away. Brenna looked up at her husband and saw his jaw tick. "You have no reason to concern yourself about Mister Everhart, Husband. He is not the sort of man I'd wish to call friend."

"The man raises my suspicions," Richard said. "I think Jones should look into his past and what day he arrived."

It took a moment to see the path of his thoughts. "You cannot think Mister Everhart is the killer?"

Even as she protested, she realized the man could not be ruled out. She thought about how well she knew him, and there was not much. She'd heard that he enjoyed the company of women and had a reputation for taking what he wanted from ladies, at no consequence to himself.

At least two young women in the last three years had been

sent to the country, rumored to be carrying his child, though that was unconfirmed. They were both quickly married off soon after. Otherwise, she had not given him much notice before the unwelcome kiss.

"Do you know him well enough to vouch for his character?" Richard asked, his expression accusing.

His tone rankled. She gritted her teeth. "I only bedded him a dozen times after I discovered I was carrying your child. So other than his proclivities in bed, I know very little about the man."

With that, Brenna stomped off. She spent the next several hours dancing, flirting, and ignoring her husband—that, and keeping her dance partners' hands in appropriate places. Secretive glances Richard's way confirmed he was seething. She took immense satisfaction in his anger.

Despite his wish to dance with her, Everhart did not approach her. In fact, she did not see him again all evening. His nephew and friends, including George, were there, and each took a turn with her for country-dances. She did not waltz, fearing the intimacy of the dance would tweak Richard further.

As the evening pushed past midnight, her feet throbbed in her slippers. She decided to step outside to rest before moving on to the next man on her dance card.

Without a shawl, the night air chilled her skin. She walked down the terrace steps and into the garden. Finding a quiet spot with a bench, and well within screaming distance from the house, she sat, slipped off her slippers, and rubbed her feet. A small groan escaped her.

Disappointed in the outcome of the ball brought a frown. The torment of Richard seemed to have failed, and Brenna wanted to stay in the garden so as not to have to face him again.

Perhaps she should forgo the rest of the evening and ask to return home. Her feet would thank her, and her pride had taken enough of a battering for one night. The dress proved unsuccessful. Nothing could rouse her husband to grand passion.

"Waiting for your lover, Wife?"

Brenna startled. Then her surprise turned to annoyance. "I am indeed. So you'd better trot off lest you ruin my secret lovers' tryst."

"If I thought Everhart truly was your lover, he'd currently be in need of a physician. If I let him live at all."

She came to her feet and brought her hands to her hips. "How dare you act like a jealous husband when you have banned yourself from my bed? You want a marriage of convenience, yet you forbid me from taking a lover."

"I will lock you away before I'd allow that to happen."

Her temper churned to boiling. She stepped forward and poked him in the chest. "Either you bed me or I will find a man willing to do so. I suspect there are half a dozen men inside who would eagerly do the deed, in a closet or under a bush, if I asked. Perhaps I can even try out a new lover each week. It would certainly add much-needed excitement to my life."

"Brenna."

"Do not scowl at me. I am weary of your politeness and your scowls." She stalked back and forth. "You want me. You don't want me. You kissed me, but you won't bed me. You want me to return to London, yet you lead me to believe you want me to stay." She stopped pacing. "What is it you want, Richard? Do you want a wife of convenience, or do you want a wife in truth, for I am weary of waiting for you to make up your mind. I will have your answer now."

The long pause that followed shattered her heart. She met his eyes, defeated. "James and I will be packed and gone before sunrise."

Turning on her heel, she took a step. A hand on her arm brought her to a halt. Richard spun her around and slammed his mouth over hers.

Brenna struggled. He held her in an iron grip. The kiss inflamed her body and ignited a confusing mix of emotions. She wanted to hate him, yet she quickly conceded and kissed him back with days—no, months—of built-up passion inside her.

The kiss in the dower house had not satisfied her need for this man, her husband.

She clawed at his shirt, pulling the hem from his waistband. He tugged at her bodice, freeing her breasts. Brenna walked backward, leading him to the bench, and pulled him down atop her. He broke the kiss and kissed her shoulder, then her neck, and moved lower still to suck a nipple into his mouth.

Moaning, Brenna reached to open his trousers. His erection sprang free. She lifted her legs, splaying them out like a wanton, uncaring if anyone else was enjoying the garden.

"I want you, Richard; I need you now."

He grinned, shoved aside layers of underclothes, and sought her damp center. Without preliminaries, he rubbed his hardness against her. She gasped out something that might have been "yes," and he obliged. He eased inside her with a groan and reclaimed her mouth.

Rocking against her, Brenna gasped again and again as he teased her with both his erection and his fingers. This was no coming together with love, but a mutual mating for passion's sake. His kiss kept her from crying out when she found her shattering release. Then with a few long strokes, he joined her, shuddering as he spilled himself into her willing body.

With a deep groan, he slumped over her, taking care not to crush her beneath his weight. Brenna slid her hands under his coat and down his back, to where his shirt rode up to expose his lower back. She reveled in the feel of his bare skin.

"I apologize for the speed of our coupling," he said, with his warm breath against her neck. "It has been some time since our last encounter."

Brenna freed a hand and eased his head up so she could look into his eyes. "Then you and Bethany are not lovers?"

"Why would you think that?"

"I saw you in the library," Brenna admitted. She tried to keep her voice emotionless. "I saw her in your arms."

Richard pushed up off the bench and adjusted his trousers. Then he put her skirts to rights and dragged her onto his lap.

"I have never wanted Bethany. Not before our marriage and certainly not after."

A heavy weight lifted off of Brenna. Lucy had seen what she could not. "Why, then, have you not shared my bed?"

He cupped her face in his hand. "Beckwith Hall is no place for a lively young woman to live. I cannot ask you to give up the excitement of the city, and the close proximity to your family, to live here with me."

"I cannot once recall complaining about my life at the

hall." Brenna now understood his hesitation to reclaim his conjugal rights. A separation would be more difficult were they to share a bed. "I want to be your wife and to raise our son together. I have even become fond of sheep."

Richard held her gaze. Could this be true? Was Brenna satisfied with her lot? "What of your life in London?"

"Unless you intend to lock me up here and never allow me to visit my family, I will spend time in London—with you, I hope." She played with the hair at his nape. "A few weeks a year should more than satisfy my youthful need for the social whirl."

"Are you mocking me?"

She leaned in to nip his ear. "Not in the least, love."

His cock aroused to attention. He hungered to see her naked. The bench was good for no more than a quick romp. He wanted more, much more. Brenna was his. There was no longer a need to keep himself from her.

"Come, Wife." He slid her from his lap and stood, pulling her to her feet. He bent and lifted her up into his arms. "I have plans for the rest of our evening."

Brenna let out a small giggle of surprise and wrapped her arms around his neck. "What are you doing?"

"Our coach awaits." With long strides and the desire to ravish his wife driving him onward, it did not take long to round the house and find the coach. Without more than a clipped instruction to the driver to take them home, he nudged Brenna inside, and they were off.

Taking liberties brought Brenna's laughter during the too-brief ride. He did not wait for the coachman to alight but helped Brenna down himself. They ran into the house and up the stairs, startling the footman outside his bedroom door, and Nanny when Richard pushed open the door.

"Go to bed, Nanny," he said, and the woman hurried out. James stirred in his crib, and Brenna went to him before he could awaken fully. Richard went through to his bedroom and disrobed, giving Brenna time to tend to their son.

When he returned, he went to the crib, kissed James on the head, and grinned, finding Brenna on the bed with the sheet pulled up, barely covering her nipples. Clearly she was wearing nothing beneath.

His cock sprang to attention. With long strides, he hurried to the bed, yanked back the sheet, ogled her nakedness until she flushed pink all over, and then pressed her down on the mattress and took full advantage of her welcoming nature.

Chapter Thirty-one

The sun hadn't a chance to fully arrive when James awoke his parents with a squawk, followed in short order by a loud and demanding cry. Brenna groaned and dragged herself from the bed, Richard reaching out to caress her bare buttock before her feet found the floor.

Turning to tease him with a scolding look, she smiled and slipped into her chemise, which she found lying on the stool.

"Hush, darling." She scooped up James, pressed kisses on his downy soft head, and claimed the chair. While she fed him, Richard rolled to a sit on the edge of the bed and scratched his jaw with both hands.

Brenna's heart welled. With Richard's hair mussed and the sleepy-boyish look on his face, father and son were the image of each other. And she deeply loved them both.

"We must teach our son to wait until morning is in full bloom before demanding his breakfast," Richard said. "His hours should match those of his parents."

James closed his fingers around Brenna's fingertip.

"If his father were not so demanding himself, he might not be so tired this morning. He kept us both up to the wee hours slaking his own hunger," she teased.

He narrowed his eyes. "The noises you were making during those same wee hours were not words of complaint. I'd know the difference."

Brenna laughed softly as Richard shot her a warm look and padded out of the room. She cooed to the baby and thought of the change in her life over the last several hours. Richard was hers now, forever, and she vowed to carefully tend to his, and her own, happiness.

Dressed in trousers, Richard returned and walked to the crib. He grabbed one end with both hands and, without a word, dragged it toward the open sitting-room door.

"Richard—?"

He didn't pause but vanished within, the feet of the crib scraping loudly across the polished wood floor. After a few minutes of the sounds of the crib being moved around his room, silence fell, then the pad of his bare feet coming back.

"What are you doing?" she asked.

"From this moment forward, the three of us will be sharing my room. Permanently. Your bed is too small for my comfort, and I grow weary of moving you back and forth." He stretched his back as if to prove his point. "I've discovered that I like waking with you in my arms. I intend to do so every morning from here on."

Without allowing her to comment, he walked back through the sitting room, unaware of the happy grin he'd left behind.

Tears welled in her eyes as she smiled down at her son. Richard had not declared his undying love for her, but knowing he cared enough to insist she share his bed was enough for now.

"I love your father," she whispered to James. "I certainly do." She lifted his hand to her mouth. "And I love you, too."

Richard arrived at breakfast before Brenna and found the table empty save George. The man was red-eyed and yawning over his coddled eggs and toast. He appeared to have been run over by a coach-and-four. Richard and Brenna weren't the only members of the household who did not rest well last evening.

Richard muttered a good morning and went to the sideboard.

Piling up his plate, he took a seat across from George. "Where is Miriam?" he asked. "She is usually the first up."

George gave him a funny look. "She has not been seen in two days, since she rode off to the village. I thought you knew."

Stopping his fork midway to his mouth, Richard slowly lowered it to his plate, his mouth slightly open. "She is missing?"

The other man shrugged. "Bethany told me she has a lover. Someone whose name she would not say. We assumed she's run off with the man. Miriam is just desperate enough to do so. She falls easily in love."

A wave of guilt prickled through Richard. With the turbulence of his relationship with Brenna and his concerns over the dead maid, he had not noticed that Miriam was gone.

He pushed to his feet. "Where is Bethany?"

"She packed and left this morning," George said. "She's decided to stay with a friend in Bath." He shrugged. "She finally gave up hope of becoming your viscountess."

"Damn." He went in search of Jones. The man was shrugging into his coat when Richard banged the bedroom door open and entered without leave.

"Good morning to you, Milord," Jones said, and waved off the valet. "I assume you did not come to tell me the ham is especially tasty this morning?"

"Did you know Miriam was missing?"

"I did," Jones said. "Freemont went into the village to look for her and was told she was seen riding west with a man in a black coat and hat. Since she was known to have a lover, and she has not been found murdered, we deduced she'd run off."

Richard shook his head. "Am I the only one who did not know she had a lover? That she's missing?" He clenched his fists. Beckwith Hall was his, and he knew little about the goings-on inside these walls.

"I believe the missing Miriam matter was briefly mentioned at supper last evening," Jones said, with a knowing smile. "I believe you were too busy staring at your wife like a besotted schoolboy to catch the exchange."

With his patience at an end, Richard chose to ignore the

comment. Truthfully, his mind had been so occupied by Brenna and the murder over the last few days, there was little room for anything else.

Guilt formed. Miriam was his friend, and he'd failed her. "Are there any indications to the identity of this man?"

"None." Jones tugged at his cuffs. "Unless she decides to return, there is little we can do. She is a woman grown."

First Anne, then Miriam, and now Bethany was gone, too. Sighing, Richard dropped into a chair. He could not dwell on the flighty nature of the women of Beckwith Hall—excluding Brenna, of course—as there was a murder left to solve. Miriam would contact them in her own time.

If only he'd talked to her before she'd run off. Now he might never have the chance.

"Have you discovered any new clues about Clara's murder?" he asked.

Jones walked to the wardrobe and reached inside. He pulled out a pistol and slid it into his waistband. "Only one maid knew anything about her. She said Clara had been secretive over the last week, like something was amiss. However, the woman did not have any details, as she did not know Clara well, and they did not share confidences."

"And the Bow Street Runners?"

"Freemont managed to find out something. The Runners examined Clara's body and concluded she'd died of strangulation. They are sending men out across the area to see what they can find. So far the killer has left little to point to his identity."

Richard tapped a fist on the chair arm. "This is frustrating. We are chasing a ghost."

His mind went to his family, his staff, and his tenants, everyone who lived on his property and needed his protection. With a madman lurking, no one was safe.

"Our killer has been hiding for several years now," Jones agreed. "He has perfected his game. It will take a mistake to flush him into the light. We must keep alert and wary."

"Alert is not enough; we need guards. I want to hire your men to guard the property. I want everyone you have. The cost is no issue."

Jones nodded. "My men are trained fighters and former

soldiers. There is no better group for this task. I shall send for them immediately."

Richard watched him go. One worry was taken care of and many more competed for dominance in his mind. Brenna and James would soon be heavily guarded, Bethany was safely away, and with guards roaming the grounds, the likelihood of the killer returning to his property was slim. Still, there was one concern he could not shake: Miriam's disappearance.

Had she gone off willingly with her lover as suspected, or had she fallen under the influence of a killer, who'd used her to glean information about his family and staff, and then led her off to an uncertain fate?

B renna watched the arrival of the guards from the bedroom window. Several coaches pulled to a stop in front of the hall, and the men alighted.

They were all different in age and size, and gave off an air of confidence, as the trained fighters they were.

Pleased with Richard's plan, she left James with Nanny and the footman, and joined her husband in the foyer. Up close, the men were even more intimidating. They were all stern-faced and ready to protect Beckwith Hall.

"The guards look positively menacing," she whispered to Richard, as Jace led them into the hall. She did not need to see the weapons under their coats to know they were armed. Jace would leave nothing to chance.

"Jones picked each one for his skills." He drew her hand to his mouth. "You and our son will be safe."

The tension between her shoulder blades eased as Brenna watched the last man enter the hall. There were a full dozen men, excluding Jace and Mister Freemont. Mrs. Beal and Joseph began the process of getting the men settled into the empty rooms on the servants' floor.

The maids rushed about, carrying bedding and trays of food. Though the men were considered employees and not guests, they would be well taken care of.

Lucy watched the commotion from halfway down the stairs. She pulled her skirts aside when the men passed, and took care not to take special interest in Mister Freemont. The more she ignored him, the more he watched her.

Mister Freemont frowned but said nothing as he passed her. When he was out of sight, a small secretive smile escaped her.

When she finished her descent and joined Brenna and Richard, Richard excused himself. Brenna's eyes narrowed. "Must you torture poor Mister Freemont?"

Lucy shrugged. "He paid far too much interest in that awful Bethany. I will not be his second choice now that she's gone."

"He paid attention to her because you ignored him." Brenna crossed her arms. A pair of maids rushed past. "I remember a certain companion who pointed out to me that my husband had no interest in Bethany and that I should see what was in front of my eyes. I think she should take her own advice when it comes to Mister Freemont."

"Hmm." Lucy sniffed. "You act as if I have some interest in the man. Just because I find him handsome does not make him a proper man to court me. I was a courtesan. That will make some men flee."

"You will not know unless you speak to him." Brenna tapped her foot. "His reaction will tell you much about his character."

Sobering, Lucy looked up the staircase. Mister Freemont was no longer in view. "Even a good man can be put off by my former profession. I fear seeing condemnation in his eyes."

Brenna's heart tugged. She hugged Lucy. "You are a wonderful person and friend. If he cannot see what I see, then he is not the right man for you."

They leaned back, holding each other's arms. "I am still in mourning. I think it is too soon for another suitor," Lucy said. "Perhaps I shall take the path of spinsterhood. It is much less troublesome than risking my heart."

The dejection in her friend's voice pricked Brenna's temper. "I never thought of you as a coward, Lucy." She watched Lucy's face flash from miserable to angry. This pleased her immensely.

"I am not a coward," Lucy snapped. Then she must have realized Brenna's game. She let out a thoroughly exasperated sigh. "I do not know why I keep you as my friend. You do know how to rile me up."

Brenna hooked her arm in Lucy's. "We are too much alike not to be friends, and you know I adore you." She led Lucy through the foyer. "Since the day is sunny, I think we should collect James, and a guard, and enjoy some time in the garden."

M ister Freemont was subjected to over an hour of torment in the form of a pair of women and a baby. Brenna had deliberately chosen him to watch over them, then spent most of their time together asking him questions about his life, generally interjecting herself into his privacy. He answered most queries politely while pointedly ignoring Lucy.

Lucy tended James, pretending disinterest, though Brenna knew her ears were locked on their conversation.

"I understand that you were a soldier?" Brenna asked.

Mister Freemont looked pained. "I was."

"And you fought against Napoleon?" She wondered when he'd be pushed to the end of his patience, but he forged on with calm indulgence.

"I did."

Brenna glanced over at Lucy seated on the garden bench rocking James. The baby began to fuss. Lucy tried several ways to soothe him, but the boy was not pleased with her efforts.

"I think it's time for his nap." Brenna walked over and reclaimed her son. The interrogation of Mister Freemont was over. "You two are welcome to stay and enjoy the garden. The flowers are particularly fragrant."

Without pause, she hurried off, giving Lucy no choice but to accept Mister Freemont's company.

Once she returned to the bedroom, she went to the window and looked down into the garden, giving into her desire to snoop. From her position, she could see Lucy and Mister Freemont strolling briskly up the path. Neither appeared happy.

Her shoulders slumped. Her attempt to match-make had failed. Perhaps Lucy was correct and Mister Freemont was not the man for her.

"Shall we feed you, love?" Brenna moved away from the

window and curled up with him on the bed. Once James was fed and asleep, Brenna rose to remove her dress. She returned to the bed, pulled the quilt over them, and joined him in his nap.

Richard spent several hours with Jones, planning where the guards would take positions around the manor and grounds, and the shifts each would cover.

Once he was satisfied that Jones had everything taken care of, he went off in search of his wife. He found her asleep on the bed, cuddled up with their son.

He stood in the open doorway for several minutes, his heart softened by the scene. Never once had he thought the impulsive, sometimes reckless, and stubborn Miss Brenna Harrington would turn into such an excellent mother and wife.

The bed drew him, and he lay down on the other side of James, reaching across the boy to place a hand on Brenna's hip. Her soft scent and warmth washed away all the tension he'd felt over the last few hours. When he was with her, she had the ability to make him forget anything but her.

Brenna drew in a deep breath, and her eyes opened. She saw him watching her and smiled. "Richard."

In that moment, with his eyes on hers, Richard realized that in spite of his protests to the contrary, and all his best efforts to keep his heart protected, he'd done what he feared most.

He'd fallen irrevocably in love with his wife.

Chapter Thirty-two

✦

Brenna wanted to know how his afternoon fared but did not want to wake the baby.

"Come with me," she whispered, and carefully eased off the bed. After placing a pillow on each side of their son, she led Richard through the sitting room to her old bedroom. They left the door ajar, in case James awakened.

She climbed onto the bed, and he joined her. She snuggled close. "How goes the planning? Are the guards in place?"

"They are." He ran a hand over her bare arm and over her hip, covered with only the thin chemise. "Mister Jones is well qualified to watch over Beckwith Hall."

"He is a good man," she agreed. He was also becoming a close friend. "I trust him completely."

Richard played with her hair. Brenna bit her bottom lip and drew a fingertip down his chest. His muscles twitched. Then she moved lower, careful to avoid anything below his waistband.

She took pleasure in teasing him to inflame his passion. The end always led to their mutual satisfaction. And she did so enjoy being satisfied by her seductive husband. Since the night of the ball, he never refused her wifely demands.

"Simon once told me that Jace used to be a marshal in

America and hunted down wanted criminals," Brenna said. "And Jace was a trapper and a soldier. I do not know how much of that is true, but it certainly makes for a colorful history."

"Hmm." His hand casually cupped her left breast. He rubbed the nipple gently between his fingers.

"Can you imagine the danger in hunting wanted men?" Brenna said, pretending to be immune to his advances. She twitched as he kissed the spot below her ear. "I wonder if he was ever shot at by the criminals he hunted?"

"Hmm." His hand flexed. Her nipple hardened.

"That must be why Jace is good at searching for killers," she said, hiding a smile. "He has experience in that regard."

Richard grunted, his lips on her neck. His breath tickled her skin. "Must we talk about Jace Jones?"

Brenna shrugged. "Is there something else you wish to discuss?" She finally placed her hand over his erection. "A highwayman with a dusty coat and a huge, er, pistol, perhaps? I've heard he likes to chase down coaches and ravish young innocents."

He lifted his head and grinned wickedly. "The highwayman of Beckwith Hall does like to ravish." Brenna laughed. He pushed her over onto her back and ripped off her chemise.

The evening meal was lively. Jace had been convinced, by Brenna, to tell some tales of his days as a marshal. Mister Freemont appeared pleased to find her attention off of him. Lucy flirted outrageously with George, who seemed delighted by her sudden attention. Richard sat next to Brenna and was the recipient of her stocking-covered foot, teasing his leg while they shared warm glances.

"How terrible," Brenna said. She struggled to focus on the conversation, with memories of a certain highwayman-viscount driving into her heat just two hours previous, with her ankles positioned somewhere near her ears. "An arrow in the side? How did you survive?"

Jace rubbed the spot covered by his coat. "An army surgeon tried his best to kill me with his inferior treatment, but I
won the battle to live. I did learn to keep my head down once
the arrows started flying."

"How fascinating," Lucy said. From her position at the
table, Brenna wasn't certain, but she thought Lucy batted her
lashes at Jace. She almost felt sorry for Mister Freemont.

"I was once almost decapitated by a tray thrown during
breakfast when I was at Cambridge," George interjected.
"Two of the lads were arguing over a girl, and trays, and food,
flew."

"You were lucky you weren't killed," Lucy said. She placed
a hand on his arm. "Who knew Cambridge was so dangerous?"

Brenna nodded and removed her foot from Richard's thigh.
"Who did the young lady choose?"

George's face was serious, but his eyes showed good humor.
"The chit ended up choosing someone else, with a more even
temperament."

Laughter followed. The rest of the meal went along those
lines, with Brenna telling the tale of how she and Richard
met, and how he'd killed a thief. Once the conversation turned
in that vein, the men shared more stories of brushes with
death.

Even Mister Freemont managed to hold Lucy's interest
when he spoke of killing a man who'd pulled a knife on him
in an alley. "He wanted both my purse and my life. Instead, he
came to understand the error of his decision."

Lucy gaped. This was a side of the quiet Mister Freemont
that Lucy had never seen, a bold and dangerous side.

Brenna hoped her friend would give the former Runner a
chance to woo her. He was just the sort of fascinating man
Lucy needed to keep her intrigued.

Later, in the drawing room, the men shared glasses of port
while Lucy and Brenna settled on the settee and talked softly
over tea. As the evening aged, George went off to bed, after
bowing over Lucy's hand.

"You have an admirer," Brenna said, frowning as George
left them. "I hope you do not encourage his attentions. He is a
nice man and should not have his affections toyed with."

Lucy grimaced. "He is a friendly sort. However, I will make certain he knows we can be nothing more than friends."

Brenna looked over to where Jace and Mister Freemont were whispering together as Richard refreshed their drinks. The two men had serious expressions. As Richard returned to them, Mister Freemont nodded to Jace and took the drink, tossed back the port, and excused himself.

"Ladies." He bowed. "Thank you for the interesting evening, but I must go. My duties require me elsewhere."

As he walked out, a curious Brenna turned to stare at Jace. He shrugged. She suspected there was something about Freemont's abrupt departure that he had no intention of sharing.

"That was odd," Lucy said.

"Yes, it was," Brenna said. "Jace does have his secrets."

Lucy twisted the thin necklace around her neck. "I think we should torture him for information. Then perhaps he'll tell us where Mister Freemont had gone off to."

"What are you thinking? A torture rack? Tied to a post and covered with ants?" Brenna got into the spirit. "Unfortunately Beckwith Hall does not possess a dungeon. We could chain him to a wall in a dank cell until he cracks."

"A delicious prospect, that," Lucy said. "He does like to tease me. Yesterday, he said my gown was too drab and my hair too severe. As if I care what he thinks. I am in mourning."

After two months of wearing black, Lucy had decided the color too horrid to continue wearing and changed to grays and browns. Though she continued to mourn, and did miss her husband, Brenna knew that beneath her drab gowns she was wearing a chemise she'd purchased in bright blue.

Brenna could not fault her. She'd not been married long enough to truly consider herself a wife.

Richard walked over. "I think I shall retire. The day was long. Would you care to join me, Wife?"

The warmth in his eyes spoke of something far more salacious than sleep on his mind. Heat sluiced through her. Richard presented himself as a bit of a staid presence to the world outside their bedroom, but behind the closed door, he was a man of great passion and seductive skill. And he was hers.

She took his outstretched hand. "Good night, Jace, Lucy." Brenna waited until they were up the stairs, and had dismissed Nanny and the guard, before she lifted her skirts with a laugh and raced him to their bed.

It was much later, when their passions were satiated and James was fed and sleeping again, that Brenna turned on her side and placed a hand over his heart.

"Why did Jace send Mister Freemont away?"

Richard caressed her back. "I'm not certain. It did rouse my curiosity, too. He said Freemont has gone off to investigate a new clue to the case and will return in a few days."

"This is curious," Brenna said. "And so sudden."

He rolled Brenna onto her back and reached for the laces on her bodice. "We will have to wait until Mister Freemont returns for our answers."

Brenna walked into the sunny garden, having found time for a few minutes to herself. She enjoyed the spring flowers as they bloomed, smiling at each new arrival.

Several birds splashed in the fountain as she passed. The lovely morning lifted her spirits.

After about fifteen minutes, she thought she heard two male voices speaking in hushed and angry tones behind the hedge that separated two sections of garden. She froze, unsure of her next course of action.

Not wanting to spy on a private conversation, she called out, "Hello." The voices went silent. "Is someone there?"

Still nothing. Though she was within sight of the manor, and several guards lingered nearby, a sudden feeling of unease brought her hands to her skirt. She readied herself to spin about and flee.

The desire proved unnecessary. She heard the crunch of footsteps, and George appeared around the hedge.

"Brenna."

Her shoulders slumped. "Thank goodness it's you," she said. "I'd thought I'd stumbled upon the killer."

George's smile wavered. "That would be unfortunate. Luckily, there are no killers here today." He glanced over his shoulder, then back to her. "How long were you standing there?"

"Not long," Brenna replied. "Who were you speaking with?"

Stepping forward, George took her arm and steered her back toward the manor. "It was a guard. I thought he'd left his position, but I was incorrect. He'd only stepped out of sight for a moment to, ah, take care of a delicate matter."

She did not need any more information. "I see." She hoped the delicate matter did not involve the desecration of the rose bushes.

They walked slowly back to the hall, chatting about nothing in particular. Eventually the conversation turned to the missing Mister Freemont. "Have you heard any news about his mysterious trip to who-knows-where? He has been gone over a week," George said.

"I have not learned why he is gone, though I did manage to learn his destination," she said, in a low voice, as if she had learned a very important secret.

George leaned in. His eyes gleamed. "Do tell."

"Cambridgeshire," she whispered, behind her cupped hand. "I overheard Jace discussing it with one of the guards. I was eavesdropping, though I do hope you will keep my secret."

"Cambridgeshire?" He stopped walking. "What sort of clues does he expect to find there?"

Brenna shrugged. "I cannot fathom what. But it was clearly of some urgency, as Jace rushed him off after supper without a word to anyone." It took a moment to realize George had gone pale. "George, are you ill?"

He shook his head and pressed his fingertips to his temples. "I am suddenly struck by a headache. I ask that you please excuse me."

"Of course." Brenna squeezed his arm, and he hurried away. She made a note to have someone take him up some headache powder. Mrs. Beal mixed it herself, and it worked quite well.

She paused to examine a topiary shaped to look like a fish. Somehow she'd missed the creation in previous ventures into the garden. Either that or the gardener had suddenly become artistic. Thoughts of George faded.

Smiling, she continued on toward the manor, nearly colliding with Richard as he rushed from the house.

"There you are," he said, and took her hand. "Mister Freemont has returned with news."

"What did he say?" Her heart raced.

"I knew you'd be put out if we did not wait for you. If you want to be included, you had better hurry."

"Yes, Husband." Brenna lifted her violet skirts and rushed after him. They were both eager to find out if the trip was successful and to learn any new clues.

Richard led her into the study, and she saw the two men standing together, sober faced, by the fireplace. They stopped conversing when Richard closed the door.

Mister Freemont was rumpled from his trip. He'd not taken time to change. The matter must be of some urgency. Brenna sat on a chair and clasped her hands together. "I understand you have information pertaining to the case?"

Jace and Mister Freemont walked over.

"Yes." Mister Freemont drew in a deep breath. "The journey proved to be both puzzling and interesting, though I'm not certain what to make of the information I've received."

Jace nodded. "It appears as though a member of this household may know more about this case than he's let on." Jace ran a hand over his hair. "I sent Freemont to find out if there were any murders in Cambridgeshire during the last ten years, and there was one several years ago. A laundress who worked in the village was found strangled and left in a field."

"How dreadful," Brenna said. Her stomach tightened.

"What has this to do with Beckwith Hall and my staff? Most have been in my employ for many years," Richard said.

"Not your staff," Mister Freemont replied. "This person attended Cambridge at the time of the murder."

Suspicion grew as Brenna dug through her memories for

something she'd heard recently. It took a moment for the thought to clear. Her stomach dropped.

"Who is this person?" Richard pressed.

Brenna met his eyes, disbelief in her face. "George," she whispered, and felt her world tilt.

Chapter Thirty-three

R ichard scowled. "What do you mean, George?"

Finding her voice, Brenna focused on Jace. "George mentioned attending Cambridge a few nights ago, which is why Jace sent Mister Freemont off to Cambridgeshire. Now Jace is convinced he's the killer."

"I'm convinced of nothing at this moment. However, I do find the timing suspicious," Jace said. "A laundress died there at the same time he was in residence. And a maid died the same time he was in Dover."

"That does not make him a killer," Brenna insisted. George had always been so kind to her. He was becoming a friend. "The image of him strangling a woman, or many women, does not fit my experiences with George."

"And he was here at Beckwith Hall during the time of the London murder," Richard insisted. "He's lived here for almost three years now, and I have never seen any hint of evil in him."

Jace and Mister Freemont exchanged a glance. Jace leaned forward and settled his elbows on his knees. He faced Brenna. "There is more. Through the records, Freemont discovered another interesting fact. There was another man you know who was a school chum of your George Bentley."

"Who?" Richard pressed.

"Clive Everhart."

Brenna's body went cold. She began to shake. Clive spent time in her home, ate her food, was around her son. George, too. George played with James, held him, and laughed with her over James's funny baby antics.

Richard came over and took her hand.

"Calm, love," he said softly. "None of this means we have a pair of killers in our midst." But even as he tried to settle her fears, Brenna knew, just knew, that Jace would not be telling them this information if he wasn't convinced there was some connection between the men and the murders.

Deep inside her, she drew on her strength. She'd not fall apart, not here, not now. "You think it was Mister Everhart in the nursery." Jace nodded. "And one of the men was Clara's lover."

"We think so," Jace said. "When the laundress was killed, Everhart was suspected of the deed. He'd been seen with her in the village. But his father was a baron with highly placed connections. Without direct proof, the matter was dropped." He sighed. "Had George not mentioned Cambridge the other night, coupled with Freemont's knowledge, through the Runners' investigation, of the similar death in Cambridgeshire, we would never have discovered this connection."

An arrival of a guard interrupted them. "There is no sign of Bentley," he said to Jace. "He has slipped away."

Brenna's throat tightened. She swallowed past the lump. "He has fled because of me. I overheard you mention Mister Freemont was in Cambridgeshire and told George this afternoon. I did not think it would cause any harm. He was my friend."

"This is not your fault." Richard placed his hands on her shoulders. He sent Jace a scathing glare. "Why not tell us of your suspicions earlier? You put us all in danger."

Jace stood. "You were protected. I made certain of it." He crossed his arms. "I could not accuse the men of murder without proof. I still have nothing that will see either of them hang."

Brenna pushed from the chair and went to the window. She ran through her memories of the months she'd spent here at the hall and her time with George.

Was it possible that he had hidden an evil soul? Could she have been so wrong about him?

"Before Freemont's return, he alerted the Runners to our findings. They have sent men to hunt Clive Everhart. We hope George has not gotten word to him about our suspicions. Everhart is a dangerous man."

The guard left, passing Lucy in the open doorway. Her eyes widened, falling on Mister Freemont. She glanced then to Brenna and her stricken face. "I have missed something." She hurried across the room to Brenna. "What has happened?"

"Jace and Mister Freemont think George and Clive Everhart are the killers," Brenna said.

Lucy twisted to look at Mister Freemont. He nodded. She turned back to Brenna. "I cannot believe that. Not George."

Jace briefly explained the situation. Lucy went pale. Brenna led her to the settee, and they sat.

"What can I do to help?" Richard asked. The strain of the last hour etched lines around his mouth. "I cannot sit by while George and Everhart are loose to kill again."

"I agree," Jace said. "If Everhart has run, we'll need several men to aid in the hunt." He turned to Mister Freemont. "Collect six men and have horses saddled. Ask the rest to come into the hall to stand guard. We ride in an hour."

R ichard pulled Brenna into his arms and kissed the top of her head. "I will return safely, love."

"You had better." She smoothed a wrinkle on his shirt. "James and I need you." She wrapped her arms around him and felt the pair of pistols in his waistband. There was some comfort knowing he was armed. He'd killed a man once. If need be, he'd do so again.

He tipped her chin up to look into her eyes. "I cannot leave you widowed. There are too many young bucks slavering to get into your bed."

She smiled. "Remember that, and also take Jace's experience to heart and keep your head down when the arrows start flying."

Richard grinned. "I will." He released her with a last quick kiss, and Joseph helped him into his greatcoat.

Before he could turn and follow Jace out, she caught his

arm and lifted up onto her toes. "I love you," she whispered, in his ear. "I always have and always will."

Without waiting for his reply, she walked away.

She loved him? In spite of his ill tempers and the shameful way he'd treated her, for several months from their first meeting to their wedding and after, Brenna had fallen in love with him.

Richard watched Brenna take James from Lucy and press kisses on his tiny head. His heart tugged. If he survived this hunt alive, he'd make certain she knew she was loved in return.

For now, he needed to keep his wits about him.

George and Clive were running and desperate. They'd know they were being hunted and would not hesitate to kill their pursuers to stay free.

He left the hall. His horse, and Jones and his men, were waiting on the drive. He mounted, and with one last glance at the hall, they were off.

Richard and Jace led the search. They scoured the forest, the sheep barn, and anywhere they could think of where two men could hide. Nothing led to new clues. "Wherever they are, they will be well hidden," Jace said.

"Let us check the abbey," Richard suggested. They hurried down the road. Though there were signs someone had recently visited the stone ruins, a quick scan of the building turned up no one hiding there.

"Boys play knights of the keep in this place," Richard said, his shoulders tightening with his frustration. "Lovers meet here. If George or Clive passed through, their footprints would mingle with any number of others."

The men gathered in the overgrown courtyard. "We should spread out and contact your neighbors and give them an update," Jace said. "Their families and servants need to take shelter in their homes behind locked doors."

Richard agreed. He gave directions to the men, and each was assigned several neighbors to contact. They rode away.

"I'll feel more confident knowing everyone in the park is

watching for the men." He and Jace returned to the road. They met a pair of Bow Street Runners there. The men shared information and separated again.

"There is a place we have not checked," Richard said. In his haste, he'd forgotten the dower house. "My mother's dower house is at the far end of the property. Brenna and I found clues that someone was meeting there, lovers most likely. The bed was unmade."

"Lead on."

The ride was not long, but they went slow, keeping vigilant. It would be a horrible ending to their search if either or both of them were shot from their saddles.

When they reached the small copse of trees, they dismounted. There was no smoke from the chimney, as the day was warm, and no evidence of either boot prints or horses to show that the house was occupied.

"They would be foolish to hide here," Jace said quietly. He pulled out a pistol anyway.

"Yes. However, if George and Clive were dim enough to kill Clara near where they resided, we are not dealing with two brilliant men."

"True. Still, they did get away with murder for ten years," Jace said. "That could not have been all luck."

"Then let us find out who is correct," Richard said.

Richard claimed his own pistol, and they slowly walked up the short drive. Tiny stones shifted under their boots. As silently as was manageable, they neared the dower house. Richard paused. He could not remember if the curtains on the lower level had been open or closed when he and Brenna were there.

"Hold," he said, and Jace stopped. He ran his mind over the last visit. He was now reasonably certain the curtains were open, as he had no issue with seeing into the empty house when they'd explored it.

"The maids cleaned but would not have closed the curtains," he said, his voice low. "Someone else has been here."

He and Jace bent and closed in on the door. "We have surprise working for us," Jace whispered.

Richard nodded. He reached for the door handle. It was

locked. "Someone is inside." He stepped back, met Jace's nod, and kicked the door off its hinges.

A feminine scream pierced the dim interior of the house. He ran up the stairs toward the sound, Jace on his heels.

A shadowy figure met him at the door of the darkened bedroom, an upraised candlestick in his hand. Richard could not get a shot, so he hit the man on the side of the head with the pistol. The attacker crumpled to the floor on his face.

Richard knelt. The man breathed. He knew by the color of his hair that this was neither George nor Clive.

Jace brushed by him and went to the bed. He leveled his pistol on the lone occupant. The woman cried beneath the thin sheet she'd pulled up to her chin. Clearly naked, and on the verge of hysteria, she begged Jace for her life.

"Please do not hurt us," she said, through sobs. "I have money. I'll pay you anything you want to leave us unharmed."

Her voice broke through Richard's consciousness, and he turned away from the fallen man, blinking to clear the image of the figure on the bed.

"Anne?"

T he sheet came down enough for Richard to see the tear-streaked face of his sister. Her eyes widened.

"Richard?" Her sobs instantly subsided. Her cheeks flushed, likely troubled to be found naked by her brother, though her attention was on the man on the floor. "What have you done?"

Richard turned and reached for Lockley. Had the man not already been dazed by the pistol blow, he would currently be suffering a beating. He jerked the man to his feet and shoved him onto the bed.

Clad only in trousers, hastily buttoned and partially open, a familiar face showed beneath his disheveled hair and smeared blood trickling down the side of his face from the cut on his temple. Richard froze.

This was *not* Lockley. "Andrew?"

Anne slid over to check his wound, the sheet tangling around her. She brushed his hair out of his eyes and dabbed the cut with a corner of the sheet.

"Of course, Andrew." She shot Richard an accusing glare. "Are you daft, Brother? Did you honestly think I'd actually marry that horrid Stewart Lockley?"

She cooed and tended the injured Andrew. Richard walked over to stare down at Andrew. Through slit eyelids, his steward stared up at him. Richard felt the hot rage of betrayal.

"I should kill you, you bastard."

Anne eased Andrew back against the pillows and stood up on the bed while clutching the sheet tightly to her bosom. Her hair swirled around her shoulders and red face. "He is my husband, you idiot. I have not been ruined."

Jace chuckled and backed out of the room. Richard went over to the nearest chair and slumped onto the stuffed surface.

"How did this happen?" he asked.

Anne climbed from the bed. "I will tell you everything once I am dressed and certain you have not permanently damaged my husband." She pointed to the door. "Now get out!"

Richard rose, stalked through the house, and went outside to find Jones leaning against his horse, chuckling and shaking his head. Richard's scowl did not deter the man from his mirth. Instead, it seemed to entertain him further.

"I have never been more grateful that I do not have a sister," Jace said, and gave the horse a scratch. "Though the surprise on your face when your nearly naked sister told you of the marriage was most entertaining indeed."

Thoroughly exasperated by recent events, Richard was not in the mind-set to shrug off the other man's good humor.

"Cease your prattle, Jones," Richard warned. "Or there will be another murder for the Runners to investigate today." He collected his reins and swung up into the saddle to what sounded like a cat being strangled behind him.

Chapter Thirty-four

❦

Brenna heard the front door burst open and hurried to the banister. She looked down to find Richard entering the manor, followed by Jace and two strangers, one, a man wobbling slightly on his feet.

"You nearly killed him," the woman said, her arm linked with the wobbling man. "And you expect me not to be livid?"

"How was I to know you'd turned the dower house into a love nest?" Richard replied, his voice only slightly lower than hers. "You could have sent around a note."

"And watch you shoot my husband?" the woman scoffed. "You have always been hotheaded. As it is, we are lucky you were not able to pull off a shot."

Their upraised voices carried through the foyer to Brenna—and beyond, she suspected. Her curiosity rose about the woman who was clearly not intimidated by Richard. Their bickering continued unabated as they headed down the hallway and disappeared from sight.

Interested and unable to hear the continuing argument clearly, Brenna lifted her skirts and ran down the stairs. She saw Richard lead the trio into the drawing room and walked briskly after them. She was lady of the manor, she rationalized, and if something was amiss, she had a right to know what it was.

"I can do what I wish with my life," the woman was saying, as Brenna paused in the open doorway. Jace sent her a sympathetic glance and stepped into the hallway. Brenna barely acknowledged him as she watched the woman help the injured man onto the settee. "Who I marry is none of your concern."

"It is not the marriage I object to, Sister," Richard argued. "You've been missing for months, without a word, and then you move into the dower house without making your presence known to anyone."

Brenna's eyes widened. So this was the missing Anne. Upon further inspection, she did see a resemblance. And clearly sister and brother shared a similar temperament.

"We were not hiding from you when we tied the horses around back of the house. We only just arrived this morning after a grueling ride," Anne said, glowering. "I planned to rest for a bit, then come to the manor and explain myself, well knowing that you would not be pleased with my news. How was I to know that you'd burst in and pummel my husband senseless?"

This battered man was the horrid Mister Lockley? He did not look at all like she'd expected.

Brenna needed to defuse the anger before blood was shed. She stepped forward and cleared her throat. Four pairs of eyes turned in her direction.

Richard sighed. He indicated she join them. She went to his side. He took her hand.

Anne gave her a look over. Her gaze lingered on their clasped hands. "It appears as if some things have changed during my absence. Would you care to introduce us?"

"Anne, this is my wife, Brenna. Brenna, this is my sister, Anne." He turned to the man on the settee. "This is her husband, and my missing steward, Andrew Pearson."

"Andrew?" Brenna frowned. "I thought Mister Lockley was her husband."

Anne's mouth thinned. "And I thought my brother would never remarry. It appears we were both misinformed, Lady Brenna."

"What a turn," Brenna said. She walked over to pull the

bell cord. When the maid appeared, she requested tea and cakes. "I think we should sit and untangle this puzzle."

Brother and sister refused to acknowledge each other while waiting for the tea to arrive. Anne tended her husband, assuring him that she loved him and everything would work out. "Richard is nothing but a bully," Anne said softly, to Andrew, but not quietly enough not to reach her brother. Richard stiffened. She continued, "If we have to return to Scotland to escape his reach, we will."

Brenna hid a smile. Their relationship reminded her of the way she and Simon argued. She realized how much she missed her brother. Once George and Clive were captured and life settled, she'd insist they pack up James and make a visit to London.

Richard ignored Anne's jabs and poured a brandy for Jace and Andrew. He handed a glass to his steward. After a few sips, the poor man's color returned.

"Thank you, Your Lordship," he mumbled, careful to keep his eyes averted. He'd been trusted to find and rescue Anne from Lockley and had somehow ended up married to the woman. Brenna's patience stretched thin when the tea seemed to take an eternity to arrive. This was a story she very much wanted to hear.

The maid finally came and set out the small repast. In addition to the tea and cakes, there were small sandwiches.

Brenna smiled. "Thank you, Brigit, you may go."

"Yes, Milady."

Reaching for the teapot, Brenna poured tea for herself and Anne. As Anne stirred cream into her cup, Brenna took a moment to examine her sister-in-law. Anne was tall and pretty and—as evidenced from their earlier, loudly voiced argument—strong willed. Richard needn't have worried about her. His sister was obviously no ninny who'd made an imprudent match.

"Enough tea stirring, Anne," Richard commanded. "Tell me everything that happened after you ran off."

Anne sipped her tea. "I cannot believe you thought I'd run off with Lockley. That toad. If he were the last man in England, I'd still chase him off."

"Why, then, did you flee?" Richard pressed.

She glanced over at Andrew. "I was in love with someone who barely gave me notice. I knew that if you chased after me, you would bring along the one man you trusted most to help you."

"Andrew?" Richard stared. "You were in love with Andrew?"

Brenna was transfixed.

"I was from the first day, when he arrived here to accept your offer of employment. I looked into his eyes and knew I would marry him someday."

Andrew smiled at his wife. "I felt the same." He glanced at Richard. "However, I was not able to voice my feelings. A steward is not on the same level as a Lady. I could not ask for her. So I kept my feelings to myself."

"You've been in love with each other for the last four years?" Richard stared in disbelief. "You kept it well hidden."

"What part does Lockley play in this?" Brenna interjected.

"Nothing," Anne said. "At the Farnsworth musicale, I overheard him tell Mister Braun his plans to flee to France to avoid creditors. I assumed, rightly, that if I left at the same time, Richard would think I'd run off with the man." She grinned, and Andrew took her hand. "To my surprise, Andrew found me instead of Richard. It was my chance to speak my feelings."

"How romantic," Brenna sighed.

Richard frowned at her. Brenna chewed down a cake to hide her amusement. "Your frown does not change my mind. This *is* very romantic." She turned back to the couple. "Please continue."

Andrew took up the story. "I had ridden into Scotland, determined to find her. I'd given up and was about to return to England when I literally stumbled upon her at an inn. She, too, had decided to return home. We argued, she told me of her feelings, and I knew that no matter how angry you'd be, My Lord, I'd make her my wife."

"We do not move in society, so our marriage should be accepted without much notice," Anne added. "We hope we will be allowed to live quietly here, at the hall."

Brenna sighed. Richard scowled. Brenna covered her mouth with her hand. Anne winked at her. Brenna grinned.

"We decided to stay in Scotland over the winter and return in the spring." Anne met Richard's eyes. "I apologize for not contacting you. I know you worried. But I feared what you might do if you found us. I hoped the passage of time would work in our favor and settle your temper."

Andrew rubbed his head. "Still, you managed to injure me anyway, Milord. I hope my cracked skull has satisfied your desire for justice."

Richard did not answer. Instead, he walked to the window and looked out. The three waited in silence for him to speak.

What happened next surprised Brenna and, by their faces, the other three occupants of the room, too. A low rumble sounded from her husband, which turned into a chuckle. He turned back to them, shaking his head.

"Had I known of your feelings, Andrew, I would have begged you to take her. Anne has always been a thorn in my backside. Now she has someone else to deal with her emotional upsets and ill tempers."

"*My* ill tempers?" Anne stood. "You are as humorless as a goat. No, the goat has more humor."

Richard returned to them, bent to pull his sister off the settee and into a crushing hug, and swung her around. "Welcome back, Annie."

Anne laughed and smacked his shoulders. "Put me down, you brute. I'm getting dizzy." Doing her bidding, Richard set her back onto her feet and went to Andrew. The man pushed to his feet. Richard took his hand.

"Welcome to the family, my friend."

Sniffing, Brenna stood and dabbed her eyes with a knuckle. She was pleased to have Anne home safe and happily married. Richard would no longer worry that she'd come to harm.

Anne snuggled against her husband and turned to Brenna. "Our love story is not the only one. I want to know how you two met and how Brenna managed to harness my brother under the marital yoke."

The story had to wait, as Jace stepped back into the room with Mister Freemont on his heels. Freemont drew in a few quick breaths before he could speak. "The Runners have the men on the run afoot. A huntsman from Brighton Manor saw them passing through their property. They cannot go far. The Runners have the roads blocked."

Richard stepped forward. "Trapped, they will be more dangerous." He glanced at Brenna. "I have to go."

Reluctantly, she nodded. "Be careful."

"I promise." He and Jace followed Mister Freemont out. Brenna slumped into the chair. A small cry brought her attention back to the door. Nanny held a fussing James.

"He wants his mother," she said, and brought James to Brenna, who cradled him in her arms.

"There, there, sweetheart." She made a silly face, and he smiled a toothless smile. "Who is my handsome little man?" she cooed, and lifted her eyes to see Anne and Andrew staring agape.

She chuckled. "I have more than a marriage to explain. Anne, Andrew, meet James Ellerby, Richard's son."

B renna paced from the one window to another in the drawing room, watching for Richard's return. After telling her story of how she and Richard met, eating supper with her new family, and getting James to sleep, she had nothing else to distract her from worry as the evening aged.

"Any sign of them?" Anne came up behind her after seeing Andrew settled for the night to sleep off his headache, and peered into the darkness outside the glass. A misty-rain fell. "Wherever they are, they must be miserable."

"No, there is no word." Brenna twisted her fingers and paced some more. "Where can they be?"

Anne fell into step beside her. "From what I've seen, my brother and your Mister Jones are quite capable of taking care of themselves. They will return unharmed."

"I hope so," Brenna said. "I do not want to think macabre thoughts, but two killers are trapped in the park. They'd not hesitate to shoot my husband."

The front door opened, and Brenna and Anne rushed into the hallway. Richard, Jace, and Mister Freemont stomped into the manor, damp from the mist and appearing exhausted.

They pulled off their hats and coats and handed them to Joseph and Mrs. Beal. Brenna hurried to greet her husband.

He caught her against him. She felt dampness on his shirt and waistcoat. "Come, let us get you by the fire."

Tucked under Richard's arm, she led him to the drawing room. Anne and the other men followed.

Once the men were seated, Mrs. Beal brought food for the starved trio. Questions waited until they finished eating.

"No sign of George or Clive, then?" Brenna asked. She sat beside Richard and linked their fingers.

"The bastards are slippery. We think the huntsman foiled their escape," Richard said, and kissed her knuckles. "We all believe they have reclaimed their hiding place, but know not where. There are many places scattered around the park to hide: hunting lodges, dower houses, manors all but empty from the owners heading into London for the beginning of the season. They could be anywhere."

"The Runners are stationed throughout the park," Jace added. "Unless they manage to slip away in the rain and darkness, we have them trapped."

"We will ride back out at sunrise," Richard said. "For now, I need sleep."

"Of course." Brenna noted the tension lines on his face. "If you all will excuse us." They said their goodnights and went upstairs. The guard was seated outside their door, and they sent Nanny off to bed. Brenna waited until Miles stripped the wet clothes off Richard before sending the valet away and tucking her husband into bed.

"I am chilled and weary," he said softly, his lids drooping. Brenna stripped to her chemise and climbed in beside him. She thought he was asleep until his hand slid up to cup her buttock. She smiled.

"Your hand is cold," she protested.

"Everything is cold," he replied. "Warm me, Wife." She snuggled against him. Whatever his intentions when he cupped her buttock, fatigue proved a greater force, and he fell into a deep sleep.

It was still dark the next morning when Richard awoke Brenna with his mouth on her breast and a morning erection. They barely had time for a brief encounter when James started to fuss. Richard took him from the crib and rocked the boy while he carried him to Brenna on the bed.

"He is just as bossy as his aunt," Richard said. He leaned to kiss them both. She changed and fed their son and watched Richard go to the wardrobe.

"He does show early indications that he will be stubborn, like the Ellerbys," Brenna said. She glanced at her husband. "Thank goodness I am so even-tempered."

Richard snorted. "You start every morning grumbling about the early hour. My ears ache from the abuse."

"How can I not grumble?" she protested. "You and James wake me up most mornings before sunrise." To prove her point, she gestured to the window and the blackness beyond.

"I did not hear you complain a few minutes ago," he teased.

Brenna frowned. "The same thing can be accomplished at a later hour," she scolded lightly. "Once the sun has come up."

Richard chuckled. "A man's passions do not follow a clock." He pulled on his breeches. "You will just have to accept your lot."

Rolling her eyes skyward, she listened to the rain click against the window glass. "It's still raining out," Brenna said, after a moment. "Must you go?"

He nodded. "Every moment they're free puts more women in danger." He came to Brenna and kissed her. He lifted his head and stared into her eyes. "I love you, Brenna."

Her mouth dropped open. With a grin, he left her.

Brenna slumped back on the bed, her heart beating at a rapid pace. Her shock was genuine. He'd given her no hint of his feelings. Now he spoke of love?

"When did he come to this conclusion?" she muttered. It was not a declaration with poetry and candlelight, or during a romantic walk around the lake. But theirs was no ordinary relationship. The three words were heartfelt and wonderful. That was what mattered.

James looked up. She smiled down at him. "Your father loves me, yes he does." She caressed his soft cheek. "Is that not an interesting turn? He swore he'd never love again."

James kicked his feet and squealed. She laughed. "You are such a silly boy." She came to her knees at his feet. She pressed her lips to one foot and blew. The funny sound and tickle caused him to squeak. They played for a time before Agnes came to help her dress. Nanny followed a few minutes later.

"The men have gone out?" Nanny asked. She took James.

"They have." Brenna went to the window. With rain on the glass, the outside world was a blur. She leaned her forehead on the pane and prayed for Richard's safe return.

He loved her. She could not lose him to a killer.

Chapter Thirty-five

Andrew was at the breakfast table when Brenna went downstairs. She was relieved that a night's rest was beneficial to his health. He seemed fit as he and Anne chatted over their meal. After filling her plate, she took a place next to them at the table.

"Your headache is gone?" Brenna asked, and received a nod.

"Thankfully so." Andrew rubbed his temple and winced. "I suppose I deserved a whack for marrying his sister without permission."

"I am just pleased that Richard accepted the marriage and that you both are back at Beckwith Hall," Brenna said. "Richard missed you."

"I missed him, too," Anne said. She took a bite of eggs. "Though sometimes he can be as angry as a feral cat."

"Yes, he certainly can." Brenna thought of how different he was since they first met. He was not as stoic and laughed more often. "He was unhappy for a very long time."

"He was," Anne agreed. "You and James brought hope and happiness back into his life. For that, I'll always be grateful."

A sober cast hung over the household as Brenna finished her meal and went to check on James. The staff was quiet while they worked. Everyone was on edge over the hunt for the killers.

The manor was protected with armed guards posted everywhere. Brenna hated that her home felt like a prison. The only positive was that James, and the rest of the family and staff, were safe.

"What do you have planned for the day?" Lucy asked, when they met in the hallway outside Brenna's bedroom.

"Other than fretting over my husband being in danger and chewing my nails to the quick?" Brenna said. "Nothing."

Lucy made a face. "We could write letters. I have not written Miss Eva in almost two weeks." She covertly glanced around them, as if looking for onlookers, then pulled something from behind her back. "Or we could take this map into your room and try to figure out where our killers may be hiding."

Brenna's eyes widened. She snatched the map out of Lucy's hand. "Where did you get this?"

Taking Brenna's hand, Lucy pulled her into Brenna's former bedroom. "Remember back when we first came here and His Lordship mentioned that had Andrew not been missing, he'd find you a map to the hall so that you would not get lost?"

"I do remember," Brenna said.

"Well, I asked Andrew if he had one for the park. He did. The man apparently has an interest in maps. Ask him about a place anywhere in England, and he'll probably have a map to show you."

"This is wonderful," Brenna exclaimed, then lowered her voice when Nanny shushed them from the other bedroom.

Brenna dragged Lucy to the bed. They spread the map out on the coverlet and knelt for a better view.

Though somewhat simplistic in its drawings, it showed many of the houses and landmarks she recognized from her explorations. "I know some of these places. This is Beckwith Hall." She ran her fingertip over the map. "This is the abbey, and this, I believe, is the Cookson cottage."

She lifted her eyes to Lucy, awed. "You are brilliant."

"I like to think so," Lucy said, and flipped her braid over her shoulder. "Now where would our killers hide?"

Finding a few familiar markings was easy. Figuring out the other notations proved daunting. There were smaller buildings Brenna took to be cottages or perhaps stables or dower houses. Branching out from Beckwith Hall, the properties nearby were also marked with the same careful detail. Too much detail. It soon became clear that they needed an expert to untangle the intricacies of the map.

Excitement prickled through Brenna. "Please fetch Andrew. We will meet him in the library."

Ten minutes later, the three were hunched over the map, spread out on the desk. To her surprise, she discovered that Andrew not only had the map in his collection but also had drawn it himself.

"So you know what each of these buildings are?" she asked. She was nearly giddy. And Brenna was rarely giddy.

"I do," he replied. He pulled a pair of spectacles from his pocket and slid them on. "What exactly are you looking for, My Lady?"

"We want to see if the men have missed any hiding places during their search. Since many of the properties in the park are vast, there may be small outbuildings hidden from the road or tucked into wooded areas that are unseen unless someone knows where to look. And there is no time to press the neighbors for details of their properties."

Andrew lifted his attention from the map. "What an excellent idea," he said, his eyes bright. "Hand me the pen and ink, and I will write what each of these markings are. We will give it to His Lordship, and they can do a more detailed search."

"Won't it ruin the map?" Lucy said.

He shook his head. "I have several other copies."

The steward took the pen and ink from Lucy and went to work. The two women watched, fascinated, by his vast knowledge of the park. "How do you know all of this?" Brenna asked, her curiosity overcoming her desire to see the task completed.

"The property owners allowed me to walk their properties to find the correct positioning for each building, pond, stream, and whatever else I wanted to include. It truly is very accurate."

Brenna wanted to hug him but thought better of it. She did not want to startle the poor man.

After an hour, he lifted his head and grinned. "Done."

The two women clapped happily. "Now we must wait for His Lordship to return."

They did not have to wait long for someone's return. When Brenna heard boot steps in the foyer, she hurried out to find that it was Jace and not Richard who'd arrived.

"Where is Richard?" She tried to keep her voice calm.

"He is with Freemont at Tarleton House. The family has gone for the season, and the manor is being searched." Jace slapped dirt off his breeches. "I returned for a fresh horse. Mine picked up a stone. I came inside because I thought you'd want to know that your husband is safe."

Brenna stepped close and pressed a kiss on his cheek. "Thank you. I was worried."

Andrew stepped forward. He held out the map and explained what they'd done. Jace looked impressed. "It has everything marked, down to the smallest hut."

Jace rolled up the map and tapped it on his open palm. "This will be of great help." He tipped his hat to the steward. "I should get back."

"Be careful," Brenna urged. Jace had become a good friend. She'd hate to see him injured. Or worse.

"I will." Then he was gone.

Brenna stood for a moment in indecision. She hated waiting. Her adventurous nature felt trapped within these walls. There had to be some way for her to assist.

A thought took root. She turned to Lucy. "I need your help. Quickly!"

Tarleton House was empty but for a few worried servants. They allowed the search, even as they assured Richard that they'd kept the doors locked, as a precaution after the murder.

As expected, there was nothing to indicate anything untoward. Richard suspected that the Runners were unwittingly playing a game with the killers. The men were moving from place to place to keep ahead of the two dozen or so investigators and Jace's men. Since the huntsman's account, they'd vanished.

"I fear their desperation may drive them to kidnap someone in order to get away," Richard said. "I'd hate to see more innocents harmed."

"We would need a hundred men to completely cover the park. We have just enough to keep George and Clive from taking the roads out on horseback and to scatter the rest around," Mister Freemont said.

"If we do not catch them soon, they will find a way to escape our net," Richard agreed. He stared up at the façade of Tarleton House. "What are we missing?"

Jace rode up to join them. He dismounted and walked over. He unrolled and held out the map. "Your Andrew is a brilliant man. I'd marry him myself if he were free," Jace jested, and waved over several Runners. Once they were gathered, he ran his finger over the map, explaining what they were seeing. "This map covers the park in precise detail. If we go in groups of two, each pair can cover a property. It will be more efficient than guessing where the killers will go next."

All, including Richard, were impressed. "I knew Andrew had some unusual interests. I never thought one would be beneficial to crime investigation."

Mister Freemont went in search of the Runners still wandering the property. Within the hour, the Runners agreed to the plan, took torn pieces of the map, and rode out.

Richard, Jace, and Mister Freemont collected their horses. "Fire a shot if you find the men," Jace said.

The sound of racing hoof beats drew their attention. To Richard's surprise, Brenna, trailed by Lucy, rode up the drive as if the devil himself were on their tail.

Brenna drew Brontes to a skidding stop. Her hat slid forward on her forehead. She pushed it back.

"Brenna. What are you doing here?" He stepped forward and gripped Brontes's bridle. He did not wait for her answer. "Return to the hall immediately."

Her face tightened. "I will not. We are here to help."

Aware that they were the focus of every pair of eyes, he led the horse away from the rest of the party.

"It is too dangerous for you to be out here. Go home to James. He needs you more than we do."

"He is with Nanny and Mrs. Beal," Brenna said, through her closed teeth. She leaned down in the saddle and lifted her skirt. She had a small pistol tucked into her garter. "I am armed and capable of using this. Now, are we going to argue over my stubborn nature and lack of sense, or are we going to hunt for the murderers?"

A war waged inside him, and his head began to pound. He wanted to spin the mare around and send them back to Beckwith Hall, and he wanted to kiss her breathless. She was his fierce warrior wife, the Brenna who faced danger without flinching.

The second won out. He pulled her face down to his and kissed her soundly. She smiled beneath his mouth.

"What am I to do with you?" he said, breaking the kiss.

"Love me forever?"

His eyes rolled up, and he expelled a harsh breath. "That I will. Lord help me." To the sound of her soft laughter, he released the mare and walked over to gather his horse.

"Freemont and Lucy will take the Cottswood property, and Brenna, Jace, and I will take the Livingston land." Jace tore the map and handed Freemont his piece. "Fire a shot if you find anything," Richard added. "And be safe."

The Livingstons were in residence when the trio rode up. Mister Livingston agreed to the search and sent a pair of footmen to assist. It took two hours to cover the property, and they found no clues to George and Clive Everhart.

"They are as slippery as fish," Brenna grumbled, as they traveled back to the road. "How can they hide so well?"

"It is a large park," Richard said. "We believe they are on foot. That makes it easier for them to hide."

"And you are certain they have not fled the area? Clive's uncle could have spirited them away," Brenna pressed. "They could be on a ship to the Americas."

Richard stopped in the road. He pulled off his hat and scratched his head. "We are not certain of anything."

"What a dismal situation," Brenna said. "I still cannot believe George is a murderer. I've met some very devious and calculating men in my life, and he showed no signs of a black heart."

"We were all fooled." Richard replaced his hat. "He lived at the hall. His sister lived there. We were all blind to the truth of his nature."

Deep in her heart, Brenna wanted to believe this was a mistake, not for George but for her. She despaired to think her instincts were so flawed.

"Do you think Bethany knew the truth?" Brenna tried to imagine Bethany keeping such a secret. "She was a witch, but could she close her eyes to his misdeeds, knowing her brother was killing women and letting him continue on that path?"

"Perhaps she left to keep from giving him away," Jace said. He looked down at the map. "We will probably never know."

Jace scanned the torn paper. "We have covered our property. There are only two common areas left. The village is the largest, the church, and the abbey. We checked the abbey already."

"Let us check the village," Richard suggested.

"I'll go," Jace offered. "You two check the church the tenants use. When you finish, you can join me." At Richard's nod, he spun his horse and rode away.

Brenna adjusted her hat and retied the ribbons under her chin. "Shall we?" Brontes turned her head, and Brenna looked behind them. "We have a rider coming." She squinted. "I think it's Andrew."

It *was* Andrew. He joined the group. "No sign of them?"

"Not yet," Richard said. "We were about to leave for the church. It is one of the few places we have left to search."

"Not exactly." Andrew pulled out another copy of the map. It was folded into a small rectangle. "I was looking over the map and found something I'd missed."

"What is it?" Brenna asked. She nudged Brontes closer to him.

Andrew held up the map so they could see it. "Long ago, before the abbey was built, a keep was on the property. Sometime in the mid-seventeenth century, it burned. Eventually, the remaining stones were used in building the abbey over the old keep."

Richard motioned impatiently for Andrew to get to the point.

"What is left of the original keep is all underground. The dungeon." Andrew's voice rose. "Don't you see? It's a perfect place to hide, if the killers found an entrance."

Brenna's heart thudded. Richard stared. "How did I not know about this? I have lived here all my life."

Andrew put the map into his pocket. "I have always been interested in both maps and history. I researched all of the buildings in this area. There was a small mention, in a dusty old book, about the keep and the dungeon. At one time I planned to see if I could find it, but my work kept me busy, and then I was off hunting for Anne."

"Can you find it now?" Richard asked, with unconcealed excitement in his voice.

"Possibly." Andrew did not sound confident. "If Bentley or Everhart stumbled upon the entrance, there should be signs of activity—footprints, scrapes from a concealed door, disturbed cobwebs—or there may be nothing at all."

"We must try," Brenna said. "We will not find the passageway if we waste time speculating." She nudged Brontes forward in the direction of the abbey.

"Brenna, wait!"

Chapter Thirty-six

It took Richard a burst of speed to catch up with Brenna. "What do you think you're doing?" he shouted, over the sound of hoof beats pounding on the road.

"I'm racing for the abbey," she shouted back. "We have to search the ruins. It may be our last chance to find our killers."

She knew he was displeased. It was in his voice. He'd demand that she return to the hall and hide behind locked doors. She would not accept his directive, and they'd quarrel. Eventually, he'd agree with her point rather than wasting time arguing further.

There would be no hiding in the hall for her. After all that had happened, she had to see this through.

The road flew beneath Brontes's hooves. The mare must have sensed her urgency and gave her all. Brenna's hat flew off her head to dangle between her shoulder blades from its ribbons. She could hear Richard behind her, and she did not slow.

Within minutes, the abbey spire came into view. It was nearly impossible to believe the tumbledown ruins still held secrets. However, she trusted Andrew to know. They needed their three minds to find the dungeon if it did indeed exist.

She stopped at the edge of the property. There was a possibility that one of the men was keeping watch, and they needed caution when approaching the abbey.

Before Richard could protest, she was off Brontes and tying the mare to a bush.

"Brenna." Richard swung off his gelding. He led his horse up beside the mare.

She removed her hat, tossed it onto the bush, and quelled his argument before it began. "Would it not be in the best interest of us both if you watched over me, rather than me pretending to ride away and instead secretly following in your wake?"

Grumbling under his breath about stubborn wives and some such, he reached for her arm and faced her. "You will do everything I say from this moment forward, or I will drag you back to the hall myself and tie you to a chair if I must."

She knew he'd not let her accompany him if she did not agree. "Yes, Husband."

They waited for Andrew to catch up, then scanned the abbey for any sign of George or Clive watching from the open windows. Set against a backdrop of gray clouds, the abbey was eerily quiet.

"I see no one," Richard said, and pulled the pair of pistols from his waistband. "This is good. Follow me closely and keep vigilant."

Staying in the taller weeds, they walked slowly toward the abbey. The only signs of life were crows perched on the edge of a stone wall. They flew off as the trio approached.

"If the two men were here, would they not have disturbed the birds?" Brenna whispered.

"Not if they've been underground for a while," Andrew whispered back. "With the Runners all over the park, they will remain hidden for as long as possible before making their escape."

Richard led them along the same path he and Brenna had taken last fall. The abbey was much the same as she remembered, though the weeds were tromped down from many men passing through during the searches.

"Where should we start?" Richard said softly. He scanned the large room. Brenna walked the perimeter, hoping to find something to indicate a dungeon below. She did not truly expect to find anything here. If a door or passageway was that easy to find, it would have been found long ago.

No, it was the need for a distraction that drove her forward. She did not want Richard to see her fear.

"This part of the building is a good place to begin." Andrew looked up at the patches of open sky from the damaged roof. "I think the west walls were part of the original keep." He walked in that direction. They went through a low doorway into a small, dark room. Andrew pointed to broken bits of wood on the dirt. "This used to be a wood floor. It was probably broken up by the tenants for firewood."

A quick search of the room turned up nothing but a mouse nest in the corner. Similar searches of the rest of the rooms on the ground level were equally disappointing.

Andrew rubbed his eyes. "We have to continue searching. I know there is a dungeon under this abbey." He walked away.

Brenna and Richard shared a glance. Neither wanted to give up hope, but there was no indication that the killers had taken shelter here. "We must continue," she agreed, and he nodded.

They joined Andrew and climbed the staircase to the second floor. Careful to watch out for the two killers, they went from room to room, peering into each crack and corner.

The abbey was built for pious women who lived simply. The rooms were a reflection of that. There were no hidden doors in the walls or the floor. At the far end of the hall was the large room Brenna remembered from the earlier visit, with the huge fireplace at one end. She imagined the amount of wood and peat it would take to keep a fire burning in a fireplace of this size.

Brenna walked to the fireplace and stepped inside the massive structure. It was almost a separate room by itself.

Her boots crunched over tiny bits of old debris.

"The nuns must have gathered in this room for food or prayer, and enjoyed the warmth provided by this fireplace." Her voice carried up the chimney. She bent to look out. "There are no killers in here, though it's big enough for a half dozen men to stand in."

"There is nothing here," Richard said. "Let us move on."

Before exiting the fireplace, and out of curiosity, she examined a crack in the back wall. In novels, manors and castles always had secret panels to rooms filled with hidden treasure, or passageways in which to hide from invaders. Why not an abbey?

She pushed against the crack and felt a slight movement under her hand. Stunned, she pushed again. The wall clicked and slid back just a bit.

Her heart raced. She bent to look into the room. "Richard, Andrew, come quick!" she said, in an excited whisper. "I think I found something."

Brenna stepped out of the fireplace to allow the two men to see where she indicated. "The back wall moved."

They all stared at it, as if Brenna had found a skeleton lying among the ash. Truthfully, this was much more exciting.

Richard stepped inside and ran a hand over the crack. "I cannot believe this. You found the secret door." He craned his neck to look back at her, disbelief on his face.

"Excellent work, Lady Ashwood," Andrew said in awe.

"I would like to credit my intelligence and deductive skills for the find. Unfortunately, I found it accidentally. I do like to read adventure novels."

"How it happened is of no concern," Richard said. "You may have found a killer's lair."

There was no time to wait. Andrew and Richard pushed the stone, and the wall eased open with a scrape. The door to the dark and very narrow staircase inside was too small to walk through. They'd have to crawl in on their knees.

"This must be a secondary entrance to the dungeon," Andrew said. "The main door and staircase would be larger."

"We'll need light," Richard said.

"I think I saw some torches in a storage room down the hall." Andrew rushed off.

Richard turned to Brenna. "I will take Andrew and see where these stairs lead. I want you to stay here and hide. The men may not be in the dungeon."

Though she wanted to protest, she realized that once her husband and Andrew vanished into the hole, no one would know where they were. If anything happened, their disappearance would forever remain a mystery.

Andrew returned with a pair of lit torches. "I suspect our villains left these for their use."

Anxious for his safety, she pulled Richard down and kissed him soundly. "Be careful. I love you."

He held her gaze. She saw the love in his eyes. "I will." Richard handed one of the pistols to Andrew. "Ready?"

Andrew nodded. With one last quick caress of her cheek, Richard went back into the fireplace, with Andrew on his heels. The men dropped to their knees and crawled through the door.

Lifting her skirt, Brenna crouched and peered inside to see them take the steps down. After a bend in the staircase, the torchlight faded and then vanished.

Backing out, she said a silent prayer for their safe return and checked the pistol in her garter. If either George or Clive tried to enter or exit the room, she'd be ready.

The dungeon was damp, cool, and dark but for the torchlight. Richard and Andrew reached the bottom of the staircase and moved quietly into the middle of a narrow room. There was nothing but a stone ceiling and walls. No sign of occupants.

In the distance, Richard could hear the drip, drip of water leaking into the chamber from above. The idea of spending days, weeks, or years as a prisoner in this dank place chilled him.

"I hear nothing," Andrew whispered.

"This may be a futile trip," Richard replied. He slowly swung the torch around. To his relief, there were boot prints on the dusty floor. "No, someone has been here recently."

Andrew gripped his pistol tighter. "Then lead on, My Lord."

Richard knew that Andrew showed a confidence he did not feel. His steward was not a fighting man, nor a soldier trained for battle. He was a man of books and maps and numbers. Still, Richard knew he would fight vigorously if in danger.

"Tread carefully," he said. "The floor is slick."

The room led straight to another corridor and another downward staircase. Uneasy, Richard's heartbeat echoed in his ears. The dungeon gave all the appearances of being empty. His senses told him otherwise. Still, he walked on.

They were two floors down when a faint sound drew his attention. Hardly more than a whisper, at first he thought it was rats. Yet with a second consideration, he was not convinced that rats were the cause.

It sounded like the whisper of fabric on the stone floor. Was the killer lying in wait to attack them in the darkness?

He turned to press a fingertip to his mouth. Andrew froze.

Richard lifted the pistol. He handed Andrew his torch and whispered, "Stay a few paces back, just enough to give me some light but not enough to alert the killer I am coming."

Andrew nodded. He stepped back until Richard was out of the direct light. Richard carefully moved forward, careful to silence his footsteps. His senses were on alert.

He neared the cells and glanced into the first one. It was empty but for a pair of rats. There was nothing but ancient pieces of what may have once been a cot and a broken and rusted chain hooked to a link on the wall. The second and third cells were empty, too.

Maybe the sound *was* rats. A low moan dispelled him of that notion. He carefully made his way to the fourth cell and glanced inside. On the floor was the form of a woman, lying prone on the damp stone.

"Andrew," he called, in a harsh whisper.

He hurried inside and knelt beside her. She moaned again when he touched her. Her skin was cold and her hair tangled. Careful not to hurt her, he slowly rolled her onto her back.

The steward ran up behind him, torchlight flooding the cell. Richard's stomach recoiled.

"Miriam?"

Chapter Thirty-seven

Brenna heard footsteps in the hallway outside the room. She hurried to take a position next to the door, pressed herself flat against the wall, and readied her pistol to fire.

Just as quickly as she worried that she might have to take a life, she realized the person who rushed past the open door was not male. The scent of lavender gave her sex away. Brenna darted a glance out the door. "Anne?"

The woman stopped and spun around. Clutched in her shaking hand was a large knife.

"Brenna." She blew out a breath and put a hand over her heart. "I saw your horses on the road and knew you were here. Where are the men?"

"We found the dungeon door." Brenna led her to the fireplace and indicated the open passageway. "They have gone below to see if they can find George and Clive."

Anne's face fell. The knife slipped from her fingers. She placed her trembling hands over her mouth. "What a foolish idea. What if the murderers hear them coming and lie in wait? They could be killed."

Brenna patted her arm. "We must have faith—" A blast from below cut off her words. It echoed up the staircase and startled them. "It's a gunshot!" she cried, overwhelmed with sickening dread. Richard!

Brenna stood, immobilized with panic, unsure of what to do. The terror of knowing Richard was in danger snapped her indecision into action.

Spinning on Anne, she grabbed her arms. "Go to the village and find Jace." Anne whimpered. Brenna shook her, hard. "Do as I say. Now go!"

Anne turned and ran.

Wasting no time, Brenna dropped to her knees. She sucked in a deep breath and scrambled inside the fireplace and through the door.

The press of chill air prickled her skin like the touch of the dead. She clambered to her feet, wobbling slightly in her haste. She put one hand on the door for balance and jerked up her skirts with the other.

With panic cutting through her veins, she took the narrow stairs at a rapid clip, willing herself not to fall. She rounded the bend in the staircase, when the folly of her impulsiveness suddenly hit her. Without the light from the room above, the inky blackness surrounded her in its grip.

She'd forgotten to collect a torch. She paused for a moment, weighing her options, when a second shot jolted her backward. She held her breath, then made her decision. She'd continue forward, letting the wall be her guide.

The journey was grueling. Each step deeper into darkness twisted greater fear through her body. Her hands shook, her heart beat erratically, and she became more and more certain with the passage of time that she'd lost her way.

Struggling against the urge to curl up on the floor and submit to the horror of being lost forever in the darkness, the slightest hint of light appeared in the distance. Relief flooded through her. She cautiously stepped forward and took a second set of stairs downward.

A voice brought the pistol up. She could see a torch on the floor outside of an open cell and heard the weak sound of a male voice. At first she thought it might be the caretaker, Mister Crane, but she quickly recognized the voice.

Andrew. Brenna kept watch for a trap, following his voice until she could collect the torch. She slid it into a sconce outside the cell door and looked inside. Andrew was propped against a wall, blood on his breeches, a woman lying next to him on the floor.

He stared up at her. "It's Miriam."

Brenna rushed to kneel beside him. "How? Why?"

"I cannot say. We found her like this," Andrew said. He pulled off his cravat and tied it around his leg. "She is in a stupor." Brenna reached to touch her arm. She was cold. She bent to brush the hair from Miriam's face. She was breathing. "Where is Richard?"

"He chased after the men after one of them shot me. The second shot went wide."

Brenna tamped down the desire to scream. She would do Richard no good if she gave in to her anxiety. He was alone in the dark dungeon with two killers. He needed her to be strong. And the only person who could give her answers to this puzzle was lying at her feet.

Bending over Miriam, Brenna tucked the pistol into her pocket and patted Miriam's cheek. "Miriam? Miriam? Can you hear me?" She tapped her harder. "Miriam, wake up."

Slowly Miriam roused, too slowly. Brenna gently shook her, her impatience growing. Miriam had gone off with a man. Somehow she was involved in all this. How, she could not know, until Miriam explained her actions.

"Wake up." Miriam's eyes fluttered open. She stared, puzzled, into Brenna's face. "Why are you here, Miriam? Were you kidnapped? Where are George and Clive?"

Miriam blinked. Her eyes welled. "I thought Clive loved me," she whispered.

"Good lord," Brenna said, gnashing her teeth. Miriam had willingly run off with a killer. "I do not need to hear your tale of woe. Where are George and Clive hiding? I need to find Richard."

Rubbing her bruised face, Miriam whimpered, "Clive beat me."

Brenna grabbed both sides of her head and lowered her face until they were nearly nose-to-nose. "Tell me where the men are hiding right now, or I will beat you myself."

The woman blanched. Under Brenna's threat, she nodded. "They have a hiding place down the corridor and to the left. It is a small room where the guards tortured prisoners. There are chains on the walls."

Brenna stood, retrieved the pistol, and glared down. "If anything happens to my husband, I will come back and make good my threat."

Miriam turned her face away.

Andrew pushed himself off the wall. "If you give me a moment to rise, I will go after him."

"Nonsense. Stay and watch her." Reaching deep for courage, Brenna fled the cell, her mission clear. Save Richard.

G et out of the way, George." Richard's limp arm dangled at his side, and the other gripped his pistol. Leaning against the wall, he forced himself to stay upright. The pain in his shoulder was excruciating, yet he could not succumb to the driving need to slip to his knees. Not while Clive was alive.

"This is between Clive and me," George said. The two men held pistols on each other. George's voice wavered. "I will not allow you to kill anyone else. This is over."

Richard's eyes widened. George was protecting him?

"You are a coward," Clive sneered. "You have always been a coward." He lifted his pistol level with George's forehead. "You cried when I killed that laundress. What sort of man are you?"

"You forced me to help you," George cried out. "I thought after Cambridge, I was free of you. But you came after me. You planted Brenna's writing paper under the dead woman to taunt me, you broke the wheel and set fire to the tree, and you killed that maid in Dover and Clara, to make me look guilty." His pistol shook. "You threatened James, you bastard. I will kill you for that alone."

Clive grinned. Richard tried to get off a shot, but George stood between them. "You will do nothing of the sort. You are weak. Controlling you was almost as enjoyable as killing those women, perhaps even more so. It gave me pleasure to know that you were suffering with night terrors because of me. You will never be free. Never."

"You are the devil, Clive Everhart." Brenna stepped into

the room, her pistol aimed at Clive. His surprise quickly turned to laughter. He turned his pistol on her. "It appears the Lady Ashwood has decided to join us . . . and we have a standoff. Who will take the first shot?"

Richard wanted to call to her but feared she'd lose her focus. She needed to keep her eyes on Clive.

A sob caught in George's throat. He dropped to one knee, and his pistol clattered to the floor. Richard lifted his pistol and aimed it at Everhart. Worry that the man would fire at Brenna kept him from making the shot.

"I meant you no harm, Brenna," George said, tears in his eyes. "You were my friend."

"I know that now." Her voice softened, but her aim stayed true. "You *are* my friend. You cared for my son. I never wanted to believe you were a killer."

George put his hands over his face.

"You make me ill," Clive said, to George. "I'd kill you myself, but I need the bullet for Lord Ashwood. Then I can play my little games with his pretty little wife—"

A shot exploded through the room, and Clive went down. Brenna dropped to a crouch with a cry, her hand over her ear. Behind her and just off to the side stood Miriam, the smoking pistol she must have taken from Andrew in her grip.

"I will take the first shot, Clive." With that, her eyes rolled up, and she crumpled to the floor.

Richard forced himself forward and stumbled to Brenna. He pulled her to her feet and bent to examine her face. "Are you hurt?"

She shook her head. "Only my right ear. It's ringing." She covered her ear with her hand and winced. "And you?" she asked, her gaze going to his injured shoulder.

"It will heal," Richard replied. Brenna reached for him, but they were pushed apart when George stumbled past, jostling Richard. He ran down the corridor and out of sight. "I'll get him. You guard Clive." She bolted after George.

"Brenna, come back!"

With her hand on the wall, she hurried through the darkness, gaining light where she left the torch at the cell. She darted a quick glance inside, saw Andrew as she'd left him, and continued forward at a brisk pace.

Now familiar with the dungeon, she knew the direction of the staircase and listened for the sound of George's footsteps in front of her. He meant to escape.

"George," she called. He didn't slow. Brenna was not about to give up. With one hand on the wall to guide her, she followed him through the darkness and up the staircase. He scrambled into the fireplace, leaving the door open behind him.

Brenna poked her head out and saw him exit the room. She went after him. But he wasn't going down to the lower floor to escape the abbey. Instead, he went up toward the bell tower. Brenna paused. Was he leading her into a trap?

This part of the ruins had no route to freedom but for the staircase. She lifted her pistol and took the steps slowly. She did not have to look far for him. He was in the bell tower, sitting on an open windowpane.

"I am unarmed," he said, and lifted his hands. Brenna lowered the pistol but kept her distance. She could not afford to trust him.

"Brenna, I truly am sorry." He pressed a hand to his mouth. "I made the wrong friend, and it has haunted me ever since. If only I'd seen his villainous nature before he had me trapped in his web of murder." His voice trailed off.

"This was not your fault, George," she said softly. "You killed no one."

"But I did nothing to save those women, either." George rocked forward and back. "I was afraid of Clive. It was my cowardice that let him continue killing. I should have turned him in to the Runners, but he threatened to tell them that I was the killer. They'd believed him once; they would again."

"No, George. I will help you," Brenna said, and reached out her hand. "Everything will work out."

He lifted his face to her and shook his head. There was resignation in his eyes. "Tell Bethany I love her."

Brenna saw his intention too late. She cried out as he pushed backward out of the window. There was no cry as he fell.

With a hand clamped over her mouth, she went to the window and looked down. George was sprawled on his back on the stone pathway below. From the angle of his head, he'd broken his neck.

She spun away from the sight. Bile burned her throat.

Richard entered the room and walked to her. "Where is George?" She pointed out the window. He looked out, cursed, and pulled her to him with his good arm. Brenna clung to him, her tears flowing. "He could not live with his guilt."

"Shhh, love. It's over." He nuzzled his mouth in her hair, comforting her until her sobs subsided.

"Is Clive dead?" she asked.

"He lives. Miriam is a terrible shot. I locked him in a cell and met Jace, Mister Freemont, and Lucy below. The men will take care of Everhart. He will hang."

"And Miriam?" She brushed her tears away with her sleeve.

"Andrew is watching her. After she's seen a physician, we will get answers. Until then, she is under arrest."

"What a mess." Brenna thought having the case concluded would bring relief. Instead, she grieved for the lives lost all because of one evil man. "I must go to James. He is probably starving."

"I will take you. There is nothing more we can do here."

Jace arrived as Brenna slid up under Richard's good arm. He glanced around the empty room.

"Where is Bentley?"

"Dead," Richard said. "He jumped from the window."

Jace tucked his pistol away. "It appears that I have missed all the excitement." He looked at Richard. "Miriam is not the only one in need of a physician. How were you injured?"

"Clive came out of the darkness and slammed me into a wall. I think my shoulder is out of joint."

"Let me have a look." Jace probed the area with his fingers. Richard winced. After a moment, Jace nodded. "I can fix it if you promise not to scream too shrilly."

He was rewarded with a scowl. "I'll do my best."

Jace instructed Richard to brace himself against the wall with his good hand. He moved the arm this way and that until he was satisfied with its position. Without warning, he jerked the arm. Hard. It popped. Richard cursed Jace, his mother for birthing him, and his entire family tree.

However, there was not one shrill scream. Brenna smiled.

"Well done, Jace, Richard," she said. Richard moved the

arm around, his teeth gritted and his face screwed up. Once she was satisfied he was able to use the arm, she walked into the hallway. "I'm going home to our son. Are you coming?"

The two men followed her down the stairs and out of the abbey. When they reached the road, they met up with several Runners. Jace stayed behind to clear up matters at the abbey. Brenna just wanted to get home.

James was sleeping peacefully when they returned. Nanny explained, "When you did not return, he was inconsolable. Mrs. Beal sent for Mrs. Cookson, and she happily fed him. She said it was the very least she could do for you, after your kindness toward her family."

Brenna blinked, her eyes filling as she stared down at her contented son. "I shall thank her when I see her."

With all her jests about living with the sheep, she did not realize until just that moment how deeply attached she had become to the hall and the residents who lived within.

She tried to imagine her life, had she never gotten with child and decided her marriage was worth saving.

And no one would take this away from her. Not ever.

Chapter Thirty-eight

Andrew's wound was tended to, and the physician sewed him up. Barring infection, he had survived his first bullet wound and now had a tale to tell his children someday about his harrowing experience with a killer.

It was nearing dusk when Jace and Mister Freemont returned to the hall, dirty, exhausted, and needing food. Brenna ordered baths prepared and trays to be brought up, wanting both men settled with all the comforts the hall could provide.

Brenna left Jace's room and saw Lucy catch up with a maid who was carrying the tray toward Mister Freemont's room. She took the tray from the startled girl.

Lucy lifted her nose as she and Brenna passed in the hall. "I have decided Mister Freemont is not as uninteresting as I first thought," she said, shrugging. "I think I might give him a chance to woo me."

Laughing, Brenna shook her head. "Poor Mister Freemont."

The next few days were a whirl. The Harringtons—Walter and Kathleen; Simon and Laura; Eva, Nicholas, and baby Catherine; and Noelle and Gavin—had all came to the hall en masse to assure themselves that Brenna, Richard, and little James had not come to harm.

A Convenient Bride 313

Once the Bow Street Runners concluded their investigation, it would take some time to put the clues together. Clive's crimes were spread over many years. Brenna suspected that George had been correct. Clive had killed the maid in Dover, when George was there, and Clara, here, to make it look as though George had done the murders. That way, he could keep George under his control.

Much about Clive's life, and his connection to George, would always remain a mystery.

There'd been some worry that the caretaker, Mister Crane, had been done in by Clive, but he was found to have been visiting a certain widow two villages over and thus had missed the turmoil of the investigation.

George was sent back to his family to be buried. At Brenna's insistence, his death was determined to be accidental. Clive was arrested and sent to London for trial. With the gallery of witnesses against him, there would be no doubt of the outcome. He would be executed for his crimes.

"There you are," Richard said. Brenna looked up from the crib and placed a finger to her lips. James had been fussing, and it had taken almost an hour to get him to sleep.

She led Richard into the sitting room. "Did you get Miriam settled?" It was determined that Miriam had been duped by Clive. When she became suspicious of his activities, he'd kidnapped and intended to kill her. Once she'd recovered her sensibilities, Richard, with her in agreement, decided she would best be suited for a pious life.

"She is not certain she will become a nun but should find peace at Newbury Abbey," Richard said. "She will work in the kitchen until her injuries fully heal."

"I wish her well." Brenna slipped into his arms. "Have I told you today how much I love you?"

"You have now," Richard said. He looked deep into her eyes. "I love you as well. Who knew our marriage of convenience would turn into a love match?"

Brenna ran her hand down his chest. "I knew." She smiled and brushed her lips over his. "I am happy to have our lives settled. I look forward to returning to our quiet existence here, among the sheep."

Richard lowered his head and nuzzled her ear. "It will be quiet once I run off your family. They are a raucous lot."

"You wouldn't dare," Brenna scolded, laughing softly. She reached back to remove his hand from her right buttock. "You will have to wait until later to slake your needs. I am expected downstairs to ride with Mother, Laura, and Noelle into the village."

He grumbled against her neck. "We've had very little time alone over the last few days. Everywhere I turn, I trip over a Harrington. How can I seduce my wife when she tends to everyone's needs but my own?"

Brenna eased out of his grip and gently slapped away his exploring hands. "Then you must get creative, love. I am positive there are dark corners somewhere in this manor for private romantic trysts with your wife."

She flounced away, leaving the challenge lingering in his mind. She wanted seduction, too. However, between James and her family, she usually dropped exhausted into bed at night.

Romance had fallen aside, in favor of sleep.

Brenna was on the stoop, awaiting the other women, when she heard the sound of pounding hoofbeats coming around the house. On the back of a chestnut gelding, bedecked in a dusty coat and carrying a pair of pistols in his waistband, Richard tore up the drive, scattering dust as he came, and drew the horse to a skittering stop before her.

She gasped and waved away a cloud of dust, her heart skipping a beat. He looked exactly the way he'd looked when they'd met: handsome and dangerous.

"What is the meaning of this?" she asked.

"Some months ago, a highwayman was propositioned by a tart-tongued chit with green eyes, who asked him to compromise her." He sent Brenna a salacious grin. "I think it long past the time when he should take her up on her offer."

Brenna's lips parted, and her eyes danced. The women could find their way around the village without her today. She stepped forward, taking his outstretched hand. "Certainly you do not intend to take me here, in the mud, Milord highwayman."

"I do not." He swung her up behind him. "I know a much better place for a compromise than a muddy drive."

With carefree laughter and a heart full of love for her dashing highwayman, Brenna clung to Richard's coat as he spun the horse around and kneed him in the direction of the dower house.

And Brenna's very thorough compromising.

Read on for a special preview of
the next School for Brides romance

The Wife He Always Wanted

Coming soon from Berkley Sensation!

S arah squelched the scream racing up the back of her throat. The man standing before her was unshaven, dressed in some sort of fringed garment, and was so dusty that he looked as if bathing was an unknown concept. However, what truly made her knees knock and her body tremble was the fact that he loomed over her like some mythical beast.

The man could easily crush her with just his two hands.

She instinctively knew to show no fear. Alone in the cottage, with neighbors too distant to summon for help, she'd be vulnerable should he attempt something nefarious. So, as calmly as she could manage, she reached toward the hook beside the door where her hat hung and fingered the item until she found the hatpin. Then very carefully, so as not to give away her intention, she clasped the pin between her thumb and forefinger. She was about to slide the weapon free when he spoke.

"You are Sarah Louise Palmer?" he asked, the harsh timbre of his voice giving her no ease. When she did not, or rather could not answer, he stared. "Albert did not tell me you were mute."

Albert? Her lips parted and what came out was a breathless gasp. Knowing that she'd just all but confirmed his assessment that she *was* mute, she shook her head to clear her mind and regain some control of herself.

"How do you know my brother?" she asked, and slowly let loose the hatpin. She could not imagine any circles in which Albert and this man would ever converge.

He pulled off his rumpled hat and ran a hand through his abused brown locks. "We are, or were, friends." He drew in his breath and twisted the hat. "It is sad tidings I bring you, Miss Palmer. Your brother is dead."

Sarah frowned. "You are a bit late with the news, sir." She tried to imagine her brother friendly with this unkempt savage. The idea was absurd. "I have known of his death for over a year."

"How? I came here straightaway."

"By way of the moon?" she asked, sharper than she'd intended. The pain of her brother's death was still fresh, despite the passage of many months. "He has been dead since a year ago last January." She scanned his bearded face. "I thank you for coming to tell me this, and do not mean to be rude, sir, but I have a pot of stew on the stove and I fear it may be burning."

She intended to close the door, but a scuffed boot stopped it in mid swing.

"Your stew will have to wait," he said, and placed a flat hand on the panel. With a firm push, he slowly eased the door wide open.

Heart thudding, Sarah stepped back and darted a quick glance at the hatpin. It was still within reach on the hook by the door. Thankfully, the man remained on the stoop.

"There is more for us to discuss than Albert's death. You see, as he lay dying, he made me promise to take care of you. That is a vow I intend to keep."

Sarah stared. "My brother has been away for ten years, with only a few letters to assure me he was alive. Now he decides on his death bed that he should show me some brotherly concern?" Her sadness dissipated and a fire burned in her chest. She'd loved her brother dearly, but he had not been the best caretaker for her. "I release you from your vow, Mister—?"

"Harrington. Gabriel Harrington."

"Mister Harrington." She stepped fully into the opening lest he see how shabby her living conditions were. After her aunt died two years ago and her tiny pension was cut off,

Sarah's funds had dwindled to an alarming degree. She was within weeks of being penniless. Still, her pride would not allow her to accept help from a stranger. "I am quite capable of seeing to my own needs."

"As I can see," he said, peering over her head.

Sarah's spine straightened and her neck prickled. "I do not care if you and Albert were as close as brothers, I do not need your help. Please go."

He grumbled under his breath and his face became a blank mask, as if he was pondering his next argument. Then he said, "I am more than Albert's friend." He sighed deeply. "I am your fiancé."

G abriel watched her pretty mouth pop open. As quickly as he'd spoken the lie, he wished he could take it back. Guilt raced through his bones. He *had* promised to care for the chit. He had not promised to marry her.

Find her a vicar or farmer to marry and care for her, Gabe, Albert had said. *Keep her safe from rogues like us. She deserves a far better life than what I have provided.*

A second wave of guilt followed. Albert had been correct. Gabe *was* a woman-loving, adventure-seeking, irresponsible rogue; he didn't have the stability to care for a wife. He was wrong to offer to marry Sarah. Albert would never allow the wedding if he were alive.

Hell, if the chit had not been so eager to see him gone, he'd have asked her to come with him to London and left her in the care of his mother. However, the girl was stubbornly refusing his assistance, even as she clearly teetered on the edge of desperation. Now he'd all but proposed to her on impulse, and honor would not let him take it back.

"We are betrothed?" Her face went white. He reached to take her arm, fearful she'd faint at his feet, but she brushed him away and whispered, "I cannot believe Albert would marry me off to a barbarian." She turned and wobbled toward the nearest chair, dropping down onto the frayed surface.

Taken aback by her insult, Gabe stepped into the cottage. The top of his head brushed the doorframe of the low door.

"A barbarian?" He looked down. His buckskin was dirty,

streaked with salt and dust and who-knew-what from his trip from America. He'd intended to change to suitable clothing after he boarded the London-bound ship from New York, but his trunk had disappeared somewhere between the wharf and the *Lady Hope*. By the time he noticed it missing, they had left port.

This left him in buckskin, a second shirt from his pack, and the kindness of his fellow traveler Mrs. Johnson, and her lye washing soap to keep him from smelling most foul.

No wonder Sarah thought him barbaric. He did look rather fierce.

Chuckling softly, he examined her from her faded gray dress up to her stricken face. She was not unpleasant to look at—somewhat pretty really, albeit too thin for his consideration and dressed in the severe manner of a spinster, though she was not old enough yet to wear that title. Still, he could do worse in a wife. And since it was too late to withdraw the lie and the damage was done, he silently vowed to make her a respectable husband. Sarah, and Albert, deserved nothing less.

"I assure you, Miss Palmer, I do not usually look so barbaric." His attempt to reassure her did not stop her lower lip from trembling. "I do own a razor. Or I used to. I will shave as soon as we reach London."

The effort to calm her worries failed. Sarah lifted her sad eyes to his. There was hopelessness in the violet depths. She'd lost the flicker of spirit he'd first glimpsed when she'd tried to run him off.

Truthfully, he couldn't fault her dismay, or her tears. She'd been born and gently raised to a quiet life in this small village. And according to Albert, she had never traveled far outside its boundaries once she'd been secreted away here as a girl, thus limiting her experiences with strangers. He knew he must appear to her like the savage he'd been for the last three years he'd spent in the American West.

"Come, Miss Palmer. With a shave and some decent clothing, some women find me quiet pleasing to look at."

The attempt to lighten the moment gained him no quarter. Her shoulders slumped forward. He tried again. "Would it help if I told you that my father is an earl and my family is well respected throughout England?" She remained as she was. "That we have more money than the Prince Regent?"

That last seemed to rouse her a bit. She rubbed her eyes with her palms then lifted her gaze to peer around the dismal room. He could almost see the very last of her spirit flee.

Even the poorest citizen would find the sparse accommodations somewhat lacking. He was certain she'd sold off whatever she could to survive, leaving only that which had no monetary worth behind.

"I suppose I can do no worse," she said after a long pause. She pushed from the chair. Then, without acknowledging him, she walked with a stiff gait from the room.

He'd risk it all to keep her safe . . .

NATIONAL BESTSELLING AUTHOR
CHERYL ANN SMITH

The Scarlet Bride
• A SCHOOL FOR BRIDES ROMANCE •

Notorious bad boy Simon Harrington, third in line for his uncle's title, has finally conceded to settle down and find a noble wife. When he stumbles across Laura Precott, a courtesan in peril on a dark London street, his life takes an unexpected turn. Fearing for her safety, he brings the mysterious beauty to his cousin's School for Brides, where compromised women are taught how to be suitable wives. But he finds it impossible to simply walk away.

Simon knows he must forget his feelings for such an unsuitable woman or risk disgracing his family. But when Laura's former lover turns out to have been murdered the very night of her escape, suspicion falls squarely on Laura. Now it is up to Simon to prove her innocence—even if it leads to his downfall . . .

cherylannsmith.com
facebook.com/cherylannsmithauthor
facebook.com/LoveAlwaysBooks
penguin.com

M1158T0712

AN ENTICING ESPECIAL NOVELLA
FROM NATIONAL BESTSELLING AUTHOR

CHERYL ANN SMITH

The Bride Who Fell In Love With Her Husband

. . .

As a courtesan, Rose Bailey learned how to seduce men by playing the coquette. As a student at Miss Eva Black's School for Brides, she learned the manners of a proper wife. But her husband, Thomas Stanhope, was drawn to her spirited nature, and does not want her to merely play a role. Now Rose has one final lesson to learn—how to let herself love, and to truly be loved.

Available for digital download!

cherylannsmith.com
facebook.com/cherylannsmithauthor
facebook.com/LoveAlwaysBooks
penguin.com

Discover Romance

berkleyjoveauthors.com

See what's coming up next from your favorite romance authors and explore all the latest Berkley, Jove, and Sensation selections.

See what's new
~
Find author appearances
~
Win fantastic prizes
~
Get reading recommendations
~
Chat with authors and other fans
~
Read interviews with authors you love

berkleyjoveauthors.com

M1G0610